CW01513278

'Rarely has a book delivered so spectacularly on the promise of an unlikeable lead character, but Anna Harris is every bit as artful and awful as this reader could wish. Highsmith herself would raise a glass'
Sarah Hilary, author of *Someone Else's Skin*

'An intriguing cat and mouse game, which will keep you reading into the early hours'
Tina Baker, author of *Call Me Mummy*

'I devoured *The Artful Anna Harris* in a single sitting. Pacy, thrilling and fun ... An excellent debut'
J.M. Hewitt, author of *The Life She Wants*

'*The Artful Anna Harris* drew me in from the very first page and had me hooked throughout. With brilliantly complex characters and a plot that unfolds with unnerving inevitability, Anna's story is chilling and deeply engaging by turns'
Philippa East, author of *Little White Lies*

'Twisty, elegant and darkly addictive. I didn't just read this book – I let it quietly rearrange my assumptions about everyone I know'
Joanna Wallace, author of *You'd Look Better as a Ghost*

'Beautifully written and suspenseful with sinister Highsmith vibes – this book will get under your skin'
Caroline Hulse, author of *The Adults*

the
artful
anna
harris

TRACY MATON

 VIPER

First published in Great Britain in 2026 by
Viper,
an imprint of Profile Books Ltd
29 Cloth Fair
London
EC1A 7JQ

www.viperbooks.co.uk

Designed and typeset in Garamond by CC Book Production

Epigraph on page v from PATRICIA HIGHSMITH,
PLOTTING AND WRITING SUSPENSE FICTION, First published in 1966,
Copyright © 1993 Diogenes Verlag AG Zürich, All rights reserved

1 3 5 7 9 10 8 6 4 2

Printed and bound in Great Britain by
CPI Group (UK) Ltd, Croydon, CR0 4YY

Our product safety representative in the EU is BGC Sustainability & Compliance,
7 avenue du Général Leclerc, Paris, 75014, France
https://baldwinglobalconsulting.com

ISBN 978 1 80522 3818
eISBN 978 1 80522 3825

'. . . for neither life nor nature cares if justice is ever done or not.'

Patricia Highsmith

The dog walker – for it is always a dog walker – is impatient. Tricked by the mellow yellow of the rising sun, he came out without gloves, but the wind is bitingly cold. He tries to retract his hands further up his sleeves; changes his mind and sinks them into the pockets of his jacket. There is no comforting fleece lining, only poo bags and house keys.

'Lenny!' he shouts, knowing his cry can't compete with the noise of the ocean. The dog is playing in the waves; he won't come. Not until he's forced. They walk this spit of land every day and, every day, the dog greets the sea like a never-seen-before miracle.

Lenny loves to swim. Clever dog, he doesn't stray out of his depth, choosing instead to go across, as though he understands the geography of the steeply shelving storm beach with its dangerous undercurrents.

But today, Lenny is not swimming. He is thrashing about in the shallows.

As the dog walker negotiates the shingle slope, he realises Lenny's loud bark is one of urgency, not joy. The dog walker speeds up, his stinging fingers forgotten. What has Lenny found this time?

Focus is slow to come thanks to dancing reflections on moving water. A dark shape. Large. A seal, perhaps. This makes him break into a run, boots slipping on pebbles. He is already thinking who he can call; if the creature is alive, he'll need help to coax it into the deeper water.

His acceleration is short-lived.

The dark mass, clearer with every stride, has no comedy flippers. It has no bulbous body. No whiskery snout.

Lenny is whining now, tail flapping: dog language for unknown crisis. The dog walker hangs back, reaches for his phone – but when does he ever remember his phone on a dog walk? He looks around. There is a woman who walks a Staffie; she is sometimes out early.

No. There is no one on the beach.

Only the dog walker. His dog, Lenny. And a very dead body.

1

Come and Praise

Today, I am going to meet Sofia. I don't know it yet. I don't even know she exists. As I get ready to leave, I have no inkling that this Sunday morning will not imitate all others, excluding special occasions like Mothering Sunday or Easter when the wider family gets involved. (Ben's family that is.)

Growing up in South London, religion meant nothing more than a tick in a box. My family always opted for Church of England but the real answer was Not Applicable. I'm not sure we knew anyone who went to actual church, as in a service with wine and wafers, which probably explains why the one by us ended up converted into swanky flats.

And yet, in this saccharine Somerset village, the church bells are every bit as effective as the one Pavlov rang for his dog. The first peal is a ten-minute warning; you can feel the flurry – gulping the last mouthful of tea, drawing a quick stripe of lipstick, reaching for a wool coat. The hungry-for-spiritual-feeding dash out of their doors and so the promenade begins.

There are two routes, depending on where you live: clockwise down Main Street and along Church Road or anti-clockwise down

Highlands Avenue. I go clockwise, calling for Dee – who will be my mother-in-law if Ben and I ever get married – on the way.

Today Dee is wearing the Fair Isle scarf I bought for her birthday. The greens and golds look lovely against her camel coat, but when doesn't she look nice? Her silver-grey hair is cut in a long bob and she is never seen without a pair of shiny earrings and a made-up face.

'Hello, Anna. How are you this morning?' She smiles, touches my cheek.

'I'm good, thanks, Dee. Although I'm looking forward to the first Sunday we can dispense with the layers.'

Spring feels slow to show itself this year. I am hidden in my puffer coat, hair in a ponytail, face the one I woke up in. I don't have anything against the idea of improving my appearance but have somehow raced through my twenties without acquiring either the tools or the inclination.

'There's definitely hope,' she says. 'My hostas are poking out of the soil.'

'Glad to hear it,' I say, unsure what a hosta is.

The two of us fall in step. Mrs Chalmers is ahead. Sally Wood is behind, but will soon catch us up. On the last stretch we will come across the Saville family. Mr Fellows is invariably last to arrive. If you catch sight of him on the way, you're late.

Dee and I stand on the gravel path and wait our turn to enter the fan-vaulted porch of St Michael's, where we will be greeted by Hannah from the B&B because it is the last Sunday of the month: her week to open up and mine to close.

Hymnal and service book in hand, we head for our usual pew: close enough to see and hear but not in any way entitled. I breathe

4

in the familiar citrus and spice and let my body fold to fit the shallow pew, designed when people were smaller in all dimensions. Dee drops her head and shuts her eyes. She says a little prayer, lips barely moving. I wonder, every time I wonder, what she prays so earnestly for.

I don't have faith. I find it hard to understand how anyone believes, but perhaps it's not as simple as that. I have faith in the goodness of people (and evidence of the badness of others) and can see being Christian in the adjective sense makes for a cordial society. No one can really buy into the idea an ethereal being is listening to the names the congregation proffers up for prayers every week, although there is probably something cathartic in hearing the pleas voiced out loud. I find the fascination with forgiveness particularly problematic: being wronged does not foster feelings of grace and mercy, quite the opposite in fact. And, just to be clear, the meek do not inherit the earth.

Anyway, at worst, church is harmless, and at best, community.

Despite the open invitation from Dee, only when her breathing became a problem did I start escorting her to the morning service. Ben has football so he can't go. Ben's sister, Milly, who also lives in the village, has the twins so she can't go (although she does pick Dee up afterwards and give her lunch) and the rest of the clan didn't offer. I wasn't exactly thrilled by my new responsibility but, to my surprise, I have grown to like it. There is a peculiar freedom in having no choice; in spending an hour being told when to sit and stand, when to sing, when to bow your head, while all the time your thoughts polka about. I save things to think about on Sunday mornings – the wild variations in sentencing for similar crimes, why biscuits are round when square is surely more space-efficient, whether lost dogs find their way home using smell, sight or an internal compass – and never run out of topics.

Dee has finished her silent communion and is now rifling through the tissue-thin pages of *Common Praise* to see which hymns the numbers on the board refer to. My hand strays to touch my belly, palm flattened against the zip of my jeans, thumb resting in the dip of my navel. I wish for the soft swell of flesh to harden, to stretch tight over my full abdomen, to declare itself. It is the end of March and the baby is due at Halloween. The previous one would have been a Christmas baby. Loath to dwell on what feels like a lottery, I direct my attention to the divisions caused by the proposal to extend the graveyard; 'the practice of burials is outdated and unsustainable', I have been told, but I also know the vicar has his eye on a plot.

All too soon the grace of the Lord Jesus Christ and the love of God declare the service over. Those words are as robust a stimulus as the church bells, catapulting me back into the room. I watch the choir – an eclectic line of people homogenised by red gowns and white collars – pass by, before standing up to follow.

Thanks to Meryl (chief churchwarden and doesn't she know it) the transition from place of worship to coffee shop is slick. The urn is miraculously hot; the cloth is crowded with crockery; a selection of cakes appear – all before the congregation has had a chance to weave down the aisle to the rear of the church.

Like the host at a party, I skate over conversations – yes, it was a lovely sermon; actually, I think it's carrot cake; I know, not long until Easter – in between servicing people's needs. I pass Dee a cup of black coffee before taking a second milky one to Old Mary together with a generous slice of fruitcake. She has mobility issues, so the world comes to her.

The unwritten rule is that forty-five minutes socialising is ample. Any longer might imply church exists to feed the gossip and not the soul. When Old Mary and Hannah from the B&B leave, I begin clearing up. Being helpful has proved a very straightforward way to ingratiate myself. Dee regularly refers to me as a 'treasure'. The other day she said she can't understand how they coped without me. It was a compliment, but felt prophetic. Growing old in the village, stepping into the shoes of my much-respected mother-in-law, Ben hanging up his football boots but keeping his hand in by managing the fixture list, our children starting at the village school, moving to secondary.

A future I'm not aware of choosing.

By noon, I'm quite alone with only the pews left to tidy. I'm nudging the kneelers into parallel when the heavy wooden door makes its quiet squeal followed by a creak. I look across to see who has forgotten what.

A woman is standing quite still, framed by the arch. She looks ridiculously dramatic – not dressed, as much as curated. A riot of red corduroy dungarees over a traditional Aran sweater, a short bottle-green velvet cape slung around her shoulders and fingerless turquoise gloves, the whole affair topped by a tremendous pile of dark hair, the knots and twists streaked with ash blonde. Her chandelier earrings almost reach her shoulders.

'Hello,' I say, walking towards her.

'Heavens, it's so pretty.' Her beautifully clear voice, ice-cold water freed from a deep spring, travels to all four corners. 'I'm just going to breathe it in.'

She raises her eyes. It's hard not to expect a lightning bolt. A stranger in the church is a rare enough event without that stranger being so remarkable.

'I'm afraid you're too late for the service.'

'It was intentional. I watched everyone leave but didn't expect a straggler.' She beams at me. 'I hope it's okay to come in.'

'Of course. The church belongs to everyone.'

'Even atheists?' Her conspiratorial whisper makes me smile.

'I believe so, although my responsibility doesn't extend beyond putting away the china.'

She holds out her hand. 'I'm Sofia, by the way. Relative newcomer.'

'Anna.' I shake her hand. 'Do you live in the village? I don't think I've seen you.'

'I'm renting Keeper's Cottage.'

'Ah, yes.' I knew someone had moved in – a student I thought, but Sofia looks about thirty. 'The family are undecided, aren't they, about whether to sell?'

She giggles. 'I love that you know that. I didn't imagine villages like this actually existed, where everyone knows everything – except in a book, of course.'

When I moved here, I remember having exactly the same thought. I consider saying so but it might lead to questions I don't feel like answering. Questions about why, one rainy day, I traded all that London had to offer for a miniature life in the country. In the village, there are people who have never ventured to the Big Smoke; people who think going into Bristol – heaven forbid, the traffic! – is best avoided unless in dire need of a service only a metropolis can provide. I have seamlessly slotted into this little haven, but only because I altered myself to fit.

'How old is the church?' she asks.

It is ludicrous that I know the answer. The old me was only a reliable source of where to buy some weed on a Tuesday afternoon. 'It was entirely rebuilt, save the font, in 1450 . . .'

Our conversation sets sail, Sofia interjecting as I regurgitate the audio tour I have heard Meryl give many times.

'I love a church,' she says, when our stroll ends back at the door, 'although I have to squash the compulsion to behave badly. Steal something, or scratch my name somewhere.'

'I did that once.' I don't know why I am about to share this memory. I am a private person: that is how the locals would describe me. 'They'd laid new concrete at the park and like idiots, my friend Pippa and I wrote our initials with a stick.'

'Were you caught?'

'Of course. Within half an hour.'

The echo of her loud laugh is incongruous in this place of hushed voices. Similar to a library, the building tends to impose a muffle. I am tempted to expand, list the many misdemeanours of Anna Harris and Pippa Williams in the hope of hearing her unchecked pleasure ring out once more. But I resist.

As I turn the lights off – a habit not a hint – she says, 'Sorry, I hope I haven't kept you,' and reaches for the huge round handle.

I want to show her that I am friendly, that this has been a nice interlude, but I am out of practice. Being an adjunct to Ben's dynasty means I am accepted wherever I go without making any actual effort. There is no need for personal details, or indeed personality, because I am vouched for. I am, in all but name, a Slater now. The halo that shines bright over their pack encompasses me too. Misplaced in my case, but there nonetheless.

Dee, with no hesitation, would invite Sofia for lunch – she would have a handy quiche in the fridge and half a cake in the tin.

9

I have neither, but am toying with asking her to try out next week's service – hoping she won't think it's a ploy to convert her – when she takes the initiative.

'I don't suppose . . . do you want to come over for a cup of coffee?' she asks. 'I haven't got any milk, but—'

'Yes,' I say, snatching the invitation out of her mouth. 'Coffee would be great.'

'Excellent. You can be my first visitor.'

2

Dish Dash

From the outside Keeper's Cottage could be made of cake: a thatch of spun sugar sitting on wonky royal icing walls with a marzipan door, but walking straight into the front room the promise disappears. The ceilings are low, the windows tiny, the soft furnishings surely plump with mites. Sofia leads me through to the kitchen where black flies line the strip light and grease lines everything else.

'It's gross, isn't it?' she says. 'But I'm told it'll be gutted when I leave so I am going for a complete whitewash. Have you met the daughter?'

'Yes.' Sofia is waiting for embellishment. I choose: 'She's efficient.'

'I like you already. She's monstrous. No sign of a heartbeat. Sign here. Twelve months. We won't be extending. My brother needs time to process our father's death. Dish dash.' Sofia uses pursed lips to make the staccato delivery. 'No parties. Obviously. The cottage is too small. Dish dash. I won't tolerate any complaints. Don't burn it down. It's thatch.'

'Why did you take it?'

Sofia throws open the top of the stable door and light streams in, showcasing every smear and scuff. 'Because of the garden, of course.' She slips off her cape and hangs it on the door handle. 'Don't disappoint me. Can't you see the potential?'

The garden is knee-high weeds backed by what might be fruit trees; in the corner is a dilapidated shed. 'It's disappointment from me, sorry. I'd get a man in.'

'Honestly, no romance and a helping of everyday sexism. I'm going to make a clearing – a circle, I thought – and leave the rest of the garden to live its life around me. I've already chucked those miracle wildflower seeds that come in clever little coats full of everything they need to flourish. It'll be bee heaven.'

'If you want any help, my boyfriend's mum – four doors down – is a garden whizz.'

'Which direction and what's her name?'

'Dee.' I point. 'Royal-blue door and neat pots.'

'Excellent. I'll say you sent me.' She picks up the kettle and turns the tap; there's a throaty gurgle followed by much spurting. 'Do you think there's a toad trapped?'

'Unlikely.'

The ritual of coffee making begins. I take off my puffer, drape it over the back of the chair closest to me and sit. In our short journey from the church, I have established that Sofia, like me, grew up in London but, unlike me, is excited by 'the countryside's rich and varied tapestry'. She is raving about the importance of pollinators, when the gnawing starts. There's nothing, and then something. A dragging, gravity drawing on what should be held tight. I know this feeling. My attention disappears inwards, staring deep into my abdomen to interrogate the sensation. It isn't pain, not yet. More of a firm stretch, a yawn, a steady tug.

'Anna?'

'Yes.'

'Where did you go?'

The only answer comes from my flat, forever fucking flat, stomach. The grip seems more determined, but I am an unreliable narrator. Hypervigilant. Alert to any danger. Maybe this is indigestion, or bloating. This baby cannot follow its unborn sibling. I cannot bear to see Ben's face. Dee's face. Milly's face. I don't want to hear what they say: Ben picked a dud; Milly had no problems making babies.

Stop it, Anna.

Sofia places her hand on top of mine. I look up at her face – lovely dark eyes, quite a narrow nose, dainty lips – but no words come. Her expression is wide open, ready for whatever it is I am about to tell her. And I am going to tell her. When I can.

Without losing contact with my skin, she sits down and crosses one leg over the other. Her dungarees ride up to reveal her sock, dark green with two grey stripes at the top.

I focus on the sock as I say, 'I think I'm going to have another miscarriage.'

'How many have you had?'

'Just the one.'

'How do you know?'

'Gripey feeling.'

'How many weeks are you?'

'Nine.'

She audibly puffs. 'I won't insult you by reeling off easy platitudes.' Her hand picks up mine.

'Thank you.' And I am thankful: thankful she hasn't told me to think positively. Or insisted the next one will hold, be twins even; or embarked on an anecdote of a woman who had a hundred failures before giving birth to an Olympic bobsleigh champion; that she isn't recommending pomegranate shakes or beetroot juice.

'My sister, Tamsin, had an ectopic pregnancy,' she says. 'That was pretty shit. She lost a fallopian tube.'

'Does she have children now?'

'No. But they have a really beautiful Airedale terrier.'

How can I be laughing? She joins in and, between spates, tells me tales of Hippo-the-Airedale who has a waxed Barbour coat and a wigwam and weekly cranial osteopathy to curb an irrational dislike of Dalmatians. I don't believe her, obviously.

The situation should be awkward but this stranger has taken my woe in her stride. I want to go to the toilet and check the progress but I also don't want to. If I wait, the grumbling might settle down.

'Are there any more of you?' I ask her.

'I'm the youngest of three. And living up to the stereotype.'

'Spoilt?'

'That's a trifle harsh. I prefer leaning more towards rebellion than responsibility.' I stutter inside – the younger me could have worn that description, but the current me is the polar opposite. 'What about you? Hang on, I'll guess. Oldest of two?'

'Bingo. One brother, eleven months between us. Wayward.' Keen to avoid any talk of Simon, I point at the pile of non-fiction books and papers on the round wooden table. 'Are you a student?'

'I'm doing a PhD at Bath – I'm interested in pain.' She rolls her eyes. 'It's a classic reaction to seeing my mum suffer but at least I realise that. She has fibromyalgia.'

'Sorry to hear that.'

'Thanks.' She sighs. 'I'm actually taking time out, doing some shadowing at a pain clinic. I need to regroup.'

'That all sounds very responsible to me.'

'Don't be fooled. Education is the classic shirk. Learn don't do. What about you?'

The coffee has arrived in two incongruously beautiful mugs, clearly Sofia's own.

'I'm a teaching assistant at the school.'

'Wow. Rather you than me.'

'It's okay. I work with nice people.'

'What about the loathsome children? And don't tell me there aren't any.'

As wanting to throttle children is unacceptable, I say, 'I find a way to like them.'

'Come on, there must be some you despise?'

Despise isn't in my lexicon, too melodious. I would use hate, shorter and harder. Word choice is an endlessly fertile topic. Fertile, that's ironic.

I shake my head, take a sip of the weighty black coffee. Wonder at how ordinary this is, and how extraordinary. This filthy kitchen, which used to belong to a grumpy man who died of a heart attack aged seventy-four and temporarily belongs to Sofia, is an odd place to begin the process of losing – an example of the wrong word, let's try expelling – expelling Ben's lookalike. Funny that I think of it as a mini-Slater already. As though their dominant genes would negate all my influence. Soon I will have to go home and tell him. My shoulders slump at the thought. The disappointment will burn across his face before he has a chance to fix his expression into something more stoical.

Sofia seems to sense I am back on the topic of the hour. 'How long have you been trying?'

15

'A year and a bit. I can get pregnant but they don't seem to want to stay.'

'I have a similar problem with men.'

'That can't be true.' I choose to believe she is attempting levity and not wildly insensitive. 'You're so . . .' I want to say arresting or vivid but am too embarrassed.

'Opinionated, intolerant, childish, impatient, irreverent—'

'Easy to talk to.'

'It's not the greatest compliment I've ever had. You make me sound like elevator music.' She screws up her nose. 'I'm not being absolutely truthful. I was married for about five seconds.'

'Really?'

'Really. Although it was five months, not five seconds.'

'What happened?'

'Nothing. We were eighteen – I'm not sure it wasn't a dare. I did all the legals to become Sofia Hemingway but the rhythm sounded strange so I reverted to Carstairs. What about your partner . . .?'

'Ben.'

'Ben. Will he be distraught?'

I nod. 'As will his mum and his sister and his brother and Uncle Eric and—'

'Ah! You've married a clan.'

'Not quite married. Attached.'

'We're a clan. The Carstairs swallow people whole. Dad becomes everyone's best friend on impact and Mum plies them with drink and salty pretzels and my sister makes them personalised cards and my brother takes them racing. The attack comes from all sides and there is no defence.'

Families are my thing. I already want my personalised card

16

and a day at the races, regardless of whether that's horse, dog or pigeon. Maybe, like Sofia, it's a classic reaction to a childhood of dysfunction. Ben's tight-knit flock was definitely a part of his allure. They welcomed me in and closed around me. Safe. Warm. Reliable. Steady. Other words pop into my head without invitation. Predictable. Sensible. Dull.

'They sound nice,' I say. 'Good people to be swallowed by.'

She huffs. 'You're a lost cause. Clearly, it's better not to be swallowed at all.'

Her manner, or more specifically the teasing, is engaging. We have somehow bypassed the canapés and are chewing the medium-rare steak. I wonder whether she is like this with everyone. And that thought is tailgated by the idea that I am being swallowed. That Sofia, like her family, has a talent for relationships.

'I enjoy being part of a big family.' I am determinedly upbeat. 'There's always something happening.'

That sentence temporarily stalls us both. My baby is what is happening. With perfect synergy a cloud shifts to block the light, robbing the kitchen of its only merit.

'I'd better go,' I say, draining my mug.

I'd like to stay. Hover in this liminal place where neither of us belongs. Put off the inevitable. But Ben will be home soon. We are meant to be going to the garden centre to invest in comfortable garden furniture. I don't mind the knackered wooden bench we already have. If I place a cushion at one end and lie down, the backs of my knees can rest on the other arm, leaving my lower limbs to hang in a completely pleasing way. Ben fancies rattan with over-stuffed cushions.

3

Vodka Bucks

Ben is out – someone's birthday at work – and I should be at Dee's because the entity that is family deems it not good for me to be alone given the circumstances. The circumstances being that I am no longer pregnant.

But I have texted Dee to say that I am going to have a bath and an early night. This is a lie. The truth is that Sofia is coming round, but she is still my secret: one I want to keep. Soon enough she will debut at a village event and be shared among us. Until then, she is mine.

She arrives with two handfuls of dark purple tulips, vodka, ginger beer and a bag of limes. I usually drink wine or beer, the occasional gin and tonic. Nice, middle-class choices. The vodka is perfect. She gets to work, making the kitchen her own. I watch her reject our utility tumblers and choose the latte glasses instead; watch her fingers grip the lime and squeeze, talking all the time.

'I adore the recycling centre. Hurling stuff and hearing it smash unleashes that destructive force adulthood tries its hardest to dampen. Ultra-cathartic.'

'What have you got rid of?'

'Everything that wasn't nailed down. I went three times yesterday. I'm washing the walls with sugar soap next – that's what the woman in the hardware shop recommended.' She raises her glass high and I do the same. 'Onwards.'

The few people who know have tiptoed around me, wincing as they speak. Sofia, who'd caught me putting out the recycling earlier, had aimed straight for the bull's eye. 'Is it over?'

A nod reciprocated by a shrug and she had segued into telling me about the sticky mulch she'd found down the side of the oven that so resembled mango chutney she was tempted to taste it. And now she's here and we are drinking on a weeknight. Not that it matters because it is still the Easter holidays.

'What will you do when you've got your PhD?' I ask, as though having a PhD is something I understand.

'No idea. The point of a PhD is to delay the grind of real work.'

'Have you ever had a job?'

'Of course. Many, but don't ask me to list them. My most interesting was doing art therapy at the Maudsley Hospital.'

Sofia grabs the pad from the kitchen counter and creates what she calls 'a happy drawing' with a sun and a smiley face. She turns the page and starts again, a jagged scrawl, pressing so hard the paper tears. 'See. The pencil never lies, Anna.'

'Don't sad people ever draw fields of flowers?'

'You heretic. How dare you question the established doctrine?'

The first glass of what is evidently a Vodka Buck slips down. As does the second. I decide a hangover is a price worth paying.

'Do you wear anything but navy?' Sofia asks, her disapproval accentuated by the deep crease in her forehead.

'I honestly don't know how my uniform became this,' I say,

looking down at the V-necked navy sweater, navy T-shirt and dark jeans that have replaced distressed denim and crop tops.

Tonight, Sofia's hair is loose, draped over her shoulders like a badger-fur stole. She is wearing a large man's shirt with a bold orange stripe, slung over a white vest; her baggy jeans are rolled up and, without me noticing, she has taken off her bovver boots. Her brown and green Argyll socks with their cheeky red thread mock my black ones.

'Clothes make me cheerful. If I hate the world – which is most days – all I have to do is stare at my wardrobe and some combination leaps out at me and suddenly I'm sprayed in sunshine.' Sofia takes a swig and wipes her mouth afterwards. 'It might also be called vanity.'

'I'm not sure I like clothes.'

'That's ridiculous. You're ridiculous. And gorgeous, despite trying not to be – you could wear anything and yet you choose plain, plain, plain.' She has her palms out, imploring me to agree. 'Is it all a front for a secret life?'

Dee would say the inside is what matters, but I know that my invisibility is as deliberate as Sofia's flamboyance.

'Maybe I don't want to stand out. Someone has to be in the background.'

'Is that really what you think? That some people are born solely to provide a backdrop?'

If my argument had any conviction, I would have a countermove. 'I'm not playing,' I say, 'because you will win.'

She sighs. 'I don't want to win. I want Anna . . . what's your surname?'

'Harris.'

'I want the affable Anna Harris to drop her reserve.'

'I'm not reserved, I'm just not you.'

She takes a few of the prawn-flavoured crisps that Ben buys for his lunch when he's going into the office. Like a kid going on a school trip, he packs a sandwich, crisps, an apple, a flapjack and a sugary drink. Never will a roasted vegetable wrap grace his Tupperware.

Mouth full, she says, 'I know, let's swap.'

'Swap what?'

'Well, we can't swap partners. Clothes, you idiot.' She has already pulled her shirt over her head. Under her vest I can see lacy fuchsia straps that clearly attach to some delicious underwear. Without her capacious coverall she is slight, proud collarbones, pert boobs with only a hint of cleavage, a tiny waist. 'Come on.'

Because I'm afraid Sofia might do it for me, I wriggle my arms out of the sleeves to offer her my jumper and, in turn, accept her shirt. It is warm and smells of salt and peach and English rain. I lose myself in its expanse. When my head emerges from the neck, she has tied her hair back using the string bag from the limes as a fastener and is, in my plain navy jumper, fundamentally altered.

Sofia is grinning widely at me but all I see is my best friend Pippa Williams, aged anywhere between ten and sixteen. She is goading me to climb onto the roof, steal the chewing gum, ask the boys in the year above for a cigarette, dye my hair pink, eat a doughnut from the inside out. I don't have a friend like Pippa anymore, one who pushes you to places you're not sure you want to go, one who makes your pulse race and your laugh urgent. She has been replaced by women who care about refugees and planning applications and who universally despise SATs; and by Ben, who asks nothing of me except to bear his child. I have missed this feeling. The thrill of being attracted, wanting to entertain, the

21

sense that this connection is special: a purer hedonism, unsullied by the shadow of sex.

Sofia's hand reaches across, freeing my hair from its scrunchy before grabbing my elbow to drag me to standing; she takes a selfie of us, heads tight together. In the photo, my skin is flushed, thanks to the vodka, and my sometimes-stern face is softened by the sweep of dark hair falling across my forehead. By contrast, Sofia has lessened; with her mane of hair tamed she is more waiflike and drained of colour. I am surprised that we are the same height. Her undeniable presence had made her larger in every way.

When Sofia is gone, when I can't see her ever again, I will wear out the image of our happy faces; the lights and shades, humps and hollows, engraved on my memory.

Later, my voice thick with alcohol, I find I am talking about Ben, about his certainty that we will manage to make a full-term baby, about how supportive he is. She makes no comment.

Conscious it has become a monologue, I dry up.

'Tell me something you don't like about him,' she says.

'Why?'

'To make him real.'

I flick through a list of trivial dislikes: his slipper boots, his obsessional interest in house prices, screaming at sport on the TV, none of which satisfy Sofia.

'I don't like the way you sound so grateful. As though you bring nothing.'

My mum could be a mean drinker. The high spirits would be followed by a visible need to peck at me, her head bobbing forwards to moan about how untidy I was, what a picky eater, too lazy, too thin. I become wary.

'He's a nice person.'

'Apple pie is nice. Wouldn't you prefer . . .' she thrusts her chin skywards, arms outspread, '. . . stallionesque?'

'Stallionesque is a made-up—'

The key in the door makes me jump. Time has travelled fast. In my head I'd imagined Sofia would leave after a couple of hours and I could clear away the evidence and omit to mention her visit.

'Hi,' Ben calls. I hear him kick off his shoes before he walks in wearing the aforementioned camel slipper boots. His double take is understandable. Sofia is sitting on my stool, in my clothes. I am in Ben's place, wearing strange clothes. 'This looks like fun.' He holds out his hand. 'I'm Ben.'

'Sofia.'

I observe the efficient way they become acquainted – two practised people.

The younger Ben, the one who first chatted me up, had shorter hair, a grim football shirt and a skinful of beer; but he also had deep pockets and I'd been sacked from the pub and had no immediate plans apart from sinking my head into as much alcohol as I could get for free. I've asked him, many times, what possessed him to pursue me – a mouthy drunk, propped up by the bar in The Mayflower, rough as fuck and going nowhere. He insists it was when I said he was simply a means to an end. Undone by my brutal honesty. (I was less honest about the existence of my boyfriend, Smiffy.) Ben was twenty-seven, visiting a friend from uni. He dumped the friend and came back to mine, both of us utterly wasted. A chance encounter. Call it fate. Call it convenience.

'What do you think, Anna?'

'Sorry?'

'Sofia wants to remodel her garden.' He looks at me, my blue-eyed Ben. 'I've said I'll introduce her to Dave.'

'Yes. Good idea.'

The tendrils of the village have begun their creep. Dave will do your lawn. Jack from the estate will fell your trees. Hannah from the B&B will give you a room. Stella Jefferies will make a superb cake for a special birthday. Alan has drain rods in case you get a blockage. Ariadne is a vet; take your dog, budgie, guinea pig. Jenny can hem trousers but best not trust her with anything complicated. Fenella does the food for every wake in the village hall but likes the money upfront. If you've got any other problem, the village will either come up trumps or rain down on you, depending on who you are. We are Slaters. We make the sodding rain.

4

Playing Dead

Ben's hand is stroking my left thigh, his mouth is in my hair. On another night I might press back against him. Or I might tell him I'm tired and, as compensation, turn to peck his cheek. But tonight, I am pretending my nerve endings don't work. Breathing steadily is an effort when your legs are clamped shut and your mind is screaming, but I persevere.

When he gets no response, he will give up. Ben is nice. (Must stop staying that.) He is testing the water. The water is still icy.

We both heard the doctor. Leave it a couple of weeks, she'd said, for the risk of infection to pass. We are well past the deadline and I am physically and mentally ready to resume our sex life, but I am definitely not ready to make embryo number three.

The hand begins to creep, slow and stealthy. In my head his fingers become something other: a predatory snake, a slick of oil suffocating the seabirds. They come to rest, lightly cupping my buttock. I concentrate on remaining immobile, hoping his hiatus is a sign he has correctly read the temperature.

Ben usually falls asleep quickly, purrs rather than snores. I listen, keenly, waiting for the rhythm of his breath to change. The rise and fall of my own chest is, I think, convincing, but inside the pressure is building. My whole body is primed, eager to stretch, roll onto my other hip, wrest free of his touch. Soon I will have to take a discordant lungful of air, the urge to shift will be too great to ignore, the compulsion to grab his hand and push it away will win.

'Anna.'

I don't immediately answer, weighing up whether any part of him believes I am asleep. But this is Ben, I remind myself. The Ben I love.

I try a dozy reply. 'What?'

'Can we talk?'

No.

'I'm very tired, Ben.'

'Please.'

We have not talked about the baby. Because we have not talked about the baby we have not talked about sex, or more specifically, contraception. Because we have not talked about contraception, I cannot have sex with Ben. I am not good to go again.

'I don't want to make love, if you don't.' I liked his voice from the off. Low, slow, but also light, curious. I replay the syllables in my head.

'Is it too soon?'

'It's going to take a little while,' I say. 'Making love is too tied up with everything else.'

He kisses the back of my head. 'I get it. I'm sorry, I don't know how to be with you. We haven't really spoken about it, have we?'

'We will.' Only now do I turn to kiss him.

'You know . . . we both lost the baby.' He takes a quick, desperate snatch of air. I touch his face, feel the slight stubble. I cannot tell him. I cannot tell him that I'm not sure anymore, that the heartbreak has been replaced by another, less acceptable feeling, which might be relief. Relief at failing at this early stage rather than failing later on, as I undoubtedly would. Ben has no qualms about fatherhood because his upbringing gave him a blueprint, whereas I only have a fuck-up of a mother to emulate.

He rolls away from me and I spoon him. And his sleep comes. But I remain awake, surfing the waves that picked me up and deposited me here.

I am twenty-two again, lodging in an attic room. It is the morning after the night I first met Ben and he is in my bed. The sober sex is better, deft and deliberate, and he talks, which adds a certain something. I'd like to remember what his lips whisper into the back of my neck, but the words vanish like the bubbles in a glass of lemonade. We go out for breakfast and, in daylight, I realise how attractive he is. Like a pedigree dog that has been fed a nutritious diet and regularly exercised, Ben radiates wellbeing. It occurs to me that he might be what happy looks like. After he leaves, promising to return on Friday from wherever it is he lives, I go to meet my boyfriend, Smiffy, in the pub. By comparison he has become a mongrel. What I had found edgy – his dark hair and pale skin, his skinny body, ever encased in faded denim – now looks like neglect. We have an afternoon shag – always best to make sure – before I break up with him.

For the third Friday running Ben comes to see me in London. I meet him at Paddington Station and we have sex in a deserted pub garden and go on to a club. We party hard every weekend; on Sunday nights he goes back to his other life.

Six months later I go to Ben's village for the weekend. I am treated like visiting royalty, following a tight itinerary that takes in his siblings and their kids and, on Sunday, lunch at his parents'. I wear a borrowed dress that Ben peels off as soon as we've left to check the real Anna is still underneath.

I am twenty-three, eating dinner at Dee and Richard's. We don't know Richard will have a heart attack the next week, dead in his sixties, or that Ben will find him, face down in the garden. Drowning in grief, Ben begs to meet my family but my mum hooks up with a bloke who works on the oil rigs and after forty years in Southwark, Helen Harris fucks off to Glasgow and I don't see her again for two years. My brother is already dead and none of my extended family would measure up, so I am saved.

I am twenty-four and Ben rarely comes to London. Instead, I get the train to Bath and he picks me up and brings me to the village. We drink in the pub, go to his sister's or brother's for dinner, drop round to Dee's. It is me who, eventually, helps her empty Richard's wardrobe, his briefcase, his wash bag. I am the chosen one, and I like it.

It is Christmas and London holds no sparkle for me. My housemates have, like most normal people, gone to see their families. My mum is, I assume, in Glasgow, not that we've spoken in a while. The Slaters are all going to Milly's and I'm invited. It's astonishingly civilised – no one pukes, no one falls out over the contents of a cracker, no one reignites a smouldering family fire: the one about buying an enormous TV that had no sound from a man in a pub; the one about Mum reporting the neighbours to the RSPCA because their mongrel kept waking her up; the one about me going missing. (They knew where I was – just didn't come to get me.)

I stay at Ben's for a week and see, at first hand, there is a way out.

An escape from the messes I've made, the damage I've caused, the person I've been.

Ben nudges me. I'm leaden with sleep. Don't want to wake. Scramble to keep the happy feeling, dancing in a pink minidress.

'Anna.'

I think I murmur.

'Anna.'

'Yes?' My lids are sandbags. Definitely can't open them, not even a slit.

'I've made you tea.'

My 'Thank you' takes a humongous effort.

He sits and I roll towards the dip slightly. Reality slides into place. It is Friday. Maypole day.

'I've been trying to say something, Anna.'

Only now do I actually look at Ben. Really look at him. Not glance, relying on the memory of the face I know, but scrutinise. His eyes seem smaller, or maybe the skin around them has lost some elasticity, his blond hair is darkened by the long winter, there's the hint of a jowl. He is thirty-two. He is not happy.

'What is it?'

'Mum came round yesterday. She was hoping to see us together.'

I was at Sofia's, hanging a blind in her bedroom but really just hanging out. 'She's not ill?'

'No. She wants to help.'

Ah! We are back to baby. 'She can't carry one for me, Ben.'

'She offered to pay.' The pause is in an unnatural place; he's not sure how I'll react. I don't help him out. 'For us to see a fertility specialist.'

Buying your way out of everything doesn't sit well with me. There were times growing up when fifty quid would have made the difference between abject misery and euphoria. I can still channel the feeling of watching a girl in the year above buy the Adidas Gazelles I coveted so much I repeatedly hid them in the back of the JD Sports in Croydon. I tried them on once, walked towards the door with a view to carrying on and forfeiting my shitty trainers but 'shoplifter' was written all over me.

If I hadn't been perpetually broke, who knows, I might have paid attention at school and become a software developer like Ben, or a dentist like Milly, or a teacher instead of the unqualified assistant.

'Anna?'

'That's kind of her, it is, but I'm not ready to think about trying again, Ben.' I know, really I do, that Dee isn't offering to buy a baby, but that's how it feels . . . and my switch trips. 'How about we let the last baby grow cold?'

He stares at me. The epitome of struck dumb. This is not his Anna speaking. I match his look. I want us to row. That would feel good. But we haven't rowed since, oh I don't know, maybe since the pub landlord was ranting about the travellers who had set up camp on the playing field. I remember, halfway down my wine, daring to show discord: 'You're like those people who put ugly spikes on their windowsills to stop the pigeons.' I'd smiled – we were all chatting, weren't we? 'Why not let them tiptoe on your precious ledge?'

The village voice was high-pitched with outrage. Back home, Ben went into a tailspin: children weren't safe to play out on their own, the rubbish would attract rats, the field would be cut up and what would that mean for the cricket? Community doesn't necessarily extend to other communities; I understand that now.

30

'I hope you'll be more polite with my mum.' He leans over to kiss me, not because he wants to but because he has never not kissed me goodbye, even after #travellergate. 'I've got to go.'

The lessons of marriage were well taught by Dee. All the Slaters are civil, mindful, respectful. I lie in bed, marvelling at the restraint, marvelling for so long that there's no time left to shower.

5

Spider's Web

This year the maypole ribbons have been replaced; no longer patriotically red, white and blue, they now include purple, orange and green. The dances, however, can never change because the learning curve is too steep for the staff. So, once again, the kids have performed The Barber's Hat, The Plait and The Spider's Web to an audience of parents and caregivers, the rest of the school and any locals keen to wander down memory lane. And, as usual, the weather has been kind. God shines on this village.

Sofia, who let out a squeal of delight when I told her we have an actual wooden maypole, is here, standing with Dee and Hannah from the B&B. I catch her eye and wave but am ringed by parents. In the middle of a trying conversation with Ralph's mum – Ralph who wasn't picked to dance because he's a little shit – she interrupts us.

'Sorry, excuse me.' Sofia smiles to offset the rudeness. 'Anna, that was brilliant. How did you corral the little creatures to make those clever patterns down the pole?'

'Beatings,' I say, turning away from Ralph's mum. 'Interspersed with praise.'

'I'd like to have a go. There should be evening classes.'

'I think going round and round when you're our age causes vertigo.'

'That sort of attitude deserves early arthritis.'

'Why, thank you,' I say. 'I'll live in hope.'

'I'd get those grab rails installed. Can never be too well prepared.'

Since I've known Sofia, we have transformed the cottage by painting her kitchen and living room entirely white, had two Chinese takeaways, been for several walks, been to the pub a few times with Ben and, in between, perfected our own method of conversing while drinking every type of alcohol. With Sofia, I am dry and funny and she is garrulous and ridiculous. I cannot imagine my life before she came.

I see Dee approaching and prepare a precautionary shield. Ben's crack-of-dawn fertility chat is in storage and I'd like it to stay there.

'Anna, they were absolute darlings, every one of them.'

'Except behind the scenes,' I say.

'All that matters is how they behave in public.'

'Is that also true for adults?' asks Sofia.

'Most definitely.' Dee laughs and touches Sofia's arm. They look gorgeous together, both in flowery dresses, both boasting lush red lips. I know how much they like each other because they have each told me. Dee shares with Sofia how she feels about her chronic obstructive pulmonary disease because chronic illness is, after all, Sofia's bag, and Sofia breaks Dee's confidence and tells me, but I don't tell Ben. I don't tell him that Dee is increasingly scared of the future, that the tight band that stops a full breath comes more often or that she would rather die than be plumbed into an oxygen cylinder via tubes up her nose.

The crowds dissipate, taking the children with them. The pole is dismantled for another year and I am free to go. I grab my bag and the three of us begin the walk home, taking the shortcut through the alley. To camouflage Dee's snail pace, to make it less apparent, we act as though we are on a nature tour. I mention the way the verge has narrowed the path and comment on the glut of wild garlic and Sofia remarks on the canopy made by the bowing trees and eulogises about the bluebells before, supposedly, spotting a jay. (I will repeat this later and it will be riotously comic.) Dee, whose step is as deliberate as a marching soldier, is only required to affirm or deny.

At the corner, we bump into Alan, tell-tale green dog lead slung around his neck. He walks twice a day, early morning and late afternoon, setting off with Rocket, his bluey-grey Weimaraner, but often returning without him. The ravages of arthritis dictate that Alan's bowed legs can only get him as far as the little bridge where he lets Rocket off the lead and sits and smokes on the bench for half an hour with the faint hope his dog will reappear. Why would he? There are rabbits for heaven's sake! Rocket either returns when he feels like it or is lured home by a fellow dog walker with treats or, on one occasion, by me, using my belt as a lead.

'Hi there, Alan.' I smile. 'No Rocket today?'

'Bloody wretch,' says Alan. 'Serve him right if a bloody car gets him.'

The last stretch is a trial but, safely back at Dee's, Sofia makes tea and I cut three slices from a freshly made banana cake with a pleasing crust. Our idle chat allows the disquiet to leave Dee's eyes and the ease to return to her breath. I realise I have become a medical monitor, observing her vital signs and recording changes.

Dee is, it appears, doing something similar: 'You're looking so much better, Anna.'

34

We are at right angles, elbows nearly touching. Instinct draws me away.

'I'm fine.' My tone is brusque, designed to deter discussion of my fertility.

'I've got ants,' says Sofia, apropos of nothing. 'Do you know any remedies that aren't poison?'

Dee diverts onto vinegar and cinnamon, before getting back on track.

'I'm so proud of the way you pick yourself up.' She switches her gaze to Sofia. 'And you've been such a welcome friend to our lovely girl, Sofia.'

She reaches for both our hands. I want to throw hers in the air and slap it back down. Dee has my best interests at heart, I have to remind myself. Our best interests.

'It's the other way around,' says Sofia. 'I'm atrocious at friendship. I either piss people off by being too direct or I find they're not who I think they are. Anna is the friendship fairy.' She turns her head to smile at me.

'I think you were sent, Sofia,' says Dee, eyes plump with meaning.

I do well not to scoff. Believing in the intervention of a deity smacks of madness. Sofia was not summoned by an unseen hand; she is here because she has a placement at the pain clinic. End of.

In the absence of any response, Dee embellishes. 'You were sent because we needed you at this difficult time.'

'What we need, Dee, is more cake,' says Sofia. 'I wish I could get a decent rise.'

'I haven't been feeling myself,' says Dee, as though she hasn't heard Sofia. 'I might have many years in me, but I might not and,

35

Anna, I want to see you and Ben settled with your own little family. It would mean the world . . .'

Her eyes have watered, glassy blue Slater eyes. My face is solid stone, can't force any expression into it. Inside I'm beseeching Sofia to step in but she appears stunned by Dee's insensitivity. And it gets worse.

'Richard would want me to help. I know he would.' Recruiting a dead husband is a master move. I can't argue with the saintly dead.

Thankfully, Sofia has no such compunction – 'Anna hasn't had two miscarriages because of a lack of help. It's biology' – which gives me the courage to meet the topic head-on – 'Sofia, Dee has offered to pay for me to see a fertility specialist' – but I can't muster a shred of gratitude.

My body. My choice. My life.

Up to speed, Sofia takes over. And I love her. Truly, in this moment, I love her.

'That's kind of you, Dee. But it's so recent, the miscarriage, I think you need a moment, don't you, Anna? When my sister lost her baby . . .'

She runs with a story of how her sister, Tamsin, booked a week's silent retreat and dyed her hair, bridging the gap between Dee's magnanimous gesture and my obvious reluctance. Ruffles smoothed, I cut more cake. When our mugs are empty, Sofia and I make good our escape, leaving Dee intact, but in limbo. It is too soon to make me embark on another journey with an unknown destination. She understands that now.

Drinking is the answer. Drinking on a stomach lined with cake. Drinking with wild abandon. If you're trying for a baby the recommendation is that you avoid alcohol. After what feels like years of moderation, with periods of complete abstinence, the Anna who used to buy half-bottles of vodka from the convenience store has woken from dormancy. I smile at the memory of being charged a premium because the guy knew I was underage.

The tipple of the night is one of the bottles of Chardonnay Sofia intended to take to her parents' tomorrow. I am pleased of the excuse to quiz her, put flesh on the stick people that comprise her sister and brother, her stoic mother and charismatic father. We cover her brother's messy divorce after only ten months, her sister's teenage infatuation with older men and her father's penchant for lost causes.

'That was awkward with Dee,' says Sofia, bored, I think, of my insatiable desire for familial details. 'Kind, but stratospherically insensitive.'

'Oh look,' I say, pointing at the door. 'I think it's a jay.'

Sofia is, for once, slow to catch on, but joins in with gusto when she gets the joke. We see jays everywhere, fashioning the chat to purposefully trespass on areas that are verboten so we can declare the sighting of a jay.

In the middle of a story about how I sold my mum's diazepam at school, Ben texts me and I reply that I am at Sofia's. He asks if I'll be home soon and I ping back that I'll be a while as I'm eating here – *If that's okay?*

Sofia orders a whole Peking duck that we devour, the sticky hoisin sauce washed down with a second bottle of oaky golden wine.

'You can come if you like,' says Sofia. 'Be my plus one.'

'To your parents'?'

'Yes. Then you can see for yourself. I know you're fascinated by me.'

I hesitate. She knows why, of course she does.

'Do you need a pass? Permission to leave the gated community?'

I don't need a pass as such, but apart from Ben's annual ski trip we tend to spend our free time together. A quick résumé of a typical weekend involves family, football, the pub, shopping, occasional rudimentary gardening, washing, church. Nothing that can't wait. In fact, nothing that won't be repeated every weekend in perpetuity. And I want to go. Of course I do.

'Well?'

'When are you leaving?' I am stalling.

'Elevenish. Back Sunday.'

I bite my lip.

'Don't worry. I guess it's tricky to abscond at short notice.'

Running away is never the answer, unless you have the permission of a mum who fucked off to Glasgow with only a five-word text.

'I'll come,' I say, and my smile erupts. 'Thank you.'

'Fantastic. You will be their best present. A stranger to deconstruct.' Sofia reaches across, hooks her hand around my neck and draws me close. She stares for a second before kissing me on the lips. 'It'll be fun. Be prepared, Tamsin will be madly jealous and Dad will invite you to the Dordogne in the summer.'

With my lips a-tingle, a graze with a nettle, I ask what I should bring, and when we'll be back and whether I should pretend to not know personal things about her family like the messy divorce and the ectopic pregnancy.

'They know I can't keep anything to myself. Just be your lovely self.'

It is late. Brimful of wine, salty sauce and fat, I start to clear away.

Sofia would happily leave the detritus to deal with in the morning but she lets me restore order – we've been through this before.

'Do you feel more like a surrogate than a girlfriend?' she asks.

My back is to her, my hands dunked in hot washing-up water. Sober, the question might seem more insulting. 'I didn't, but now you've pointed it out . . .'

'Sorry.'

'No need. Anyway, surrogates get paid.'

'Only expenses.'

'But reasonable expenses.'

'Yes, like new clothes with elastic panels.'

'And therapy.'

'And wear and tear. That would be huge.'

A month ago I was pregnant, willing my belly to be space-hopper size, and now I can't imagine how that felt. 'Maybe I won't have a baby.' I turn around. 'Maybe I'll be a pilot.'

Sofia sprays wine with her laugh and slaps her own thigh. 'You can literally be the jay.'

I spread my arms, tilt, add an engine noise. 'Fly with me, Sofia.'

The flying becomes dancing – young, free and wild.

I have found my soulmate.

6

Maneki-neko (Lucky Cat)

The kitchen in Sofia's parents' house has masses of open shelving with no apparent sense of organisation. A copper colander sits next to a bag of flour, some digital scales hold a plastic pot of basil, a gold cat with a waving arm narrowly misses a box of decaf tea. I am sitting in the bay window at a dark wood table that was, when Sofia and I arrived, similarly cluttered, but is now laid for seven, the detritus simply added to the pile on the sideboard.

The three women in the family – Sofia, her sister Tamsin and their mum Viv – are busy preparing lunch at the other end of the large room. Sofia's dad, Rollo, is looking after me. The other two lunch guests – Sofia's brother and brother-in-law – are walking Hippo-the-Airedale around the block. A very smart Clerkenwell block, I could add.

'I do adore it when the children bring strangers,' says Rollo, pouring me a glass from a newly opened bottle of Crémant. 'We behave much better in company.'

'That's a shame. I'm quite comfortable with bad behaviour.'

'Why? Do you work in the House of Commons?' His quip elicits appreciative chuckles from the cooks.

'Worse, she works in a school,' says Sofia, gliding over to steal the bottle before returning to stir whatever is in the saucepan. She is wearing a diaphanous red dress, wholly unsuitable to be near a flame. Entirely suitable for a ball. I am glad I have, for the occasion, also found some colour in the form of a khaki jumpsuit (despite Ben's insistence that I look like someone on manoeuvres).

'What drew you to teaching?' asks Rollo.

'I'm only an assistant.'

'The "only" isn't necessary. We don't have to crave more responsibility.'

'In my case it might be. My boyfriend's mum is a governor and she shooed me in.'

'Nepotism gets a bad press but we all try to help our families.' He smiles, forgivingly. Such a nice face – just enough wrinkles, just enough bulk to his lips, hair just grey enough at the fringes to set off his warm skin. I'm enjoying the company of that rare thing – a dad-figure – so I continue to tunnel down.

'I've never had a job I didn't get through a friend.' I say this for effect but, running back through my CV, find it to be true: the bar work, the waitressing, the stint at the language school, the care home. Not a single application filled out; simply pitching up on someone or other's say-so.

'Well, you must be good at making friends then.'

I love that he finds the positive.

The temptation to confess my largely absent, now dead, dad and my chaotic mother is stymied by the arrival of food: a Spanish omelette streaked with ribbons of red, sprinkled with green confetti; a wide blue bowl full of leaves – maroon, bottle green, acid lime – dotted with spring onion pearls; green beans; posh bread – impossible to cut an actual slice; pickle.

41

'We're vegetarian,' says Viv. 'Did Sofia say? Meat is murder.'

Sofia makes a beak with her hand and I smile at the reference to last night's duck.

As Viv bends to sit, I catch a shot of pain cross her face and am reminded that she has fibromyalgia. A condition that is under-diagnosed, undertreated and its impact underestimated, according to Sofia.

A bout of barking heralds the arrival of Hippo-the-Airedale, who bounds into the kitchen and runs between the many pairs of legs, frantically checking us out. Sofia's brother, Archie, is close behind, eccentrically dressed in top to bottom checks.

'Archie!' Sofia wraps her arms around him. 'Mum said you'd got chunky. Why haven't you been to visit me?'

'Because you say things like that.'

The final guest, Ed, fills the doorframe. He is supersized, not fat but Teutonic tall and broad, and clean-cut.

'I hope we're not late,' he says.

'Your timing is perfect. Let's eat,' says Viv.

While dishes are passed between us, I study the Carstairs family. Rollo and Archie clearly belong to their own branch, both stocky with masses of brown hair and beguiling brown cow eyes. And florid in their style: Rollo is sporting those red cords rich men favour. Whereas Viv is slim, short-haired and classically dressed in black jeans and a charcoal linen shirt. Tamsin, who has taken the seat the other side of me, is Sofia's clone – a shade shorter and a size rounder but the same expressive face, lots of hair and wearing a neon-yellow boyfriend shirt.

'Top-up?' says Tamsin, and I nod, 'Yes, please,' offering her my glass.

'So, you're Sofia's latest passion.'

'We've become good friends,' I say, slightly unsure.

'She has a trail of friends that appear from nowhere and vanish as quickly. Try not to bank on her, Anna,' she takes a generous mouthful of fizz, 'or my sister will break your heart.'

Sibling rivalry in action, I think, as I answer, my voice light, my smile easy. 'My heart is titanium. But thanks for the heads-up.'

'I think you must be from South London. Originally, that is,' says Viv, from across the table.

I nod, wondering what her ear has spied in my manufactured accent. 'Rotherhithe.'

'What on earth took you to Somerset? I'm welded to London and wilfully deaf to any suggestion life can exist elsewhere.'

There is a short delay while I watch videos from my childhood: with Pippa at Camden Market eating churros; sunbathing in Greenwich Park, both with our heads in a book; ice-skating at Ally Pally.

'There is definitely life in villages, just packed into fewer streets.'

'Sofia says in a month she knows more people's darkest secrets than she did in four years at Cambridge. But she exaggerates, as you'll know.'

'Not this time. Pop your head above the parapet and you get a part in the proceedings.'

I am rewarded with several laughs. 'What do you mean?' asks Viv.

'If you show your face in the pub or at church—'

'The pillars of any community,' says Rollo.

'Exactly. The village scoops you up and gives you a role. Although to be fair, the population is pretty static so someone like Sofia arriving is big news.'

'Oh, she's big news wherever she goes,' says Archie. 'It's youngest-child syndrome.'

The touchpaper is lit. Accusations and anecdotes, funny and fiery, are traded for laughs. The energy is high, the volume higher. This is what I like. The teasing born of intimacy, the knotted-together past that informs all aspects of the present, the underlying knowledge that they like . . . love each other and that they are secure both in themselves and as a whole.

'You were all little bastards,' says Rollo. 'Just at different times.'

'Actually, Tamsin and I have something to say about little bastards,' says Ed, who has spoken the least. 'Don't we?'

Tamsin nods; there is a hiatus while she visibly swallows. 'It's been two years since the ectopic emergency and, as you all know, no baby.' She smiles. 'Thank you for not constantly asking.'

'We weren't interested,' says Sofia, a patent attempt to take the sting out.

Archie follows suit: 'I don't think about you from one day to the next, Tamsin.'

I badly want to chip in, to share my experience of Ben's family who, while careful to not badger me, have freely forwarded links to folic-rich foods and articles on the relationship between stress and hormones, but I am not the subject.

'So, we've thought through all the options and . . .' Tamsin takes a deep breath and locks eyes with Ed. He reaches across with his giant hand.

'I love you,' he says.

She continues, eyes bright with tears. 'We are lucky. We are happy as we are. And if it doesn't happen naturally, we've decided we don't want to bludgeon my body into making a baby.'

Ed takes the baton. 'We don't want to exist from month to month, waiting for the next test. I don't want Tamsin pumped full of hormones that might wreak their revenge in the long term or made to feel like a breeding machine or have her entire life medicalised.'

'I know how that one goes,' says Viv.

'We're going to live now. Every day. Every second of every day.'

'Bravo,' says Sofia, glass in the air. Archie gets up and smacks Ed on the back, before hugging Tamsin. I see Viv and Rollo share a look of approval.

'It's a good decision,' says Viv. 'There is something very powerful about accepting the life you're given and not coveting other people's.'

I am captivated by this public display, by the openness and unity. And dismayed by the light it shines on my own situation, making Ben and I appear positively constipated and his family tone deaf.

Time skips and I see the wall of Slaters encouraging me to be poked and prodded, dyed and dissected. They are probably all together right now, using my absence to discuss the crisis. Not only have I failed to grow a Slater baby, I have abandoned Ben's family to play teenager with Sofia; although enormously likeable, might she be – the schoolteacher phrase – a bad influence? No one wants to mention my drinking, but surely everyone has noticed. At a time like this my body needs all the help it can get. Isn't it a tad reckless, this behaviour? Dee admits she is a little disappointed I haven't taken up her offer. Everyone knows the NHS is a lottery. A baby mustn't be a lottery. If money can help, money must. Poor Ben . . .

'So, Anna,' says Archie, hauling me back into the room. 'When did you give up on London?'

'Three years ago.' The memory of packing up my clothes, chucking everything else into a wheelie bin and stepping into Ben's car,

45

destination Somerset, arrives as fresh as yesterday's maypole dance; too fresh, because on its heels comes the reason I was prepared to leave the only home I'd ever known. I focus on the checks of Archie's shirt, and order my thoughts to not stray.

'Do you not miss it?' asks Archie.

'London?' I say, forcing my mouth to smile. 'Sometimes. The anonymity mostly.'

'Why? What are you hiding?' He is being playful, I know that. He waits for a reply in the same vein.

I could say anything: I could say I am an outlier of a notorious crime family or an ex-child star of the West End; I could, if my soft palate, tongue and lips would comply, announce a connection to royalty; but the only answer dancing on my breath is the shocking truth. The shocking, distasteful truth that I must repeatedly swallow and forever keep down.

In the end Sofia speaks for me.

'She was buried under thatch. But I'm exhuming her.'

7

Distressed Purchase

The attic room in Sofia's parents' house has the comfiest, most pillow-heavy bed ever, despite which my sleep has been fitful. The physical act of leaving the village, leaving the Slaters, has broken a spell I didn't realise I was under. Being back in London, tucked away at the top of the house in an echo of my old lodgings, knowing my soulmate is downstairs, honestly feels as though I have been dug up. Cleared of claggy earth and fully ventilated.

Sofia's stated dedication to my exhumation is cause for much celebration. Buried in deepest Somerset cannot be the final chapter of my fucked-up story.

Safely snuggled under the cloud-like duvet, vaguely aware that I should venture downstairs for a Carstairs breakfast, my mind retraces the steps that led me from the streets of SE16, half encircled by the Thames, to a village of eight hundred people, flanked by fields. Steps that begin and end with Pippa.

In Year 11 we had three weeks' study leave before our big exams. My grand plans included sneaking into the multiplex at Westfield and hitching to Brighton but Pippa bought revision guides with shiny covers and decided to show the numerous teachers who had given up on us that she could teach herself. Arriving at the back door to find her making notes on an A4-lined pad in front of a textbook fringed with Post-its was shocking. I left her to it, figuring she'd soon get bored and come begging. But she didn't. No more truanting for us, because her results were brilliant, whereas my only notable achievement was securing a credible enough ID to work in the pub underage. She went on to sixth-form college, killed that too, and got a place at university: Warwick, which I gathered was a bit of a coup. Some part of me must have wished I had followed her lead, but I resolutely stuck to my line: why get a huge student loan when you can get a job? The bluster was classic Anna. If you refuse to compete, you can't fail.

The spring I turned nineteen, Pippa texted (again) inviting me to stay in her halls and this time I decided to go. She, along with half the teenage population of Rotherhithe, had come out on the lash after my brother's funeral and I'd realised how much I missed her, thought we might find a way to reconnect.

If I spin back to that weekend, I can smell the sabotage.

It's the day before I am due to go and I'm trying to pack but my denim skirt goes in and back out and back in; and if we go clubbing, I could wear the skinny black dress but what if all the students wear jeans and a top? I don't even have proper luggage, only my school rucksack, because where do I ever go? The task is insurmountable because I am trying to fit courage and hope and the vestiges of our friendship into a space that bears the scars of all my failures: failure to attend, to achieve, to make an effort, to keep Pippa close.

It's the night before and I'm in a pub. Every time my glass empties, I sidle up to anything male and get a refill. I snog an older guy at the bar. End up down by the river in the early hours, sick as a dog, and am rewarded by the mother of all hangovers. In no state to catch a coach.

Confronting what I was afraid of was impossible; instead, I convinced myself that hanging out with a bunch of posh students would have been a tragic waste of a weekend.

With Pippa's parents living nearby, our paths were, however, bound to keep crossing. It must have been that Easter I saw her in Surrey Quays. She was wearing a frumpy blue cardigan and her hair was cut in a bob. I still had my fade, sculpted by the barber on Jacob Street. In my red Fred Perry, I remember thinking we'd become fans of opposing teams; she was Chelsea and I was Brentford. She might have waved but I determinedly didn't see. My signature strut was stiff with bravado, designed to ward off any suggestion my life wasn't what I wanted.

I shift in the bed, uncomfortable at the memory. I looked peacock-proud, but inside I was lost. Being without Pippa also meant being without her family. Smiffy, who was new on the scene, was no substitute.

After that, avoiding her became a game. I'd leave a pub if she came in, cross the road, duck down an alley. Her texts went unanswered.

And then, one Sunday morning, a few months into my relationship with Ben, Pippa is literally in my face.

'Anna!'

Ben is a dead weight, scuppering any hope of escape. But I can't speak to her.

'It's really nice to see you.' She looks at Ben, smiles. 'I'm Pippa.'

I am mute, so Ben bridges the gap.

'Ben. Anna's better half.' He holds out his hand. I am completely triggered by this gesture, this recognition that she is of the same tribe. A tribe that shakes hands rather than nods or curls their lip. When we first met, he didn't offer me his hand; he put it up my skirt.

I have wet hair from the shower, a sore head from a spontaneous vodka fest and am wearing a pair of joggers. She is pretty in a lilac dress. Reincarnated as a completely different species. One I can't, won't, acknowledge.

The conversation happens around my sulky face. I think Pippa says she has moved to Nottingham, is working in finance, but I can hardly hear above the roar of abandonment, deafening and devastating. She was my twin. She made sense of me. We are both twenty-two but I am stuck, glued to the spot where she left me. I hate her.

'I thought she was your friend,' Ben says, as we walk away. And I know I have embarrassed him.

Pippa's metamorphosis was a case study in social mobility. She didn't only become educated, she became Philippa and, according to Instagram, developed a love of the great outdoors.

I'm self-aware enough to know I have done something similar, adopting the Slater way, eschewing my lairy life for one of modesty. But I am slipstreaming whereas she did it on her own. Hers was genuine; mine, a disguise.

The sun has inched across the sky, bringing morning light to the bedroom. I idly wonder if Sofia will tell me when to come for breakfast, but stay in the cocoon because I'm not finished thinking.

Despite her increasingly sporadic visits, Pippa and I remained indelibly stuck together in the neighbourhood memory. Everyone knew how tight we'd been: our schoolfriends, their parents, bar staff, shop staff, teachers, police, which meant I couldn't move for being reminded of the scrapes we'd got into, the people we'd pissed off and the ones we'd shagged. More insufferable still was the constant comparison, the golden girl and the reprobate. It was stifling, and would continue to be. Pippa might have gone but her monkey was firmly attached to my back.

Ten days after I'd spent Christmas chez the Slaters, I accepted Ben's long-standing invitation and moved to Somerset. New year, new life. An act driven not by love, but by the very deepest disenchantment.

Surely this is the nub of the problem. The Slater package always was a distressed purchase.

Flinging back the duvet, I reject the idea of showering and instead clean my teeth, tie up my hair and pull on my jeans. I am suddenly in a hurry for the day to start. With Sofia as a catalyst, I know I am on the cusp of change. And I'm excited for it.

Maybe, as Dee would like to believe, Sofia was sent by a higher power, but not to support me in my struggle to become a mother. No, sent to save me from my humdrum life.

It is after eleven when Sofia eventually appears in the kitchen, not that I care. Rollo has fed me fancy mushrooms on toast along with the life histories of his three kids. Evidently Sofia's five-minute husband was an heir to the Hemingway brewing dynasty – an interesting detail she chose to omit.

Sofia refuses the offer of a cooked breakfast, choosing coffee and a slice of toast, and by midday we are on the way home. She is quiet, which I put down to tiredness after our late night, or maybe

51

a hangover. No matter. Having a captive audience suits me, because I am buzzing.

As we have many miles to drive, rather than leap straight to my desire for change, I decide some background will make for a better discussion. My lack of application at school was, arguably, the most influential factor in shaping my early twenties, so I start there.

'. . . no one explained that exam results could open doors. I honestly didn't realise ordinary people could become doctors and lawyers, imagined there was an exclusive club for people with professional parents and plenty of dosh.' I rub my fingers together for emphasis.

From her exalted position, I wonder if she can relate to this in any way. The invisible net that keeps aspiration at bay is complex, woven tight over years until the mesh becomes matted like felt.

'Does this mean you're thinking of going back into education?' she asks, her first utterance in a while.

'God, no. I don't even have a BTEC.'

'You know there are access courses for people who, for whatever reason, didn't connect with education as children.'

'I'm honestly okay with having no qualifications. I was just explaining how I ended up doing minimum-wage work.'

Sofia is, for once, deaf to my words.

'Universities are genuinely keen to attract people like you.'

'Surely there's no one like me.'

'I'm talking about mature students in general, Anna. A diverse intake makes a very robust learning environment.'

'I don't think I would have the energy.'

'You might surprise yourself. Learning brings benefits far beyond the actual subject matter.' And she lists: better sleep, greater empathy, improved self-esteem, increased blood flow.

I am desperate to shut her down: 'Sofia, if I didn't work, I wouldn't have any money.'

'You would qualify for a student loan – the clue is in the name – and the temporary loss in earnings would be compensated by better job opportunities. Or you could study part-time.'

I don't respond, hoping that finds her off-switch.

'I expect Ben would support you,' she says, 'if you asked nicely.'

'I couldn't ask him to do that.'

'No, perhaps not.' She turns her head to look at me. 'At least, not straight from royally ridiculing him.'

Her barb catches on skin. Entertaining Sofia's family last night by painting Ben as a mummy's boy and Milly as a pageant queen has, without the glow of candlelight, considerably more malice and less jest. The twitch of guilt is, however, quickly negated by the memory of the Carstairs' mirth.

Despite no natural segue, I announce: 'Your dad invited me to France like you said he would.'

She is still not diverted. 'Do you intend to ossify in the village school, Anna?'

I prickle at her ready dismissal of my job. 'From where I was, where I am now is an achievement. You have no idea what it's like to be me.'

'You're right, I don't. I really don't.' She smiles at the road ahead. 'I hardly know you.'

These are the last words either of us speak because when I don't immediately respond, she pointedly turns on the radio.

8

Ossification

From the moment the kids troop in from the playground, one activity rolls into the next; add in some pockets of poor behaviour that require attention and some prepping and the endless admin and, honestly, squeezing in a wee can be a push. But, this Monday morning, I cannot stay on task, repeatedly going over yesterday's conversation in the car and how abruptly Sofia dropped me home.

Flashing red is the threat of ossification. The mere fact that I know the word is taunting me, daring me to make something of myself. I am quick, bright, more well read than any of the Slaters despite my lack of schooling. I am only twenty-seven. Life must have more to offer.

At lunch I text Sofia, thanking her for the weekend, but get no reply. She is probably busy at the pain clinic. While I eat my tuna wrap, I try to work out whether I was also at fault yesterday, too closed to her barrage of well-meaning suggestions. In hindsight, her radar was spot on: I do want to make a change. It was her remedy that took me by surprise.

One change is already in motion. Last night Ben and I had sex using an almost out-of-date condom. It was like fucking a stranger, in a good way – no agenda, no baggage. Before work, I filled in an online consultation form asking for a doctor's appointment to arrange contraception. Ben understands I need a break. This would not be a good time to become parents.

My mum, Helen, was seventeen when I was born and eighteen when Simon arrived. Despite being young, she managed okay: we attended school in an approximation of the uniform, had meals with green or orange in them and the odd caravan holiday in Broadstairs. Our dad came and went, working, I suppose, but I don't know what at. (It might suit me not to know.) In my memory his wide smile is bound with the joy of fatty batter cut through with vinegar and salt because he'd often turn up with fish and chips.

Most Saturday nights, my mum and dad would go out drinking. When I was about eight they started leaving Simon and me without a babysitter. We were old enough not to choke on a marble, so what else was there to worry about? Even now, black rocks weigh down my stomach when I think of those nights. The second the front door closed, I'd position myself halfway up the stairs, hardly breathing, alert for any creak or crack of glass. Simon didn't care that we were alone; never woke up although I willed him to.

As I got older, I learnt how to curb intrusive thoughts, but as a kid I delved deep into big, burly men in balaclavas, fires ripping through our terrace, sometimes ghosts. Hours would pass but I would never creep back to my bed, not until the key turned in the door.

After Dad died – a car crash at two in the morning on the A3 near Kingston – we were left on our own a lot more; and when Simon found brothers in the form of the Channing Road Gang, the house was emptier again. Mum was working in the betting shop and, after hours, enjoying the teenage years she'd missed out on. More than once we came across each other in the early hours, both shit-faced. Pippa's family saved me. It didn't matter if she was there or not, I was always welcome to pull up a chair at the table, borrow a book from her mum's vast collection of paperbacks and curl up on the sofa or crash on the mattress in Pippa's room.

The afternoon bell interrupts my reveries. I finish my apple and jog to the classroom, replacing the hollowness my teenage years evoke with a mental scan of the two poems we are about to compare and contrast. Galvanising my group of less able students to both understand, critique and produce something of their own is always a challenge and today we do not do well. My end-of-day classroom tidying is begrudging.

Knowing my general demeanour will not be improved by going home and stewing, I decide to call in at Sofia's. She still hasn't replied to my text but I have something to say that I know will please her.

Her car is outside the cottage but she doesn't answer the door and a phone call draws no response. I dither outside, before deciding to go for a walk. If I follow the well-used circular route, there is a chance I'll come across her. I head off, ignoring the warning from my temporal lobe that Sofia might not want me to come looking for her today. Instead, I tell myself yesterday was a blip; her being direct with me was a sign of how close we are.

At the first field I vault the gate like a teenager and stride through the long grass with no care that my plimsolls are porous. I cross the little bridge where Alan's cigarette butts decorate the scrub and navigate the narrow strip between the stream and the wheat field. At the far end I take a right towards the manor house. My cardigan is too hot, making my armpits prickle. I tie it around my waist and the warm breeze tickles my elbows. I shut my eyes, appreciating the first heat of the year.

A high hedge surrounds the manor house. I skirt the wall of dark green in order to loop back towards the road through the fields, vaulting another gate on my way just for the hell of it. I am a few metres along the rough track when I notice the cows and remember there are calves in the field. Someone in the pub mentioned they were skittish. If the cows approach, the locals yell or clap their hands, but I tend to give a wide berth, ever watchful.

A dozen more strides and I lose my nerve. The cows have formed a wall between where I am and where I want to go. I begin to back-track; only a vague notion that too fast a pace might signal fear prevents me from running. I swing my legs over the closed gate and land with my feet in parallel, bang in front of Sofia.

'Hi, Sofia.'

She smiles. 'Hi.'

'How was your day?'

'Good.'

'I rang you earlier. I've been thinking about our conversation in the car.'

'I'm not sure it was much of a conversation. I was a battering ram and you were a very heavy door.'

'That's probably a fair summary but you got me thinking. I might look at some sort of further education.'

The enthusiasm I am expecting doesn't materialise. Instead, Sofia says, 'Golly gosh, you've made a rapid turnabout.'

The 'golly gosh' may have a tinge of sarcasm but I carry on, concerned only with delivering my information. 'I hadn't really imagined there were options for people with hardly any qualifications.'

'That's great.' She takes a step – is she intending to walk past?

'If you've got time to help me work out the best way forward, I'm ready and willing.'

'Okay,' she hesitates, 'or maybe see if you feel the same when you've done some research.'

I catch up with her distanced tone. 'What do you mean?'

'Come on, Anna. Yesterday you were firmly not interested and now you are. Who knows what tomorrow might bring?' She is positively shrill.

'That's uncalled for.' In the face of her antagonism, keeping my voice steady is a challenge.

'I'm not sure it is. You can be quite mercurial, you know.' It is very Sofia to use a pleasing word for an ugly sentiment.

'I've had other things on my mind.' I sigh, adopt the air of a confidante. 'I'm not sure how I feel about . . . about everything, actually.'

She is determinedly silent. I am determinedly intent on restoring our usual ebb and flow. The situation must be salvageable if I can only read her mood.

'Seeing Tamsin and Ed together made me realise Ben and I don't talk about things.'

'I don't really want to get into the intimacies of your relationship,' she says. 'I like Ben.'

'I thought you said stallionesque was more your taste.'

'I'm not the one in a relationship with him.'

'You seem keen to stand up for him.'

'Which is interesting, isn't it? One would hope you might adopt that role.'

'I do, but at the moment we're struggling a bit.'

'If you say so.' Sofia moves to the side but I mirror her, blocking the track.

'I might call in at Dee's.' I am fumbling for common ground to rebuild from. 'Do you want to come?'

'You're quite the chameleon, aren't you? Do you think Dee would recognise the raconteur from Saturday night as the Anna she is so fond of?'

Saturday evening flies in my face, colours bright, audio loud.

Old Anna is back, the Anna who weaved a good story, never shying from the unacceptable – and she is on fine form. Tamsin is laughing and laughing and Rollo keeps pouring more drinks while Viv, tucked up in her armchair, encourages me to divulge more episodes from a London that bears no resemblance to her own and from the village that I dumb down for comedy purposes. No one escapes from my forked tongue, from the character assassinations that betray everyone except those in the room with keen details and funny observations. Only if I move the camera angle does Sofia come into view – her position in the wings, which I took as an invitation to occupy the stage, could equally be a determination not to collude. The realisation grows, thunder rumbling to a crescendo. I am a necrotising bacterium destroying anything healthy in search of popularity, affirmation, attention. And she has seen me under the microscope.

Actively ignoring the icy hand squeezing my heart I concentrate on being contrite. I am contrite. One uncensored evening can't be allowed to jeopardise our friendship.

'I don't know what to say. I'd had too much to drink and got carried away.'

'Is that your excuse for mocking Ben and his family? That you were tipsy?'

'Your parents are so lovely – I just wanted them to like me.'

'You have to let people like you for who you are, not manufacture a character to please them.'

'You make me sound very calculated.'

'Is that why you've decided to be interested in education, Anna? A calculated move to ingratiate yourself with me?' Her question creates a shortcut to other places: pretender, fibber, fake.

'Of course not. I hadn't thought about it before, that's all.'

'Are you sure? Because I think this is your mode of operation. You adopted Pippa's family, you swapped some poor boy for Ben—'

'Smiffy, he was called Smiffy.'

'Swapped Smiffy for Ben and got busy making babies and then you meet me and from nowhere it's academia, all thought of motherhood forgotten. If you meet a Tibetan monk, will you start wearing orange robes?'

Her smugness, her tone, her dismissive expression are too much to bear, threatening to unleash what must stay inside. I take a tiny breath, tighten the corset of control.

'Why are you twisting my words? Where has this come from?'

I want to slap her, to watch her fall to the ground in that ridiculous red dress with its little-girl puffed sleeves. How dare she pick on me, her with the privileged family and overeducated skull.

'You made me sick at the weekend, Anna. The village is delightful, Ben's family are thoroughly decent people. Why would you be so cruel about them?'

I want to tell her that she had a part in this – didn't we both make fun of the Slaters? – but can't shape the sentence. Too fevered, too frantic.

'I don't want to be the teaching assistant in a primary school but if it suits you, own it. Don't pretend to reject your life to inveigle yourself with mine, with my family. You can't have them. You can't be me. And you certainly can't tag along to France.'

The rage, needle sharp, perforates my veneer. 'What part of your fucked-up head have I prodded to make you so angry? You, who flits from here to there, no baggage, no boyfriend, swanning around collecting certificates to stick on Mummy's fridge—'

'Shut up. I'm sorry I thought to introduce you.' The look that accompanies her calm and collected rejection is a hard punch to the chest. 'I think we're done here.'

Ordering my face not to reveal the hurt, I flounder for a reply but my mind is white noise and my lungs won't inflate. Sofia pushes past me, grabs the lever and throws open the gate to the field, leaving it to swing shut. I watch the metal bar bounce against the catch twice – clackety-clank – before the gate comes to rest slightly ajar. Instinctively, I go to fasten it.

Rocket appears from nowhere, a streak of grey dog. My hand is on the cool metal – a firm tug will secure the gate and stop him in his tracks. But my hand stays still.

In a shot he has breached the gap and run into the field.

A dog racing through a field of mothers caring for their young is a dog asking for trouble. I leave him to it.

9

A Caravaggio

The siren is incongruous. I can't remember ever hearing one in the village. If I assume anything, it is that there is a cat on a roof or a dog in a drain. Whatever the reason, it is of no concern to me. The ugly burst of noise is quickly over and the hum of the countryside restored.

I am sitting on the bridge rearranging Alan's many cigarette ends with the toe of my plimsoll. Both walking here and making the decision to sit are a blur. I check my phone for the time and am surprised by how late it is. I should go home, but the idea holds no attraction; the best place for me to be is here, with only my head for company. For there is plenty to think about: I have let down my guard and Sofia has seen inside and knows me to be a limpet, attaching to the sturdiest rock, moving only when in sight of a safer home. Truly, I am nothing without someone to stick to.

The siren returns, blaring for three short bars. I turn around, look in all directions and, somewhat bizarrely, upwards, searching for signs of a crisis.

If there is a whisper, a suggestion of what the emergency might be, I adamantly don't hear it.

I really should go. The later I arrive back from school, the more questions Ben will have. Our life runs on the wheels of routine.

Standing up, my legs, independent of mind, decide not to carry me home, heading instead back towards the field of cows. The dog will be fine, I know that, but I indulge a fantasy where I find the quivering creature cornered by snorting cows and, in front of an audience of villagers, firemen, police, I bravely disperse the herd and – *go for it, Anna* – carry the dog to safety.

As I emerge from the soundproofing of the high hedge for the second time this afternoon – or I suppose it's evening now – the purr of traffic becomes brakes, banging doors and voices.

The drama is nearby.

I cover the stretch to the metal gate at speed. The disaster is unfolding ahead of me. Dark green uniforms. A chequerboard of neon yellow and green on the side of an ambulance. Black for police. A man in brown. The cows, a huddle of rust and ivory. A patch of poppy red in the long grass. I accelerate, concentrating on these flashes of colour because the individual parts refuse to make a picture.

I am running now, running fast – balls of my feet pushing off from the dusty ground, knees high, mouth dry.

The voice of authority. 'Stay back.' A hand, palm facing, raised high.

Do I know at that point? Is that why I keep going? Why I bull-doze past two men who should surely have been able to stop me?

The tableau, for it must surely be staged, deliberately contrived to shock, has the horror, the ugliness and the palette of a Caravaggio we once studied in school. The livid swell of deep red is not blood or poppies but a cotton skirt, spread ragged and threaded with grass dyed verdigris by the clouded light. A trampled bone-black foot is still held by the lead-tin-yellow straps of a sandal but the ankle is flayed – a cut of meat for the butcher's window. One arm is leaden white, flung wide, perhaps in sleep, but the other is shadowy, bent awkwardly. There is a polished knob of silvery white in a place where there should be uninterrupted skin. Her hair, carbon black striped with ash, is fanned around the space that was her face, now umber, vermilion, red ochre.

My legs disappear and I am falling.

10

Holy Cow

Inquests take forever, not the proceedings themselves but what goes before. I can't imagine what takes so long; what there is to do after the body has been unpeeled from its wrapper, inspected and sewn back together; after the stagnant blood has been tested for any synthetics that might pertain to the cause of death; after the report has been written, full of medical jargon that in no way informs the reality of a violent death; after witnesses, if there are any, have been identified and interrogated. By the time Sofia has her day in court I will have left the village, so, although I'm getting ahead of myself again, here are the facts. They are my words because the clinical equivalents hide the brutality.

A shattered pelvis and snapped femur, all her ribs broken, some in several places, her right lung punctured, her abdomen horribly swollen, distended with blood, her right shoulder dislocated and humerus broken, her spinal cord severed by a crushed vertebra in her neck, her skull a broken eggshell, her face obliterated, stamped out of existence by hooves, her accomplished brain forever dead.

Twenty cows were grazing in the field that day together with three calves; calves that their mothers were programmed to protect.

The average dairy cow weighs the same as eleven of me. Their hooves are specially designed to bear that weight on the move; the surface is rock hard and the filling is the equivalent of biological cement. They walk on tiptoe, which means the force is further concentrated. And, despite their bulk, cows can run fast, faster than humans. Although they're not good at dodging – a tip, in case you're ever chased.

Apart from the farmer's wife, who found the body, the only witness was the pub landlord. He had been to post his acceptance of a speeding fine, he said, when he saw Sofia heading out of the village at about four on Monday afternoon. He had shouted across to her that she wasn't kitted out for a walk, still wearing that voluminous red dress and strappy sandals, and she had replied: 'I like to look my best. You never know who you might meet.' No one else went on record but the rumours suggest that Alan was seen returning home not long after, without Rocket. In London there would be CCTV at every junction and the comings and goings would provide factual evidence. A dog, foaming at the mouth after a race with an army of thundering cows, would feature, as would Alan, as would I. But this is not London.

I arrived in unison with the emergency services: that is the accepted version of events.

The coroner will declare an accidental verdict. Death by cow, rare but not unknown, commonly involving a dog.

Your mind can act as a friend or an enemy. Catastrophising is an example of an unhelpful mind, wishing you ill, whereas amnesia can be very welcome. I can't remember anything about arriving in the field. The image I strive to bat away is the one I have created for myself: Sofia as accidental matador.

Cows can't see red; the colour was originally chosen to mask the blood after the beast has died. But they can see flapping. I make Sofia's skirt billow as she strides through the field, teasing the wall of livestock, goading them to charge. Already excited, the beasts grate the earth with their killer feet. Rocket provides that extra something, a tornado in their midst. In my reconstruction Sofia has no idea that she is in danger. However unlikely, I have chosen to believe her life is obliterated in an instant.

For me, the reality only switches on after a police officer drives me home. Ben is in the road, waiting, the grapevine having done its work. We go inside and I get straight in the shower. When the water finally loses its heat I pull on my old gingham pyjamas and crawl into bed. The loss is deep purple bruising round my heart, the tenderness so acute that I mustn't move a muscle, must stay silent and still to have the slimmest hope of healing.

I refuse dinner on a tray because I can't possibly chew and don't want to taste. I speak in monosyllables. Nothing must dislodge this stupor because if my senses start to fire it might all be true.

My sleep is opaque, thick and complete, like anaesthesia. On Tuesday I wake to the alarm and begin the morning routine. I have reset and am in working order.

'Are you okay to go in today?' Ben asks.

'Of course.' I put the tablet in the dishwasher and press Start. 'Compassionate leave doesn't extend to a pal you've only known for half a term.'

My guard is back in place, strong and all-encompassing. The affair is over; normal service was interrupted but is ready to resume.

Everyone lets me down, I know that. Everyone except Ben.

11

Object Constancy

It is Friday afternoon and – praise the Lord – school is over for the week. I am lying on the garden bench letting the sun's laser beams bore through my skin and fry my organs. I have been thinking about how, although I am utterly still, my body is busy using every adaptation to regulate my internal temperature. I like the idea of homeostasis: the relentless pursuit of a stable environment, the perfectionism of endlessly tweaking the conditions to guarantee optimal function, the unwinnable nature of the battle to preserve constancy.

Children who have unreliable parents can lack something called object constancy, which, according to the article I read in the *Psychologies* magazine at the dentist about two years ago, means they are used to being let down and they carry that distrust into their adult relationships. This damage makes it hard to retain a bond when a partner or friend acts in a way that is upsetting or disappointing. Controversial though it may be, I don't think the bond with someone who is upsetting and disappointing is worth retaining. Take Sofia – even if she hadn't died, she was dead to me the minute she lashed out so cruelly. This is not because of a deficit of object constancy but because of a surfeit of self-worth.

The ringtone that Ben selected for me (because only lazy people keep the default) makes its irritating chirpy-chirp. Reluctantly I open my eyes – ouch! ice bright – quickly close them before sitting up and trying again. I fumble and my phone falls through the slats of the bench; in the scramble to rescue it from the rough concrete – Ben would like decking – I scrape my knuckles.

'Hello.'

It is Sofia's landlord. She deals with the condolences in one sentence and we are on to business.

'I gather from Sofia Carstairs' father that you are going to clear out the cottage. Might you manage that by Monday?'

The vastness of the monochrome blue sky, devoid of even a wisp of cloud, reminds me of how insignificant we all are: mere pixels.

'Yes, I suppose so.'

'Leave the key, please. And many thanks, Anna – I realise this is an unpleasant undertaking.'

I resume my position but can't recover my contemplative state. My Adidas shorts have ridden up and my thighs are sticking together; I flop over onto my front and bury my face in the cushion. The mini-heatwave came yesterday and is forecast to last until Tuesday. School has gone into overdrive marshalling gazebos and demanding children arrive with hats and sun cream already applied. I can't get excited about what is an everyday temperature for half the world.

The morgue keeps bodies at the same temperature as supermarket meat. Being asked to identify a chilled, sanitised version of your loved one seems a very unenviable task. After seeing Sofia's body, Rollo went straight to her cottage and evidently that was his undoing; I got a call from Tamsin saying as much. She said he had taken a few items but, would I mind? Keep, donate, discard, as I like.

69

'We don't want mementos. It's maudlin and she'd have hated it.' Her tone was clipped. 'My sister was anything but forgettable.'

'Of course. Understood.'

Being pleased to have been given the job feels wrong, but I am pleased. Tamsin's call came yesterday and I have savoured the prospect ever since. I will go tomorrow, set up camp in the front room and take my time ordering Sofia's belongings into piles. Perhaps I'll dither over the velvet cape she was wearing that day in the church before I decide to hang it in my own wardrobe where it will be forever unworn; maybe I'll find letters from friends, or an old lover, that will lay bare the parts I didn't get to know. A diary would be the best find, or a series of them charting her charmed life. Sofia wrote with extravagant loops and curlicues. I asked her about that once, assuming she'd been to some fancy school preoccupied with cursive handwriting, but she said she'd found a homemade cookbook in a charity shop and liked the look of the pages so she copied the style. Reinvention, she'd said, was fun.

The anticipation of going to Sofia's, touching her possessions, is anchoring; a fixed point that stops me from looking further ahead. I don't want to look further ahead.

Not being excited about anything can be a sign of depression, but I have diagnosed disillusionment, which feels both less awful and more permanent.

'Surely you're baking out here?' says Ben's voice. I roll over and, forewarned this time, cup my hand over my eyes before I open them.

'I think "cooked" is the word.'

He perches on the edge of the bench, puts a hand on my thigh. 'Shitty week.'

I nod.

'Come in and I'll make us some tea.'

I stand up to follow him indoors. 'I don't think this is a moment for tea.'

'Well, what about wine then?' he says and I like the way his expression lifts.

I watch him unscrew the top of a bottle of Sauvignon. I could fetch the glasses, suggest we have breadsticks too and reach into the cupboard, but I let him wait on me. The measure he pours is generous, and I'm glad of that.

'Back outside or staying in here?' he asks.

'Outside,' I say, because we will sit next to each other not opposite and that feels easier.

We take the bottle and an extra glass with some ice.

'I know you said you don't want to talk about Sofia but I think we should. It's not normal to have a tragedy happen in front of you and just carry on.' He takes a swig. 'I think you loved her.'

I nod; tears pinch the corners of my eyes, making me blink. He nods too.

'It's hard to believe she's dead.'

I shake my head, not yet ready with actual speech.

'She was one of those people who has more personality than it seems there's room for,' he says. I glance. From the side, his smile is measured and kind; his cheek is tanned with the perfect level of stubble, manly but not overly hirsute. 'It's going to take a while. I could see how close you'd got. I liked it. She made you happy.'

I want to ask him if I wasn't happy before, but nothing materialises.

'It was terrible that you saw her in the field.'

The palette of colours flashes in front of me; a Gothic abstract of tar-like paint. I don't want to look, so I shut my eyes.

71

I wish, wish so hard it hurts my sternum, that one thing could have been different that day: the cows had found a lush patch of grass away from the path, Rocket had found another dog to play with in a faraway field, a villager had caught up with Sofia on her stroll or a call had delayed her altogether. Most of all I wish she hadn't been so unkind to me, hurling vitriol when all I was guilty of was the tiny, tiny crime of being ingratiating. If she hadn't been so poisonous, I'd have shut the gate and she would still be alive.

I am sobbing. Ben puts his hot arm around my shoulder and draws me in. I fit perfectly between his biceps and his chest. Lodged in his embrace, some dire portent, uninvited but as clear as if chiselled in stone, shouted from a rooftop, tattooed on my arm, shows me that life will continue as it was before Sofia came. The certainty that I will ossify, as she predicted, encompasses me like acrid fog. I will stay in this cloying, airless cloud, too cowardly to dive down in case I crash and too frightened to rise up in case I can't fly.

12

Look straight at the camera and don't smile

The coffee looks and tastes the same – bitter Bialetti black in a porcelain mug – despite being made by my hand. I am sitting at Sofia's whitewashed table, the stable door open. The garden is a pantomime of reds, oranges, blues, pinks, whites and yellows, exactly as advertised on the wildflower seed packet. Someone somewhere is mowing – hardly a surprise on a Saturday in May. I came straight through into the kitchen and have not moved since. Sofia has popped to the shed, is in the loo, has run upstairs to fetch a cardigan; she has gone to borrow blackfly spray from Dee or to fetch her sun cream from where I noticed it in the door pocket of her car a week ago.

If I start amassing her possessions, she will truly be dead, but for now she is teasing me about my outfit of grey T-shirt and navy shorts; complaining about Sally Wood's regimented flower beds; asking me whether the rumour Old Mary used to be a swinger is true.

Sofia delighted in befriending the older residents. I can hear her glee-filled voice – 'Personalities filed to a spike by a lifetime of 'iteration' – but know her remarks will fade, the life blanching out of them.

I can't recreate Pippa's voice, not anymore. Perhaps that's a good thing.

The post lands on the floor with a flump. Conditioning, I suppose, makes me stand up. The movement, a few steps, is galvanising. I carry on, walking up the narrow staircase with its sharp bend and take the right into Sofia's bedroom.

The intake of breath is sharp, too fast for my lungs. Her bed has a depression, an ammonite curl. She slept on her right side, must have hardly moved so well defined are the edges. I slip off my flip-flops and position myself in the hollow, knees high.

At some point, on autopilot, I stretch, swing my legs over the side and walk across to Sofia's wardrobe. I shrug off my shorts and top and peruse the selection. I rifle, touching slippery silk, a furry collar, rough wool that must surely itch; I slide my fingers along a rib of jumbo corduroy, finger a buttonhole, hesitate over a black and white checked pinafore before carrying along the rail, hanger by hanger.

The choice I make is typical Sofia although not something I ever saw her wear – wide-legged jade linen trousers topped with a pinstripe navy waistcoat. My reflection in the mirror isn't quite right; it lacks something, so I return and take a square scarf that I fold and tie at my neck, very French, or maybe very pirate. I untie my hair, reach for an earring that may as well have been placed for my attention and am surprised to find a layer of skin has grown that I have to pierce. I swing my head from side to side, enjoying the weight of Sofia's sparkly chandeliers.

Her trademark bovver boots demand to be part of this ensemble. Adding an incongruous element was part of what made Sofia's look so noteworthy. I shove my bare feet inside and lace them up.

I stay in this outfit, adopting a deliberate air of efficiency, as though I've been meaning to get on top of this sorting for a while. *Tum-te-tum.*

The wardrobe is relatively straightforward, as is the chest of drawers: the charity shop will make a handsome profit. The pile for me to keep is sparingly small.

The bedding disappears into a black bin liner. I pretend I'm letting the bed air and move on to the deep windowsill, where her make-up mirror lights up as I approach. The lid of her maroon hard-sided vanity case is propped open to reveal a large collection of eyeshadow palettes, pots of blusher, tubes of cream, pencils, wands of mascara and lipsticks.

Never again will she take off her make-up as preparation for going to bed. The idea she will be eternally awake boils in my brain, bringing a vision of her in her tattered red dress, feet bare and streaked with blood, arms outstretched, head bent in abject weariness. A crucifixion. As though she senses my presence, her head rises. No face.

My hands reach for the wooden sill. A long, loud growl comes from somewhere deep. The noise, disconcertingly feral, adds to the horror. I stay at the window, unseeing, and wait for her to leave me alone.

It is a strange day. Time loses its structure. I was in Sofia's bed and then I was dancing in her clothes and I think I slept and now I am standing in the living room with several bin liners of varying degrees of fullness and the upstairs is empty of any trace of its most recent occupant.

Only in here can I detect what is missing. Like the game where an object is removed from the tray, I notice the gap on the coffee table where there was a jade Buddha and the space on the shelf where Sofia kept her battered Concise Oxford Dictionary, a huge navy book with gold lettering she bought when she went to Cambridge. I know, before I look, what else her father has taken because there is no background metallic tick. Yes, the cuckoo clock is no longer hanging on the wall.

I wonder if he has hung it in his study – a heartbeat to replace his daughter's.

Jesus, Anna!

What felt like comfort dissolves into something sickening. I need the job to be finished, to close the door on this episode and forget it happened. The contents of Sofia's kitchen is packed into cardboard boxes without pause for consideration.

Ben has offered to transport everything to the charity shop; I text him to say I'm ready.

I should learn to drive; I've got a provisional licence but my motivation waxes and wanes and lessons are expensive. Money is a funny thing in a relationship. When I moved in, I offered to pay rent but Ben said I wasn't a lodger. He didn't say I'm a kept woman but given he earns four times my salary, I am one. A joint account has been on the to-do list since the first pregnancy but never reached the top. If he died, I'd be homeless.

Ben taps a couple of times before opening the front door.

'All done?' He hovers on the boundary between outside and

inside, filling the little doorway. In front of his feet lies the forgotten post.

I nod.

'Shall I put it in the car?'

'Yes, please.'

The boot of his Audi isn't very big. Ben places the last of the bags and the two boxes on the back seat.

'I've got a meeting, but I'll take it straight after?'

His lilt implies flexibility – if I want him to go this afternoon, he will; if I want him to go on Monday, he'll do that; if I want him to pirouette on a pinhead, he'll try.

'May as well.' I kiss his cheek. 'I'll make sure I've closed all the windows and see you at home.'

The hesitation is barely there. He wants to double-check I'm all right without appearing to fuss.

My smile is heartfelt, and he leaves. I pick up the post: three flyers, all garish colours on flimsy paper, and a brown envelope addressed to Sofia Hemingway.

I run my finger over the rectangular ridge made by the contents, slide my nail under the flap.

There is something fake about the fabric of a passport that reminds me of battered leather on a pub chair or maybe crazed china, as though the designers were briefed to convey authority through antiquing. I open the cover, flick through the freshly minted pages to her portrait.

This version of Sofia, her bush of hair tidied away and her face purposefully unsmiling, looks nothing like her. I stare, savouring the realisation that, in this photograph, Sofia looks more like me.

13

Unfed Hope

My stash of Sofia's possessions is a secret from Ben. It wouldn't matter if, when rooting around for some old cricket whites, he found her things. Maybe he already has. But I chose not to tell him, squirrelling away my hoard while he was tasked with offloading the rest, because it felt mawkish, unhealthy, maybe even unwise.

I don't remove the vacuum storage bag from its home in the wardrobe of the spare room; I don't unzip its perimeter and let the air whoosh in, plumping out the sides. But I know it's there. A shrine, comprising Sofia's velvet cape, her dungarees and her battered boots, the striped shirt she pulled over my head and a flouncy white blouse with blue tassels that epitomised her flamboyance, the chandelier earrings, a copy of *Middlemarch* (because she underlined the quotes she particularly liked: unfed hope) and her passport.

Despite being dead, Sofia's frustration at my small life continues, shadowing me on the walk to school, sighing at the village-centric chat in the pub, mocking Ben's plans to invest in an outdoor lounging set. For most of the week I work hard to ignore her, but on Sundays I allow her a discreet window: the length of the vicar's sermon.

This Sunday, the village football team has won 3–0. Ben is overjoyed. We celebrate with our staple cheese on toast, eaten in front of different sections of the newspaper. I float out of my body and see Sunday after Sunday stretching before us. And make a decision.

Casually, oh so casually, I raise the idea that I might want to consider changing my job, perhaps get a qualification. I gabble, blurring my intention by the addition of extraneous words.

He doesn't immediately understand; thinks we're talking about my health. 'It's a great idea. You've been through a lot. Some down-time might really help.'

'I don't mean downtime,' I say, 'I mean time otherwise employed.'

My words are a riddle. He solves them as best he can.

'Being with kids all day is probably the last thing you need.'

Is he alluding to our absence of children or to the full-on nature of working with them? I can't tell and he doesn't elucidate. He has a dash of red sauce on his cheek that I wipe when I could be replying, clarifying his remark and putting him right. But I don't know that we are about to be interrupted. Nor do I know – how could I? – that this tentative attempt to ring the changes will gain momentum and amplify, sending clappers a-swinging.

'Actually, I was thinking of going to college,' I say, because my comprehensive-dropout mouth won't say university.

'Mum did that. Enrolled on a computer course when we were at secondary school.'

'No wonder she's so spreadsheet-orientated.'

Ben likes this comment. 'Where would Christmas be without Mum's present matrix?'

'Full of duplications.' I smile, gauging how to explain my ambition

79

without belittling Dee's foray into adult learning. 'I was thinking more mainstream education than evening—'

A cursory tap on the back door and Milly and Finn have let themselves in. They both look athletic in denim shorts and shirts; blonde, sun-baked Milly in pink, ginger Finn in green.

'We won't stay,' says Milly. 'Finn wants to borrow a power bank, if that's okay?'

'Of course,' says Ben.

'How did you get on today?' asks Finn.

'We won!' A full and fiery commentary follows, and then, 'Anna's thinking of doing an evening class.'

They all stare. I feel as though I missed the preamble.

'Or maybe a college course,' I say, but the nuance is drowned by a deluge of suggestions that include one-pot cooking and researching your ancestry, God help me.

Only when I have shaken my head at ballroom dancing and batik, at volunteering to tag trees and trap moths, do Milly and Finn leave, taking Ben and the power bank with them.

The ready assumption that I am in search of a hobby is mildly disconcerting, but I have at least opened the dialogue. Next time I will be clearer, I think.

But what happens next is not down to me.

The teaching assistant in Year 5, due back from maternity leave in September, has asked if she can drop down to two days a week. Her maternity cover, a sporty boy with film-star teeth, is keen to stay but needs to work full-time. The school is keen to keep him, men being a precious commodity. I could counter that most children have, by the age of eleven, ample experience of the patriarchy but

I am not consulted. However, Dee, as school governor, is privy to the discussions. Thanks to Ben, she is also aware of my ambition to re-enter education and, for clarity, not to learn to hand-build with clay. The genius solution presented as a fait accompli is that next term I move to Year 5 and job share, working three days a week, and sporty boy continues in a full-time role. My role.

The pressure to comply is intense. The lives of a dedicated mother and a likeable lad both depend on my whim. Ben says it's a no-brainer. Two days to devote to self-actualisation. Isn't that what I want?

'It might be better for Milly and Finn's kids,' he says. 'Or they'll be in your class next year.'

This is clearly the collective Slater opinion. And so I agree.

In preparation, I scour the internet, gradually getting the gist of foundation years, access courses, student finance. I send off for copies of my exam results but don't register an interest at any establishments or request a prospectus. There are open days, I tell Ben one morning, and he says we could go together, 'make a day of it', but no actual dates make it onto the calendar and May becomes June.

I'm about to leave for church when Dee texts to say she's going to give the service a miss. Popping in on my way home I find the cold she is supposed to have is not a cold. Ben is at football and Milly's family are away for the weekend so I call Ben's brother, Jamie, who lives three miles away in an almost identical village.

'Getting in the car now,' he says, to my relief.

I sit beside Dee and maintain a steady narrative while studying my patient. Her lips, devoid of Blushing Rose or Soft Coral, have merged with the surrounding skin. Without her trademark blow-dry, her hair is two curtains either side of her face. There is no glint of earrings.

'. . . the whole year is going to the ecumenical church, which will be a challenge . . .'

As each breath labours past the next, her panicked eyes tremble. Yet her frame appears frozen, until she coughs, an unwilling spasm that brings several more.

'. . . getting through the packed lunches takes forever . . .'

Jamie's car tyres announce his arrival. He strides in, kneels beside Dee and takes her hand. She forces a smile. The visible effort brings a tightness to my own chest. I don't want anything to happen to Dee.

In true Slater fashion, Jamie bypasses the agony of contacting 111 and waiting for a call-back, instead texting the doctor who lives on the executive estate at the edge of the village. I have never met her, although I know of her from her philandering husband. She replies that she is playing tennis but will drop in on her way home.

News of the imminent arrival of someone with a stethoscope acts as a placebo. The static making my nerves crackle drops a level.

'Would you make some tea, Anna?' asks Jamie, adding a little wink of camaraderie.

Everywhere in the kitchen there is evidence of Dee's distress: the blind on the back door is still down, the milk has been left out, the toast abandoned. Having delivered the tea, I get busy restoring order.

I hear the doctor and Ben arrive in quick succession, but stay in the kitchen, praying it's not pneumonia. Dee will not want to go into hospital. Only when voices reach me from the hall do I go to join them.

'A chest infection,' says Jamie, waving a piece of paper. 'I'm going to get the antibiotics now.' He heads off, leaving me with the doctor (who looks sensational in her all-white kit).

She spends a few minutes repeating what she has, presumably, told the brothers: take a double dose today and thereafter three times a day, make sure to complete the course; plenty of fluids; sleep propped up; the occasional infection is to be expected because of the impairment to lung function; any problems, call the surgery tomorrow.

'Thank you so much,' I say, opening the front door.

'My pleasure.' She stops by the pots of what I now know are hostas. The sweeping variegated leaves lick her bare legs like flames. 'It's Anna, isn't it?'

'Yes.'

'I know Dee is reluctant but it might be time to join the Breathe Easy sessions at the hospital – they're an excellent support group.' Her manner is lovely, full of concern. I feel a pinch of regret that, when I was new to the village, both full of unease and easy prey, her husband played with me while she played tennis. Rumour has it he's now bedding the manager of the leisure centre.

'Apart from symptom control, someone to talk to outside the family can really help with mood,' she says.

'Thank you, I'll talk to her.'

In the living room, Dee seems to be asleep. Ben has moved the ottoman to sit at her feet, so I leave them.

When Ben's dad died he appeared to cope but, at night, would cling to me, his body voicing what he couldn't. All the kids were stoic in the face of Dee's grief. Their self-control felt unnatural, but who am I to judge? A few days after my dad died one of his mates gave me and my brother new bikes and I can't separate the shock of Dad disappearing from the utter delight at owning a blue BMX. And my mum, well, she may be alive but she's a virtual stranger.

Two summers ago, all out of excuses, I finally agreed to introduce Ben to my mum. He was unbearably jolly, despite the long drive, whereas I was unsteady, stomach too tight to force down breakfast, fingers playing an imaginary keyboard on my thigh. Explaining how I felt wasn't an option because I didn't know myself. Mum was, still is, a shapeshifter. I can make her a daredevil or as caring as the most devoted nurse, vicious or indifferent; I can paint her face and straighten her unnaturally blonde hair or leave her languishing on the sofa in a stained dressing gown. One minute she's laughing as she swings a bucket of water over me and Simon while we run around our postage-stamp garden, shrieking with delight; and the next she's the one shrieking, and I am a slut, a whore, a piece of shit, and she hates me, truly hates me, for being exactly like her.

My mum's address in the West End of Glasgow was smart, a run of conker-brown houses with clean windows and shiny door-knockers. She buzzed us in and we climbed the stairs to find her waiting in the open doorway of the flat she was sharing with her new partner, cruelly also called Ben. Her hug was firm, mine was frigid, unsure of the rules. She took us through to the kitchen where a fruit loaf was waiting – shop-bought, thank Christ; home-baking would have crucified me – and we made polite conversation. She didn't reel off her favourite anecdotes depicting me as a problem and her as a saint, choosing instead to congratulate me on a steady job, a nice boy, our country life. In answer to Ben, who was doing a fine job of making conversation, she said she was the office manager in her Ben's financial services business and I resisted the obvious quip about shagging the boss. I wanted to poke her, this new mum with her expensive-looking hair, to check she wasn't a figment of my imagination, but she'd have poked me back, because I too had changed beyond recognition. Plastic people: that's what I thought. Moulded to fit.

My Ben was appeased – it being important to meet your partner's family – but I couldn't wait to leave and never return.

Although we don't share DNA, Dee is more real to me.

I'm lost in that thought when Jamie returns holding a white paper bag with the chemist's sticker.

'How is she?'

'I think she might be asleep.'

'That's good. Thanks for looking out for her, Anna.'

I follow Jamie through into the living room and gesture that I'm going home. Ben nods, whispers that he'll stay till Dee wakes up.

Closing the door, I am hit by the realisation that these exacerbations will continue, her condition will worsen and she will need more and more help. The whirring in my head speeds up and a scenario arrives, fully formed, of me pushing Dee's wheelchair up the aisle of the church, her trusty oxygen cylinder cleverly concealed by a shawl. At coffee, the congregation takes turns to praise me for giving up work to care for my dear mother-in-law.

What did Sofia say on that last car journey?

Don't ossify in the village, Anna.

Back home, I go straight upstairs and unzip the shrine. It takes a breath and the contents swell, waking after their long sleep. I bury my face in the velvet cape.

14

Tête-à-tête

At the beginning of the school holidays Ben and I spend two weeks in Ibiza where we drink and eat like pigs and I take a pink contraceptive pill every day and we don't talk about anything that matters. The rest of the six-week break passes in a flurry of crises: Dee has two more courses of antibiotics and six days on steroids that finally restore her to a recognisable self; my mum gets married, texting after the event – two witnesses and a curry; Old Mary dies and Fenella recruits me to help organise the food for the wake; the rotten arm falls off the garden bench leaving a sharp, jagged stump and Ben takes it to the dump before I can plead its case. As a result, I abandon my habit of lolling outside in the afternoon with my nose in a paperback and instead lie on the sofa. This is where I am, engrossed in a grainy war movie, when Milly texts asking if I'm at home for the next half-hour for her to drop Ben's power bank back. I'm glad of the warning – the Slaters tend to operate an open-door policy. Reluctantly, I turn off the television. Only a certain type of person watches daytime and I am not supposed to be that type.

She arrives to find me in the kitchen, kettle hot, breakfast hidden in the dishwasher. Lunch has passed me by, I realise.

'Hi, Milly. How are you?'

'Good, thanks,' and so we begin the social niceties. She is looking very fresh and summery in an aquamarine sundress and white sandals. I am in dossing-about clothes, which Milly doesn't seem to know is a thing.

'Are the twins looking forward to going back to school?' Somehow it is already the last Saturday in August.

'I have no idea. All the talk is about tomorrow's animal-petting party.'

I laugh. 'Do they get to take one home?'

'Let's hope not.'

'You'd better check their party bags.'

. . . and we continue, genial and aimless.

'Anna.' Milly leans forwards and I instinctively lean back. Her body language is not aimless.

'Yes?'

The thrum of blood rushing is loud. I can't imagine what she is about to say but am fairly certain I won't like it.

'There isn't an easy way to say this.' She pauses. I hate her for the melodrama, for the cliché, for the exaggerated pause that heightens the dread. In this moment I am too incensed to even guess what the bombshell is going to be.

'Get on with it, Milly,' I say, my voice unpleasant. Holding her eye is difficult but I stay the distance.

Her cup-shaped hand moves towards her middle. 'We're—'

'Having another baby,' I say for her.

She smiles but I can't. My mouth is stuck open. I feel too exposed to be able to work out how I feel. Maybe I'm jealous that Little Miss Milly has it all; maybe I'm angry that she thought telling me face to face was kind when it really, really isn't; maybe I'm sad for Ben because – oh more maybes – maybe we won't have a family; maybe we won't even stay together. She needs to leave so I can think about that some more. Maybe he should find a nice fertile filly with big hips who can carry any number of babies at the same time.

'I wanted you to know before it becomes common knowledge.'

Ben is out, helping Jamie fit a new derailleur on his bike. This is not serendipity. This is manipulation.

'Have you already told Ben?'

She has the decency to flush.

'How many weeks?'

'Fourteen.' The Slaters have not been in the dark all this time; only I have. In some clandestine meeting the family clearly agreed that waiting until the first trimester was over made sense. No point upsetting me unnecessarily.

'I'm sorry, Anna, I didn't know what to do for the best.' Although loosely cognisant that I should be cross with Ben, only Milly is in my sights.

'The best might have been to tell me when you told everyone else rather than whispering behind my back, working out how to break the terrible news. A baby should never be terrible news. It shouldn't be an apology.' I'm on a roll and there's no stopping me. I hear my voice rise and sharpen. 'Maybe stop assuming you know how I feel. If you actually care, try asking. You can talk to Ben about whatever you choose – of course you can, he's your brother – but don't gang up on me, Milly. Don't try to manage me like a problem child.'

The lull is short. I can almost see her deciding whether or not to retaliate. She slips off the stool, picks up her car keys. While I wait, I watch the furry pink pompom on her keyring swing.

'You don't let us in, Anna. That's why we tiptoe around. Ben has bent over backwards to make you happy – we all have – but you won't give back.'

'Give back a baby?'

That does it. She matches my tone. 'For Christ's sake, grow up. Princess fucking Anna.'

She leaves without me congratulating her. And I'm not sorry.

15

Lapsang Souchong

Dee, who was initially reluctant, now looks forward to her Thursday afternoons at the Breathe Easy Club. She has bonded with a fellow garden enthusiast called Steve who is a similar age and, more importantly, further along the lung-disease journey. Seeing how well he copes, and how positive he is, has buoyed Dee, making her less fearful of the future. She has embraced the physio exercises, has started to meditate at home and next week several of the group are meeting for a cup of tea before the session. What's not to like?

Accompanying Dee to the hospital and back has fallen to me; it makes sense given I'm not at work. I take a book and kill time by a walk followed by a piece of cake in Woodies Kitchen, which is where I am now, all the while battling the feeling I should be in my old classroom, helping the children settle into Year 6.

Being part-time has robbed me of a sturdy hook to hang my life on, giving work the status of a hobby. My three days in Year 5 with Miss Emery are perfectly tolerable but at the end of the week I tend to beat myself up. It isn't that I begrudge helping Dee. No, the deep discontent is entirely due to the fact I had a chance to carve out a different future, but did nothing. Actually that's not fair – I bought a black plastic folder and filled it with paper: a CV, my qualifications, print-outs of course details, hand-written lists on hole-punched pieces of A4 and, in homage to Pippa, primary-coloured cardboard dividers.

I take a mouthful of cake and let my mind edge towards Pippa, the young one, the one I loved. In junior school, she ran a sideline exchanging the frill-free facts of life for chocolate. Some of the girls cried, terrified by her description of a penis stabbing away at their insides. I like this memory, can almost feel the laughter as we replay the reactions of the kids whose innocence we destroyed.

My mind, unbidden, skips to the last time I saw her. This is a dangerous game – a game to see how close I dare creep before the blackness comes. I consult my internal saboteur, take another forkful of date and walnut cake, and decide to play.

It is ten days before Christmas. And, therefore, twenty days before I become a modern-day evacuee, leaving a London full of exploding bombs to take refuge in a Somerset village. Pippa and I are both twenty-four but have nothing else in common, apart from both happening to be in Russia Dock Woodland on the same dank, dismal evening. She is running, the reflective stripes on her super-sleek kit somehow flashing despite the lack of light. I am running too, but in my waitress outfit of black trousers and black canvas pumps, late for work at the brasserie. Unspeakable emotions start to rise and rise – the loudest, the most acute and most deadly is the thing I can't abide: the knowledge that life has no obligation to be fair. I didn't choose to have a crap family. I didn't choose to constantly flirt with poverty. I didn't choose to serve fucking Fettucine Alfredo to people my age who wear suits and may or may not deign to tip me. I am fired up, looking for someone to blame, and the fire makes my feet fast. I would like Pippa to notice me; I would like there to be some kind of showdown. But as I close in on her, I can see she is wearing wireless earphones, happily pounding the ground with no idea I am at her heels.

At this juncture in my reconstruction, as with every other time, the footage refuses to load. I take the last triangle of cake and linger. I can rewind, picturing the slight rock of her hips, the neat swing of her arms, the straight back, but can't go forward. I am at her heels, and then—

'Excuse me.' In a blink Pippa has vanished. 'Do you mind if I sit here?'

I nod and gesture at the spare seat because my mouth is crammed with crumbly sponge.

The man sits opposite me and I hurriedly swallow and clean my teeth with my tongue, in case I have to speak. The two grey-haired women on the next table choose this moment to explode with laughter and the man and I share a smile even though we can't share the joke. These women have been here every week, demolishing the Woodies cream tea while they loudly chat. Another day, I might ask to join their table and laugh uproariously with them.

The smell of smoky bacon makes me wrinkle my nose in disgust. I look up from my book, a mediocre Nordic noir, to find the source.

'Sorry. Lapsang is an anti-social choice, isn't it?'

'Should be banned,' I say, 'along with Bovril.'

'And anything with cardamom.'

'And kiwi fruit.'

'And nail polish remover.'

'But what would you take your polish off with?'

He laughs. 'Wire wool.'

92

'You've obviously never had acrylic nails.'

'I'm going to risk a personal comment and suggest you haven't either.'

It's impossible not to glance down at my sensibly short unadorned nails. When my head bobs back up he has raised his eyebrows, inviting confirmation. My smile is spontaneous and wide.

'Actually, the idea makes me claustrophobic.'

'I get that,' he says. 'I don't know if nails breathe but they should definitely be given the option.'

'A naturist in the making, if I can also risk a personal comment.'

'Something that has never appealed, I'm afraid,' he says. 'Most people's bodies are better hidden.'

Involuntarily I scan what I can see of him. His legs, tucked under the table, are a mystery but his torso is dressed in a long-sleeved stripy Breton top – not an item a Slater would wear, or most men come to that. The backs of his hands are hairy, suggesting there is more fur lining his body. No ring. His face is slim, sun-weathered, with wrinkles that frame his smile; his eyes are dark and his hair, which is a melange of browns, would benefit from a cut. He might be a tree surgeon or a landscape gardener. Something outdoorsy and wholesome. Although he doesn't have dirty nails. (*Maybe he's a ceramicist*, says some little voice in search of a tortured artist.)

'What about you? Ever had the urge to play table tennis in the buff?'

'I feel the cold,' I say.

'I've always thought that's more of an attitude than an actual thing.'

'You think cold is imagined?'

'I think cold is a fact and feeling the cold is a decision.'

This man has poured the last of his tea from the pot. I find myself panicking he might leave before I want him to.

'But there are biological responses to cold – shivering, goose-bumps, pale skin. Surely you're not a science-denier?'

'I'm not a creationist, if that's what you mean. Although it does have a lovely sound.' He repeats the word slowly and I stare hard at his mouth. 'I like words with lots of syllables. Mellifluous. Sartorial.'

'Diaphanous.' Sofia's dress, a billowing red sail, dances in front of my eyes.

'Yes. That's not a word I ever use but I like it very much.' He cocks his head to one side; it is unaccountably adorable. 'Diaphanous.'

He drains his cup and rubs his right eye hard like a tired toddler; signs our time is drawing to a close. I have a compulsion to give significance to this accidental meeting, this collision of nimble tongues and vivid ideas. So, I hold out my hand.

'It was nice to chat,' I say.

We shake hands. And I dare myself. (Never will I turn down a dare.)

'I'm Sofia, by the way.' I mimic her intonation: a short first syllable, almost missing the 'o', and a long swishing tail.

'Sofia. That's gorgeous.' He means the name: I know that. 'I'm Mark.'

'Goodbye, Mark.'

On the walk back to the hospital, titillated by my impromptu subterfuge, I imagine I am Sofia. I hold my chin a little higher and swing my arms energetically.

'Pretend' always was my favourite game.

16

King of Strokes

This week, my three days in the Year 5 classroom have flown by, the brittle newness replaced by something more settled. Miss Emery is getting used to me, I am getting to know her rhythm and habits and the kids have worked out their dominance hierarchy. The top dogs are a gang of three boys, made in my own mould. Smart, spry and sassy. I manage their constant disruptions with a stern face, but inside I find them funny.

As I watch them run out of the school gates, having been reprimanded for throwing conkers at a cat, my mood bombs. For me, the working week is over. Thursday and Friday dangle in front of me: dead pheasants outside the butcher's.

Ben's habit of quizzing me about my two days of freedom brings a degree of pressure to achieve something. I have attacked the bindweed in the garden; I have made my own pesto – who knew it was so easy? I have tidied the spice cupboard and thrown away the many out-of-date jars; I have had coffee with Hannah from the B&B twice. Relying on my own initiative to fill the time is draining. With no structure, the day is interminably long.

Dawdling home, I think what I'd really like to do is lie on the sofa and eat a tub of ice cream while thinking about the man from the café. The man who brought back the butterfly excitement Sofia engendered from the moment she announced herself in the arched doorway of the church. It is interesting the way a stranger can elicit such a strong reaction. I was determined to make Sofia my friend . . . but based on what? The look of her, her manner, her diction. And the same goes for the man in the café. What was so intoxicating? And did he feel it too? With hindsight, our conversation was blatantly flirtatious. I badly want to have more conversations with him; and to occupy his thoughts as he is occupying mine.

I try, again, to visualise him but can't recall his face, conjuring only his stripy Breton top and a sense of . . . impishness.

Letting myself into the house, I consider indulging this train of thought by taking to my bed – Ben has gone into the office today and won't be back until about seven – but decide against. I need something more concrete to hold on to than a teenage crush on someone I'll probably never see again. So, in desperation, I do what I adamantly didn't want to.

I go online to find something regular to commit to. If hand-building with clay is my destiny, so be it.

The next morning, I have a fluttery sensation in my stomach as I get ready for my first ever swimming lesson – the alternatives on offer being line dancing and Knit-and-Natter. Ben is absurdly pleased that I am voluntarily going to exercise. Milly has lent me a racer-backed swimsuit – a triangle bikini would never do in a public pool, I'm advised – and goggles. I have thanked her with the sincerest expression I can summon because we have not fully recovered from #babygate.

The motivation to learn to simultaneously breathe, submerge my head, perform an effective stroke and gain some propulsion from kicking is completely and utterly missing, but I refuse to bail. I cannot fail at everything.

Slightly stout, broad-chested, balding Frank is waiting by the pool in disturbingly small Speedos. Equally disturbingly, I seem to be the only taker for October's adult improvers course at the leisure centre. There is, however, no time to feel awkward because he asks if I can swim a length and, when I nod, he says, in you go then. I attempt a fast breaststroke, head well clear of the water, reaching the far end with my arms already aching and heart thumping.

'Good start,' he says. 'You can stay afloat and you're not scared.'

We are, however, not going to bother with breaststroke until we have mastered the king of strokes, crawl. Breaststroke done badly can wreak havoc with knees and lower backs, he says, and I nod. Wanting to please people is a curse. I like breaststroke best but the need to agree with Frank trumps my actual opinion.

We duck our heads to establish that being underwater is not a threat; we blow, audibly, to practise expelling air; he goes through the arc of a stroke of crawl and I copy; when it's time to take a breath I must remember to twist my head sideways not up – with firm hands he demonstrates by turning my neck for me.

We finish the half-hour lesson with two lengths of crawl, breathing every three strokes. My legs are too low in the water and my stroke too short, he says, but otherwise, not bad. I am ecstatic. I am not ballast; I am selkie.

'What brought you here today?' he asks.

'I like the idea of cold-water swimming but I need to know I'd be safe.' I am amused by my own lie, the truth being so very dull.

'Have you had a bad experience in open water?'

I trawl my seaside holidays but find only bars, boys and sunburn. 'No. I've hardly ever been in the sea.' Ben prefers the pool, less sand and more waiters.

'That can change when your technique improves.' He levers his body out of the pool. 'See you next week.'

On the way to get changed, I feel extremely pleased with myself for doing something other than watching daytime television. Maybe I should embrace my lie . . .

My mind draws an endless expanse of ocean, cerulean blue with frothy white frills. I place myself on the beach, dressed in a woolly hat, a sensible swimsuit and wetsuit gloves. In my practical rucksack there is a flask for afterwards. I add some fellow hearty swimmers, part of a group with a pun for a name. Blue Tits. Chilly Dippers. We make our way towards the tempestuous sea. I look to my companion.

The face, miraculously formed by rods and cones I didn't know I had, is my café man, Lapsang-Souchong Mark.

I let the changing-room door slam behind me, making an ugly clang. Scold my brain for producing unhelpful nonsense. After my shower, feet firmly planted on dirty tiles, I rub myself dry and count my blessings. I have a kind, loyal partner, I have food and shelter, I have a nice place of work, I have straight teeth, I don't smoke anything anymore, I can still touch my toes.

On the bus home, I make a mental list of how to restore my mojo that doesn't involve fantasising about a stranger.

See the baby doctor and have another go.

Get a job to fill the two days a week. (Not a charity shop.)

Go to college and do A-level English.

Go to college and do an access course and become an astrophysicist.

(My confidence in the list is ebbing.)

Learn sign language and work with deaf children.

Ask Ben if he can take a sabbatical and go travelling.

Travelling is a middle-class pursuit I can't unpick. Two weeks at an all-inclusive, I get. But where is the pleasure in moving from place to place, no routine, another bloody museum, dodgy tummy, no idea what anyone is saying. People boast about suffering a rash of insect bites while trekking in Nepal or being struck with dengue fever in Borneo, but in my opinion, it would be hard to beat the weekend Mum got a load of out-of-date freebies from Iceland and we threw the biggest impromptu party the street, or Police Community Support Officer collar number 8460, had ever seen.

I'm laughing out loud as my phone beeps. Time to go to Dee's.

17

Bakewell Slice

This week the breathing group are meeting for a cup of tea before the session so I arrive at Dee's house super early. Respiratory problems gobble time; rushing is not an option. Using the bathroom, locking up, walking to the car: they all deplete Dee's shallow reserves.

Once on our way, her breathing steadies; she capably negotiates the twisty roads before picking up speed on the A-road. If parking at the hospital wasn't such a problem, she could cope on her own, but her anxiety can be as debilitating as her pulmonary issues. Worrying about not being able to breathe is a shortcut to exactly that.

Today, luck is on our side. We secure a prime spot and walk the short distance to the entrance, arriving at the same time as Dee's new friend, Steve. Dressed in tan and olive, he looks like a cosy creature displaced from his woodland habitat. His manner is equally warm, clasping my hand between both of his and saying, 'This must be the lovely Anna.'

They reject my offer to fetch them drinks and shoo me away.

'I'll be back at four,' I say.

Without warning the dam holding back my hopes for the afternoon breaks, unleashing a galloping heart and tacky armpits. The man won't be at the café, I tell myself, but some part refuses to listen. Some irrational, hedonistic streak has no care for the fact I am all but married, might in different circumstances be a mother. Good God, I've even dressed up, choosing the green jumpsuit, leaving my hair down, adding a dash of rose-tinted lip balm. My teenage self, who overlapped every boyfriend she ever had with the next, is alive and well despite the decade that has passed.

'Sofia!'

My borrowed name ricochets through the lobby, bringing a wave of light-headedness that might, if I were Victorian, be called a swoon. The possibility of our crossing paths at the hospital had not occurred to me, despite the proximity to the café.

'Sofia!' he calls again. The voice is commanding; an order to stop where I am. An order I will obey as soon as I can work out how to feign surprise.

Sorry, do we know each other?

Rabbit-fast feet come from nowhere. Yellow flip-flops leading to brown legs and the skirt of a pink tutu. The girl runs past me and I follow her path to the outstretched hand of a suited man: 'Sofia, you mustn't run off.' They disappear but I remain where I am, a silly woman who has forgotten who she is and why she's here.

The outside is welcome. A fresh breeze, not cold, but a reminder that we are on the cusp of coats and boots. I walk towards the café, searching the sky for a glimmer of blue in the blanket white.

Maybe the tables will be full, forcing me to sit with the two old ladies who laugh so joyously – that would be a good result. Or maybe Mark will be there with his wife, freshly bald from chemo. A visible confirmation that any connection is merely a figment of my imagination. Regardless, there will be cake.

As I walk inside, the significance I have given to a passing chat with a stranger is laughable. So laughable that when I see him, sitting at the same table as before, I stare, unsure whether he is imagined.

The woman in front of me takes her elderflower pressé, no ice, and goes to sit down.

'Flat white, please,' I say, turning away from Mark, 'and . . . one of those.' I point.

'Bakewell slice?'

'Yes, thank you.'

Prickling with the knowledge he might be looking at me, I pull my shoulders back, which feels artificial, so I straighten up. *Where is straight?* I think.

'I'll bring it over,' says the woman behind the counter. 'Where are you going to sit?'

Don't ask me that.

'Which table?' she says.

I should look around, that is what people do, they look around and they say 'in the window' or 'the one by the bookcase' or 'the one with the ugly bastard scoffing a sausage roll'.

'Is it to take away?'

I shake my head. She waits . . .

'I'll share his table,' I say, pointing over my shoulder.

I glide over, willing him to look up, but he is intent on his phone. This is incredible to me. I am alight, shiny with expectation, and he is oblivious.

'Hello,' I say, but am too quiet. I lick my lips to try again, change my mind and tap his shoulder.

He looks up, doesn't appear to immediately recognise me. And then . . . my name comes to him. 'Sofia?'

'May I join you?'

'Yes, by all means.'

He seems bemused as he watches me pull out a chair, hang my coat over the back and sit. 'Why do I have the sense this is an arrangement? When I know we haven't made an arrangement.'

I like this statement. I like it a lot. It emboldens me. Despite my many other insecurities, my sexual confidence is unfailing. If I want him, I will have him.

'Let's pretend it is an arrangement. Would that be okay with you, Mark?'

'Yes, Sofia. That would be nice.'

I smile, a smile without any brakes. Game on.

'So how is your day going?' he asks.

Fluent now, I regale the story of the swimming lesson. Anna's preference would be to be spare but amusing, whereas I feel Sofia would over-share. I wince at her mention of Frank's trunks. Seamlessly Mark takes over with his own experience, paddling on the open sea. We fill the café with mutual appreciation.

Though not a ceramicist, as I'd hoped, he is an art therapist. The coincidence – I remember Sofia's depiction of happy drawing versus angry drawing – floods me with pheromones.

'What?' he says.

I may be smirking. 'I had you down as a ceramicist.'

'As in you thought that just now or you thought it before?'

I side-step, not wanting to confess the level of my preoccupation.

'It was the stripy top,' I narrow my eyes in mock disapproval before adding, 'and the hair.'

'Most of us have a uniform of sorts, don't you think?' Today he is wearing a faded red shirt with a half-placket that might be called an artist's smock.

'I do,' I say, thinking of Ben's programming colleagues who all seem to wear chinos and a semi-casual shirt.

'Although you're not giving much away,' he says, taking in my outfit, 'unless you're a mechanic.'

'I'm off duty,' I say.

'You don't work?'

'I'm a student. Third time around.'

He asks me about my PhD and I answer as Sofia answered me, embellishing the aspects I'm more confident of and skimming over others. I'm grateful to be a quick study – chunks of our conversations remain intact and accessible. She would be impressed.

'So, what does a typical day look like for an art therapist?' I say.

I store the phrases: therapeutic art intervention, the physicality of art-making, art is a form of truth.

'. . . but my favourite gig is at the PRU.'

'I thought pupil referral units struggle to get academic staff let alone therapy.'

'There's an enlightened head who somehow alchemised funding to start the programme in exchange for being part of a study.'

'Does that pile on the pressure to succeed?' I quickly correct myself. 'Not succeed as in solve, but provide evidence of results.'

'Actually, we all rather like the attention. You've never seen six excluded teenagers display such conforming behaviours.'

He is charming. (We are both charming.) 'Doesn't that interfere with the therapeutic aspect?'

'Smart question.' He touches my arm. 'Sorry, I didn't mean to be condescending.'

I want to take his hand and slot my fingers between his as confirmation of our union, but patience triumphs.

We sit, heads ever closer together, and I listen to his words and watch his mouth and in between take in every feature from his largish ears to his visible filling, back right, that I only get to glimpse when he laughs. When it is my turn to speak, he stares intently, lips slightly apart, but I don't feel any need to blink, or look elsewhere, happy in the skin I've created. As Sofia I am more forthcoming, less self-censorious. I may also be slightly posher, my speech more flowery with nice enunciation.

'. . . so what brought you to my favourite café two weeks running?'

I explain about Dee, my lovely neighbour, aware of how rose-coloured I sound, aware that I am omitting the pertinent fact. Aware enough to create a diversion.

'Tell me about the head of the PRU you so admire?' I can tell my interest pleases him.

He run his fingers through the wayward hair that flops over his eyes. 'She has this aura of authority and bone-deep conviction. Elemental, somehow, like . . . weather.'

'A force of nature.'

'A cliché doesn't do her justice.'

'Too glib.'

'Clichés are always glib.'

'At the end of the day.'

'To cut a long story short.'

'Everything happens for a reason.' I smile, eyes locked on his.

He swallows, a bob of his Adam's apple.

'I need to go,' he says, shifting his chair backwards, readying to leave.

'Perhaps I'll see you next week.' I am an audacious woman, virtually spreading my legs beneath the painted wooden table.

'I'm here most Thursdays,' he says. 'My morning belongs to the hospital but the afternoon is mine.' He stuffs his khaki jacket into his bag and slings it across his body. 'One of the benefits of portfolio working.'

I plunge straight in. 'Perhaps the afternoon could be ours?'

'This is a surprising conversation, Sofia.' He is unsure but not, I feel, uncomfortable.

'Surprises are good, aren't they?'

'They are.'

He leans towards me and I stop breathing – *is he going to kiss me?* – but he steals an icing-covered crumb from my plate.

'Goodbye, Sofia.'

When he is most of the way to the door, he turns around and stares; a stare that might make another woman avert her eyes. But I stay as I am and I don't blush.

18

Chequerboard

My, what a skip there is to my step. I am set to permanent boost. The grass is greener, the air is sweeter.

Because I have a secret.

Recognising the difference between good and bad secrets is something we teach in class. The lesson is very black and white: good secrets, we tell the children, make you feel happy; bad secrets make you feel uncomfortable, confused and unsafe. This may be true at the very darkest end of the spectrum, but I think the reality is more chequerboard. Kids have very little agency; secrets bring that seductive sliver of power.

Mark is a bad secret that feels good, better than good. So much better that I would contest there is anything bad about it. Chatting to a stranger, attractive or otherwise, does not constitute a crime. What is a crime is the lift in my spirits. It is Wednesday and the usual woe at my two days off is absent, because tomorrow I have a liaison in Woodies.

Miss Emery and I have taken to eating our lunch together in the classroom; this feels like a tentative move towards becoming friends. She is telling me about her irritable bowel when a notification pops up on my silenced phone; it's from Finn to the family chat. I tap. Milly has bleeding. They're going to the hospital. I know I need to reply but can't immediately decide on the words. I tap a reply, delete, tap some more, add kisses and send.

'Is something wrong?' asks Miss Emery.

I tell her about Milly and she asks how copious and what colour and whether there is pain. I don't know the answers, nor am I about to quiz Finn. Since #babygate this is all landmine territory.

'I lost a baby in the summer,' says Miss Emery, and so begins our most personal chat to date.

I am sympathetic, but don't offer my own experience. In school, only a couple of people know about my miscarriages and I'd like it to stay that way.

'I was devastated. My daughter already had long hair in a fat plait and slightly pudgy legs. Her whole life took shape without me even trying.'

I have never envisaged plaits, or a bob or a mullet. Nor could I ever picture Ben and me pushing a pram. Given the colourful nature of my internal world, this feels like a sign. We aren't meant to have babies. At least, not with each other.

'Did you know it was a girl?'

'No!' She smiles at the ridiculousness. 'But my daughter came complete with a gap between her front teeth and a love of riding.'

'I like the sound of her.'

Eyes a little shiny, Miss Emery places her outspread hand on her stomach in the same way I have seen other women touch their full wombs, empty wombs, hopeful wombs. Me included. 'We're trying again.'

A second alert comes up on my phone. Miss Emery leans in,

clearly invested in the outcome. It is Dee. She is in school this afternoon interviewing for the new caretaker. Can she pop by and see me? She hopes I'm not upset.

It takes me a moment to realise I am meant to be upset about Milly.

'You're so lucky to have Dee,' says Miss Emery.

'Yes, she's hardly the wicked mother-in-law.'

'You're not married, are you?' Her forehead creases and I'm aware of some flaking of the powder she uses to present a veneer of porcelain.

I shake my head.

'Nor me. It's too expensive.'

'You could have a registry office and a pie in a pub.'

'That's not my style.' She opens her palms to suggest I take in her everyday look which is full-on flounce, full-on make-up, full-on blow-dry. 'It's bridezilla or nothing.'

'It's good to know what you want,' I say.

Sofia, like Miss Emery, knew what she wanted: from work, from the cocktail menu, from a pillow – 'Feathers every time, Anna. If there's a chance of microfibre, I take my own' – which is one of the reasons she found me so frustrating.

'I hope Milly doesn't lose the baby,' says Miss Emery.

I murmur, on balance, more interested in her irritable bowel.

'Do you and Ben want children?'

My answer – 'Not yet' – which has been ready throughout, coincides with the arrival of Dee. Saved by serendipity.

'Hello, Dee,' says Miss Emery. A quick exchange of pleasantries and she excuses herself, giving Dee and me some privacy.

'I wanted to check you're all right,' says Dee.

Whatever feelings the news of Milly's precarious pregnancy is meant to engender, I don't have them. So I improvise.

'I'm trying not to think about it. How do you feel, Dee?'

'Worried, obviously. But trying to stay optimistic.' She smiles. 'I'm hoping by the end of the afternoon we'll know more.' She takes a chest-heaving breath. I remind myself that the clump of cells in Milly's womb is Dee's grandchild.

'How many interviews do you have?'

'Three. I'll have to leave my phone on.'

'Put it on silent and you'll still be able to see if Finn sends any updates.'

'So sorry, I don't mean to interrupt.' Miss Emery is back. 'Can I just ask Anna something?'

'Of course,' says Dee. 'I need to get going anyway.'

'Anna, can you possibly work tomorrow?' She goes on to explain my job share has called in full of cold. 'I'm sorry to ask but we can arrange a day in lieu.'

'Sorry. I'm afraid I go out with Dee on Thursdays.' I don't mention the hospital because Dee's illness is not public property.

'I can easily get a lift with Steve,' says Dee, who is hovering in the doorway. 'He goes past the village so it's no bother.'

'I also have a swimming lesson in the morning,' I add, my chest tightening at the prospect of not going to Woodies, not seeing Mark, not populating the pages of our story. I do know what I want, at least in the short term. I want him.

The two of them wait – owl eyes staring – for me to say I will cancel.

'Can you at least do the afternoon?' asks Miss Emery.

110

Resisting is difficult, but the alternative is more unbearable. 'No. I'm afraid—'

'Anna, you really mustn't worry about me,' says Dee. 'Just let me know one way or the other in the morning.' And she disappears.

Without Dee's scrutiny, I am braver. 'I'm very sorry, Miss Emery, I'd like to help but I have a busy day planned.' She looks like she might press me so I continue. 'I don't want Dee to have to change her plans. She does enough for the school already.' I stand up and walk briskly towards the staff toilets and lock myself in a cubicle. I am suffocating – a forced tomato in Dee's greenhouse, crammed into too small a pot, roots already reaching the bottom and sides, nowhere left to go. My time is not my own. My life is not my own.

19

Celestial Bodies

Mark is not at his usual table or any other. I order the same as last week, a flat white and a Bakewell slice, then sit and fret. Perhaps the afternoon could be ours, I repeat to myself, squirming at Sofia's self-assurance that could be taken as hubris. Rerunning our whole exchange, I realise I was way too forward. No one wants the fish to jump onto the plate, they want to dangle a fly for a while first.

So when he does finally appear, sporting his favourite Breton top, hand already waving, the relief makes me doubly happy.

'How was your morning?' I ask, as he joins me.

He provides a snapshot of being the only art therapist, and part-time at that, in an environment crying out for more therapeutic interventions.

'What about yours, Sofia?'

'Chaos.' I toss my head and the chandelier earrings (that I swapped with my studs on the walk here) swing like pendulums.

'Those earrings are beautiful.' I am also wearing Sofia's flouncy blouse, hidden from Dee by my puffer coat. Dressing in a dead woman's clothes feels illicit. Illicit is good.

'Thank you.'

'What was chaotic?'

The truth is I drank a lot of pool water because this week we tried tumble turns, which frustrated my body's spatial understanding. The lie is that a patient fainted while having acupuncture at the pain clinic. Lying, like a bad secret, should probably make you feel uncomfortable, confused or unsafe, but none of those apply.

'I quite like it when everything goes wrong,' he says. 'It reminds me that I'm not in charge of the world. That I'm a pixel.'

He has used my thought, my exact word. After Sofia died, I distinctly remember lying on the garden bench staring at the sky, thinking, *I'm a pixel*. This is proof. Some crucial astrological lines have crossed, some celestial bodies have overlapped their moons to bring us together.

'Does that mean you can abdicate responsibility?' I ask.

'Not completely. You still have to try, but there's no comeback if it doesn't work. Success, or otherwise, is down to pixels.'

'I might adopt that approach.'

'This is what therapy gets you.' He pats his own shoulder. 'Acceptance.'

'Acceptance can sound like settling for less.'

'In the eye of the beholder, perhaps. I think acceptance is the key to wellbeing. Striving is . . . just listen to the word. Full of effort, audibly straining.'

We have a second drink and the conversation strays into our personal histories. The anticipation is a wasp flitting in and out of hearing – what will he divulge, and what will I?

He mentions growing up in Devizes with his sister and working in a bakery as a teenager. I share a wealthy version of London, throwing in a sister as well as a brother, and describe Keeper's Cottage and my plans for the garden. Our ringless fingers dance around the table. A table that feels like an impediment to progress.

My eyes stray to the window. 'Do you have time for a walk?'

His hesitation is almost undetectable, but there nonetheless. 'Yes, I do.'

We stand and I feel, rather than see, several pairs of eyes track our journey to the door and beyond. In three short weeks we are an item.

Mark is taller and slimmer than Ben, and his gait is longer, fairly obviously. The few strides we take to settle on both a pace and the distance of separation are interesting. If I were a clever student of psychology I would research the minuscule ways in which we adapt to fit a new social situation without any discernible communication, whether that is a side-by-side walk or a conversation with a stranger where we have to observe the pattern of speech to recognise what is merely a pause and what is the end of the piece. My remit would cover which antennae send and receive signals, how people manage not to overcompensate, and whether some people are oblivious, maintaining their usual behaviour and leaving the opposition to meld to them.

'What are you thinking?'

When I tell him, he grasps hold of the notion and shakes it loose. We are all experts already, he insists, and in no need of a study to explain what occurs organically.

'It has to be a mistake to want to dissect, to deconstruct. That we can bend to accommodate another human being is a beautiful thing. Shame on you, Sofia, for wanting to unravel the mystery.'

No man I have ever known, biblically or not, has spoken like this.

'I think it could be a beautiful thing to study the mechanism,' I say. 'Think of the innards of an old clock.'

114

'Innards makes me think of flesh – I don't get wheels and cogs, quite the opposite.'

'Try harder,' I say. 'Shiny brass, whirring cogs, a nice, clean tick.'

'No. Innards is a synonym for intestines. I reject your word. And your argument. Some things are better left as a whole.'

'How very gestalt of you.'

This is play, which stops because our wanderings, a left here, a right there, bring us to a terrace with an impressive array of coloured front doors. Sulphur yellow through prison grey via a livid lilac.

'What an inspiring little neighbourhood,' I say.

'And the light is nice today. Blue cold.' He takes out his phone and starts taking photographs, at one point standing on a low wall to capture a midnight-blue door choked by ivy. My gaze follows his, emulating his experience.

'Do you think new residents have to ask the committee to approve their Pantone?' I ask.

'I hope so.' He is distracted, doesn't really want to chat. His absorption is charming.

The inhabitants of each house give themselves away not only by their colour choices but by their shiny knockers, video doorbells, window boxes. Dee's house tells any passer-by she is a keen gardener with archetypal English rather than exotic taste.

'Do you use photography in your work?' I ask.

'I'm constantly reinventing what I do. Clay, crayon, doors, the sea, triangles, biscuits – the truth comes out whatever the medium, whatever the subject.'

Truth is a much-used word of Mark's. If he were built from words *truth* would be his backbone, strong and unequivocal, but the other bones would be flightier: ethereal, impetuous, scandalous.

'What will you do with these photos?'

'Endless possibilities.'

'Give me one.'

'Okay, pick a favourite door.'

I let Sofia choose. 'The red with the shiny knocker.'

His sudden, animated rummaging in his messenger bag is funny, reminiscent of a granny rooting for a safety pin in an oversized handbag.

A rabbit held high by its ears wouldn't surprise me but out comes a pristine box of white chalks.

'I didn't think anyone used chalk anymore.'

'They do if they have a chalkboard in the kitchen.' He opens the box and hands me one. 'Now draw what lies behind the door.'

He has already sat down on the pavement and crossed his legs, so I follow suit.

'I can't really draw.'

I get a disdainful look. 'Everyone can make a mark, Sofia. Do an outline.'

I oblige, drawing four lines on the bumpy tarmac.

'What are you waiting for?'

'A briefing,' I say.

He embarks on a spiel about how creativity loves constraint and, mid-flow, I begin.

My rectangle is quickly filled with balloons, recognisable more by the string than the attempt at a knot. I use a dab of wet finger to imply some light source somewhere. And, as instructed, sign my work, rejecting Sofia's family name in favour of the more romantic Hemingway.

He reads my clumsy letters, rolling the name around his mouth like a boiled sweet. 'A descendant of Ernest, I hope.'

'Sadly not. My family is in pubs rather than publishing,' I say, adopting Sofia's short-lived husband's brewing heritage to grow my status. 'And are you Mark Twain?'

'Turner.'

I hand back my chalk. 'Okay, Mark Turner. Analyse me.'

'Analysing a drawing is not what I do, numpty. I'm not a tarot reader.'

'Do it anyway.'

'You've made it too easy, balloons are universally celebratory.'

'Do you feel celebratory?'

A pause.

All it takes is a slight lean to my right and a turn of the head, like taking a breath when swimming. And I kiss him. His cheek is in my palm and I can feel each blunt-ended hair and the smoother skin above. I want him to grab the back of my head and pull me towards him with the potency of a teenage boy, but he moves away.

'You need to be sure.' His pulse is visible at his temple, but all else is still. I am rapt, quite possibly drooling. 'Because I can't stop thinking about you, Sofia.'

20

Cry Wolf

'Pass the wine, Anna,' says Ben.

He is sitting between Milly and Dee; his older brother, Jamie, is at the head; Bridget, Jamie's wife, is one side of me and Finn is the other. We are out to dinner to mark the happy resolution to the scare everyone had this week. Milly's pregnancy is deemed stable (placenta not previa) and it's a girl. Finn is threatening to call her Wolfie because she cried wolf. I realise this is a form of self-defence but the light it shines, once again, on my and Ben's inability to communicate prevents me from enjoying the joke.

This is not the only way in which I am not in harmony with the true Slaters. While pleased by the news, I didn't hold my breath, I didn't pray, I didn't spend every minute catastrophising on Milly's behalf because I knew her baby would stick or twist, depending on biology. My reaction is probably a sign of some unresolved emotional issues. Regardless, I can't muster the relief that is writ large this Saturday evening.

Ben fills his empty glass, tops up those around him. He is drinking at a pace.

'How's the calamari?' Dee asks. I have demolished my starter, smearing each ring of batter in aioli.

'Delicious. What about yours?'

Her plate has the remains of a beetroot, apple and fennel salad. 'Healthy.'

We giggle.

I have a pang of guilt. This family has taken me in, supported and subbed me, and I am repaying them by rejoicing in the beginnings of an affair. (For it will be an affair!)

To offset this grumble of disquiet, I turn to Bridget and actively engage. 'How are the girls?'

She recounts their latest achievements at gymnastics, at Brownies, at after-school art.

'Tell me, Bridget, what aren't they good at?'

This is not Anna speaking. This is a throwback to Sofia demanding I reveal something I don't like about Ben.

'They aren't very co-ordinated,' she says, nervously, 'at ball sports.'

'I'm joking, Bridget,' I say. 'It's wonderful that the girls are so accomplished.'

Ben narrows his eyes at me. I make mine wider in response.

If I left him, would he simply provide stabling for another mare, I wonder, or would his heart be scooped out, leaving only the husk?

A steak knife is passed to me and I tear into the fibres and watch the milky red myoglobin that people routinely mistake for blood leak onto my plate. My mum would be astounded at the facts I have picked up outside mainstream education and at my extensive vocabulary (and let us not dwell on the disappearance of my estuary accent).

119

Another bottle appears. This time round I match Ben glass for glass. We reject pudding in favour of grappa.

Dee insists on paying the bill and we all thank her profusely.

'Shall we walk home?' I ask Ben. 'It's not raining.'

The goodbyes are excruciating given we live in each other's pockets. When we are finally free, I say, 'Let's have a nightcap in The White Hart.'

Ben, whose breath is chemical and eyes slightly pink, is game.

I pour us large glasses from a bottle of house red, taking the top inch in one mouthful. Being drunk is the perfect way for the weekend to accelerate past. Being drunk means a fry-up after church followed by a nap and a film in the evening. Monday means a new week. A new Thursday. *I have kissed him*, I think. The physical shiver is delectable.

'You must have been reliving the miscarriage this week,' says Ben's timorous voice.

Pain and blood and industrial sanitary towels come easily to mind; my attempt to find sorrow fails. I have moved on.

'I didn't let myself think about it.'

'I couldn't . . . can't stop myself. Our first baby would have been walking by now.'

This is not a calculation I have made. I am shocked he has.

I drain my glass and let the alcohol wreak havoc. 'I didn't ever picture our babies.'

'Didn't you look ahead?' He is crestfallen, visibly broken. 'Imagine a spin bowler or a pain-in-the-neck teenager?'

I shake my head. Miss Emery's virtual daughter with her fat plait is more real than any of my unborn children.

There is a period of silence in which he does nothing and I fill my glass with maroon. I don't like maroon as a colour, it's depressing, but I like the taste.

He wipes his face on his sleeve. 'Are we in trouble, Anna?'

I am not prepared for this. Nor, given an opening, do I consider honesty. I may be about to sample an alternative but have no plans to throw the Slaters away.

'I don't think so,' I say.

'What kind of answer is that?'

I am deciding whether to empty the last of the wine into my glass, or to share, when he stands up. 'I can't do this. I'm going home. Are you coming?'

'I'll come in a bit,' I say, not unhappy at being left with my own head for company. If this is a crossroads, or I suppose a fork, I need to choose well.

Although, best not to decide anything when drunk.

I concentrate on remaining drunk enough to not have to decide.

Later, maybe after midnight, I lurch along the stretch of road to the village, too far gone to care about Ben. My heart of stone can only be cracked open by my soon-to-be lover, Mark.

The walk is sobering, as is the group of loud-mouthed lads that I have to pass. I instinctively bunch my keys into my fist – slotting them between your fingers doesn't work – and picture myself making a backhand hammer punch with a blade sticking out. Growing up with a bully for a brother polishes your self-defence skills.

When I open the front door, a meaty belch followed by a wave of nausea sends me straight to the downstairs loo. The violent vomiting brings a healthy dose of self-disgust that cleaning my teeth doesn't negate. I can't bring myself to creep into our bed, not tonight. So much more is at stake than when I last bailed on a boyfriend. As Mark said, I need to be sure.

The first breakfast doesn't stay down, but by the time Ben appears my second attempt – the biggest bowl of granola ever seen topped with a whole banana and swimming in milk – is hitting the spot.

'How's your head?' he asks.

'Attached by a thread. Yours?'

'Similar.' He fetches a coffee and sits down opposite me. 'We don't talk, Anna. But I don't know why.'

On a scale of boldness, I decide where I am. Quite bold is the answer. 'We don't talk because you want me to keep trying for a baby and I don't think I want to do that.'

This is the clearest sentence I have ever uttered.

'Don't think you want to, or know you don't want to?'

Or maybe not the clearest.

I want to say 'Know I don't want to,' but Ben looks different this morning, or perhaps my fragile self is more appreciative. He looks like someone I know, someone I like. I am reminded of the journey we've navigated from pleasure-seeking layabouts to stalwarts of society, of the closeness, the security he has given so willingly that I have forgotten what it is to lack that security. In an instant the drunken dream of fleeing with a man I met in a café becomes preposterous silliness.

'I know that I can't begin that cycle again anytime soon.'

'If it's never, you need to tell me.'

'It's not never, not as absolute as that. That's all I have right now, Ben.'

I wouldn't be surprised if the family has been lobbying Ben for an answer, keen for all the cousins to grow up together. Jamie and Bridget's girls are eight and six, Milly and Finn's twins are ten and the new baby will be here in March.

Ben coughs and I stand to attention. 'How about we agree to have a proper conversation after Christmas? See how you feel then?'

'Don't you have any doubts, Ben?'

'About a baby?'

'About me.'

'No,' he shakes his head for emphasis, and doesn't ask the obvious question.

The bells begin their peal. Time for church.

I have grown to like hymn music – traditional rather than evangelical. Dee and I warble away, often sharing a look when I soar to the higher notes she can't reach. 'How Great thou Art' is on the hymn board today, which is one of my favourites. When we sit back down for the sermon, I find my tranquillity is troubled by some flecks of conscience, contaminating what had been unbridled joy; so, for a change, I try not thinking.

The 'Amens' are emphatic and heartfelt because Sally Wood's husband, newly diagnosed with bowel cancer, is named in the prayers. On the way down the aisle, Hannah from the B&B nods at Sally's back. 'She's doing well, isn't she?'

'Yes, let's hope he responds to the treatment.'

'There's a rota for lifts to the hospital.'

'I know, but I can't drive.'

'Of course.' She tuts at her own stupidity. 'I think I saw you near the hospital last week.'

'Was it Thursday?' I am immediately wary. 'That's the day I go with Dee.'

'Yes, but you were with someone else. A man.' The casting of her hook is clumsy, splashes everywhere.

I look dumb, I hope, while I busy myself, passing coffee cups to outstretched hands. 'Must have been my double,' I say. 'But I like the idea of a strange man. Was he good-looking?'

She takes a slice of coffee cake. 'I'm sure it was you.'

'I have one of those faces. A bloke ran after me at the station once – I thought he was going to assault me but he'd mistaken me for his cousin.' I giggle. 'That could never happen to you, Hannah, because of your hair.' Autosuggestion makes her hand rise to touch her very unattractive crop of coiled springs.

'Anna, can I have a word?' Meryl's voice is a welcome interruption.

I take the opportunity to turn away from Hannah. 'Yes, Meryl.'

'Can I count on you for the activity day at half-term?' She is in full churchwarden mode, pen poised to add my name to the clipboard.

The question is superfluous: I always help.

(Or do I?)

'Oh, sorry, Meryl,' I hear myself say, 'I'm afraid I'll be away.'

'Never mind, we'll manage. You do enough, my dear.'

'I didn't know you were going away,' says Dee from somewhere behind my head.

The sense of suffocation, never far from the surface, bubbles up.

'A last-minute decision, Dee.'

'Late summer sun?'

'No, I thought I'd go and see my mum.' Where this devilry has sprung from, I have no clue. But once it's out, the prospect of disappearing for a few days is exciting. Obviously, I have no intention of going anywhere near Glasgow.

'That's nice. I'm sure she'll be pleased to see you.' The family are always careful not to pry. A teenager for a mum, a deceased dad and a brother who dies of a drug overdose all combine to propel the Slaters well out of their comfort zone.

On my walk home I replay Hannah's barely disguised accusation that I have been canoodling with a man and conclude I was completely believable, but note the warning. It wouldn't do to be caught, not unless there's something worth being caught for. I am thinking about the stupid risks I took with the doctor's husband as I swing open our front door—

'Anna! In here.' Ben's voice is coming from the front room when he should be at football.

'What are you doing here?' I ask, at the same time as my eye travels to the swollen ball that was his kneecap.

'I've hurt my knee.'

'Ouch, that doesn't look good. Shall I get some ice?'

'Finn's going to take me to A&E.'

'Shall I come too? We can make up bad things about the wounded.'

He laughs. We used to create elaborate stories of people we noticed in restaurants or on holiday. The woman with the extraordinary fangs is an old favourite.

'No point, but if there's a fanged woman, I'll send a photo,' he says, perfectly in tune.

When Finn has manoeuvred Ben into the car and I have dispatched the remains of my hangover by eating a fried egg sandwich, I waste

125

the afternoon trying to find a trace of Mark Turner on social media. Unfortunately, there are more Mark Turners than anyone could possibly want. If only his mum had chosen Tarquin. I give up and instead scrutinise the part of me that is never satisfied, always on the lookout for greener grass.

21

Self-portrait

Thanks to the wonders of his work's private healthcare scheme, Ben has already seen an orthopaedic surgeon and had an MRI; the verdict is a partially torn meniscus. The options are physiotherapy, which might work, or keyhole surgery, which is a definite fix. A life without football and skiing is no life, evidently, so he has opted for surgery. Therefore, next Tuesday he is having an arthroscopy, leap-frogging all the cripples with knackered joints in order to safeguard his hobbies. Health inequality playing out before our eyes.

His operation is peculiarly well timed, coinciding with half-term when, thanks to my spontaneous lie, the family are expecting me to go to Glasgow to visit my mum. I now have the perfect excuse to stay home. I did consider going away on my own – for a full five minutes I felt intrepid and adventurous – but where would I go and what would I do when I got there? I don't have any old friends, there is no extended family to visit, no Lake District tor I'm desperate to climb. Much better to appear to forgo my trip to selflessly look after Ben.

I nip up to his home office to say goodbye. It's Thursday morning and my swimming lesson is calling.

'Do you need anything before I go?'

He has his leg on a stool with a pillow below his knee. The swelling has reduced but the flesh, on poking, feels boggy.

'No, I'm good, thanks.'

'Okay.' I pull my navy rucksack further up my shoulder.

'Anna, we haven't talked about next week. You can still go. I'll need a lift to the hospital and back anyway so may as well stay at Milly's.'

'No, no. I can go and see my mum in the Christmas holidays. I want to look after you.'

'It's all arranged, Anna. Milly says the twins are going to be my nurses.' He grimaces.

'I want to be here, Ben. You're having an operation.'

'It's more like having a tooth out.' He takes my hand. 'It means a lot to me that you thought of spending some time with your mum. You're going – I'll be fine.'

I want to insist, but can't hope to match the talents of marvellous Milly. On the bus to the leisure centre, I tell myself they can't make me go. (I sound like a sulky child.)

What is also childlike is the way I seek out and store Frank's meagre praise. Trying to impress him has, however, reaped benefits: I can now do a tumble turn and emerge facing the right way, I can kick from the hip and not the knee, I can swim a length underwater.

Today's reward is 'Shoulders are getting stronger.'

I don't feel strong-shouldered as I pitch up at Dee's, too preoccupied by my supposed trip to Glasgow. Perhaps Mum could come down with a contagious disease.

'You're quiet, Anna. Is everything all right?'

'Just tired.'

While we wait for a gap in the traffic, Dee says, 'I know I hit the wrong note when I offered to pay for fertility treatment.'

'It wasn't wrong, Dee, it was generous.'

'It was insensitive and worse, there was an element of selfishness.' She pulls out and accelerates. 'I would like to see you and Ben settled with a family but I realise this isn't necessarily the right time. People have children in their forties nowadays.'

'Thanks for understanding. Two goes has left me a little battered.'

I spend a moment reliving the highs and lows of a failed pregnancy and wonder if I have convinced myself I'm ill-equipped to be a mother because I'm too terrified to try?

'I have another suggestion, a better one.'

'Go ahead.'

'I'd like to pay for driving lessons. Half a dozen to get you on your way. You need the independence.'

I look across at her. 'I should say no – it's too generous, but I'm not going to. Thank you so much, Dee.' She is a proper mother, I think. Lucky Slater children, having a nurturer all their lives. Lucky me, having a share of her.

'Good. Perhaps you could get a lesson next week.' She pats my thigh. 'Little tip. Don't be too confident to start with. Milly nearly wrote off my car when she was learning.'

'I'm all ears.'

Dee recounts Milly taking a tight corner at speed, two wheels on the ground, two in the air. She laughs but it quickly becomes a cough. I've noticed before that laughing is a dangerous occupation when your airways are compromised. To ameliorate the situation, I share one of my joyrider stories, framed as apocryphal. Rites of passage differ, depending on your tribe.

After I've deposited Dee I amble towards the exit, skirt the car park but flounder at the main road. My duplicity seems so odious in the light of Dee's kindness. Earlier, when my mood was better, I packed Sofia's red dungarees to change into but they are no longer made of corduroy but of deceit, their weight in my rucksack doubling with every stretch of pavement. Was I really going to slide my legs inside, do up the straps, continue this charade?

I stop where I am because Sofia rises up in front of me. Her face on that last day, mocking, sneering, putting me right back where I belong.

The self-loathing arrives like smog, all-enveloping.

With neither the inclination nor the capacity to be the dazzling Sofia that Mark expects, I retrace my steps to weather the gloom in the hospital canteen.

I order tea, which comes in a stainless-steel pot with a stupidly small cup and saucer. Irritatingly, there is no empty table so I perch at the far end of one which is occupied by a middle-aged couple, and, while my tea is brewing, scroll through the posts Instagram thinks might be of interest. Water bottles, dog beds, non-surgical eyelifts.

Their conversation reaches across the divide.

'He has a lovely way about him. I think Jordan really looks forward to the sessions,' says the woman.

'Funny what they come up with,' says the man.

'He prefers it to singing.'

'Anything would be better than Jordan singing.'

They both laugh.

I find I am waiting to see if one of them elucidates. They are maybe forty, dreary clothes (who am I to talk) but lively voices. I assume Jordan must be their son.

'That clay face didn't look anything like Jordan.'

'I don't think it was meant to.'

'He said it was a self-portrait.'

'It's art therapy,' she says. 'Not fine art.'

'I still don't understand what art therapy means,' says the man.

'You don't listen. It gives people another way to express how they might be feeling.'

'Well, Jordan obviously didn't feel like himself when he made that face.'

It's impossible not to join in with their laughter.

I swivel and lean slightly towards them. 'Excuse me, I couldn't help hearing you mention art therapy.'

As is often the case, these strangers are happy to talk. Their ten-year-old son has been in hospital for some weeks – he has had surgery to release something or other, a consequence of his cerebral palsy – the boredom and loneliness are a problem – they can't be here all day – and he has been feeling quite low, away from home and not seeing his friends . . .

'Jordan really likes Mark,' she says. 'He's the therapist.'

I grow taller in my chair, all senses primed. Of course Jordan likes him. He is extremely likeable.

Jordan's father nods. 'I don't understand how mucking around with clay can help but if it does, I'm all for it.'

'They don't always do clay.' She looks at me. 'Jordan made a collage of the nurses on the ward – it's on the fridge.'

'That sounds wonderful.'

'Mark's one of those that has a knack with kids.'

'He sounds great,' I say.

'Do you have someone in the hospital?' she asks.

Her husband twitches, a reprimand, perhaps, for being too personal.

'My mother-in-law comes every week for her COPD.'

'That's a horrible disease,' she says. 'My uncle had COPD.'

In a natural pause I wish them the very best and disappear to the ladies', pull on the corduroy dungarees and go to meet the inspirational man Jordan is so keen on. I tried to do the right thing but this is clearly meant to be.

22

The Thrill of the Fairground

Sofia's dungarees are an invisibility cloak, obscuring my normal life to the point where it dissolves. I stride into Woodies and join Mark at his table. He probes the reason for my lateness, some sixth sense at work, and I admit to a degree of reticence. Acknowledging that we are on the cusp makes me feel vulnerable, a feeling I like. The tension between us thins the air; taking a decent breath is difficult. I can't look at any of the other customers, certain they too have shallow breath, fixed gazes.

Convinced my reading of the cards is accurate, I dispense with the preliminaries and say it. I just say it.

'Will you come on a date with me?'

My disregard for the usual rules of engagement momentarily silences him. I am neither coy nor cautious. I am assertive and available.

'I could be persuaded,' he says.

'And how might I persuade you?'

He holds my eye for an impossibly long time before he answers.

'When were you thinking?'

'I've got next week off. What about . . . Tuesday?'

To give him his due, he recovers nicely. Once the principle of a date is agreed, the progression becomes entirely logical – a vague suggestion to go to the seaside leads to a debate about whether the nicer beaches would be too far for a day trip. An overnight stay would make more sense, wouldn't it? I moot. His assent is also based on sound rationale. Oh, how seamlessly we collude.

'I just need to check something.' He retrieves his phone from his canvas bag and sends a series of texts. I sip my coffee and wait for his verdict.

'All good at my end. It'll be fun, Sofia.' He makes it sound innocent, as though we are going to build a dam from wet sand or go rock-pooling.

For planning purposes, we swap numbers. I claim to know too many Marks, instead filing him under Woodie. This amuses him so he files me under Bakewell.

When our mugs are drained, we leave the café hand in hand. Mark leads me to a leafy park designed specifically, it would seem, to provide shady corners for lovers.

There is nothing quite like those first kisses. Maybe even when you're eighty, the lips of a stranger, the sandpaper grade of their hands, the close-to smell – a warmed nest – the bobbles on a sweater, the slip of a shirt against skin, all remain utterly intoxicating. He unashamedly presses against me. God it's good.

'I wish I could wrap you up and take you home with me,' he says.

'I'm not for sale.'

Kissing, the sound of the word and the act, are well matched, as are we. I am fully committed to kissing him forever, when he creates a degree of separation. 'I can't believe this is happening.'

'Do you want me to pinch you?'

'Yes.'

I pinch hard, twisting the skin on the back of his hand. He yelps.

'Better?' I say.

'Never better.'

He is kissing my neck, one hand in my hair and the other holding me close. The flood of feel-good hormones is exquisite. I sink into him, eyes shut.

'Sofia.'

'Yes?' I mumble into the skin of his face.

'I'm sorry but I've got to be somewhere.'

'Me too.' I rock back to stand on my own two feet, slightly embarrassed by how wholly I have submitted to him.

'So, Tuesday.' He kisses my lips, feather-light this time, and leaves.

The complications of this arrangement will have to be dealt with another day; for now, I try to hold on to the fingerprints he has left on my body and the metallic orange taste of his mouth. Next week feels forever away – I want it to be tomorrow. If my libido ever left me, I'd be distraught. (Or do drugs.)

How I forget, I cannot reconcile. I am not someone who forgets because I overthink everything, but I turn up to fetch Dee still wearing Sofia's trademark dungarees.

'Hello, Anna.' She checks me over. 'Didn't you have jeans on earlier?'

Too stunned to answer, I leave the floor to her.

'Those are Sofia's, aren't they?'

She is bewildered. Understandably.

'Yes.' She waits for more. 'I was going to take them to a charity shop, but . . .' I falter, 'I can't really explain . . .'

'Keep them if they bring you joy, Anna.'

135

'I've got a few of her things.' I look ashamed. 'I needed something to hang on to.'

'Do you remember when you helped me sort out Richard's stuff?'

I nod.

'You were so kind. We put those ties in a pile to go and then we both stared at them.'

'And I rolled each one up and put them in a shoe box.'

'And on went the lid. Teamwork, Anna.'

Back home, I glide past Ben's study, only poking my head in when I am safely dressed as Anna. 'Shall I make carbonara?'

He nods, raises his face for a kiss. I oblige, aware of the stain of Mark's lips.

As I cut the bacon and grate the parmesan, I am astounded by how simple it is to separate the part of me that is Ben's girlfriend from the Sofia who is going to somewhere on the south coast with, let's face it, a complete stranger.

Perhaps he'll murder me. Perhaps I'll murder him.

'What are you smiling at?' asks Ben, stroking my hair en route to get the water jug.

'Just happy.'

We go to bed early but I can't sleep. I feel I won't ever sleep again. For I am the thrill of the fairground; I am drinking vodka on an empty stomach in a backless dress; I am in that car, my first joyride, and the clench of my stomach is terrifying and exhilarating.

I always was reckless.

23

There is no tree

And finally, Tuesday comes.

The studio where we are staying sits at the end of a long garden and overlooks the sea. As soon as we are through the door, we have sex. Mark is confident, almost too smooth. Maybe I am too. We've both done this before, I think. Is this the first time that my doubts hover over Mark as opposed to myself? When Mark is no longer able to dive between the legs of any more waiting women, I will, using my fly's-eye view, pull apart the sticky filaments of web to understand the spider's craft, but for now, I let this twitch of uncertainty pass.

Having broken the ice (smashed might be more apt) we dress again and head out. He has brought me to Exmouth, a huge beach with a long promenade that is busy with kids and dogs and ice creams and laughter. Most exciting is the sky, littered with huge arcs of every colour kite. I have never seen kite surfers before – their athleticism, leaping unfeasibly high above the waterline, is surreal. Mark has to drag me away, insisting the cliffs are beckoning. We rise and fall and by mid-afternoon come across another massive beach; this one has a row of wooden huts, pastel, pretty. I like the name – Budleigh Salterton – and turn it into a ditty to sing to him.

'Sofia, Sofia, you are something else.'

'What I am is cold. And it isn't an attitude – it's a full-blown reality.'

Mark buys us both a hot chocolate from a handy hut. We share a table with another couple, all of us nursing our drinks for the wind has taken hold, blowing my hair across my face, making me eat strands as I talk.

'Are you local?' asks the grey-haired man.

'No, just taking advantage of a few days off,' says Mark.

I literally feel a pulse between my thighs as he says advantage.

'What about you?' I ask.

'We live in Exmouth. There is a lovely bike ride you can do to Topsham and back over the ferry, if you're cyclists?'

'Can you ride a bike, Sofia?' Mark asks.

'I can. Can you?'

'I can.'

This exchange puzzles our companions. She is the braver. 'Are you newly connected?'

'We are,' says Mark. 'You could say this is day one.'

'How lovely. You make a perfect pair, don't they, darling?' She is attractive, sixty-something with big tortoiseshell glasses and wearing hot pink. He is unremittingly mid-blue.

'Thank you,' says Mark, his knee pressing my thigh. He is enjoying this.

'We're forty years in,' says the man and they beam at each other.

'Congratulations. Do you think we might marry, Sofia?' says Mark.

If he wants games, I can do games. 'What about your wife?'

'She won't notice as long as I continue to do the bins.'

The woman nudges her stunned partner. 'They're teasing us, darling.'

He chuckles. 'You had me going then.'

'What else would you recommend we do?' I ask, keeping my eyes averted in case Mark has a lascivious grin.

They mention a cake shop and advise us not to visit a particular pub unless we like deafening music, before levering their bodies off the bench – 'Enjoy your stay.'

'Nice people,' says Mark, watching them walk off, collars high, backs slightly rounded.

Our return journey is less enjoyable, blustery with the threat of rain. The bottle-green velvet cape of Sofia's, despite garnering compliments, offers little protection – I long for my puffer coat and the wherewithal to drag my airborne hair into its non-descript ponytail. Mark, in his flannel and moleskin in shades of blue and mustard, is at one with the scenery – rugged and wholesome.

Back at the studio, I check my phone again and am relieved to find a text from Ben confirming he is alive. I send many kisses.

Mark lights the wood burner and opens the wine he brought, handing me a glass before fetching more provisions from the boot of his car. This is better.

'You don't mind if I cook for us?' he asks.

The shaking of my head is vigorous. He is the whole package, I marvel, before chastising myself. Everyone can show their best side for a limited period. (Or a prolonged period, in my case.)

He sets to work, sizzling something in a frying pan, boiling water, chopping, clattering in a drawer in search of some kitchen utensil or other. I drift off.

*

I am woken by a strange hand that I physically scuttle back on the sofa to get away from. Locating a tether to the present takes longer than it should.

'You sleep like the dead,' he says, placing a hand on my thigh.

'A clean conscience,' I say, finally finding myself. I am Sofia. I am in Exmouth. Anna is in Glasgow. Ben has had surgery. It is the Tuesday of half-term.

'I doubt that. Supper is served, milady.'

The small table is laid with cutlery, glasses and a candle. In the centre a rectangular dish is sitting under a cloud of steam.

'What is it?'

'Cheat's moussaka.'

'Yummy, I love cheats.'

'That's a relief – it's an acquired taste.'

'What is the cheat?' I say, unsure whether we are sharing the same joke.

'Yoghurt instead of béchamel.'

The smell reaches my nose and I leap off the sofa, suddenly ravenous.

'Help yourself,' he says, taking a slug of wine.

Anna would want to avoid looking greedy but I dish out an enormous portion, and the same for him. The dressing has a squeaky lemony taste that is divine with the smoky lamb. We clean our plates, empty the wine bottle and open a second. The conversation is easy, if spare on personal details. He tells me a story of one of the patients he sees in the psychiatric hospital and I provide a profile of a typical patient attending the pain clinic. Neither of us asks the obvious questions – where do we live and with who. I know why I'm not proffering information and can only assume he has similar reasons. By ten we've had our fill and approach the bed for the second time.

'What side do you prefer?' I ask.

'Below,' he says, and I oblige.

In true man style he falls asleep quickly, whereas I lie awake. In this moment I should be engulfed in guilt: a normal emotion that is, in my case, entirely absent. It's possible my chaotic childhood interfered with a vital developmental stage but I prefer to think I am of a different order, programmed to exploit opportunities unburdened by futile feelings. Ben is fine, already back at Milly's with a bandaged leg and a pair of crutches. Tomorrow he will wake surrounded by family and eat nice food and be waited on. I, too, am happy. Mark is undoubtedly happy. I dare you, show me the harm?

For no apparent reason I am reminded of the much-quoted tree falling in the forest – does it make a sound if no one hears?

No is the answer, because sound is what happens when a vibration meets an eardrum: no eardrums around, therefore no sound.

Yes is the answer, because there must be a living creature somewhere within earshot.

Anyway, no one can hear us. For there is no tree.

24

Hot Sauce

Mark and I return the bikes to the hire shop just after three o'clock, having cycled nine miles and eaten a delicious lunch of smoked salmon on sourdough with grated fennel and hot sauce at a riverside pub. When we finally make it back to the studio in the garden what I have in mind is a restorative nap but . . .

'We'd better get going, I suppose.' He sighs.

I stretch like a cat, unashamedly angling to stay longer. 'Do we have to?'

'Real life calls.'

'Can't it call tomorrow?'

'I'd love that, but I have to go.'

'Should I be grateful to have secured a slot?' I stay chirpy – no one likes needy – despite the problem this throws up. I can hardly pretend to be back from Scotland already.

'The gratefulness is all mine, numpty.' His arm reaches out to envelop me. I thought I was perfectly suited to nestle inside Ben's limbs but it seems I'm one-size-fits-all.

Our leaving is efficient, the boot packed and the kitchen tidied, the bin emptied. I offer to strip the bed but Mark says there's no need. Only at this point do I think to ask, 'Did you rent this place?'

'It belongs to a friend's parents.'

'Handy.' *Handy for bringing women*, chides some other Anna. 'Shall I write a glowing report in the visitors' book?'

'Best not. I'm not sure they realise I get freebies.'

'It must be nice in the summer.'

'We'll come back – eat outside and watch the sun go down.' The indication that this is not an interlude but something ongoing brings a soupçon of delight.

On the drive back, Mark opens up a little more – 'I would have liked to stay – more than liked – but I agreed weeks ago to babysit at my sister's tonight.'

Even though this puts a hard stop on my hopes of a bed for the night, I like that he likes.

'How many children are you in charge of?'

'None that warrant that label – my sister has a herd of squealing piglets that demand hourly slops.'

'Is there a father?'

'I assume so, but one look at Robin and several virgin births seem more likely.'

'They're not together, then?'

'Carrie and Robin are very much together despite my attempts to create a rift.'

'Why don't you like him?'

'I do like him, but ribbing him is more fun. He's a loyal, reliable gem of a man who makes my sister happy, but the tragedy is that he has no comedy. Do you get on with your sister?'

'I do,' I say, picturing Tamsin's zingy yellow shirt but not letting the vividness bleed into the rest of her family.

'I always think that's a good sign – siblings who get along.'

'A sign of what?' I watch myself trying to kill my brother with a wrench and, on another occasion, a vodka bottle. I watch him holding a pillow over my head and hear him calling me psycho.

'Good people, able to rise above the natural rivalry. Is your sister married?'

'Yes, but no births, virgin or regular.'

He glances across at me. 'Is that a problem?'

I nod.

'Shame. But you don't always get what you want.' He takes his hand off the steering wheel and, with good aim, brushes my cheek. 'Then again, sometimes you do.'

'Would you like children?' I ask.

'God, no,' he says, looking positively alarmed. 'Never, ever.'

Although I say, 'Nor me,' I don't think I mean it. (I park this mini-revelation for the future.)

'Shall I drive you home?' he asks. 'Wherever home is.'

'There's no need, the bus is easy.'

'So is driving.'

'Thanks, but no.' The refusal is noted.

'Why don't you drive?'

'I lost my licence. Accidently drove off a bridge high on mephedrone.'

He laughs. 'Truth or lie, I don't care.'

Mark parks by the bus station and leaps out to fetch my bag from the boot, but doesn't hand it over. All of him is fidgeting, from his feet to his fingers.

'Actually, I can't keep this up.' He drags his hand down his face, distorting his mouth. 'There's something I need to tell you.'

I know, of course I do. He is about to declare a wife, or five kids from five different mothers, or a boyfriend: none of these options faze me. What would faze me would be an unattached Mark – that would be much more tricky.

'Save it for next time,' I say, relieving him of my bag. I don't want to hear his confession, because I don't want to make mine in return.

For I am Sofia, who is not in a relationship.

'I know we haven't discussed what this is but I have to be open, should have been from the start. When we first shared that table, Sofia, I could never have dreamed we would become lovers.'

I don't tell him that it was my dream, my instigation, my orchestration.

'I don't believe you. I think you ordered bad-smelling tea expressly for my benefit.'

His solemn face gives a little, tiny creases forming at the edges of his eyes. 'I have to admit, tea was the cornerstone of my grand plan.'

'I'm glad we've sorted that out. Now get off to your sister's.'

Still not derailed, he takes a breath and out it spills. 'I'm not free, Sofia. I should have said so before – I know that – but I couldn't take the risk. I'm infatuated with you – proper teenage infatuation. But I live with someone. I'm sorry and I'm not sorry because it has been wonderful and I very much want this to continue but I don't know how. I don't know anything.'

'I am going to catch my bus,' I say. 'I have enjoyed our sojourn by the sea and will look forward to seeing you again.'

'You're not angry?'

'Do I look angry?'

'No, you look amazing.'

'You look like someone who should be somewhere else.'

'Next week, then?'

'Lovely.'

He waves as he drives off in his red Honda Jazz, the happy smile of a man given the green light to conduct an affair.

My immediate dilemma is whether to invent a disagreement with my mum and turn up at home, further disappointing the Slater dynasty, or to get a cheap hotel room. Until a third option occurs to me. I take a taxi to the village, asking to be dropped in the cul-de-sac, slip through the alley by Dee's house, walk briskly up the road and let myself in the back door. As long as I don't use the rooms that face the street, no one will notice I'm here.

With Sofia's clothes safely back inside their airless cocoon, I run a bath and, in the semi-dark afforded by the street lighting, sink into my thoughts.

Head submerged, intermittently coming up for breath, I dissect both Mark's physical reality – animal words come freely: haunch, loin, rump – and the less tangible aspects – what made him laugh, how slowly he ate and how closely he listened.

When I woke this morning, he was still sleeping, lying with his back to me, his hands together in what looked like prayer. Probably praying not to be caught out. I took a photo of him and, on my way back from the loo, had a peek inside his messenger bag as he hadn't stirred. I was hoping to find some clues to his love life or, at the very least, his address on his driving licence, but found only condoms (an optimistic number given we'd already used two) and a wallet with a bank card in the name of M L Turner that expires next February. Had he rifled through my possessions, the search would have been even less illuminating – you can't glean much from keys and a locked phone.

Eventually, hunger forces me out of the bath. I slip into pyjamas and head downstairs. While the pasta cooks, I text Ben, as I have done periodically over the last two days. He replies with an update on what he had for supper and wishes me a safe journey home tomorrow. I send back a kiss. I also send a text to Woodie; he doesn't reply, but dealing with piglets is probably quite labour-intensive and possibly mucky.

There isn't any open wine in the fridge but the rack has two bottles of red, both with corks. The corkscrew with lever arms broke last Sunday but there is definitely a waiter's friend somewhere. Having checked both of the obvious places – the drawer, the other drawer – I'm stumped. Once you've decided you're having a drink, a drink must be had. I eye the bottle, consider smashing the top before googling better methods. I am about to push the cork in when I remember Ben has a multi-tool. (Every man, practical or not, is gifted a multi-tool at some point.)

Hoppity-skip back up the stairs, I slide open both of his desk drawers but find only memory sticks and old phones and dental floss. His desk-tidy (a misnomer) also disappoints. Without hope, I flip open the lid of the walnut box that stores cufflinks and tie pins and there, nestled in the magpie's trove of shiny metals, is a small navy-blue velvet box. If I didn't know it to be fantasy, I would swear the Anglepoise turns on and self-adjusts to shine on the pleasingly concave lid. Could be earrings, could be a collection

147

of his baby teeth, could be a christening bracelet for our unborn child.

Obviously, I check. And then I go back downstairs and push the cork in.

25

Fairy Lights

Late on Thursday afternoon, I walk the long way around the village to Milly and Finn's pretty house with its olive front door and ring the bell. I have been on trains most of the day, I remind myself, changing at Birmingham. Glasgow is not an easy journey from the south-west.

The rapid thump of feet on wooden stairs precedes Daisy flinging open the door. She is ten years old and blessed with tangle-free Swedish-blonde hair. Dylan, her twin, has the same colour but with a wave.

'Excellent outfit, Daisy.'

Her nurse's uniform consists of a white paper apron safety-pinned onto blue pyjamas and a white cardboard hat. The apron has been decorated with an upside-down watch and blood. Very funny.

'Dylan's the porter,' she says as he appears in a fluorescent-yellow tabard. 'He carries Uncle Ben's things.'

I can see Ben has provided excellent half-term entertainment.

'How is the patient?' I ask.

'Bad,' says Daisy. 'He won't keep his leg in the air.'

'You weren't complaining about me, were you, Daisy?' says Ben, swinging in to the hall on his crutches.

'Yes, I was. And Mummy was too.'

'How was your trip?' asks Ben, kissing me on the lips to the disgust of the twins.

'Good,' I say. 'Ben seems to have smoothed Mum's rough edges.'

'That is what Bens are for.'

'I didn't have any rough edges.'

'What do you mean about edges?' says Daisy, indignant.

'He means angry bits,' says Dylan, doing a few star jumps for no apparent reason.

'Stop jumping near Ben or I'll have you put down,' says Milly, poking her head out of the kitchen. 'Hi, Anna, come in. I'll make some tea.'

'Only dogs get put down,' says Dylan.

'Can we play dog treats again?' says Daisy. Milly says they can and a tin is passed to their waiting hands and off they scramble.

'What is "dog treats"?' I ask.

'They throw mini-cookies into each other's mouths.' Milly shakes her head.

'I played yesterday,' says Ben. 'Didn't miss a single one.'

I clap, hopefully with sarcasm. 'How does the knee feel?'

'Painless, unbelievably. And hardly swollen.'

'When does the bandage come off?'

'Tomorrow. And the dressing next week. Give me five minutes to finish my exercises and I'll give you the full lowdown,' he says, heading back to the sitting room.

'How was your mum, Anna?' asks Milly.

'Very well, thank you. Enjoying being married.' I almost stutter – please let my Ben not propose any time soon.

'We've loved having Ben here. He's like the third twin.'

Over tea and home-made cookies, the conversation moves on to twenty-three-week-old Wolfie (the name has stuck.) Dee arrives with Finn in time to hear the end of Milly's mimicry of the midwife: 'Baby can hear your words, Mrs Slater, and don't you think baby would prefer a nicer name?'

'You won't call her Wolfie, will you?' asks Dee, bristling at our loud laughter. 'Not when she's here.'

'It won't be on her birth certificate,' says Milly, 'but it might be her nickname.'

'Wolfie has a certain panache,' I say. 'You could engrave it on her collar.' My words are Sofia-flavoured.

'I'll ask when I have her micro-chipped,' says Milly.

As Dee looks askance, I abandon my retort about wormers.

'Are you looking forward to your driving lesson, Anna?' she asks.

'Very much, thank you.' I make a brum-brum noise and my hands turn a pretend wheel; acting as though I'm in school is the Anna they recognise.

My phone comes to life – a message from Woodie. This is one of the few texts I've received. My favourite was *I am still pinching myself.* The normal me would mock such romantic nonsense, but the prickles on my skin thought otherwise.

I show the screen my face and read Mark's text. He can't wait until next week – *Can we meet tonight or tomorrow?* Tonight is out of the question but, after a quick calculation, I decide I can probably manage tomorrow. The smile has to stay inside.

When Finn has driven us home, Ben and I have a convivial Chinese takeaway and, for a change, sex on the sofa. Ben has no option but to be the eager recipient. For those of you who haven't dabbled, honestly, an affair can be the fairy lights that make you appreciate the wallpaper.

Later, with Ben spark out by my side, I consider how to absent myself tomorrow evening. Lies are easy but the sensible thing is to create a repeatable reason. I discount evening classes and an imaginary friend in favour of charity. My story takes shape and, as I add more detail, I begin to believe in my construct. Method lying, you could call it.

Ben is woken by an energised Anna, brimming with enthusiasm for good works.

'There's a poster in the hospital about the shelter for the homeless in Hope Square – they need volunteers in the kitchen.'

He shifts onto his back and one arm appears above the duvet. 'You're not thinking of helping, are you?'

'Why not?'

He rubs his eyes, rolls onto one elbow and places the free hand on my belly. 'How would you get there?'

'Tardis. Next objection?'

'Sorry. Let me wake up.' He almost knocks over his water glass but some dexterity honed on the cricket pitch prevents a spill.

'I'm going to ring them. For all I know the flyer is out of date and they've got loads of helpers.'

In an imitation of the perfect girlfriend, I whip up scrambled eggs on toast and by nine have settled Ben at his desk, leg propped, coffee steaming. By quarter past I too am busy, strapped into the driving instructor's Skoda Fabia. When I park outside our house, wheels parallel to the kerb, I am declared a natural. I don't explain that the car is much easier to drive than the Ford Escorts my brother repeatedly hot-wired.

On a cloud of confidence, I book my theory test, keen to capitalise on the opportunities afforded by being a driver. The garden is budding, as Dee likes to say.

26

Julian, Saint of Travellers

The Julian Shelter is very pleased to have an extra pair of hands in the kitchen. On Friday, Saturday and Sunday evenings the centre provides hot dinners for the homeless using supplies donated by local businesses. Variations on a vegetable stew – go easy on the spice – with plenty of rice and bread is the staple offering. Nadine, who gave me a tour of the kitchen on my first shift, has been a kind voice in an alien environment. It can be upsetting coming up close to those of no fixed abode; however, 'What we have in common far exceeds our differences,' I have heard myself tell Ben and Dee and Milly and Miss Emery. Tempting though it is to expand, the little voice that looks out for me advises caution. Way too much fun was had inventing Nadine's coal-black hair and skin-tight polo necks.

Tonight is the third Friday I have, in theory, absented myself to serve the public. The pace of our affair is driven by Mark but suits me perfectly. A routine of Thursday afternoons and Friday nights creates a nice frisson to end the week, our chaste afternoons as enjoyable as our grown-up evenings. Mark talks freely about the future: growing vegetables, learning Spanish, buying a fox-red Labrador. These conversations are not grounded, but a form of dance; we step together and flounce apart, lock our hips together and pirouette away. We are two of a kind, I think.

'So sorry I'm late, Sofia.' Mark rushes in and kisses me, before sitting in the chair opposite. He has had a haircut and is looking particularly attractive in an indigo shirt.

'I've only just got here myself. You look nice.'

We are having dinner in the bar of the three-star hotel Mark has booked for the night despite only needing it for the evening, although I'm wondering whether we might settle for drinks and cashew nuts. The more sex you have, the more you want. (The converse is also true, apparently.)

'Do you want to know why I'm late?'

'You're here – that's all that matters.' Sofia remains entirely uncurious about Mark's other life.

'I'd like to tell you.' He takes both my hands and encapsulates them in his. 'I haven't been in a position to ask anything about your situation because—'

'We're good as we are, Mark. Neither of us has made any promises.'

'That can change, if you want it to.'

I stay silent, willing him to do the same.

'This afternoon I told – do you mind if we don't name her?'

'Your story, your way,' I say, burying my face in my wine glass.

'I told her what we both already know – that the relationship isn't working anymore. I'm not unencumbered, but I will be. And if you want something more, I'm here.'

The fast fizz of oxygenated blood signals something that might be elation. I am already imagining Mark painting my nude in his artist's studio.

'I shouldn't be allowed to feel relieved, but I do.' He breathes in and out in a yogic manner. 'The truth sets you free.'

I drain my glass and we head upstairs. Twenty minutes later, our heads on a single pillow, we have an open and honest discussion. Or rather Mark does. He has been living with she-who-will-not-be-named for a year. She is resigned to the split, he says, but needs time to adjust.

'. . . if I had been happy, I would never have let this happen.'

'I'm glad you did,' I say. 'I enjoyed our initiation ceremony by the sea.'

'We should pay a return visit. I'll find out when it's free.' He moves his hand proprietorially over my right breast and his lips kiss my biceps. 'Can you stay the night, Sofia?'

I shake my head.

'Please. I don't have to get back tonight.'

The acrobatics in my head are too complex, too gravity-defying to attempt a safe execution. I don't know why I am so loath to declare my relationship status, but I am.

'I'm afraid there's no one else to do the milking in the morning,' I say.

Keeping my face straight while his grin slowly spreads is difficult.

'What time do you do that, Farmer Sofia?'

'Six. Routine is important for dairy cows – they have a strong internal body clock.'

'And do you have any tips for a rookie?'

'The teat needs to be stimulated one to two minutes before the cup is applied to allow for let-down and the cow needs to remain standing for thirty minutes afterwards to prevent infection from open teats. Mastitis is our primary concern.'

'I think you can stay with me tonight, Sofia.' His mouth is on mine, his hands cradling my head.

My short conversation with Ben is conducted in the bathroom, for obvious reasons.

Nadine is distraught, I tell him, speaking quietly, as though she might be nearby. A regular died this week. She wants to keep working at the centre but doesn't know if she can. She doesn't want to go home alone but if I go with her I'll miss the late bus. She says I can stay at hers.

'Thanks for understanding, Ben. I'll be back in the morning.'

'I wish I was allowed to drive – I'd come and get you.'

'Aren't you in the pub?'

'Well, yes, but in principle I'd have come.'

I laugh.

'I'm proud of what you're doing, Anna.'

I delete these words before they find a foothold.

Mark and I go back down to the bar and eat burgers and drink red wine and midnight comes and goes. He was testing me, I think, to see whether my elastic would stretch or snag. And I have passed.

When I am close to sleep, woolly-brained and warm-bodied, I half hear Mark say that he has fallen truly, madly, deeply in love with me.

27

Blue Badge

More and more often I let my mind disappear into a world where Mark and I are together and I don't work in a school and I don't spend my life waiting at bus stops and it isn't nearly winter.

'Did you hear anything I just said?'

'Not a word.' Frank's face swims into view. 'Try me again.'

'In the pull phase your hand is a scoop; drag it to your hips, ankles floppy, first length you breathe every third stroke, second length every seventh, and repeat for eight reps – we're training hypoxically.' A parallel soundtrack of Sofia describing her landlady's manner – dish dash – plays loudly in my head. I listen to her rather than Frank.

'Where are you today, Anna?'

'Right here,' I say, sniffing the chlorine as though it's amyl nitrate.

I should abandon the lessons – hypoxic training is surely over the top – but our Thursday mornings are therapeutic. In the water I am unfettered, loose of limb, powerful and dove white.

I kick off, hairline level with the water, body in one plane, slight slope down to my hips, the technique instinctive. Taking fewer breaths on the second length brings a noticeable pressure in my chest. I wonder if, for Dee, this is normal: a hypoxic life.

158

Having settled into the breathing pattern, my mind runs free. A precipice is approaching – no idea how soon, but coming nonetheless. Mark acts as though we are destined to be together. I'm not willing to give him up – the very idea sucks me down into a well of blackness – but I can't untangle my lies or my life. Sometimes I try – deconstructing the creation that is Sofia in the hope of finding a way of being her for real. Claiming to be the descendant of a brewing magnate was an unnecessary move, but both my poverty and lack of family could be explained by a feud. I could bin my postgraduate studies, Mark could work at another hospital, find another PRU . . .

From the grave, Sofia derides me for my lack of ambition so I recalibrate. In this version Mark gets a work visa for New Zealand, marrying me to expedite the documentation.

Mark Turner and Sofia Hemingway were married in a private ceremony . . .

I am not deluded. I know stacking lie upon lie makes the whole tower fragile and yet her passport teases me from the Sofia shrine.

I dare you, Anna.

'Good,' says Frank. 'Being able to swim with fewer breaths can really help in open water where your rhythm can easily get interrupted. Waves, other swimmers—'

'A shark,' I say.

Frank doesn't react – he can't do humour.

Back home, with damp hair and cold bones, I make coffee and go upstairs to the spare room. I take out Sofia's passport and stare at her photo. Propping the document against the mirror, page wedged open by a Calvin Klein perfume bottle, I let my eyes flit from my reflection to her face and back. I fetch my hairdryer and blast my hair dry before tying it up and using a clip to mimic her mini-quiff. As a final touch, I drape a silk scarf across my décolletage to mimic the fall of Sofia's shirt. It could work. Height, weight, our face shapes: they are all similar. My mouth is wider but would a passport-checker notice? Not if I breezed through with enough swagger.

'Sofia Hemingway,' I say to the mirror. 'Yes, that's right, Sofia Hemingway.'

My smile is complete mischief.

I walk to Dee's, jingling like the bells round a Morris dancer's ankle. I don't understand this feeling. I am Anna, living with Ben. I can't simply step out of my skin and into Sofia's.

Or can I?

'Good morning.' Dee is waiting at the door, coat on, scarf tied, car keys dangling. Upbeat today, she provides a commentary to help me with my driving lessons: this left is notorious for people pulling out; the right-hand lane disappears in a minute; always watch out for the bus lane.

I try to bank the precious feeling of being parented, in case the days of these journeys are numbered. That thought brings a flutter of fear to my stomach. If I need Dee, but want to be with Mark, can it be Ben who somehow steps out of the picture? Or in front of a train? Accidents happen all the time; I spend a few minutes inventing one.

The car park is full. We circle three times, tracking pedestrians in the hope they are leaving while scouring the rows for red reversing lights. The vigilance has a direct impact on Dee's breathing. A black Golf scoots past us and hovers, intent on stealing a parking spot that could be ours. I can't stand by – the agitation is strangling Dee – so I get out of her car, walk past the Golf and stand next to the little

Fiat that is about to reverse. The Golf driver, a woman, makes an aggressive gesture but moves on, and Dee swings in.

We walk at a glacial pace across the car park.

In the foyer, Dee says, 'Let's sit for a minute,' before collapsing onto a beige plastic chair. I pretend to look at my phone while my ear audits her breathing. That I might need to ask for help brings a jitter of anxiety.

'Hello there.'

The couple I met all those weeks ago in the café are approaching my row of chairs. They have done well to recognise me; I never forget a face but the majority of the population seems not to share my talent. Outside of school I constantly have to remind parents I am not a stranger talking to their kid but the person they see in the playground. Ben is no better, although he would jolly well recognise a premier league footballer.

'Hello again,' I say.

Today the couple are with their son, who is in a wheelchair. He has cerebral palsy, I recall. It seems rude but I don't introduce Dee because she is not fit for small talk.

'We're finally going home. Aren't we, Jordan?' says the dad.

Jordan's enunciation might be a challenge but his excitement is transparent.

'That's such good news,' I say.

'I'll get the car,' says the dad, slipping a large rucksack off his back and leaning it against the wall. 'Nice to see you again.' He nods at Dee and she reciprocates. I appreciate his sensitivity; perhaps he remembers she has COPD. The mum puts the brakes on Jordan's wheelchair and sits down, leaving a seat between us in the way people do. Compared to when I saw them before, the parents are brighter, literally. She has a grass-green sweater and the dad is wearing a red waterproof. Jordan is in china blue, complementing his striking blue eyes. His sallow skin, however, looks thirsty for sunlight.

'What are you going to do when you get home, Jordan?' I ask, tempting though it is to ignore anyone who has communication difficulties and focus on their carer.

I deduce from the response that he is going to play on his games console with his best friend.

'I hope you win.'

His whole body reacts to affirm that he will. As we continue our conversation, I am aware that Jordan is proving an effective distraction, giving Dee the opportunity to reset her breathing.

'We're parked miles away,' says the mother, looking again at the huge glass doors. 'The blue badge is no use when there aren't enough disabled spaces.'

'Parking is always a worry for us. We don't have a badge.'

Our discussion on the criteria for a badge is in full flood when she breaks off. 'There's Jordan's art therapist,' she nudges my knee, 'the one I told you about.'

She leans forward to release the brakes and turn Jordan's chair. 'Look, Jordan, here's Mark.'

The surge of blood pelting around my body might actually burst something vital. All inside is quick, frantic, dizzying, but my eyes are absurdly slow, moving from where her hand touched my leg to the black and silver braking system of the wheelchair before finally rising to rest on the target.

And there, his hand outstretched, is the very popular Mark.

28

Pretty Little Liar

The fixtures and fittings of the foyer of the hospital, the milling people, the ambient noise and the headache-inducing lighting all fade to grainy black and white, leaving only the main attraction: Jordan's art therapist.

'I don't want to see you for a while,' he says to Jordan, who shakes his head violently. Jordan's mum laughs. Dee also smiles.

'Don't worry, Mark, we're not planning on coming back anytime soon,' says the mum.

Jordan bangs his chest with his fist and Mark does the same.

I can't stop staring.

Jordan speaks but I don't catch the sense; whether it's his fault or mine I'm not sure. Mark has no problem translating.

'I know I'm your favourite art therapist,' he says.

Jordan holds up one finger.

'That's right, Jordan, because I'm the only one.'

We all get the joke, although I don't laugh. I might not be breathing.

'Had we better go?' says Dee, her hand pressing down on the edge of the seat in readiness.

I nod.

We leave Jordan and his mum talking to Mark and make our way to the lift. My body travels as ordered but how my limbs know to do this is magic of the highest order because I have shut down. Using the minimum of words, the fewest expressions, the smallest movements, I manage to deliver Dee safely to her session.

'See you later,' I say, unable to control the reedy squeak in my voice now that escape is imminent.

I walk, an automaton, to the ladies' – the age-old place of safety. Only with the door bolted do I let myself consider what I have just witnessed.

The Mark I have just met, the art therapist Jordan is so fond of, is a normal height for a man; he clearly cares about his hair because his flat-top is the work of a spirit level; he favours all black, from his T-shirt to his Nike trainers; and is about fifty. He says he is the only art therapist in the hospital. No matter how hard I try, logic is not my friend today because I cannot compute this information. The obvious answer is too unpalatable to consider. From the beginning, I suspected Mark might have a partner, but I never for one second doubted he was an art therapist working in the hospital. My head feels stuffed tight with wadding, too dense to allow a clear line of thought. So I fester, aware of the edge of the loo seat forming a welt on the back of my thighs.

There must be a mistake in my understanding, a disconnect between what I thought he said and reality. Except there isn't. I am Anna. I listen.

But why would he pretend? What could he hope to achieve? And if he has lied about his job, what else is a lie? I was so cocky, revelling in how capably I had kept my secrets. But I, the duper, have been duped. There is no other conclusion. Beautifully, artfully, expertly duped. I thought I was clever, but I am stupid.

The tears, slow to arrive, gather momentum and gush down my cheeks. As my sobbing becomes more urgent, I muffle the noisy gulping by pressing my fists against my lips so hard they hurt.

Only when the tears are dry streaks on my face can I see well enough to study the trajectory of our affair. I watch a silly woman falling over herself to drown in the silvery saliva of a passably attractive man, offering herself up like a sacrifice. I observe myself fawning, latching on to random aspects of Mark's character and conversation, actively searching for meaning. Never was there such an easy lay as the perpetually dissatisfied Anna Harris. My malcontent is a boulder on my shoulders. I rest my elbows on my knees and drop my head.

Dee once said that I am good at picking myself up and she's not wrong. One second I'm awash with misery, my fantasy future in smithereens, and the next I am out of the cubicle dousing my eyes in cold water to reduce the redness. I check the time. Later than usual, but nothing an accomplished liar can't explain away. Face restored to a semblance of normal, coat off to let the cool November air regulate the rest of me, I head for Woodies with a straightforward agenda: who is he and why did he lie so comprehensively? When I have the answers, I can decide on retribution. I may not know who I am dealing with, but the same is true of Mark. If he checked my form, he might feel slightly less complacent.

Mark is at the table in the window. He waves as he sees me approach the door.

'Sofia.' He is on his feet and we kiss cheeks as usual before he fetches my order. I ring in the changes by opting for a tea and a fruit scone. Having something to pour, something to cut and butter is good. In between I relay the story of how my lovely neighbour's breathing difficulties delayed me.

'I adore that you put yourself out for her. Some people wouldn't do that for *family*.'

I acknowledge the compliment before moving on. 'Where are your parents?'

'Still in Devizes,' he says. 'None of us have managed to stray very far.'

'We could stray together,' I say.

He opens his mouth, I assume to reply, but is overcome by some heartfelt emotion. I pretend to be enthralled by his fine acting. 'Where do you see us, Mark? What about off-grid in Scotland or West Wales?'

'Are you serious?'

'I'm not *not* serious.'

He exhales, eyes raised to the ceiling. With him in front of me I find I am as fascinated as I am angry. This is chess but who is white and where is the king and if we both cheat how will we spot checkmate?

'I don't think you're ready, Sofia,' he says quietly, eyes glued to mine. 'But in the new year I will be free.'

I nod.

'What does that mean?' he asks.

'It means I understand the timeline you've outlined.'

'I'm impatient for more.'

'Don't be. The wait makes the reward worth having.'

'Lessons in enlightenment.'

'True enlightenment would appreciate the wait in its own right.'

'You're like no one else, Sofia Hemingway.'

'In the meantime, maybe we could go to the studio again? A pre-Christmas treat.'

Knowing he is a fake, his moment of stillness takes on an entirely different hue. What is he juggling in his head? More importantly, what am I juggling in mine?

'Can you get away?' I prompt. 'We could go in the sea to ward off your old age.'

'Mulling wine sounds more appealing.'

'Have you got a cheat's version?'

'You can buy it ready-made.' He gives me a beautiful smile. 'Just add a slice of orange for authenticity.'

We leave the café and as we walk, out come feelers . . . on both sides.

'Why do you only work mornings on a Thursday?'

'I'm on a 0.4 contract. One full day and two halves.' He kicks an apple core into the road. 'How are your swimming lessons going?'

'I gave up. I'm a land-based species it turns out.' I am not sure why I am lying . . .

'Shame. I quite liked the *eau de piscine*.'

. . . and now not sure whether he knows I'm lying, given how chlorine binds to the skin.

'Does someone else cover the rest of the week?'

'No. We're a rare breed. Getting rarer. We used to have a music therapist but when people leave they don't get replaced. Soft therapies can't compete for funding against surgery, intensive care, neonatal.'

'Where do you work on Fridays? I want to picture you.'

'I'm at the PRU all day.'

167

'Is it attached to a mainstream school?'

'No, we're hardcore. What were you like at school, Sofia? Rebel or prefect?'

'Guess.'

'I want to say rebel, so it must be prefect.'

I nod. 'What about you?'

'A pupil referral unit for a spell. And then largely invisible.' This surprising declaration – might it be true? – interrupts my flow, but not Mark's. 'We're fine for tomorrow, aren't we?'

'Of course.' I nod. 'Fridays are my favourite days.'

He tucks a piece of hair behind my ear. 'Shall I meet you in The Royal Oak again?'

'Yes, lovely. Where does she think you go on Friday nights, Mark?'

'To my sister's.' He screws up his face. 'I shouldn't have embroiled Carrie in my mess but I needed an excuse.'

'Have you talked to your sister about me?' I need to rein in the urge to bombard him with questions.

'Yes. I had to tell someone.' The hand around my waist pulls me closer and we kiss like there's no tomorrow, fittingly.

'Does she work or stay home with the children?'

'Pig husbandry is all-consuming. What about you? Who have you told?'

'You're my secret,' I say.

'When will I not be?'

'I don't know.' My turn to feign some sort of internal wrangling.

'You're my better life, Sofia.' His grip tightens on my hand. 'I've felt it from the beginning.'

We share a look, a look that could make me forgive that he's a liar. Maybe there is a good reason for his untruths; maybe he was sacked but pretends to go to work. Men do that in television dramas.

'Am I right to put my faith in you?' I ask.

'The rightest you've ever been. But it doesn't matter to me if you have doubts because I have enough conviction to carry us through.'

'My mum would say if you've been unfaithful once you'll do it again.'

'Not when she meets me she won't.'

'Can I meet your sister?'

'Yes.'

'When?'

'What about next Friday?'

'Great.' My smile is as genuine as I can manage – I don't think he will let me meet his sister. It won't happen, or it won't be his sister.

Muttering that I mustn't be late for my neighbour, I walk off at speed, eager to create enough distance to begin to digest the events of the day. The spike of outrage is already blunted, leaving me to weigh up our undoubted attraction against our anathema for the truth. In typical Anna Harris fashion, I don't know how I feel. Is Mark Turner dead to me or have I met my twin? So he lied. So did I. Do two deceivers cancel each other out, like negatives in maths, to form a positive? Or do arithmetic rules not apply to those who spurn the conventional values of honesty and decency, leaving us in some algebraic abstract?

My fickleness fills me with despair.

Dee arrives in the hospital foyer with Steve, providing a welcome diversion. We have a jolly chat on the way to the car park, full of praise for me, for each other, for the support group, for the hospital. Steve stops by a silver Mercedes.

'Very nice to see you again, Anna.'

'And you. See you next week.'

He leans across and kisses Dee's cheek. 'Bye, Dee.'

As soon as we're in the car I launch an interrogation but, apart from her flushed face, she is giving nothing away.

29

The Perfect Getaway

After my weekly driving lesson on Friday morning, I settle down with my laptop, intent on uncovering the true identity of my lover.

Assuming Mark is not a serious swindler with a trail of identities wanted by Interpol, but some sort of opportunist, it seems reasonable to take the name on his bank card, M L Turner, as fact. Turner is too common a surname to provide much of a lead so I have to make other, arguably less robust, assumptions. Lies are surely easier to wield if there is a base level of knowledge, so I try googling his name alongside professions relating to hospitals, therapy and education – subjects he seemed comfortable with – and specify a geographical area with Woodies roughly at its centre.

All to no avail.

Frustration sends me veering off to search for Mark's sister, Carrie née Turner, and her husband, Robin, optimistic that two data points might be more fruitful; but I discover only a retired couple, a Carrie and a Robin who are both female, and, on Facebook, premature twins. Carrie could, of course, be Carol, Carolyn, Carlotta. Equally, the M in M L Turner might be Morris, Mike, Mervyn.

Too many permutations.

171

The Mark I met yesterday is easy to find. He is a Randall, works full time at the hospital as an occupational and art therapist and is married with two sons, one a doctor in London and the other living in Birmingham, profession unknown. It's surprising how many people have a virtual presence because of their work or their social media, or because of mentions in the press. My swimming teacher Frank, Hannah from the B&B and Milly all pop up with minimal effort. Typing Sofia Carstairs into the search bar brings reports of her death on multiple news sites and, before that, she peppers other people's posts at protests, with smiling refugees in Calais and at a fundraiser for fibromyalgia. Her married name, Sofia Hemingway, yields nothing. This brings a smidgeon of reassurance, should Mark ever have cause to mirror my activity.

'Do you want coffee, Anna?' says Ben, and I let out a little gasp, so absorbed in the task.

'Yes please.'

'What are you up to?'

'Christmas presents,' I say. 'Have you got physio today?'

'At three.' He immediately adopts a one-legged flamingo stance and dips forward and back up to straight, this week's challenge being to increase proprioception and strengthen the vastus medialis.

'Shall I drive you?' His hesitation is predictable – Ben has a nice Audi. 'For practice.'

'Okay. I'll put you on the insurance. You should book your theory test.'

'Already have.'

'I'll test you later, if you like.'

'I'm at the shelter, remember.'

Ben disappears with his coffee and I, bored with my lack of

172

success, try a different tack. With the kitchen door shut, I call the three pupil referral units within driving distance and ask to leave a message for Mr Turner. There are no takers but I feel the strategy has promise. Next try is the psychiatric hospital.

'Sorry, did you mean Dr Turner?' says an officious-sounding voice.

'Yes,' I say, wishing my next question was at the ready. Could Mark be a bona fide doctor?

'She's not in until Wednesday. Would you like to speak to her secretary?'

Another uneventful enquiry to a holistic clinic and I'm done. The task is futile. He could be a refuse collector, a call centre manager, a cage fighter . . .

Hunger calls me to the loaf of sourdough in the bread bin where I reject cheese on toast in favour of creating a replica of the lunch I had with Mark in the pub in Exmouth. Tinned sardines and celery are a poor substitute for smoked salmon and fennel, but Ben is appreciative. My mouth is alive with hot sauce when a possible lead to the mysterious Mark occurs to me. I can hardly wait to dive back into the internet, but I duly drive Ben to physio where he is prescribed two fast walks a day on top of his current exercise regime.

When he is safely back in his upstairs office, I, with renewed enthusiasm, search for holiday rentals in Exmouth that sleep two people. The little studio where Mark and I stayed is flagged on a map view of the town. There are thirty-two reviews under the listing, but a scan of the names doesn't throw up a Turner. According to Companies House, the owners are a Mr and Mrs Abrahams who live in London and are in their sixties. I search for a link to their son, who is supposedly Mark's friend, but the trail goes cold.

Baby steps, but I am not deterred. The harder Mark makes me work, the more determined I am to unmask him. In the absence of inspiration, I scroll back through the listing and read every review.

The studio attracts loved-up couples judging by the adjectives spattered throughout: idyllic, heavenly, the perfect getaway. I laugh out loud at the guest who felt a need to mention the kitchen whisk was a tad small, and smile at a glowing recommendation to anyone needing level access. My eye catches on that entry before I do, insane though that sounds. I click and read the review in full; read it again. Mrs J Elsworthy stayed at the studio in the summer; she was delighted to be able to get around so easily; the promenade along the beach was perfect. She has attached a very lovely photograph of the studio's painted blue table laid for dinner with a caption: *moussaka, red wine and a sunset for our last night.*

My brain does a somersault and lands perfectly on two parallel feet, slight bend of the knees to minimise the shock. This is left field but might cheat's-moussaka-Mark be in some way attached to the Mrs J Elsworthy who has mobility issues?

There are Elsworthys galore, which is odd as I've never met one. Choosing to see only recent entries and adding geographical boundaries narrows the offering. I peruse the list: Elsworthy's family-run butchers, Dr Elsworthy, properties on Elsworthy Road and Elsworthy Terrace and a single entry for a Jan Elsworthy. I click and a parish church newsletter appears featuring her name as a contact for the Christian Aid Carol Concert. A spark fires across my brain as I read her address. Jan Elsworthy doesn't live in the next county, or in the furthest reaches of this one. She lives in a little village tantalisingly close to here. Easily close enough for her to be the partner Mark claims is 'resigned to the split' but needs time to 'adjust'.

If I were a complete idiot, I might consider a little outing to see her in the flesh.

Only, that is, if I were a complete idiot.

30

Cornishware

Friday nights in the pub have become a boys-only affair thanks to my regular stint at the homeless shelter and Milly's role as Wolfie's breeder. Bridget, who has never appreciated the joys of alcohol, now drops Jamie and goes to Milly's for a girls' night before chauffeuring him home. More fool her.

Ben has his coat on, about to leave, when he notices I am still sitting in the kitchen. Normally, by six, I would be waiting at the bus stop. 'Won't you be late?'

'Nadine texted to say there's a problem with the kitchen – they don't need me because they're only offering soup.'

'Why don't you go to Milly's?' he says, quickly adding, 'Or you can come to the pub?'

'I think I'll stay in. I'm really tired and we're going to Hannah's for dinner tomorrow.'

Ben trots off, Butcombe calling from the tap.

By bike, Mrs Elsworthy's village will take roughly half an hour. So, I can be there and back, having had a poke around, in less than two hours. If I'm going, sooner would definitely be better; being out and about in the dark country lanes is very unappealing to a London girl.

I am, of course, aware Mark is expecting me – can see him, glass in hand, practising tonight's storytelling – but I decide not to cancel. The odds are the internet is doing what it does best: giving you the answer you want rather than the one you need. However, if by some miracle Jan Elsworthy is Mark's other half, I wouldn't want him to arrive home early and surprise us. Best leave him to enjoy his own company in The Royal Oak.

My bike, a cast-off of Bridget's, has a flat tyre but Ben's racer is pumped and ready. I switch on the front and back lights, lock the garage door and pedal off. The main road is too scary so I turn onto what is virtually a single-track road that runs roughly parallel.

Cycling with the wind in my face, eyes smarting, is a shortcut to childhood. Defiantly unhelmeted, I take both hands off the handlebars and freewheel, muscle memory doing the work. Although, when I cross the main road at speed, I can't arrest an image of my crushed head. But, as in childhood, I remain unscathed.

Twenty-five minutes after leaving home, out of breath and overly warm, the blue dot on my phone tells me that I am in the same circle as Jan Elsworthy's house. I get off and push the bike, only now considering how best to proceed. I toy with pretending to be lost, conducting a survey, at the wrong address, but when I see the house, no excuse seems necessary.

The grand Georgian building – white, square, beautiful – has huge windows on all sides, tailor-made for snooping. I leave the bike behind the tall, well-kept hedge and walk up the gravel drive, ears alert. In a film a huge dog would appear with a bark as loud as thunder and the audience would jump.

The first window reveals a study with a dark wood roll-top desk and many books lining the walls. I continue past what must be a bathroom window, narrow and lightless, to the kitchen at the back. The units are old-fashioned, golden pine with spindles. The next room along is the sitting room, and there I find my quarry.

I puff out my cheeks to swallow the whimper. The idea this is Mark's partner is an abomination.

Seventy, eighty, maybe even older. She is sitting, dwarfed by her armchair, watching television, a walking frame to one side. Trying to picture this infirm old lady eating moussaka in Exmouth is impossible, and the idea of her lying beside Mark in the studio's only bed is grotesque. No, this is a dead end.

Although, lingering for a moment at the window, it occurs to me the old lady might not be Jan. She could be someone's mum or aunt who is visiting, rather than living here. If I could think of a tactic that would, for completeness, confirm one way or another, I'd rat-a-tat-tat on her door, but pretending to be the police looking for an M L Turner, or demanding to know who else lives in her mansion, feels unkind. I don't want to give the old dear a heart attack.

I decide I had better text Mark – *So sorry can't get away tonight* – but provide no excuse. He texts back, hopes I'm okay. His second text asks me to ring him in the morning. His third, he is missing me.

Ten minutes later, I am still at the house. In between Mark's texts, the old lady pushed her walker out of the room and hasn't returned. She isn't in the kitchen, or anywhere else that I can see, and no lights have been switched on in any other rooms. The upstairs is in total darkness. I am desperate to go home but my vivid imagination has her lying in the hall with a head injury. What if no one comes and she's not found until Tuesday?

I am in front of the house, considering ringing the doorbell and, if she answers, asking the whereabouts of The Lodge or some other fictional address, when a car turns into the drive.

The step change in my heartbeat is so violent I become the one at risk of a cardiac episode.

Drum, drum, drum-di-drum, drum. I am presto. I am allegrissimo.

The headlights disappear along with the noise of the engine and in the seconds before the driver gets out, I try to match the outline of the vehicle to Mark's Honda. Maybe it is, maybe it isn't. Excuses for being here get stuck in the mushroom folds of my brain but, as the car door opens, I realise that for once the truth will suffice. I am here because he is a lying bastard and I've found him out.

'Hi,' says a woman, the teeth of her smile catching a stray beam of light.

Hallelujah, not Mark!

I release a stale breath. 'Hi. How are you?'

'Good. Have you been in to see Jan?'

I make a non-committal murmur. 'Do you have the time?'

'Nearly quarter to eight. I'm late again.' She walks past me and I fall in behind, keen to exploit the opportunity.

She knocks on the door, rings twice but leaves no time for the door to be answered, instead reaching for the key safe. She taps four digits – top left, bottom right, bottom left, top right – and fishes for the key. 'Damn thing.' She is unbothered by my presence, which makes me think there might be an endless roster of carers letting themselves in. Or maybe, as in our village, a stranger is someone not yet introduced.

The large door swings inwards and a rush of piano notes spill into the lobby.

'Jan!' shouts the visitor, and the music stops.

'Hello, Angie. Did you forget me?' We walk through double doors into a capacious hall and there, at the patent black upright piano, is Mrs Jan Elsworthy. Close-up she is tiny, twiglet arms in a grey round-necked cardigan, fully buttoned, and legs in black. Her hair is shoulder-length and wizard-white. By contrast, the woman I now know to be Angie is round-faced with a brown ponytail, and her body, clad in a purple fleece and jogging bottoms, is a barrel.

'How are you, today?' says Angie.

'Well enough, thank you,' she says. 'Who is this?'

'I came about the carol concert,' I say. 'It was in the newsletter.'

'Are you a soprano?'

'Yes.'

'Excellent. We have a lot of men, unlike most choirs. But you've got the wrong day.'

'Have I?'

'We rehearse on Monday evenings, seven till eight. The Bible study group have commandeered the church so it's here in my hall. Can you make that?'

'Yes.'

'Have I seen you at church?' She stares at me.

'No.' I explain that my regular church, St Michael's, isn't holding a carol concert and she tuts.

'Meryl can be overly pious – she has an issue with the irreligious sharing the joy of the devout.' Her wry remark makes me smile. This is not a benign old lady, nor is she a complete stranger, which shouldn't surprise me. The fields of green may appear to separate

180

the villages but they function like tunnels joining the chambers of a rabbit warren.

'She is a very organised churchwarden,' I say, opting for a neutral statement.

'Do you have a name, soprano girl?'

'Anna,' I say.

'All of it.'

'Anna Harris.'

'Don't be late, Anna Harris. We start promptly and finish on time.'

'Shall we get you upstairs, Jan?' says Angie.

'I suppose so.' She rolls her eyes. 'This is what it comes to. Put to bed like babies.'

She leans on her walking frame and slowly rises to a semblance of vertical. 'Although what I'd really like is a cup of tea.'

'I'll get you settled first,' says Angie.

'I could make tea,' I say.

'Thank you, Anna,' says Jan. 'A dash of milk, no sugar. Bring it up.'

'She's used to staff,' says Angie, which gets her a pretend smack. I decide I quite like Mrs Elsworthy.

In the kitchen I have an enjoyable poke about – a cupboard full of prescription medication: liquid morphine, codeine, gabapentin and tramadol; a drawer full of string, picture wire, sticky tape and another crammed tight with cards and letters; a chalkboard with a sad list: apple juice, talc, Vaseline – before emerging with a nice striped Cornishware mug.

The staircase is wide and leads to a huge galleried landing that wraps around the hall. There are six doors but only one is open.

'I've brought the tea,' I shout at the gap.

'Bring it in,' says Mrs Elsworthy.

The bedroom is a relic from an era when everything matched: cream wardrobe, cream dressing table, cream stool, cream chest of drawers, chintz curtains that match the bedspread and lampshade. Extraordinary.

'On the side, please, dear.'

Mrs Elsworthy is perched on the edge of the bed having her lower leg studied.

'Not so bad,' says Angie.

I move to get a better view but wish I hadn't. A leg shouldn't be that colour.

'I've got cancer, Anna,' says Mrs Elsworthy. 'But my immune system is dying more quickly than I am.'

'I'm sorry to hear that,' I say.

'I've promised not to peg it before the carol concert. The congregation are praying for me so I should be all right.' She moves her leg slightly. 'Although when they prayed for the organist he had a stroke.'

I'd like to ask where the cancer is but don't want to appear too fascinated.

'Check your breasts, Anna. I ignored mine and that was my mistake.'

'I never check,' says Angie. 'How would I feel a lump in this heap.' She looks down at her shelf, uninterrupted by any sense of cleavage.

Mrs Elsworthy laughs. 'Lose some weight, Angie. You'll get a new lease of life, and so will that man of yours. My husband liked me skinny.'

'And how does Liam like you?' asks Angie.

'He's only after my money,' she says, and this time they both laugh.

'Who is Liam?' I ask.

'My boyfriend,' says Mrs Elsworthy with a big wink.

'Leave it out, Jan. You're frightening her,' says Angie.

'We're all grown women, aren't we? Women with needs.'

The giggles take over. Clearly delighted by her audience Jan continues with her theme.

When Angie has made sure Jan is comfortable – pillow plumped, her water and pills within reach – and I have reiterated that I'm coming next Monday, we leave her with the radio on low and a light on the landing.

'She liked you,' says Angie. 'Doesn't like everyone.'

'I liked her,' I say, already looking forward to Monday.

I cycle home, delighted by the unpredictability of life. I have been handed Jan when looking for something else altogether.

31

The Icing on the Cake

'Really nice evening,' says Ben.

'Lovely.' My eyes are clamped shut, my body loath to move. 'What time is it?'

'Nine. Do you want tea?'

'Please.'

He lets a blast of cold air into my cosy cocoon and I respond by tucking his abandoned half of the duvet under my hip. We got home late; after two, I think. A big night out in village terms! A big enough night to warrant a lie-in if I weren't committed to my Sunday mornings at church.

Gingerly, I open the eye that isn't buried in pillow to get the measure of how I feel. Broadly okay.

I was wary going to Hannah and Hugh's for Saturday-night supper. With a few glasses inside her, I thought Hannah might make an unfunny joke about seeing me near the hospital with a strange man. But I needn't have worried. They were delightful, as were we.

I rerun the evening, from cava and canapés through roast lamb and ratatouille with deliciously velvety red wine to chocolate mousse, each course accompanied by easy conversation and much laughter.

Yesterday was, on reflection, perfect from start to finish. Ben is very keen to do as the physio says, so, in the morning we walked into town when we would normally have driven, and rewarded ourselves with coffee and pastries, and after lunch we took Milly's kids to the woods. Between us we made a wigwam out of branches, walls woven with ferns. Ben had obviously done this before but it was a first for me and I loved it.

The reminder that we have a good life is timely. Drawing the Anna who has been moonlighting after hours back into the fold.

A text from Mark arrives saying he can't wait until Thursday. I don't reply. He rang me yesterday morning – Ben was in the shower so I picked up to avoid a barrage of texts. Mark was concerned at my no-show on Friday night but seemed appeased by my invention of a puncture eight miles from home and no spare inner tube. Whether he sensed a change in my manner I'm not sure, but he made a point of confirming the café as usual and Friday night at his sister's. There is something warped, a cat determinedly targeting the most reluctant lap, about his keenness in the face of my mushrooming indifference.

'Here you go,' says Ben.

'Thank you.' I sit up and take my favourite pint-sized grey mug in both hands.

'I might come to church with you this morning,' he says, opening the blinds.

'Why? Do you need to repent?' I am expecting a punchline; Ben has to be coerced to enter the House of the Lord.

'I'm hoping we might need their services.' He reaches into the pocket of his pyjama bottoms and out comes the navy box. 'Will you marry me, Anna?'

I almost swallow my tongue, completely unprepared.

He opens the lid and, thanks to the newly risen sun, the solitary stone flickers.

My answer, because in the moment marriage seems entirely feasible, is an unequivocal yes.

Ben's response is to leap on me with the grace of a newborn orangutan and kiss whichever parts are closest. 'Hand?'

I hold out my hand and he slides the ring on without any comic shoving. A perfect fit.

'I've had the ring for ages. I wasn't sure, you know, because of everything.'

'What made today a sure day?'

'You. Happy you is back.'

I interrogate this statement. Perhaps Ben is right. I wasn't myself for a while but, yes, I am on good form.

'What sort of wedding do you fancy, Anna? Summer or winter?'

'Heat.'

'Okay. A select few or everyone we know?'

'Just you.'

'That will save money.'

The idea I might actually marry Ben, and in doing so commit to both the Slater family and the village itself, is a major development. Maybe my brain has been unusually slow to mature but the plasticity is finally hardening to form an actual personality, one that chooses fidelity over philandering. And might that choice quieten my infuriating internal monologue, allowing me to be the happy Anna that Ben has described? I am so taken with the idea of a period of calm, inside and out, that, even though there really isn't time, I seal the deal with enthusiastic sex.

*

'Hello,' says Dee with a lilt that signals surprise.

'Hi, Mum. Ready?' says Ben.

She is ready: coat, gloves, scarf. 'What are you doing here?'

He has rejected his customary sweatshirt and jeans for a round-necked green lambswool sweater and a pair of sand-coloured chinos. This alone is enough to raise alarm.

'Not watching the football today?'

He stands, wordless, grinning.

'I'm missing something,' she says.

The wait is excruciating so I take over. 'Ben found this.' I flail my hand in the air.

She bites her lip, eyes watering – takes a breath. 'You're going to be married. I cannot tell you how delighted I am. Another daughter.' She reaches out her hand and I take it.

'Will I do?'

'More than do, dear Anna. You complete the picture.'

We join the parade down Main Street, behind Mrs Chalmers and ahead of Sally Wood.

'We already think of you as family, but a wedding is the icing on the cake.'

'You're making the cake, Mum,' says Ben.

Any umbrage at his unilateral decision is quickly dealt with. Why would I care who makes what cake?

At the entrance to the church, three in line to collect our hymn-books, Dee asks whether our engagement is a secret.

'No,' says Ben, looking across at me.

'Do your worst, Dee,' I say, and she doesn't disappoint. Watching whispers whip around a room is fascinating, a Mexican wave of nods and smiles and glances. We listen to the sermon, sing four hymns, recite and pray, after which the well-wishers form a queue several rows deep. Coffee takes considerably longer than the allotted forty-five minutes.

The news has disrupted Sunday's usual order of service and instead of only Dee going to Milly's for lunch, we're all going: the three siblings, their partners and the four grandchildren.

'Congratulations,' says Milly, standing guard at the front door. 'We're all thrilled.'

Daisy is holding out a hand-made card. 'You're going to be my real aunty now.' Her statement coincides with a glass of almost transparent bubbly being passed to me.

I take a sip. From the kitchen there is a heavenly smell of roast beef. Concerned that nothing should sully this nice occasion, I make a momentous effort to banish any suspicion that Ben had forewarned Milly. His proposal seemed spontaneous, born out of our enjoyable weekend. *Go with that, Anna,* I tell myself. Don't turn the serendipitous presence of a huge cut of beef into a conspiracy.

Clinking of glasses, much refilling, the same questions asked several different ways and we take our seats, eleven of us squished around the farmhouse table. I am between Jamie and Finn.

'We thought Ben would never get around to asking you,' says Jamie. 'We all knew he'd bought the ring.'

'Maybe he wasn't sure whose finger it would fit,' I say, turning away to ask Finn how they got on at football.

In seamless Slater style the steaming serving bowls of potatoes and vegetables, the platter of pink-in-the-middle beef and the warmed gravy jug arrive simultaneously and we all help ourselves.

Ben checks everyone has a mountain of food in front of them before standing up.

'Please raise your glasses. To Anna Harris, soon to be Anna Slater.'

If Sofia were here, she would reprimand Ben for his adherence to the archaic patriarchal practice of ownership through marriage. She would stand up and propose a counter-toast to Ben Slater, soon to be Ben Harris. But she is not here and I choose not to object.

I am not sure whether I want to be Anna Slater, but what I am sure about – surrounded by the Slaters, a ring on my finger – is that I won't see Mark again. He can play his game but it is of no interest to me. We have had fun. And now it's over.

Mark Turner is history.

32

Joint Enterprise

On Monday, Miss Emery keeps the troublesome gang of three back after school. They are accused of throwing someone else's bookbag over the fence. In all likelihood only one of them is guilty, but they all have to pay. Joint enterprise in action.

That a bystander can be convicted of murder and given the same sentence as the actual murderer solely because of physical geography is, in my opinion, a travesty. Under the joint enterprise law, I should have been convicted of Sofia's murder, as should Rocket the dog. It's funny to think of an animal as an accomplice, but he and I both know who opened the gate and we know who played fast and loose in the field. Not that it matters. Neither Rocket nor I inflicted a fatal blow. It was a jittery cow that wound all the others into a frenzy.

'You can go now,' says Miss Emery, and the boys run into the corridor faster than Rocket ran into the field. She, however, doesn't rush off, keen to hear the details of Ben's proposal.

'The ring is very, very beautiful, Anna,' she says, almost salivating.

The diamond is fairly ostentatious, sitting quite proud of the band. My body is going to have to adapt to prevent the stone from hitting the doorframe, catching on my hair, snagging on anything woollen.

'Thank you, it feels a bit odd.'

'The ring or being engaged?'

'Both, probably.'

Miss Emery can't contain her envy, confessing that while she appreciates a fancy wedding is a waste of money, she badly wants one.

'When I was little, and not so little, I drew myself in every kind of dress. There was no husband, just me surrounded by flowers and frills. I can't settle for anything less.'

'Maybe find a richer man?'

'You can't help who you fall in love with.'

'I think you can.'

'You don't really?'

'I think I do.'

Miss Emery robustly defends her position, and I do the same, insisting that there's a large element of rationale involved in the choice of a life partner.

'You're a cold fish, Anna.'

When Miss Emery has gone home, I spend a few minutes analysing the pros and cons of marrying Ben. Putting aside actual feelings, the pros have a landslide. Marriage will bring financial security, emotional support, companionship, the collective knowledge, power and influence of the Slater clan and, if we subsequently divorce, half of Ben's worth.

Even though it's Monday I'm in such a good mood I raid the freezer and greet Ben, who has been into the office for the first time since his operation, with steak and chips.

'How did the knee hold up?'

'Fine. And I've cleared the skiing weekend with work.'

'No comment.' Ben, Finn and Jamie are squeezing in a pre-Christmas long weekend in the Alps because Wolfie's due date has scuppered their usual trip in mid-March. A hinged metal brace is going to keep Ben's knee safe, I'm told.

After we've eaten, he is keen to talk about the wedding.

'Sorry, I'm going to choir practice, didn't I say?'

'You'll have grown wings by Christmas.' This mini show of resentment at my earnest collection of hobbies is quite satisfying. Everyone has an edge, even Ben, no matter how well upholstered.

When he realises I intend to cycle he offers to lend me his bike, which I accept, and implores me to wear a helmet, which I decline.

'It's a beautiful evening,' I say, and am gone.

The sky is navy, pin-pricked by silver, and the air is cold, filtered clean. There is no better place to be than racing along on a bike, powered by my quads. This time I do not have the premonition of a crushed skull – the sign of a tidy mind, I decree. There will be no more clandestine meetings in Woodies because I texted Mark yesterday to say it had all been a mistake and I would be blocking his number, which I duly did. He will, I am sure, find a new muse. Infidelity is overrated; I could just as easily have more sex with Ben. What has so often felt claustrophobic, now appears uncomplicated. Working three days a week, choir on Monday evenings, swimming and accompanying Dee to the hospital on Thursdays, reverting to the habit of pub nights on Fridays – easy to claim the shelter is too upsetting – and Sunday church. A dog might be nice. Nothing as large as Tamsin's Airedale – I am wondering why she chose Hippo

192

when I remember that the name was short for Hippolyta, Queen of the Amazons. Mrs Elsworthy, for all her petiteness, has a regal air. From nowhere, I see myself visiting her on one of my days off, caring for her as she deteriorates. Appearing to be selfless is a flaw in my character that requires regular feeding. I'm not kind through altruism; no, the reflected glory is what motivates me. A psychotherapist might diagnose my need for external verification, for scaffolding if you like, as symptomatic of there being no solidity to my character . . .

'Shut up, Anna,' I say out loud.

As I brake, one leg ready to hop off my bike, I prepare to be the perfect companion for my new friend.

The front door is ajar, only piano music – Strauss, I think – permeating the quiet. I push open the inner doors and venture in.

'You're ten minutes early,' says Jan Elsworthy, without pausing or turning her head.

'Sorry, I wasn't sure how long it would take to cycle.'

That stops her. She shifts to look at me. 'The Anna girl. You came. I like someone who sticks to their word. Help me up.'

My hand firmly under her armpit, I inelegantly hoick her to standing.

'My legs are no stronger than a foal's today,' she says, taking a moment to straighten up.

I can't help but notice a gravy stain on the lapel of her cardigan. 'You've got a . . .' I point.

'Dribble.' She shakes her head, while using a licked thumb to make the smudge worse.

'Shall I get some washing-up liquid?'

Her wrinkled nose suggests she isn't particularly bothered. 'I suppose we might as well. I don't want to be accused of self-neglect and committed to a care home.'

'That seems unlikely.' I head for the kitchen, run hot water onto a cloth and add a dot of detergent. In two ticks she's clean, if a little damp.

'I was a headteacher, would you believe. Ageing is a disgrace.'

'What are you mithering about, Jan?' says a gravelly voice, and in walk two elderly men, both smart casual in blues and neutrals. In the next few minutes, a crowd gathers in the hall. I stay by Jan, amused by her quick retorts. Her body may be failing but her spirit is robust.

'Okay, everyone. Let's go,' says a middle-aged woman wearing a natty Fair Isle jumper. She is clearly the boss, running efficiently through the well-known carols on the printed sheet, hardly pausing to do more than nod at Jan on piano, except for a few times where, with no fuss, she directs the altos to purr rather than hum, or be more clipped. The sopranos need little guidance because the tune is always the easiest part to sing. The tenors have, I gather, been practising on their own. There is an undercurrent of battle between the high trilling and the deep growls that creates quite a magnificent performance from the forty or so choristers sardined into the square, high-ceilinged hall.

An hour later the session finishes as abruptly as it started. There is no mingling, merely a reminder to spread the word to ensure a full church for the concert and a modest round of applause for the pianist. I take my time, retying the laces of my trainers and tucking my trouser leg into my sock, hoping for a further interaction with our host. The hall is close to empty when the carer, Angie, appears wearing the same purple fleece as before. Like a collie, she shoos the stragglers towards the door. Awkward though it is, I hover.

'Hello, Anna.'

'Hi, Angie. How are you?' I say.

'Can't complain. No one listens.' She walks over to where Mrs Elsworthy is sitting, or more accurately, slumping. 'Do you think this is getting too much for you, Jan?'

I don't catch the reply, but I hear Angie say, 'Let's get you to bed,' and then, 'When is Liam due back?'

I sense that they are waiting for me to leave.

'Can I give you a hand up the stairs?' I say. Angie looks at Jan, who nods. An instructor in manual handling would fail us, I'm sure, but with me holding Jan's waist from behind and Angie gripping either side of her ribcage we clamber up the two flights, a six-legged beast. I wonder why she doesn't have a stairlift. And then I don't, because she is clearly unwilling to succumb to her immobility.

The contrast between tonight and our first meeting is stark. Jan is passive, can hardly bear her own weight and barks no instructions. Angie and I are also different, speaking more softly and moving slowly. In the bedroom, the care with which Angie removes Jan's clothes, checks her leg – 'We'll change the dressing tomorrow' – helps her into a jersey nightie and rearranges the bed linen is touching.

She perches on the edge of the bed. 'You'll feel better in the morning, Jan.'

Jan nods, moves her papery arm, an origami limb, to touch Angie's.

'Will you be all right on your own?' I ask, discombobulated by her weakness.

Angie answers for her. 'Liam is on a mid-shift, isn't he?' Jan nods. 'He shouldn't be too late, then. He's a paramedic,' Angie adds, by way of explanation.

'I noticed morphine in the kitchen,' I say. If I could choose oblivion over pain, I would.

'She won't take it,' says Angie.

'Until the end,' says Jan. She closes her eyes and is instantly asleep, lips parted, cheek muscles collapsed, rendering her hollow, a cadaver of her waking self.

'I love her,' says Angie, as we descend at ten times the speed we ascended. 'She's all spark, despite the pain, despite the prognosis.'

In the hall I fire my questions, unable to contain my curiosity any longer.

'Are you a carer?'

'Only for Jan. She taught me in sixth form.'

'Is Liam her companion?'

'Boyfriend.'

'Good for her.'

'He's very nice. People were sceptical when he moved in but she adores him and he appears to feel the same. He's a looker.' She winks.

'Does she have children?' I have already created a rift between the three sons and this Lothario who has won over their mother.

Angie shakes her head. 'Their careers came first. Her husband was a professor.'

'Where did she meet the paramedic? Did he do a house call and never leave?'

'Naughty.' Angie puts the key back in the key safe. 'I think she met him at the hospital. But if you ask her she says he fell into her lap, so who knows? I'd better get going. My kids are home alone.'

We walk down the drive together. 'Did you offer to look after her?'

'I did. But she pays me – way too much, actually. And I've only been coming for five months. Before that she didn't need anyone.' She opens her car door, plonks her holdall in the back seat. 'She's gone downhill quite quickly. I wouldn't be surprised if the concert is the only thing keeping her going.'

I wave. With my bike lights switched on and my coat pulled over my hands – should have brought gloves – I also head for home. Seconds . . . literally seconds later, I am blinded by a car careering towards me in the middle of the road. The way I bounce against a springy hedge yet stay upright would be amusing if I weren't so bloody livid. Fist in the air I yell at the idiot driver, who brakes hard, though he can't have heard me. (Must be a he!) I imagine he might slam into reverse and have a second shot at bulldozing me, but the car takes a hard right. A hard right straight into Jan's drive. Ah, this must be Liam – clearly a paramedic who only knows one way to drive. My mum used to say they were late for *Match of the Day* whenever she saw a cop car with the blues on.

A confrontation is not on my mind as I double back to take a peep. All I want is to eyeball Mrs Elsworthy's dedicated partner.

The shape of the car is enough, but I suspend my judgement. Common cars are common. The driver door opens. One leg and then the other. Despite being encased in two bottle-green shapeless tubes, the movement is recognisable. My body sinks, instantly heavier, as though my blood is mercury and my bones lead, while my mind scatters, light and fast and furious. The tiny cry from the

197

back of my throat is swallowed by the noise of his feet crunching the gravel.

Mark, or maybe Liam, or maybe fucking Hades, locks the car, the plink filling the still air. Three long strides and he has disappeared behind Jan Elsworthy's majestic front door.

If I had a knife, he would be dead.

33

House Burglar

My anger at discovering the extent of Mark's chicanery has brought an energy, a restlessness with no immediate outlet. Five minutes being labelled a fraudster in front of whatever audience Woodies can muster will not satisfy me – he deserves worse, much worse. From me he took sex, but from Jan he plans to take everything. For this charade has to be about money. Jan has a huge house, no family of any note, she is old and she is sick. Any microscopic possibility that it could be true love – please God let it be unconsummated – is trounced by the presence of all that wealth, and of the existence of me. The jury would not be out for long, the decision would be unanimous, the punishment the maximum allowed.

My classroom tidying on Wednesday is perfunctory because having been patient – unhinged but patient – for two whole days I am now ready for action. I considered going to Jan's last night but Ben suggested a takeaway and a film and that felt safe. And safe was what I needed.

The delay has turned out to be helpful. Yesterday I was bleakness personified, ridden with revulsion for Mark, for me, for life. The blanket of grey sky stayed throughout the shortened day, a lid pressing down while my mind replayed the way I lured him into an affair. What a gift: a ready-made mistress.

Today, however, the sunlight has lifted me out of the doldrums. *Onwards, Anna*, as Sofia would say.

At home I grab an apple that I eat as I cycle. The exercise brings a flush of wellness and I hurtle into Jan's picturesque village full of righteous indignation on her behalf.

There is a silver Golf parked on the road outside Jan's house but no red Honda Jazz on the drive. Where he is, who knows? Whether he'll come back while I'm still here, again, who knows? The risk makes my skin tingle. I chuck my bike behind Jan's hedge, ring the bell and knock twice before mimicking Angie's finger positions to release the key. Old habits die hard.

'Jan!' I shout, as I let myself in.

'In here,' says a voice that isn't Jan.

Jan is in her armchair and a brown-haired, navy-uniformed health professional of some kind is kneeling to attend to her leg.

'Hi, Jan. It's Anna.'

'I've got cancer, not cataracts,' she says. My grin spreads to a wide smile. I so love her antagonism. 'Did you let yourself in?'

'I did. I saw Angie do the code.'

'Are you a house burglar by trade?'

'No, I'm a teaching assistant actually.'

'In my day there was no need for assistants because teachers understood discipline. This one-to-one nannying is a nonsense.'

'Did you hit the kids with a long ruler?'

'I was a teacher, Anna, not the riot police.' She winces, eyes watering.

'Almost done,' says the woman at her feet, whose lanyard identifies

200

her as a district nurse. 'It's looking a little better.' She applies a big square dressing before peeling off her bright blue gloves. 'I'll pop and wash my hands. Do you want me to get you anything while I'm here, my love?'

'I can get anything she needs, if that's okay with you, Jan?' I latch onto Jan's muddy brown eyes.

'Little Anna here can minister to me this afternoon,' she says to the nurse. 'After she's told me why she is intent on visiting an immobile old lady whose deathbed is warming nicely.'

The nurse hesitates, clearly conflicted about whether I represent an actual danger.

'I'm only joking,' says Jan. 'Anna has joined our wonderful choir and we are the richer for her lovely voice.'

The nurse remains suspicious of me but leaves anyway. As the door shuts, Jan has a private chuckle. 'She's very literal,' she says. 'I think she thought you might murder me.'

'She's obviously willing to take the risk.'

'You don't look like an assassin. You don't look much like an angel either.'

'Destined to be in the middle, total mediocrity,' I say.

She is staring not so much at me as into me. 'Why are you here?'

I am here to gather information. There is a list in my head that covers Mark's regular comings and goings, Mark's supposed job, anything about his background that might contain a strand of reality and, if possible, the benefactor of her will. The loose plan was to strike up an easy conversation but this canny woman will see through me. And so, after sitting down on the Chesterfield-style sofa, I go for broke, praying the shock doesn't expedite the death she refers to so readily.

'I've been having an affair with someone called Mark Turner and I think he is the same man you call Liam.'

Her composure is unbelievable. She doesn't look away. She doesn't protest or cry. The giveaway is her silence and the tightness of her mouth, lips pressed thin. Human nature should have her pushing back, accusing me of troublemaking or spite or make-believe. I conclude she is not surprised or, at least, not floored. Perhaps, when she speaks, she will admit to knowing all about his other woman and admonish me for my naivety – a younger man has desires, Anna.

But she doesn't speak.

So I say, 'I'm sorry,' in the hope the sound will penetrate the thickened air, heavy with expectation, and provide a channel for her to use in reply.

She remains utterly silent; a little old woman who has to be helped to dress, helped to wash, helped to bed. I'd like to fetch a brush and smooth her ethereally silver hair – her wedding photograph shows she was dark – or make her a mug of hot milk with a spoon of brown sugar or fetch a wool blanket, weighty and warm, with enough texture to provide company for the bare skin of her hand or wrist.

The truth settles like snow, flakes falling achingly slowly through the air until there are enough to find purchase, to adhere, to form one layer and another, enough to turn what was grey into pure white.

'Do you think me foolish?' she says after the longest time.

'No. Or only as foolish as I have been,' I say, although I feel the age gap should have made her wary.

'No, I am the more foolish. My great age should have protected me from believing he could be sincere.'

202

Touché.

'How did you meet him?' she asks.

I relay the story of our affair, resisting the urge to make my part more palatable. The cathartic rush of sharing is worth the humiliation. Apart from nodding at the names Carrie and Robin and interjecting – 'We had a wonderful week' – at the mention of Exmouth, she is quiet. When I reveal that the thread that led me to her was their alfresco moussaka, a forlorn smile forces its way onto her face.

'My moussaka recipe. I could never be bothered with béchamel – yoghurt brings a nice tang. He made it for you?'

I nod.

She stiffens, but I carry on, hoping she can maintain her demeanour. 'It was delicious. He's a class act, Jan. I don't think we should be too hard on ourselves.'

'Are you serious about him?'

'Not anymore. I mean I was infatuated, but I think I knew it couldn't be real.'

'Because you found out?'

'Suspected. Or maybe it was always a fling.'

'Fling used to be a verb.' I'm pleased to see a glimpse of feisty Jan. 'But what about your partner?'

'I don't deserve him. I can't seem to settle. Not now, not ever.'

'You can decide to. You don't have to give in to whims. You're not a child.'

'No, but I think I'm damaged.'

'Get a grip, girl. You're attractive, eloquent, can hold a tune. You're not damaged, but it seems you're indulgent.'

The huff is involuntary, the audio to my irksome mind.

She gives me a hard stare before continuing, 'Commitment, no matter what to, is the spine, the life force that allows you to flourish. Bending to any old impulse can never bring the rewards that loyalty gives freely.'

No one has ever spoken to me in this way. I've been told off, obviously, but never in a way that felt constructive. Jan's confidence in the ability to decide for oneself and stick with that decision gives me a boost.

'I have agreed to get married.'

I fully understand why she snorts and rolls her eyes – my sentence has echoes of an arranged marriage, or of Austen. 'Do you want to marry him?'

'Yes,' I say, with only the merest hesitation.

'Then marry him and stay true and use your enthusiasm for change to keep that marriage exciting. And I don't mean sex, although that helps. Travel together. Go salsa dancing. Invite friends all the time, make new ones. You've a gift for friendship.'

'Thank you.'

'I think it's time for a cup of tea, don't you?'

'When is Mark due back?' I ask, only now considering the fallout for Jan if we are caught together.

'Not until after midnight. His shift started at two.'

'Tea would be lovely, then.'

This time I make a pot which I bring on a tray, placing it on the dark wood coffee table that holds a pile of books and a box of man-size tissues.

'How did you meet him?' I ask.

'He fell into my lap. Too good to be true – I should have realised he was too good to be true.'

'Me too. Can I ask more? I don't want to make things worse but . . .'

'Ask away.'

We unwrap him between us. He has lived with Jan for thirteen months but he works a lot of late shifts.

'He doesn't mind being awake in the small hours.'

'Is he actually a paramedic?'

Her wide eyes tell me that she has not considered more of him might be a lie. 'I believe so.'

'Only the last four Friday evenings, and one overnight, he's been with me.'

'He has the uniform . . . and some equipment.' A tremor appears in her usually strident voice, followed by a few controlled tears.

Reluctantly I carry on. 'He told me he was an art therapist, spoke very knowledgeably – well, that's how it seemed. I never saw a green uniform, Jan.'

(The paramedic racing to save unsavable Sofia sprints into view; I send him away.)

'What does he do then?' she asks.

'Apart from being a skilful liar, I have no idea.'

'Did he admit to a partner?'

I nod. 'But he gave no details except that he was planning to leave.'

'Did he mean when I die?'

I don't have a reply. The silence spurs her to share some of her own story.

'His sister was meant to come to dinner but it never happened,' she says. 'She was unwell and they are one of those families with

205

full diaries.' She takes a lungful and lets the air seep back out, slight shake of the head. 'Was it all nonsense?'

'I think so. Did he say the studio in Exmouth belonged to a friend?'

'No, I found it. I booked it.' Her scanty eyebrows form a frown. 'Odd that he chose to take you there.'

My tongue is preparing to ask about her will but it seems too brutal, too exposing. 'Do you give him money?'

'I do. He doesn't earn an awful lot and I was happy to . . . oh my word, what a babe in the woods I've been. What a numpty.'

Mark is fond of that word – another thing he has taken from Jan.

My fingertip finds its way into my mouth and I free a sliver of nail and pull with my teeth.

'That's very unattractive,' she says. 'Did no one ever rub your nails with lemon juice?'

I obediently put my hands on my thighs.

'I only saw Mark on Thursday afternoons and Friday evenings. If he's not a paramedic, where is he on his long shifts?'

She shakes her head.

'And I've only known him a short time, so where was he on those days before he met me?'

'I don't know.'

I am making things worse, so I try and make them better.

'What do you think you'll do now you know?' I ask.

'I want him gone,' she says. 'But I'm reliant on him.'

'Would you rather we both kept him in the dark for now?'

She nods. 'Yes, I'll need to make some plans.'

'Knowledge is power.'

'Perhaps.' She writhes in the armchair, the movement hinting at mental as well as physical pain.

'Do you want to get up?' According to Angie, the cancer has spread to her hip. I can't imagine how it might feel to have malevolence creeping unchecked through your body.

'Yes. The bathroom and then a hard chair and a cushion, please.'

Having delivered her to the bathroom, I take the tea tray into the kitchen and tidy away the evidence of my visit. In the narrow cupboard above the kettle I accidentally dislodge a canister and the box of Lapsang reveals itself. What a self-congratulatory bastard – ensconced in a beautiful house, adored for the way he cares for Jan, peddling lies, certain that he will stay a step ahead, certain that there will never be a rainy day for Mark Liam Turner. Well, bad weather is on the way.

My phone shudders at a text from Ben asking where I am. Somehow it is nearly seven o'clock.

When Jan is safely seated in the kitchen with a fresh cup of tea and a custard cream, I make my excuses. We exchange mobile numbers and I promise to call her after we've both had a few days to consider what might come next.

Halfway to the door, I ask, 'What did you mean when you said he fell into your lap?'

'I was sitting in a café near the hospital—'

'Do you mean Woodies?'

'Yes, do you know it? Very good scones.' I lodge the uncomfortable idea that he lurked there for a reason. Hospitals are, by definition, hubs for those in poor health.

'I've been there,' I say. The fuller picture can wait for another day.

207

'He was walking along looking at his phone and he actually fell into my waiting lap.'

'He's bold,' I say, an appreciative lilt to my voice. 'But perhaps we can be bolder.'

34

Grandmaster Kholmov's combination against Grandmaster Bronstein

Today, I am in the driving seat, tasked with delivering Dee safely to the hospital. Practice makes perfect, she said, admiring the magnetic L-plates, although now we're in the car she may feel differently. Despite pretending to be relaxed, every so often she grips the edges of her seat and stops breathing. Having a nervous passenger makes me extra cautious, waiting for enormous gaps before pulling out, only joining the roundabout when there is no other contender and scouring the road ahead for shiny ice. The sky is unremittingly blue but we had to defrost the rear window before we set off and the temperature gauge is stuck on zero. As a consequence, we arrive with only minutes to spare.

'You can drop me at the entrance,' she says and I oblige. Whether she has forgotten I am driving on a provisional licence or doesn't care, I don't know. I watch her walk briskly in, shielding her mouth with her scarf. That no one can tell she has a chronic illness is something Dee holds dear. Sofia and I once had a heated debate about whether it was better to have a visible or invisible medical condition.

There was no winner because we had such different perspectives: hers was personal, mine was theoretical. I miss Sofia – it was fun having a buddy down the road ever ready for a drink, a dance or a fierce discussion.

Instead of parking, I spend a happy half-hour cruising the streets, eyes on the road, mind on Sofia. Even if she hadn't died, I know the intensity of our friendship wouldn't have endured. Tamsin tried to warn me but I didn't listen because I was in love. Sofia picked people up as she travelled through life and discarded them like coffee grounds. If she hadn't been so impatient to slough off our friendship, we could have walked home together that fateful day and there would have been no stampede and she could be sitting in Keeper's Cottage right now, head in one of her small-print books, best buddies with someone else.

My indicator is flashing left – it makes a pleasing tick. When the queue of traffic coming the other way clears, I will turn back into the car park. I have waved people out of driveways, stopped for pedestrians and sailed past a police car with the confidence of an experienced driver, but I need to stop this silly game or my luck won't hold and I will be convicted of driving without insurance or a licence.

The day has clouded over, accentuating the bitter cold. My immediate plan is to get a takeaway coffee and read my book in the foyer where there is natural light. Mark may or may not be in Woodies; either way, I'm never going there again.

I am crossing the car park, hunched inside my puffer coat, navy beanie pulled down for protection from the ear-aching wind, when I hear Sofia's name. I carry on, fully expecting the little girl with the bare legs and pink flip-flops to appear followed by her tersely spoken father. I picture her in a winter uniform of sparkly wellies and clashing tights, but still defiantly wearing a pink tutu.

'Sofia!'

The noise of running is heavy – a slap, slap, slap of spongy soles on hard concrete.

'Sofia, stop.'

I stop, but don't turn. Mark circles in front of me.

'What's going on?'

'I decided I don't trust you.' This is not thought through – all I know is that I mustn't divulge anything about Jan. Not until she is in a position to do without him. Or dead.

'So you thought you'd ghost me, disappear without giving me a chance?' He has a mean look in his eyes and a glob of spittle by his mouth.

I stay still and quiet and watch him wrestle back some control. No one likes angry.

'Sorry. Sorry.' He goes to take my right hand – my left hand with the sparkly ring is firmly in my pocket – but changes his mind and lets it drop to his side. 'I've been sitting in the café, hoping and panicking. I understand. I do. Why would you put your faith in someone who wasn't straight from the outset?'

'And continues not to be.' Acting dispassionate is very satisfying.

He swallows. For the first time the well-tuned scanner in my brain detects genuine unease. I can almost see the whirr as he considers potential moves and likely countermoves.

'What do you mean?' he says eventually, so far on the back foot he might topple.

'Why don't you tell me about your fascinating work at the hospital?'

211

This is chess and he is in check. Wherever he moves next I have the answer.

'I am a full-time carer.' This tactic is unexpected. 'My partner is dying.' I have to remind myself of what I don't know.

'Is this a ploy? Playing the death card.' My words have a nice chill.

'No, that's why I haven't left her. She relies on me.'

'Why did you lie?'

'I thought you'd judge me. Cheating is one thing, cheating on the sick is a whole other level.'

'What is wrong with her?'

'Cancer.'

I order my face to show compassion. 'That must be very difficult.'

'The treatment has been gruelling enough, but the psychological damage – even the bloody label – feels irreparable . . .' He digs a big hole, keen to show his selfless dedication.

'That doesn't explain why you invented such elaborate lies about your work?' My tone is, I hope, troubled.

'Can we please stop this for a second and remember what happened. I thought we were having one of those random chats you have on the train or in a queue. I never expected us to become close. You did the running. You kissed me. You asked me on a date.'

'I did, but I didn't ask to go on a date with a work of fiction.'

'If it helps in any way, I *am* interested in art therapy. But mostly I wanted to impress you. If I could go back I'd admit I'm a kept man.'

'She has money?'

The set of his mouth, the hint of moisture above his lip, the dance in his eyes: he is deciding whether to jump off the bridge or climb back down to safety.

He jumps.

'Tell me, would I be a better proposition if I came with a little luxury?'

My reluctant smile is crafted to appear appalled yet enticed. 'I don't know.'

'Is that a maybe?'

'Why me?'

'Are you kidding, Sofia? You dazzle me. And we're good together, aren't we?' The flush of the skin high on his cheek is quite affecting. 'You're the missing half.'

My id has forgotten that I could be fishing for information. Fortunately, my superego bangs another nail in his coffin.

'Was your sister expecting us tomorrow evening?'

'I think you know she wasn't.'

'Do you actually have a sister?'

Another hiatus. 'No. Only child.'

'What excuse were you going to make?'

'I hadn't decided – I wasn't sure I'd see you again.' He licks his lips. 'Why did you lie?'

'What lies have I told?'

'I think you have a partner.'

'I didn't lie.'

'You lied by omission.'

I shrug.

'We could disappear. I'm going, as soon as I'm free. There's a seat on the plane for you.'

'Where does it land?'

'Anywhere. Thailand. Guatemala. Honolulu. I've been stuck for so long and I really, really need to live on a beach indefinitely.'

'Wouldn't you get bored?'

'We wouldn't get bored. We'd snorkel and eat fresh fish and sleep and wander. I'm done with all of this. Humdrum life, every day the same' – once again he takes my thought and makes it his – 'except for you, Sofia.' With no warning he pulls me towards him and kisses me, gently, hardly touching. I respond by kissing him with such intensity that he is the one who has to take a breath. The very, very last time should be noteworthy, I feel.

'Will you meet me tomorrow?'

I shake my head. 'No, Mark.'

'Is this it?'

Nodding is hard. There is something thrillingly bleak about being in a hospital car park in November kissing an utterly deceitful but delicious man who claims he is desperate to keep me in his life.

I walk away, half expecting him to hang on to my sleeve.

Having fetched a takeaway tea from the canteen, I sit, but can't immediately settle into my new book. Now that Mark has no date for tomorrow night I wonder if he will stay home with Jan, claiming his shift finished early or was cancelled altogether because they're an ambulance short. Her position is very unenviable, dependent on a con artist.

I re-read the first page, turn over several more. The prose, unbroken by paragraphs, starts to take hold and I become immersed in a breathless dystopian nightmare.

'Anna, I've been worried.' Dee is approaching at speed, leaving Steve for dust. 'I left you in the car.'

I stand up, slide my book into my coat pocket. 'I know. It doesn't matter. I was fine.'

She bites her lip. 'Goodness, what was I thinking?'

'I gather you've broken the law,' says Steve, catching up.

'Unintentionally,' I say.

'We started driving on the farm tracks from when we were about fourteen,' he says.

'I passed my test at seventeen,' says Dee. 'My dad was pleased because I could pick him up from the pub in town.' We all smile.

'Have you got a date for your test, Anna?' asks Steve.

'No, but I think I'll—'

'Anna!' The vibrant, upbeat voice is by my ear. I turn to my left, my cheeks already reddened in shame. Every other time I've been caught rears up to multiply the feeling of coming loose, falling and dying.

'Hi.'

'This is a coincidence.' Mark's face is one big smile.

He shifts to face the assembly.

'Mark,' he says, hand outstretched.

Dee takes his hand and says, 'I'm Dee, Anna's soon-to-be mother-in-law.' She glances across at me but I have nothing. 'And this is Steve.'

'Hello.'

'Very pleased to meet you,' says Mark. 'I've heard all about the club.'

They make appreciative noises, after which the collective gaze falls back on me. But I am no more forthcoming. He could destroy me in a single sentence.

'How do you know each other?' asks Dee.

'We've been frequenting the same café.' Mark angles his body towards me, oozing self-confidence. 'Nice to see you again, Anna.'

'You too.' I add a smile that barely deserves the label.

'We should get going,' says Dee, manoeuvring towards the door. 'It gets dark so early.'

Mark tags along, walking close enough to clip my heels. I stop by Dee's car.

'Be careful on the road up to St Michael's, Anna,' says Steve. 'The dip is notorious for black ice and I wouldn't want you to have an accident.'

Mark heeds the information as clearly as if he had scribbled the words on his hand.

35

Bartok the Cat

Ben is using the big screen of his work computer to show me various wedding venues, having unreservedly rejected my idea of a fish and chip van outside the village hall.

'A lot of it depends on numbers,' he says.

'I thought we'd agreed small.'

He clicks and the couple standing under an arch of roses is replaced by a terrifying list.

'Once you start writing down names, small is tricky. What about Hannah and Hugh, the pub crowd, Uncle Eric . . .?'

It is Saturday afternoon and since Thursday I have been fretting. Mark lucked out when he followed me into the hospital. Having discovered that I am not Sofia and very much not single, I can't imagine I have his blessing. The anticipation is a constant flutter. I can't concentrate, might be getting a tic. Even if he doesn't choose to come and loiter near St Michael's, every Thursday afternoon at the hospital I will be a sitting duck. I can't second-guess what he might do.

A vision of Mark running into a full church to confess our infidelity makes me shudder.

'Cold?' asks Ben.

'A bit. I'll get a sweatshirt.'

I run upstairs and, sitting on the edge of our bed, text Jan to ask when Mark is next on shift. She replies that he's supposedly working this evening, from five o'clock until three in the morning, so I invite myself over. Knowing I'm going to see her brings a solidity to a future that feels formless. Hopefully she'll have more words of wisdom.

Ben is bemused by my impromptu plan to visit an old lady I hardly know but the benefit of being a Slater is that there is always somewhere to go. By the time I'm back with a mug of tea and two chocolate biscuits each, he has arranged an early evening pint in the pub.

The next hour is spent making a concerted effort to engage with Ben's comprehensive digital scrapbook.

'. . . and here's a list of options for the wedding list.'

'I don't think we want gifts, do we?'

Ben disagrees. 'People like to buy something.'

'Are you sure? Don't they begrudge all the expense? An outfit, travel, a hotel room.'

He twists away from the screen to look at me, clearly a bit flummoxed by the negativity.

'Are you worried about how much the wedding's going to cost?'

'Yes,' I say, hoping it might excuse my ambivalence. The joy I felt at finally making a decision has vanished. In the same way I could never picture our baby, I can't photoshop myself into a white frock, walking down the aisle to a beaming Ben.

'There's no need. I know we've been useless at combining our finances but what's mine is yours. Has been from the first night you took me home, Anna Harris.'

I look at him, this steadfast man, and can't believe I've been so awful to him. Tears are itching the corners of my eyes. I could confess, I think. But quickly decide against. Even if he forgave me the shadow would never leave, forever obscuring the sunshine.

'Shall we just pick a random Saturday in . . . I don't know, April or September?' he asks.

'We don't know when the church is free.'

'Okay, let's check availability and go from there. Yes?'

I nod – because I can hardly object – kiss Ben goodbye and cycle off.

The roads are deathly quiet. Everyone sane is at home, radiators on full, curtains drawn. Balanced on my two thin tyres, vulnerability forms a cloak. A driver who has overindulged will come speeding along the lane at any moment and mow me down. The church will be full for my funeral, each row swollen by the addition to the normal congregation of those who would have attended the wedding. Ben will do a reading about how my stem was cut when in full bloom. Dee will weep.

The square white house is scarcely lit – Jan should fill the unused rooms and start a commune, says my pointless-thought generator. I chuck my bike and go to let myself in but before I can input the code the front door swings open.

'Come in. Come in.' Jan is waiting in the lobby with her trusty frame.

She walks at a pace not seen before, stopping at the piano stool

219

in the hall and sitting down heavily. 'I want you to go and find out where he is.'

'How?'

Her face is shiny bright, alight with purpose. 'I've got one of those trackers. It was meant to be for the cat but he died straight after Christmas.'

'It's not Christmas yet, Jan.'

She smacks my leg. 'Don't be a patronising little madam. Last Christmas. Angie bought it for Bartok but he was run over. Anyway, I've tagged Liam.'

My face joins hers, smiling so much my lips can't actually close. 'Shit.'

'You need to go.'

'How?'

'Drive, of course.'

'I cycled here.'

'What?'

'Can't we google the address he's at?'

'He's in a pub. I want to know who he's with.' She groans at my inadequacy. 'Take my car. If it bloody starts.'

The instructions for finding the key, opening the garage and being firm with the handbrake are barked at me. Her excitement is highly infectious, tapping into the streak of wild abandon I work hard to contain. There is no time to point out the trivial detail that concerns a licence to drive. Within ten minutes I am reversing out of her garage in a black Saab convertible – 'Keep the top up or he'll spot you' – any reservations unuttered.

I drive through the village, flying over the humpback bridge and

220

landing with a flump, before turning onto the main road. Mark is five miles away in yet another Somerset village. At the first layby I pull in and use the two very obvious release levers to take the top down. If I'm driving illegally to catch a cheating bastard, I may as well enjoy myself.

Mark's red Honda Jazz is in the car park of an old thatched pub called The King's Head, a slightly wider version of Keeper's Cottage. I crawl past and park about a hundred metres further on; the top goes back on the car.

Venturing inside the pub isn't an option – Mark doesn't need baiting – and peering through the tiny leaded windows seems unlikely to yield any information. My instinct is to drive off. I don't want to disappoint Jan but a kernel of common sense has brought me down from the high and left me in limbo.

Sitting in the dark in a borrowed car on a deserted road doing nothing is making me feel bad, hollow and stupid. I wish I was home with Ben. I don't want to be a stalker. I don't want to read any more of Jan's texts either. She says if I don't want to go in, I could wait and see who he leaves with. No, thank you, Jan. He could be hours . . .

Loath to go back without something to sate Jan's appetite, I get out and walk towards the pub, head down, hands in my coat pockets. The front door is sheltered by a lip of thatch. I saunter past – a cursory glance towards each window – and skirt the building in search of a back door but find only a yard. I pick my way through the odd shapes – crates and barrels, a woodpile, a commercial bin – to the far side where, turning the corner, the light from a half-glazed door falls in a perfect rectangle. Inside my jacket my heart is pumping madly – a warning to leave well alone – but I take a breath and in I go, already primed to run like the blazes.

This is not a customer entrance – there are boxes of crisps and shrink-wraps of canned drinks, wholesale packs of kitchen roll and a filthy mop and bucket cluttering the grubby vinyl floor. The staff toilet advertises itself by the smell emanating from the door on my right, which is slightly ajar. A glance at the triangle of stained cork tiles brings a wave of nausea. On my other side there are narrow stairs, presumably leading down to a cellar. I carry along the short corridor, aware of a melange of voices and associated clinks and knocks. The bar sounds busy. A peep is all I need, I tell my increasingly wary self; enough to describe the redhead or the dyed blonde, her age, her figure.

'Can you change the Tribute barrel?' The shout ricochets off the walls like a squash ball.

'On it,' the reply bounces back.

Despite wanting to gag, I step inside the toilet. My chest hammers in time with the thud, thud, thud of the barrel-changer hurrying past me to get to the cellar. When I notice the change from running feet on vinyl to skipping feet on stone stairs I dart out, desperate to get away. If Jan wants to know more about Mark's movements she'll have to hire a private detective. As I pass the top of the stairs, all I catch is the tiniest glimpse before he disappears down into darkness to get the Tribute back on tap, dressed in his favourite Breton top.

Safely back in the car, the adrenaline falls away, leaving me flat and lifeless. Mark is neither paramedic nor art therapist but bartender and pathological liar, inventing and living out elaborate fantasies designed to cast him in a favourable light. Knowing I was captivated by a wholly fabricated persona makes me want to stab holes in his chameleon-like skin. And suspecting I share some of his traits makes me want to race home and empty every one of Sofia's possessions into the bin. A shiver runs from my tight scalp down to the end of my toes, a symbolic shedding.

36

Coloratura Soprano

On Monday evening, I can't decide whether or not to go to choir. I text Jan and she confirms Mark will definitely not be there, and says she hopes to see me. So I go.

The two hours of what should be joy is marred by a deep disquiet. Now that Mark knows I have also lied, being in his domain feels foolhardy. I don't think I'll come again. Feeding a bear who is already sniffing around the bins is a mistake.

Given he followed me into the hospital, skulked in the shadows and watched me before introducing himself to Dee, it seems reasonable to assume he is not going to gracefully step away. Therefore, I need to take a very large step away from him.

To that end, I don't go to the hospital on Thursday. Dee is more than happy to have a lift with Steve when she knows I have an appointment at the doctor's. (I don't have an appointment at the doctor's.)

This is my strategy: complete avoidance. His interest is bound to wane. He could, of course, approach Dee again but that risk I can't mitigate.

And so, the week passes with no sight or sniff of Mark Turner.

My unease drops a notch, as do the dreams of being caught – caught stealing, caught naked, caught with a spliff. There are many beddable women; why would he pursue one who doesn't want to play?

On Friday morning I get back from my driving lesson to find Ben in the kitchen with a print-out of all the Saturdays the church is available in the coming year, which is most of them.

'. . . and I've had another idea about the venue,' he says.

'Go ahead.'

'I know you don't want a massive affair so what about a marquee in the pub garden?'

The pub feels very manageable, small and low-key. A detailed and vivid image arrives of Ben and me sitting on stools in the snug bar, late in the evening, only the diehard guests for company. The skirt of my dress is hitched up into a ball on my lap, one shoestring strap has fallen off my shoulder, I am swinging a bare leg, brushing the crease of his grey trousers with my silver sandal. He has abandoned his jacket and unbuttoned the neck of his shirt. He looks happy. We both look happy.

'Yes, I'd really like that,' I say, with more enthusiasm than I knew I could garner. The certainty in my voice feels like armour. I try more words. 'And we could all walk from the church, which would be a bonus.'

'The village would come out in force for the parade.' Ben leans across to kiss me. 'So all we need now is a date.'

Inside my head I bargain with fate – I will make a date if, in return, Mark can disappear.

On Saturday morning, as arranged, Milly picks me up to go to the shopping mall near Bristol. She wants to buy a starter pack

225

for Wolfie. (The name has grown on me; I'm hoping she'll have triangular ears.)

'I know hand-me-downs are fine, but I can't put my brand-new baby in something worn.'

Agreeing is not difficult; I've been to school in my brother's boxers before now.

Milly buys a selection of mostly green and pink items and I invest in a pair of cycling trousers with a lovely squashy pad to protect my sit bones. For my birthday I might ask Ben for a bike more like his. Having rediscovered the pleasure of self-propelled speed I'm keen to go further, more often, climb huge hills and coast back down. On the way home, having had lunch at a noodle bar, I share my ambition with Milly, who is not sympathetic.

'There's a reason we like to ski,' she says. 'And the clue is in the lift pass.'

I ignore the reference to their exclusive hobby. If we are to be related, I must practise tolerance.

'Thanks for inviting me today, Milly,' I say as she draws up outside the house.

'We should do it again,' she says.

'Yes, great,' I say, fairly sure we have finally put #babygate behind us.

The path that leads to our side door is a mulch of wet leaves. We should sweep them away. In fact, we should buy a gate – that would look much tidier. And we should have pots by the front door like Dee has, and maybe fruit trees along the back fence; we should buy two wooden benches that sit at right angles and a chiminea. How have I not thought this before?

I burst in the back door, ready to scoop up Ben – who has

226

been to buy a Christmas tree with Finn and the kids – and raid the garden centre, but stop dead, feet on the doormat, head in a salad spinner.

'Hi,' says my inner coloratura soprano.

'Anna, weird coincidence. I think you know Mark?'

'I do.' How my exterior stays calm when inside is a-gallop, I don't know.

'He saw Keeper's Cottage was for sale and came for a look.'

From Ben's manner it's clear that Mark has peddled the same story he told Dee: we are acquaintances, no more. I order myself to act as an acquaintance.

'It's small,' I say.

'I don't need a lot of space,' he says.

'How come you two have . . .' I waggle my finger between them because there are no words.

'He was in the road when I came back from Mum's.'

'I haven't only met Ben,' says Mark. 'This is an extraordinarily friendly village – I am now on good terms with the Weimaraner who walks alone and the lady from the guest house.'

'It's not friendliness, it's nosiness.' Ben looks across at me, clearly expecting a retort. When none occurs, he carries on. 'Any stranger standing in the street—'

'Gawping,' Mark interjects.

'Exactly. Is worth a prod and a poke.'

'Happy to be prodded.'

Seeing the two men side by side makes it impossible not to compare. Mark is at his amiable best, smiling and open, and handsome, obviously. But Ben has youth on his side, and is decent and loyal, and has a monogamous penis.

'Anyway, good to meet you, Ben, and thanks for the lowdown on the cottage.'

'No problem. If you decide to make an offer you can join Fridays in the pub.'

'See you around, Anna,' says Mark as Ben shows him out. When I hear the door shut, I slump onto the nearest chair, poleaxed by Mark's audacity. And yet not. I can see his mind. When I didn't show at the hospital last week, he decided to take a stroll in the streets around St Michael's church, capitalising on the For Sale sign to chat to passers-by. I was always going to be uncovered – a smile, a question, a mention of Dee or Anna. But is he simply intent on making me suffer or are we working up to a dramatic denouement?

'Nice guy,' says Ben, reappearing.

'Yes,' I nod. I am already reaching for the wine. The bottle of red disappears, followed by another with a short interval where we order Chinese – the tree decorating has to be postponed. Avoidance isn't going to work. Mark is in my face. He's in my fucking face.

37

Badger's Rise

When Dee and I arrive at church on Sunday morning, I am surprised to find Jan Elsworthy in the fourth pew from the front. I walk towards her, hand raised in acknowledgement.

'Hello, Jan. Have you come to try us out?' She is looking wonderful, pink cheeks and lipstick, a bright red scarf over a black cape. Having an ally who knows the truth, someone who was also taken in, is bolstering. I have not even a shred of doubt she will keep my secret, and I hers.

'Liam usually runs me down to St Mary's but I didn't feel like it today.'

'How did you get here?'

'Meryl fetched me. She likes ministering to the sick.'

'You don't look sick today. You look beautiful.'

'Painting over the cracks to stem the pity.'

Dee, who has been waylaid, catches up. I am about to introduce them but . . .

'It's Mrs Elsworthy, isn't it? My late husband, Richard Slater, went to your school.'

'That makes me feel my age,' says Jan.

'You're looking very well on it.'

'I'm held together by cancer, but still got a kick to my step.'

I'm flooded with a feeling I can't describe, something tender but powerful, with an undercurrent of dread that her vitality will desert her and she will desert me.

They continue their conversation – establishing that Jan taught Richard in sixth form, a connection they both enjoy; that Dee has four grandchildren, soon to be five and that I am Dee's son's fiancée – until the organ music summons the choir and we all turn to face the Lord.

When we adjourn for coffee, Jan corners me.

'These trackers are a terrible thing – a complete invasion of privacy. Imagine if you wanted to escape a violent husband. You're lucky you weren't tagged, Anna.'

'Mark seems to have found me without a tracker,' I say, relaying my panic at finding him in my kitchen with my fiancé.

'He doesn't want to let you go,' she states, unhelpfully.

'It seems not.'

'Anyway, I've tracked him again. The first time he was in the same pub as before but at one o'clock this morning he was at Badger's Rise, just around the corner. The last in the row. Number eight.'

'When did he come back to yours?' I should have realised she wouldn't be satisfied by the discovery of his pub job. I, too, had Einsteined that he couldn't be working in a pub for the whole of his supposed nine-hour ambulance shifts but my interest is non-existent.

'How should I know? It's a two-a-penny pet tracker, not MI5.'

'Doesn't it track him all the time?'

'No.' She looks at me as though I'm an idiot. 'You have to open the app and ask for a live feed and it sends co-ordinates of where it is at that moment.'

She is staring at me, expectantly.

'What?' I ask.

She raises her barely-there eyebrows.

I say it for her. 'You want me to go and ferret.'

'Don't you want to know?'

'No, he's the past. I want to forget about him.'

'I can't ask anyone else, Anna.' Her helplessness is too poignant to consider refusing. For someone whose moral compass struggles with direction I am a sucker for doe eyes.

Jan says Liam is picking her up from Meryl's house after lunch: 'It'll be a dry chicken and watery gravy but the wine will be good.' He will definitely be in for the rest of the day because they are decorating the Christmas tree. This is my window, she says, any time between three o'clock and late.

'Where did you hide the tag?'

'In that canvas bag of his.' She tuts. 'Schoolboy affectation.'

'What if he finds it?'

'I keep taking it out. I'm not a numpty, Anna. And, anyway, the battery can't charge itself.'

Dee heads off to Milly's; Jan leaves with Meryl; I walk home with Hannah. I think we're having an everyday chat but she is clutching a hand grenade that she only lobs when we reach my front door.

'Do you remember I said I saw you by the hospital?'

Dim Anna. Dim, dim Anna.

'Yes. Have you seen me again?' I am playful.

'The man you were with was here yesterday, looking at Keeper's Cottage.'

'Oh, you mean Mark!' There are too many high notes in this exclamation. For an inveterate liar I'm not at my best.

'Watch your step, Anna. We all love you but make no mistake about our loyalties.'

The loose ends are everywhere, unravelling and finding each other.

'I think you've got the wrong idea, Hannah. Ben and I are getting married, remember.'

As I step inside our house, I shrug her off like an unwanted layer. She hasn't seen my naked limbs wrapped around another man: she knows nothing.

Ben is in the living room, boy-scout ready. The stepladder is in place, the extension lead plugged in. The plastic storage box of Christmas lights, the two bags of baubles and the separate cardboard box for the treetop-star he made at school (whether ironic or sentimental, I'm still unsure) have been freed from the confines of the loft. And so the ritual begins.

When we have achieved a balance of randomness and symmetry, I use a bright and breezy voice to tell Ben I'm going out cycling later.

'Why don't you come? Cycling is meant to be good rehab.' We both know he is going to watch sport all afternoon.

'Maybe next time.' He pauses. 'Or maybe when it's not winter.'

I make our staple cheese on toast before scooting off in my new cycling leggings, mindful that, once again, I have to come up with a reason to ring a stranger's doorbell. Jan might be in charge of logistics but details of the execution seem to be down to me.

The cycle is not enjoyable; dreary sky, cold hands and an increasingly desolate mood, not helped by Hannah's insinuations. I almost hope she sidles up to Ben, asks for a quiet word and spills her concern, only for him to declare Mark a good bloke that I met doing my weekly favour for Dee. That would show the nosy cow.

I dig in and pick up speed. My goal is to get there and back in the shortest time, deliver whatever information I can glean to Jan and make it clear I can't do any more. Only she can decide how to proceed with her duplicitous housemate. I'm sorry she took up with a cad but if I engineer his downfall, he might repay the favour.

The disappearing light has cast a strange filter over the landscape; the hedgerows are jet, the sky amethyst, the ground a smoky quartz. Something touches my shoulder and I flinch, look over my shoulder and nearly lose my balance. I shake my upper body, imagining it was a bat or maybe a bird. Shoulders hunched, I pedal even faster. Ahead, the tarmac rises and the sky presses down, leaving only a narrow window for me to continue my journey. I focus on the patch of road in front of my wheel and try not to die.

The sign for the village brings the return of street lighting and a smidgeon of sanity. I lock the bike to a handy railing and continue on foot to Badger's Rise, hands cupped over my mouth to try to restore the blood supply to my fingers. The slim semi-detached redbrick house, the last in a short row that all face onto fields, is in complete darkness. If no one is home I will try next door, which is compensating nicely with three lit windows. Ideally the neighbours will confirm that Mark lives there alone but is away a lot, or the house will be his mother's, and Jan needn't worry about any added complexity. Energised by this straightforward resolution, I walk up the garden path and ring the doorbell. There is no sound, so I knock twice on the wood of the door. Still nothing. Good.

Rather than go back down the path and up the other side, I am about to step over the flower bed, when a familiar-looking woman

233

opens the door. I may not know her but I recognise her as Mark's type. She is wearing a tartan shirt over faded denim jeans, bare feet in sheepskin slippers, and has long blonde hair and huge earrings. The plan in my head, the plan to open a conversation by asking if she's seen my cat, the black and white cat I decided to call Bartok after Jan's cat – that plan vanishes so completely I may as well have never thought it.

'Can I help you?' she says.

'Is Liam around?'

'You've got the wrong house.'

'I know he was here last night.' I can sense her disquiet. Humans are a marvel, able to decipher seemingly insignificant visual cues: a cough, tucking a strand of hair away, the set of a jaw. Or, in this case, a frozen-eyed stare. 'Perhaps he calls himself Mark?'

I hold out my phone for her to see my only photograph of Mark, fast asleep in the studio in Exmouth.

She goes to slam the door, but I am faster.

38

The Other, Other Woman

Mark's very attractive other, other woman can't shut her front door because my foot is in the way. I stay as I am, waiting for her to realise she has little choice but to talk to me. The stand-off is almost comedic, two rivals, separated by two inches of door.

'Who are you?' she says, through the gap.

'Like you, I'm a close friend of Mark's.'

She hesitates, before letting the door swing back open. Her hazel eyes flick to the left and right, and beyond me, as though expecting a trap.

'I've got nothing to say.'

'I'm not looking for trouble. A few answers to a few questions and I'll leave you alone.'

'My husband'll be back soon.'

'You can tell him I'm selling windows.'

'Please, you need to go.' Her manner is quite agitated. I wonder if her husband is a bully.

'I'll be quick. I just want information.' My interest in unpicking this frankly demoralising turn of events is minimal, but if I can complete the picture for Jan, my sleuthing days will be over.

'You're having an affair,' I state.

'Maybe.'

'If you want to get rid of me, try proper answers.' My tone is pleasingly sassy. 'Does he call himself Mark?'

She nods. 'Who is . . . what did you call him?'

'Liam is the name he gave the other woman in his entourage.'

This creates a temporarily silence, although her expression says plenty.

'Are you with him too?' she asks.

'I was until last week.'

'There were three of us?'

'Three I know of.'

She breathes in and out a couple of times. I can tell she is fighting not to cry.

'How long have you been seeing him?' I ask.

'A year, a whole bloody year.' She bangs the doorframe with the heel of one hand. 'He said his girlfriend was dying. That's why we had to wait.'

'That part is true. She's got cancer and he's her part-time carer.'

'I'm leaving my husband.'

'In the new year?'

She nods.

'To go away with Mark?'

She doesn't answer.

'Me too,' I say. 'Lucky us, a threesome.'

'What a bastard.' She drops her head, raises a hand to wipe her eyes.

'If it's any consolation we all fell for it,' I say. 'The other woman, Jan, is as sharp as they come but he's a razor blade.'

'I don't fucking get it . . . what was it all about?'

She has asked the right question. 'I don't know. Well, sex, of course. And maybe the thrill of playing us.'

'Did he tell you about me?'

'No.' I explain about the pet tracker and she laughs. She doesn't, however, laugh when I explain the third woman, Jan, is in her eighties.

'Don't tell me they're . . .?' Her eyes are wide open in anticipation of my answer.

'Strictly platonic,' I say, because the alternative is too disturbing. 'She's rich.'

'He's disgusting. We should kill him.'

'How did you meet him?'

'He works in the pub.'

'How often do you see him?'

'It was three nights a week but the last month or so . . .' she purses her lips, '. . . he hasn't been able to get away. When did he start seeing you?'

'October.'

Neither of us states the obvious: that I am the replacement pussy.

'Did he ever take you to Exmouth?'

She shakes her head. 'Why?'

'No reason.'

'Do you think I'm a slut?' she asks.

'I can hardly judge.'

'Are you married?'

'Engaged,' I say and she starts to giggle. I think it must be a reaction to the absurdity of the situation because the trickle turns into a throaty belly laugh and I join in because people laughing, like people falling, is funny. But the impulse quickly fades to something more bitter.

'What will you do?' I ask her.

'I was meant to be seeing him tomorrow, but he can fuck right off.'

'You're not tempted to wait in case he comes good?'

She shakes her head. 'I probably wouldn't have gone with him anyway. He fancied Thailand but I'm not good in the heat.'

'How long have you been married?'

'Eleven years.'

'Bloody hell, you were young.'

'We were free spirits. Disobeyed our parents and got hitched in the registry office.' She sighs. 'He had a ponytail and a poncho and now he's bald and wears joggers.'

I laugh. 'Sounds like grounds for divorce.' Nosiness, not intuition, makes me ask, 'What does your husband do?'

'He's a paramedic.'

I shake my head at the gall of Mark Liam Turner. 'Mark has been pretending to be a paramedic.'

'What do you mean?'

'He leaves Jan's house in a green uniform and comes back full of gossip from his shifts.'

'Arsehole.' She looks down at her watch. 'Can you go now? The last thing I need is my husband finding you here.'

'I'd rather you didn't mention anything about me to Mark,' I say.

'Sure.'

'And Jan doesn't want him to know he's been found out because at the moment she still relies on him.'

She nods. 'I'll tell Mark I've decided to give it another go with my husband. Turns out I'm quite good at lying.'

I leave without asking her name or offering mine.

Back home, I text Jan with the barest information. Knowledge isn't power in this instance; knowledge is pain.

39

The Prisoner's Dilemma

'Have you given up on the choir?' asks Ben.

'Yes,' I say, reaching for my last slice of takeaway pizza. 'I decided I sing enough at church.'

'I thought you said you liked it.'

I shrug, and peel an escaped mushroom from the lid of the box.

Jan rang an hour ago with the news that Mark was staying in, having supposedly swapped shifts. He is, I assume, staying in because his other, other woman has cancelled their dates in perpetuity, but didn't have a chance to share this intel because Jan had already ended the call. I wasn't planning to go to choir anyway, still freaked out by Mark's staggering audacity.

While I tear and fold the pizza boxes into a more recyclable shape, I can hardly believe he has stood in this kitchen amiably chatting to Ben. His actions are so unexpected I'm not sure we're playing the same game. If he is a chess grandmaster, I am the opposite side of the board with a set of draughts, several missing. When we were kids, we used a selection of random items – bottle tops, coins, dice – to be the lost pieces. I always bagsied the cotton reel. Rust-brown thread that Dad once used to pull out my wobbly tooth. Brave girl, he'd called me.

I stay with this memory. Brave feels good.

'Shall we put a string up somewhere for the Christmas cards?' Ben asks.

I am about to agree when my pre-frontal cortex is assaulted by a stratagem with an inordinately pleasing level of pluck.

'Do you know, Ben, maybe I will go. Carols are always uplifting.'

He looks up from his phone. 'Shall I give you a lift?'

'Thanks, but I like the cycle.' A single truth in the vast sea of lies.

I rush upstairs to borrow from Ben's collection of skiwear, emerging with a base layer tucked into my jeans and mittens and a neck warmer. I'm going to be late but will at least avoid a repeat of yesterday's frozen fingers.

Everything about today's cycle is different. The air is crystal clear, cold but crisp, and my mood is bright and buoyant and my speed is sure and swift. And, suddenly, I am an alliterative poet.

Mark's car is in the drive, as expected. I throw my bike in the usual spot and, with only a deep breath to arm myself, let myself in. The songbirds are already warbling, a lovely rich sound that swells to fill every available corner. I open the lobby door and slide in at the edge of the other sopranos. Jan has her back to me and doesn't turn around for the duration of the first two carols. When she does spot me, I wink twice because once might look like a twitch. She responds with a deeper furrow of her already wrinkled forehead and a finger pointing to the bedrooms to indicate he is upstairs. I don't want her to worry so I tap my own forehead in the hope that she'll realise my presence is intentional.

This evening the loudest tenor interrupts the flow to respectfully suggest reversing the order of carols six and seven. In the pause, where he is firmly put in his place, I sidle over to Jan and convey the pertinent information. Whether she thinks I'm unhinged or a genius, I can't tell, nor does it matter.

We are on the last bar of the last chorus, mouths wide open to achieve the required crescendo, when Mark begins his catwalk down the grand staircase. He stops at the midpoint, lets his face ease into a smile, and one by one, the masses look up at him in his rightfully exalted position. He basks in the adoring gazes. A man who dons a uniform to save those most in need; a man who has assuaged their doubts through his selfless care of their precious friend, Jan.

His eyes sweep past me and I catch the stutter, the double take, but he is instantly back in character. It is my turn to beam up at him. He invaded my territory and now I have returned the favour.

The melee thins as people take their leave. Mark waits until there is only a sprinkling of us, before heading straight to Jan's side. I can't hear the exchange, but can see, like last week, she is tired, struggling to keep a straight back and a vertical neck. However, when he grips her under one arm, she firmly pushes his hand away. He should know to wait until everyone has gone; I know, and I only met her two and a half weeks ago. I moonwalk across and rise up in front of his face.

'Hi, I'm Anna. You must be Liam.'

'Yes, hello. A new recruit to the choir?'

'A few weeks,' I say. Bold. I remember telling Jan we could be bold. 'I gather you're a paramedic. That must be a difficult job.'

'Quite the opposite. People are always pleased to see a paramedic.'

Angie bowls in. 'Hello, Liam, I didn't expect to see you this early on a Monday. Been sacked?'

'Not yet, but the day may come. How are you, Angie?'

'Good.' She switches her attention to Jan. 'Hello, my love.'

'I'll be off,' I say to no one in particular and walk to the door, my mission completed.

We now have a prisoner's dilemma, albeit an adulterous version with a twist. As my legs spin, sending feelgood hormones around my body, I work through the permutations.

If Mark and I keep each other's secrets, we both win. If Mark and I both betray each other, we both lose. If Mark tells Ben, but I don't tell Jan, he wins. If I tell Jan, but he doesn't tell Ben, I win. But, friend inside my head whom I am addressing, the twist is that I have already told Jan, so there only two possible outcomes, both of which mean Mark loses. I could, in theory, also lose, but Mark won't tell Ben because, unlike the theoretical model, we are not being held in separate cells so there would be nothing to stop me telling Jan.

The smugness is good, the satisfaction of finally killing that buzzing bluebottle. Perhaps I could study game theory, develop complex variations of risk and reward that can predict behaviour and be regularly cited in academic articles. How Sofia would squirm at seeing my name on those long, dry, spidery articles she read.

I have crossed the main road to join the deserted back road that will lead me most of the way home when a possible problem occurs to me. To preserve the status quo, I need Jan to both keep schtum and continue to suffer Mark's presence. If she tells him, all bets are off, and if she evicts him, ditto. When she dies, double ditto; my ammunition will be redundant. This does not dismay me. I don't think Jan will render him homeless or pop her clogs any time soon.

I have definitely bought myself some breathing space. And Mark's ardour will cool. Of course it will.

A fringe of light appears ahead, wavering and eerie. A nano-second later this is elucidated by the noise of a car. No one uses this single-track road so I immediately picture a young man racing along with a few beers on board, maybe showing off to his mates. I brake and place my left foot on the spongy verge, intending to wait for the car to pass. There is ample room, assuming his judgement isn't addled, but as I stare at the approaching lights, some alarm centre in my brain goes from aware to amber. From amber to flashing red. The urgent thrumming inside my jacket matches my whizzing brain, calibrating, recalibrating. Speed and distance and volume and light intensity. I pray for the screech of brakes.

But the countdown reaches six . . . five . . . four . . .

The roar of the engine is predatory, firing every flight response.

Blinded by the full beam, I yank my bike across the bumpy scrub, feel my ankle wrench as it encounters a dip and reach out, grabbing barbed wire. Despite the rip of flesh and sharp sting, I hold on, eyes shut, breath suspended.

40

Tell 'em about the money, honey

'Were you trying to kill me?' I ask.

The past tense might not be apt. I am alone, in the pitch-dark, on a stretch of largely unused road.

'Of course not. I was trying to catch you,' says Mark.

'Catch me like a fish or catch me like . . . a cold?'

He laughs. 'Catch you like someone I want to talk to.'

'About?'

'I would have thought we have plenty to discuss, my lady sleuth.'

'Ben will come looking for me if I don't get home soon.'

'He seemed very nice.'

'Thank you.'

'Makes me wonder why you took up with me.'

'Same,' I say.

'How did you find out?'

'The moussaka.' Despite the cold, the lateness, the apprehension in the air, the clotting blood that has glued my fingers together, I am ludicrously proud.

'You're going to have to help me out.'

'Jan wrote a review about eating moussaka at the studio in Exmouth.'

'I'm impressed,' he says.

The sexual tension is a taut ribbon, silky and dark, tied with an extravagant bow. But it isn't real. It is the attraction of a patient snatched from the jaws of death by the actions of a young doctor, or two strangers locked out of a youth hostel on an otherwise uninhabitable Scottish island, or the lure of the forbidden, unexpectedly alone with your best friend's boyfriend or your boss.

'I'm not what you think,' he says.

'I'm not sure I'm interested.'

'I look after Jan. She has a better life because I'm part of it.'

'Nothing is true, Liam.' His other name tastes like metal against my fillings.

'My care for her is true. We share good food, enjoy each other's company.'

'But do you care about her?'

'Yes. She is a fierce, brilliant woman.'

I don't want my resolve to lessen, to dilute, to disappear. His plausibility is part of his trickery.

'So why not be honest with her?'

'She might be eighty but she is human. She must know I'm not a monk, but only a streak of cruelty would have me tell her.'

I have not considered that Jan might have been happier not knowing, that my telling her was cruel. What was straight in my mind is now tilting. If I hadn't intervened, she could have gone to her grave with a seemingly loyal man by her side.

'Don't come to my house again,' I say.

'I won't. I didn't intend to. Ben is chatty.'

'Your presence in the village was entirely intentional.'

'I was hoping to see you.'

'To what end?'

'I meant it, Anna. When Jan dies, I'm going away. Come with me.'

The temptation to scoff is strong but I am a prisoner with a dilemma and I must act accordingly. I do not know about the woman in Badger's Rise or his job in the pub. I have not told Jan.

'I need to go.'

'Thank you for not telling Jan. That was kind.'

'She's not my concern,' I say, with as much derision as possible. My fondness must stay hidden or the model will collapse and Ben and I will be burnt toast.

'Could we have a coffee on Thursday? No kissing. Just a coffee and a Bakewell slice?'

'I'm getting married.'

'I know. I met your mother-in-law, remember. Thursday, Anna, a civil conversation, that's all, between two people who, for their own reasons, lied to each other.'

Keep your enemy close, they always say. I might need a few days to work out why, but for now I need to get home. 'Okay. Bakewell, no kissing.'

My phone judders in my pocket. I glance, in case Ben is about to come looking for me. The message is from Jan, asking me to text when I'm home safely – she is concerned at how suddenly Mark left.

He insists on putting my bike in his hatchback, agreeing to drop me on the outskirts of the village. In the passenger seat, I look across and wonder. I wonder if I have underestimated him. If his set-up with Jan were jeopardised, would he turn nasty? My amateur behavioural model is too simplistic, not allowing for the other variables, the most important of which is money. I need to ask Jan the burning question: what happens to her money?

41

Unwell Women

On Thursday morning I can't go to my swimming lesson because I am completely unable to get out of bed. Every morning this week the alarm has woken me like a blow to the head. I blame the interminable nature of the winter term. The children are exhausted, there is more indoor play because of the weather and the long build-up to Christmas brings equal measures of excitement and irritability. I turn on my phone to text Frank my apologies, ask Ben not to slam the door when he leaves for the office, roll over and go back to sleep.

I materialise a couple of hours later thanks to a stream of texts from Jan: she has made a decision, wants to see me, we need to talk, but Liam has been home all week, claims to have taken holiday from work, could she come over to my house one day? Angie would bring her.

I sigh. The situation was so much more straightforward when we believed Jan was the provider of worldly goods and I was the plaything. Without the discovery of the other, other woman, Jan might have found a way to be grateful for Mark's companionship and forgiven him his little titillation on the side. Maybe she still can. He might be a liar and a philanderer but his presence does enable her to stay in her own home. Perhaps acceptance is the answer. Perhaps she has come to the same conclusion and wants to make sure I have no plans to confront the toad.

I decide not to reply until I have met Mark for 'Bakewell, no kissing', an assignation that is very unappealing but infinitely preferable to risking another impromptu visit *chez moi*.

Once again, I chauffer Dee to the hospital, parking easily and seeing her into the foyer, but I don't leave. The desire to stay close is strong, has the pull of a magnet. I draw her into a chat about the boys' skiing weekend, almost making her late.

Woodies is busy, busy. There is no free table and, as yet, no Mark, so I order a tea – a sugary cake has no appeal – and fulfil an ambition by asking to join the grey-haired women who are always laughing. They will make perfect buffers for whatever Mark has to say.

'I'm Bronwyn,' says the more vivid of the two women, 'and this is Pat.'

In order to not confuse them I make a mental note: Bronwyn is wearing bright pink lipstick and a purple scarf, Pat is slight and overly beige.

Bronwyn tells me she has had a stroke and is currently having a course of hydrotherapy; before that she had breast cancer. Pat drives her every week and in return Bronwyn buys the cream tea. I share my reason for frequenting the café and they, emboldened, comment on my friendship with the man they jokingly call Nova, short for Casanova. My nickname is Plum, because I'm a plum catch evidently. They are disappointed when I declare my ring to be an attachment to someone else.

'He sat with us a few times,' says Bronwyn. 'Such a nice man. Are you sure you've picked the right fiancé?'

They giggle.

'I hope so. How can you tell?'

'If you don't know, we can't help you,' says Bronwyn.

'Your husband was a pig,' says Pat, and they laugh again.

'How long have you known each other?'

'We were at school together. And now we're sixty-five. How has that happened, Bronwyn?'

'In a flash, and we've got a few more years.'

'I wish I had a school friend,' I say, and the dust that was Pippa spits like sherbet.

'We liked watching you and Nova,' says Bronwyn. 'Were you just friends?'

'I'm afraid so.'

'Not everyone is friendly nowadays, more's the pity,' says Pat.

'He was very kind to that posh lady – you remember, Pat, the one with the silver hair?'

I wonder if she means Jan.

'I think he has been unlucky in love,' says Pat, 'because we used to see him with Julie who had the terrible MS.'

'That was a sad case,' says Bronwyn.

'She has multiple sclerosis?' I ask, keen to keep the subject alive.

'Had.' Bronwyn puckers her painted lips in sorrow. 'Primary progressive – the worst kind. If you come to Woodies often enough you get to know all the stories.'

'We call it Wooden,' says Pat. This sets Bronwyn off again and I laugh in anticipation of the punchline. 'Because the customers all end up wooden.'

'How old was the lady with MS?' I ask, hoping the answer isn't seventy.

'Young. Was she late thirties, Bronwyn?'

'Something like that. Life can be cruel.'

They nod at each other.

'We'd better get going, I suppose,' says Pat. She stands up and helps Bronwyn with her coat and, after warm goodbyes, they walk arm in arm to the door.

The suspicion Mark deliberately lurked at the fringes of the hospital to prey on unwell women nearing the end of life solidifies into fact, making my skin shrink, pinching my eyes and forcing my nose to twitch. The only remedy is to immediately archive the information. I have the measure of him. He cannot sink lower.

The hands on the clock above the door shudder past three and Mark remains a no-show. What does his absence mean? I could unblock his number and ask, but haven't the inclination.

Maybe he always intended to stand me up. A quid pro quo for when I stood him up. A parting shot before a future where I never see him again. Finding a new fuck buddy has to be easier than pursuing one who knows his secrets. Yes, the chances are I am off the hook.

As I walk back to the hospital, my feet spring higher with each step, the weight of adultery lifting from the bottom up.

Dee is waiting in the foyer. Steve has had to dash, evidently. On our way to the car, she asks, 'Did you see that nice man today?'

'No, not today.' I wonder whether Hannah has had a sneaky word.

'Only Ben said he bumped into him in the village.'

'I know, what a coincidence. Actually, I did meet some nice people today though – two lovely women in the café let me share their table.'

'Richard used to talk to everyone. In queues, in cafés, even in the cinema.' She smiles to herself.

'I think all eating establishments should force you to share tables with strangers. Think what it could do for loneliness.'

'I sometimes feel lonely, you know, Anna. Despite having all of you.'

'I can imagine.' And I do imagine. I imagine letting myself into the house and there being no Ben, and I don't like it.

'It's nice having Steve around.'

She is dropping breadcrumbs for me. 'Are you becoming a thing?'

'Would that be all right, do you think?'

'Of course.'

'I'm not sure Milly would agree. She was very close to her dad.'

'Anyone who has your best interests at heart couldn't help but be pleased.'

'Thank you.' Assuming the topic is closed, I am about to ask her about today's session when—

'He stayed the night.'

I take my eyes off the road to check her expression, look back to find the car in front is braking. Instinct makes me slam my foot down, way too fast, way too hard, and we both lurch towards the windscreen.

As the seat belt tightens across my chest, the soreness almost makes me cry out. Wild thoughts send indecipherable messages around my body, making my tongue a stick and my armpits a lake.

'Are you shocked?' she asks.

'No,' I say, staring at the lights of the car in front to try to find some focus. 'I mean, yes, but in a good way.'

'I'll tell the family in my own time.'

'Understood.'

Dee starts to talk about Richard, and their courtship and wedding, which leads her on to Milly's and Jamie's weddings and the wedding in the village where the groom didn't turn up because he had undiagnosed concussion from the stag night and went to watch the rugby instead. Thankfully, I am only required to listen.

I refuse her offer of tea and walk briskly home. As soon as I'm inside I slide a hand up my T-shirt. My boobs are so tender I can't believe I hadn't noticed before. Maybe I am about to have a period – I have been running my packets of pills together so have absolutely no recollection of when I last bled. I go upstairs, fairly sure there is a pregnancy test left over from the last pack of two Ben bought.

I pee on the tip of the premium digital test with a weeks indicator. And wait. And think about Ben. And about Ben and me. And our wedding. And what married life will be like.

Yesterday he made me laugh by running through the pros and cons of marrying in a cold month versus a warm month – an attempt to make me hurry up and choose – but still I stalled, unable to see beyond the obstacle that is Mark.

But if Mark is no longer an obstacle . . .

Ben arrives home with a ready-made chilli con carne, two individual treacle puddings and a carton of custard.

'I can see how tired you are, so I thought we'd have a TV dinner.'

This is exactly what I want.

See, he makes you happy, says my internal voice.

Full of comfort food, I lie with my head on Ben's lap. He moves the throw to cover my legs, and the film – a stranger knocking on the door of a swanky house, a barking dog, a power cut – slips away.

'Anna.' I hear but don't hear. It is so nice in the dark and I am so dopey and so cosy and Ben's hand is playing with the hair at the nape of my neck and I could stay here forever.

'Let's go to bed.'

I take a while, but eventually lever myself up and turn to look at him. My Ben. I kiss him.

'Thank you,' I say.

'For being your pillow or for feeding you ultra-processed food?'

'Both.'

A rush of sweet, swirling dopamine collects in my decision centre, tipping the scales.

The little cluster of cells might not hold. But it might. It just might. And if it does, I may not have much of an instinct for how to parent, but I can learn from Ben. He has been nurtured by the best. He has enough for both of us.

'How much warning do you have to give to get married in church?' I frame the question as a casual enquiry.

'Three weeks of reading the banns, I think.' He swallows a lump. 'Why?'

I am still idly curious. 'What date would that take us to?'

He is trying really, really hard not to smile. 'You tell me, Anna Harris.'

I pretend to count on my fingers. 'I make it the second of January. Would you be up for that?'

42

Red Arrows

Deciding to get married in a hurry is fun. The news breaks on Friday morning via a videocall to the Slater clan and spreads faster than when four caravans of travellers appeared on the playing field.

The whole village goes into overdrive, no one denied a task. From texts to knocks on the door and notes dropped through the letterbox, all offers of help are accepted. Whether the green borders that will line our wedding parade need winter mowing or not, they will be mown. Whether the bell ringers need an extra practice, one is scheduled anyway. Whether the flowers in the church should match those in the marquee, a special taskforce will decide.

Ben takes an impromptu day off work and by the time I'm back from my driving lesson there is a schedule with each task itemised and, where possible, responsibility allotted. Red arrows show what he calls 'the critical path'.

In my role as interested observer, I say, 'Surely the aisle is the critical path?'

'What might be the critical path is my mother's outfit,' he says, and we share a smile.

Never was there a more relaxed bride: easy-going about the

menu for the wedding breakfast, about the time at which we gather to make our vows, about the choice of fizz . . . although with very definite views about the music for the service.

My mum would probably ask for a DNA test if she knew how affecting I find the soundtrack of church. How I emerge with my internal commentary hushed, my footings more sure.

Unfortunately, Mum won't be coming to the wedding. Someone would be bound to mention the half-term trip to Glasgow that didn't happen and I would be found out. So I told Ben I'd sent her a save-the-date text and pretended she'd replied saying she was sorry but will be away in Madeira.

The physical invitations – designed by Ben in a clever app – will be here next week, ready to send to the fifty-three (minus Mum and her Ben) who made the list. We'll have to dispense with the tradition of separating the bride's side from the groom's or my half will have people weeping in pity.

On Sunday morning the sky is a thick, moody grey and the ground is a confusion of puddles. Ben has joined me and Dee on our promenade because the banns are going to be read, but quickly falls behind, waylaid by tearful congratulations from Sally Wood (whose husband is back in hospital).

Dee takes the opportunity to ask if there are any colours of dress she should avoid.

'Maybe black.'

'Anna, be serious. I don't want to clash with the bridesmaids and ruin the photographs.'

'I'd like you to wear something you love.'

'Are you not going to give me a clue?' Both Dee and Milly have offered to go shopping with me but I am resisting. I don't want to look like a Slater on my wedding day.

'Well, Daisy wants pink, and Bridget says Tallulah and Sasha don't mind what colour but please can they not be itchy. So now you know as much as me.'

She tuts, which is a departure because she has hardly stopped crying since our announcement.

The walk up the aisle to our usual pew is accompanied by generous smiles from the worshippers already seated. If I'd known we were going to be the star attraction, I'd have brushed my hair.

In the quiet imposed by the sermon, I ransack the recent past for the nth time looking for a clue as to how and when my contraception failed. Mark always, always used a condom and every single day I took a pill with my morning tea. I haven't had any drugs that might interfere with the pill's efficacy or picked up a tummy bug at school or even noticed a change in bowel habits. Presumably it is because I'm in the house of the lord that my mind skitters off to imagine a virgin birth. The baby neither Ben's nor Mark's. Lunacy, clearly. I literally ground myself by pressing the soles of my trainers into the stone floor.

This baby will stick or twist based on biology. Soon enough, I will know. For now, there is nothing to be done.

At the end of the service, the well-wishers are several rows deep. Coffee takes ages, Ben and I only just making it home before a deluge of rain comes hammering down. While we drink soup from a mug – one of the few Harris habits to infiltrate his Slater life – we laugh at videos of people's first dances and decide not to do one.

Ben is going to Jamie's to watch the football and I am going to visit Jan, whose very lovely congratulations text in response to my news was followed by several increasingly urgent messages saying it's imperative she sees me. As cycling is out of the question in this horrific weather, Ben offers to take me.

'Or you can drive, if you like?' he says.

I do like. Ben's Audi has pep.

'Do you think I should bail on the boys' ski weekend?' he asks. 'There's a lot to organise.'

'No, definitely not. Jamie and Finn would never forgive you. It'll all get done somehow.'

'I suppose so.'

'But you must wear that brace. I don't want a lame husband, dragging a withered leg up the aisle.'

'For better or worse.'

'There's an exclusion for pre-existing conditions.'

'Brake!' Ben stamps on an imaginary pedal as I almost ground his car in the dip before the humpbacked bridge.

'Sorry.'

'Bloody hell, Anna. You're meant to be a learner.'

I adopt a more cautious style, indicating well in advance of Jan's drive and turning in slowly to avoid scattering the gravel. As promised, there is no red car. Mark has gone out and isn't due back until the early hours. Angie is tasked with getting Jan to bed.

'Do you want to come inside and say a quick hello?'

'Okay,' he says.

'Great.' I lean over and kiss his lovely rounded Ben-cheek and am appalled those same lips ever caroused with Mark's slimy tongue. Must remember to use newfound better judgement going forward.

We dash across the gravel and I let us in, hollering: 'I hope you're decent, Jan, only I've brought my fiancé.'

'Bring him in, Anna. I'm agog.'

Ben strides through the hall ahead of me. 'Hello, Jan,' he says. 'I've heard all about you.'

'Nothing good, I hope.'

'Fifty-fifty,' he says, and she laughs.

'Sit, young man.' She pats the seat cushion next to her and Ben settles in, no sense that he is itching to get round to Jamie's.

'There is no mistaking your lineage. You've inherited more than your fair share from your father . . .

'. . . couldn't sit still, always had a pencil spinning between his fingers.

'. . . took the baton and ran past the lot of them.'

Ben laps up every word about his dad. The absence of Richard on our wedding day isn't something I've given any attention. Perhaps I'll ask Dee how she thinks we should acknowledge him – a toast to absent friends seems underwhelming. And Ben might feel he has to mention my dad and my vile shit of a brother, which I could do without. (For the record, I have absolutely no regrets about feeding Simon those pretty little pills he loved. Not one.)

As I listen to Ben and Jan, I am aware of some spectacular disassociation at play. I know Jan has come to a decision and I'm hoping that decision is to continue to accept Mark's care and have no concern for his hidden life.

If, however, that decision is to disrupt Mark's comfortable exist-ence, there will undoubtedly be consequences for me and yet I am blissfully unbothered. I am skipping along while beneath me the fault lines are gathering potential energy, readying to unleash devastation, but that is still to come.

Even when their conversation moves on to the wedding, the

wedding Mark could so easily scupper, I remain serene, unaware of any lapping waves from the impending tsunami.

'I won't need a partner,' says Jan. 'I can dance with my walker – much more compliant than any man I've ever known.'

I interject, knowing Ben will be desperate to catch at least some of the match. 'Ben, you need to go or you'll be coming straight back.'

He jumps up. 'Bye, Jan. It was really nice hearing you talk about my dad.'

'It was good therapy for me,' she says. 'Jogged my memory, what's left of it.'

'I'll pick you up at six-forty, Anna.' At seven, we're expected at the pub where the anxious chef is going to present a selection of dishes he can scale up for our big day.

'Great.'

'There's no need,' says Jan. 'Anna can borrow my car – it's no use to me.'

'She'd need to pass her test first,' says Ben, and is gone.

The look on Jan's face is positively slapstick – a mismatch of horror and amusement, startled eyes but a laughing mouth. I have no hope of controlling my own impulse to smile. The little madam who courted trouble, always prepared to go one step further for the laugh, the attention, the glory – she lives on.

'You intimated that you were lawless, Anna Harris.'

I shrug my shoulders. 'Good haircut, by the way.' The straight edges of her new bob fall level with her chin.

'Isn't this what women do? Believe the hairdresser can solve all manner of problems.' She tilts her head to affect a jaunty pose.

'Supposedly. But I've always chosen vodka. How's the leg?'

'Very tentative healing.'

'Good. The tree is magnificent, by the way.' The whole bay is taken up by the lushest Christmas tree; teal and racing-green brushes hold metallic baubles in every sheen from sparkling crystal to the foxed finish of old mirrors. No colour, no tinsel.

She nods. 'All Liam's work.'

When nothing emerges in reply (because I am choked by the concatenation of the ugly and the beautiful) she continues, 'I'm going to evict him.'

If this declaration brings more stirrings of thunder underground, I still hear nothing.

'I don't want to leave this life I have loved in the company of a man like Liam. I've got a live-in carer coming next Saturday who will stay till the end.'

I sniff away the sob.

'None of that. I feel empowered actually. My last hurrah.'

'Who is she?'

'He. I like a man. Harry is the son of an old friend.'

Harry has been running a hostel in Patagonia for two decades and needed a reason to come home. His dad is dead and his mum, Jan's friend, is in sheltered accommodation, but retains her marbles. Jan, or rather Jan's generosity, is providing the catalyst.

'He wants to see if he can reconnect with British life,' she says. 'I am merely the stopgap.'

Once more, I stifle tears.

'When are you going to tell Mark?' (I still can't call him Liam.)

'He knows Harry is coming to visit.'

'But not why?'

'I thought I might wait until Harry is in situ – just a precaution.'

'Are you scared?'

'I don't think so, although . . . my physical vulnerability is a worry.'

Here it comes. I swallow the first attempt, but the second comes out cleanly. 'Have you left him anything in your will?'

'There are bequests to charities, to people I've known along the way, but the house and a lump sum was left to Liam.' She smiles but it has no warmth. 'I imagined he might marry and fill the house with children. There hasn't been a family in this house for too long.'

This was not a game for Jan; this was her last love. I remind myself to measure with my heart.

'You said "was"?'

She nods. 'I changed my will this week. New executor – Meryl has kindly stepped in – new beneficiaries.' She dusts off her hands. 'Signed and safely lodged with the solicitor.'

'Mark doesn't know, I assume?' Stupid question.

'Are you worried he'll blame you?'

'Maybe.' Incredibly, my feet stay dry, when all around the water is rising, warning of the life-threatening flood. My hand strays to my pulse, nice and steady.

'I will try very hard not to incriminate you, but we're dealing with a smart man, remember.'

'When exactly is Harry coming?'

'Saturday lunchtime. Angie is picking him up from the train station.'

My internal pencil draws a comic strip: four squares with black pen strokes on grainy newspaper following the face-off between a long, lean Mark and a short, bulky, hairy Harry (for contrast I assume) that ends with them both rolling on the floor, bottom cracks on show.

'Is Harry a big chap?' I ask

'Not particularly, he was a chorister.' She shows me a picture of a slim, wan man with the classic M-shape of male-pattern baldness. He is wearing a white shirt and looks like he belongs in an office, not a South American hostel.

The giggles ripple through me – perhaps this is the beginning of the panic I should have been experiencing throughout our exchange. My juddering unstoppable laughter infects Jan and we sit, the pair of us, rocking and crying.

When I've indulged the delicious feeling long enough, I disappear into the kitchen to make us both tea, re-emerging with a neatly arranged tray and more questions.

'Does Angie know about Mark?' I ask, in sober mood now.

'She knows he is not what he claims to be.'

'Didn't she ask for details?'

'I expect she will – she was dashing off.'

'What will you do with Mark's stuff? Will it be waiting in the hall in black bin liners?'

'Anna, I haven't bothered with the minutiae.'

'I think you should. Once you've told him, he needs to leave immediately.'

'I'll have a think.' Her jowls hang low, a visual burden of what lies ahead. If I weren't implicated I'd distract her with a lighter subject.

'If you were Mark, would you tell Ben about our affair?'

'I'm not a spiteful person, too old.' She sighs. 'I will do everything I can to keep the spotlight away from you.'

'He'll want a reason.'

My fingernail settles nicely between my top and bottom teeth. I am preparing to bite one edge when Jan slaps my hand. 'Stop that.'

'You could say you tracked him to Badger's Rise – it's the truth after all.'

We debate what his reaction might be but, in reality, there is no debate.

When Mark realises his long game has been scuppered seconds before the whistle, he will seek to destroy me. Despite knowing that, I remain indifferent. Jan and I could be discussing asylum seekers or *Eurovision* or the cruelty of breeding dogs that can't breathe. The consequences of her momentous decision simply refuse to sink in.

Having exhausted the best and worst scenarios we stray on to the history of the house.

'My aunt left it to me. She was also childless. Lived with her friend, Betty.' Jan raises one eyebrow.

'The love that dare not say its name.'

'People my age must have seen the greatest transformation of any generation in history.'

The longer we talk, the more her demeanour stiffens, becoming more redolent of the headteacher she once was. When Ben returns we are deep inside her life story and I'm sorry not to hear the end. But at least I leave her in better shape, the plan clearer in her head.

Knowing Mark's life is going to be turned upside down in six days rather crystallises my plan too.

43

No dogs, no Irish

Christmas week in school is convivial chaos. Miss Emery and I barely have time to breathe in between sprinkling glitter and fashioning cotton-wool beards. A reprieve comes on Wednesday morning when all the juniors gather in the hall to watch the infant nativity play and we get to stay in the classroom.

My update on our express wedding plans leaves the polished Miss Emery open-mouthed in shock. She cannot believe we have guests, we have invitations, we have a menu.

'Beef Wellington, and mushroom Wellington for the vegetarians.'

'What about the gluten-free?'

'Didn't I say? It's a prejudiced wedding. No dogs, no Irish, no fruitarians, no teetotal.'

She laughs.

'What about the dress?'

'I've managed to get appointments for Friday at a couple of places in Bath.'

'Heaven. Is your mum going with you?'

'Sadly not. I smile. 'She'd love to but she lives in Glasgow.'

Way too much of my life has been spent fretting about the

absence of a primal parental connection but the self-diagnosis stops here. Well-balanced people are those with a strong, enduring attachment. I might not have that with my mum but I have a chance with Ben. He will keep me afloat however low or high the tide, however calm or rough the waters.

'What sort of dress would you choose for me?'

Miss Emery picks up a pencil. I'm watching her sketch an unexpected 1950s affair with a solid bodice, long lacy sleeves and a high neck when my phone announces a text from Dee, asking if we want candles at the end of each pew.

'What is it?' asks Miss Emery.

'Wedding admin.'

'Lucky you.'

I don't feel lucky. At this moment I feel positively trepidatious. But I expect most people contemplating murder have a degree of nerves, even if they've done it before.

In the afternoon, the book corner provides the perfect antidote. I devour books so quickly the words hardly register, simply forming a stream of meaning. Listening to the children enunciate every syllable of every word is a joy, the stumbles, the mispronunciations all adding texture.

'What do you think is going to happen next?' I ask. I have high hopes but the consensus is the hero will be smashed to pieces by a rocket.

'Let's hope not.' I make a frowny face, and the bell goes.

For me, the autumn term is over. Miss Emery thanks me for my contribution and hands me a bottle of wine to go with my stash from the kids. I reciprocate with a holly-berry candle.

On the way home from school, I unblock Mark's number and

send a text asking why he stood me up last Thursday when we were meant to be having 'Bakewell, no kissing'. If a reply made of individual letters and spaces can fall over itself in eagerness, his does. A nail in his tyre, evidently. He has been agonising over whether he dare come to the village, was going to wait until Thursday and see if I turned up at the café.

I'll be there, I tell him. The two kisses are deliberate.

His reply is an ingratiating gush.

As I type *I've missed you* my fingers spasm in disgust.

On Thursday morning I swim and, after some toast and peanut butter that might as well be hydrangea paste on a loofah, I drive Dee to the hospital. The poor appetite could be attributed to pregnancy but the other symptoms – a complete lack of saliva, a blunt ache in my breastbone and palpitations in my neck – are definitely to do with my psyche. Despite which I maintain an adequate pretence at being Anna.

'Bye, Dee. See you later.'

I stride off in Sofia's dungarees, her chandelier earrings swinging, and Act One begins.

Rushing into Woodies, already smiling, is a promising beginning – an effective mask for my deep distaste for both Mark and the task. He picks up on my energy and leaps up, a hand on my back that follows through to a kiss on my cheek and a deliberate hesitation . . . to see if I object. I don't, obviously.

'Hi, Mark.'

'So good to see you,' he says, caramel consonants.

'I'm here against my better judgement.'

'But you're here.'

I nod. 'Better judgement is not my forte.'

My seat has a perfect view of my friends from last week so I raise my hand in greeting – 'Hello, Pat. Hi, Bronwyn.' Mark follows my lead, turning to acknowledge them before fixing me in his gaze.

'I couldn't be more sorry, Anna. I know I've laboured this, but you have to believe I had no agenda. You were serendipity.'

'Do you prefer me as Sofia?'

'No, I like you. Be Esmerelda, be Dawn, be Janice.'

This is an unfortunate slip. 'Why are you with Jan?'

'You know why.'

'Say it.'

'I saw a chance and I took it. But I stand by what I said. She has benefited, and everything she has given me has been of her own volition.'

'I'm not sure I can reconcile that in my head. Where's the line between opportunistic and taking advantage?'

'Wherever you draw it. I haven't hurt her, Anna.' He embarks on a tale of the companionable relationship he and Jan have enjoyed, emphasising the longevity, omitting any mention of the other, other woman, reminding me that I was in part to blame for our untimely connection. I am untouched by his spiel – rain on my golf umbrella.

'You made a beautiful tree,' I say, keen to feed his vanity.

'Her last Christmas. I decided it should be special.' Reflex makes me splay my fingers, all the better to poke his eyes out.

'When you weren't here last week I sat with Pat and Bronwyn.'

'Two very nice women.'

'They told me you had another friend who was unwell. That was tough luck, Mark.'

I can read his face. I couldn't describe the tiny changes but I

269

know he is not ashamed; he is amused at how cleverly he has reeled in an unknown number of women.

'She died.'

'And did you benefit?'

'I did.' My phone could be recording our conversation to hand to the police but we both know he has done nothing wrong. There is no law to prevent romantic exploitation of the vulnerable, only a moral code.

'And you'd say she did too.'

'I would. Why are you asking me these questions?'

'Because I can't decide.'

'Can't decide whether to continue to see me in parallel with your fiancé? Or can't decide whether to forsake me and marry the boy-next-door?' His choice of words seeps into my soul. 'Or, and this is what I hope, you might decide not to marry your steady man.'

'Why would I swap steady for storybook?'

'Because steady is, as we both know, stultifyingly dull.'

'What if I said a reminder of what's on offer might help me decide.' (I actually hate myself.)

'The goods can be sampled at any time.'

I hold his eye and don't falter. 'Ben is going away this weekend.'

Mark is not expecting this. 'Is he going anywhere nice?'

'Skiing,' I say. 'A long weekend in the Alps.'

Three days. Three days for me to engineer the right outcome.

'You don't ski?'

'A Rotherhithe upbringing is further from the slopes than the actual miles.' As I say this I wriggle in my foreign clothes; I should have come as Anna, not Sofia.

'You're far from home.'

'I feel quite at home with you.' I lick my lips before delivering the next line in my roughly outlined script. 'The studio is available this weekend.'

'You checked?'

'I did. You didn't book it the last time, did you?'

He shakes his head. 'People seldom bother to change the keycodes.'

'The owners could have turned up, or a cleaner.'

'They could. But I talked to the owners when I was there with Jan – they were staying in the main house. Fortunately, they winter in Antigua. The housekeeper-cum-gardener – delightful woman – pops in on a Thursday morning.'

So, so smug. So smug I'd like to suffocate him with a choux bun.

'Is the risk part of the fun, Mark?'

'I could ask you that.' He looks out of the window. 'Shall we continue this conversation as we walk?'

'Yes, let's do that.'

We head for the park. When our coat sleeves brush against each other, I have to smother the urge to recoil.

Hovering above, I watch a relaxed man with an easy gait, strolling along with a visibly less comfortable partner. I try to introduce some swagger, but misstep and turn on my ankle. I reach for his hand. The anchor is helpful.

He turns his head and his smile purrs, cat-like. My shoulders inch a little further down my back, my chest expands. He is not, at present, suspicious.

'So, what do you think about the weekend?' I ask.

'I'm not sure I can get away – it's short notice.'

'I think you can. I'm completely free from lunchtime tomorrow until Monday.'

He chews the left side of his lip. 'You know I can't leave Jan for long periods unless someone is covering.' Mentioning the arrival of Harry would be a mistake – Mark mustn't feel shoehorned. (And, stupid, stupid Anna, you are not meant to know about Harry.)

'Could you ask Angie?' I say. 'I can't imagine you'll have a problem coming up with an excuse.' My wry look won't stay so I scratch the tip of my nose.

He pulls his phone out of his jacket pocket and I exhale, slow and silent. I take a replacement breath and visualise the air plumping up my lungs, inviting my pulse to drop from boil to simmer. His text receives an instant response: ping! He composes a second text and receives another two pings in reply. He taps a longer sentence. My attention is taken by a squirrel, running at speed along the back of the park bench; the squirrel leaps fully ten times its length, lands with ease on the tip of a bendy branch that bows under the weight before bobbing back up as the squirrel flits to a higher, sturdier branch and continues up the tree.

Ping!

Mark cups my face in his cold hands. 'I've got half a free pass.'

'What does that mean?'

'From Saturday morning until Sunday evening I'm all yours.'

'I'll take it.' I am beaming. The beaming is genuine.

'This is an unexpected U-turn, Missy Anna.'

'Unexpected is good, yes?' I kiss him, because I feel exposed, but can't remember how to do what should come naturally. The movement of my lips, mouth, tongue is self-conscious – more reminiscent of dislodging a trapped seed from between two tight teeth than of passion. Chanting inside my head helps: *I am in love with Mark, I want to go away with him, I have doubts about Ben, Mark will have money, we can elope, I am Sofia, I am in love with Mark . . .*

I am the one who pulls away.

'I have to go.' I look down at my watch and see that I have fifteen minutes to spare. 'I need to pick up a couple of things from the supermarket.'

'Where shall I meet you?'

'The bus station – can we get going early? I want to make the most of our time.'

'Name your hour.'

'Nine?'

'Okay.' He leans in for another bout but my repugnance outweighs the fear of being discovered. I step back and manage a trill, playful goodbye before turning my back and striding off. The light head, the hollow insides, the boundless energy isn't fear, it isn't nerves or, heaven help me, a conscience; it is the high of the dare, it is the kick of operating outside the bell curve. Mark has no idea who he is pitted against.

For completeness, I go to the Co-op and buy carrots and a pint of milk, popping them in Dee's car before taking up my position in the hospital foyer.

'Hello, Anna,' says Steve. 'You're looking very bonny.'

'Thank you, Steve. I feel quite bonny.' Sofia's red dungarees do have a cheeriness of their own.

'I am so excited for the wedding,' he says.

'I'm glad you can come.'

'Dee says there's no gift list.'

'Come along and have the best time – that's the only gift we want.'

'I can definitely manage that.'

Dee slips her arm in Steve's. 'We're going mother-of-the-groom shopping together.'

'She'll look dynamite whatever she wears,' says Steve. 'I'm only there for the lunch.'

I wait in the car while they have a lengthy kiss goodbye. I assumed sexual attraction disappeared with the menopause but patently not.

'Are you and Steve common knowledge now?' I ask, once she's strapped in and we're on our way.

'You haven't heard then?'

'What?'

'I told Milly he was coming with me to your wedding and she started crying. Said he can't take Richard's place on the top table.'

I could assassinate Princess Milly, but choose diplomacy. 'I've got news for you, Dee. That won't be an issue because there is no top table.'

'What do you mean?'

'Ben and I have decided we want people to mingle so we're not going to have named seating.'

'I've never heard of that . . . but it sounds nice.'

'What's nice is that no one person will be lumbered with Uncle Eric.'

We both laugh. The last laugh of the day, in my case.

I arrive home to find a frazzled Ben: can't find this, can't find that. I am partly to blame, having borrowed some of his ski gear to use on my bike rides. Finally packed, he insists on checking the wedding spreadsheet and firing off a few messages. We go to bed late and he jerks in his sleep, rolls over and back, robs me of the duvet, thrusts it away. In surely the darkest hour of the night, he dresses by lamplight while I doze. He sits on the edge of the bed to kiss my cheek and I murmur a goodbye, but as he goes to move away I fling out one arm to drag him back, wrapping my body koala-style around his chunky ski jacket and kissing him hard.

I won't make it back from Exmouth. Something will go wrong. I will never see Ben again. He will come home and have no idea where I am. No one will know.

The foresight is crushing, rendering me both mute and immobile. I stay pinned in place until Ben physically unpeels me from his torso.

'I've got to go,' he says. 'It's only three nights.'

44

Romantic Tutu

Insisting on wedding-dress shopping before gallivanting off with Mark is something of a perversion. The existence of an outfit for my big day will have no effect on whether I get to wear it, but I refuse to come home empty-handed. I am taunting myself, putting everything firmly into place as though this will guarantee success.

My driving instructor drops me in Bath a few minutes before my first dress appointment and by twelve-thirty, I am sitting in a city centre bar, my off-the-peg dress sealed inside its silver cover and stashed under the table, the second appointment cancelled. I tried on three dresses: one that loosely mimicked Miss Emery's drawing, one suggested by the assistant and one I chose because the skirt reminded me of the miniature Sofia who ran past me that day at the hospital. The romantic tutu, as the assistant called it, was perfect: an achingly simple, weightless creation worthy of the ballet. I caught the assistant wiping away a tear, whether at my arresting beauty or as a sales tactic, I cared not. I was smitten.

Although mirrors are part of everyone's everyday life, I rarely study my reflection. A cursory check for food in my teeth or sleepy dust and I'm done. Broadly speaking, I know I'm slim, slightly above average height, have a nice face and no obvious flaws (except my character, of course) but wearing the dress, I stared in the way an artist might, tracing the curve of my waist, aware of the narrowness of my ankle in the shop's kitten heels and the length of my neck. I took in the slope of my hip and let my eye swoosh down the sweep of the skirt. The assistant – fawning, but not unbearable – fetched a veil attached to a comb and slotted it into my waiting ponytail. Ta-da! That is, unbelievably, all it takes to make a bride. I tried to buy the whole package but the shoes were a size too big; luckily, I found a similar pair online and ordered them while waiting for the bartender – who is my new best friend – to bring my celebratory virgin mojito.

'You bought a dress, shoes and a veil in under an hour,' he repeats.
'I did.'
'That's the sort of shopping I approve of. When are you getting married?'

While we chat, my brain leaps ahead, imagining I am already on my way back from Exmouth, unfettered and excited for the future.

But once home, bereft of either company or purpose – the dress is hung, my weekend packing complete – the exhilaration ebbs, leaving the empty hours of the day to drag unbearably. I wish Mark had been able to get away today. The wait until tomorrow feels interminable, the anticipation an insistent tick.

Tick. Tick. Tick. Tick . . .

My overnight bag, rucksack and coat are barring the front door like guard dogs. If they could speak, I feel they would urge me to reconsider: to cancel the trip and instead try to negotiate with Mark;

to confess my infidelity to Ben and hope for a favourable verdict; to let destiny decide my fate – but I can't, won't, take the risk.

I was wrong about buying the dress. Having had a preview of my wedding self, the next twenty-four hours have become more charged, the outcome more loaded, the possibility of failure more devastating.

Lying on my back on the sofa, I let my mind travel to the studio by the coast, to my memory of the terrain, to the map I have studied. The difficulties ahead are legion: partly because Mark is physically larger and irritatingly unpredictable, mostly because I am reliant on opportunity.

Exmouth has two bespoke dangers: water and cliffs, along with the universal threats of traffic, carbon monoxide, an overdose, falling, choking on a fishbone, electrocution from a passing lightning bolt or, more commonly, a faulty wire. The more examples that come to mind, the more I perceive the miracle to be that any of us survive the day. How capable we are to make it to bed without being mown down by a motorbike while taking a selfie of a cathedral or having a fatal anaphylactic reaction to an unknown allergen.

My preference for Mark is a cliff fall – a quick, clean (excluding the landing), blameless accident – but his agenda, his willingness to comply, his level of belief in my fickle emotions, they all have the potential to stymie the plan. The plan has been nicely composting since he trespassed in my kitchen, long before Jan decided to turf him out.

When I can no longer abide to indulge the infinite number of scenarios my internal cinema screen is intent on showing, I flip onto my side and turn on the television, immersing myself in late-afternoon easy-watching: antiques and property in the sun and game shows. And there I stay, with only the punctuation of a toast and marmalade supper washed down with tea, and a misspelt text from Ben, who has had a fantastic afternoon and whose knee feels 'as good as new'. He is, no doubt, oiled by mountain wine. I am effusive in reply.

At six-thirty in the morning, the alarm wakes me and anticipation catapults me out of bed. I load the boot of Ben's Audi, change the P and the L on his number plate to an R and an E using black electrical tape, reverse out of the garage, close the door behind me, and set off, the hood of my coat pulled over my head, a scarf over my mouth. I am not expecting any police involvement but better to have all eventualities covered. Ben's radio, tuned to grim news, is promptly turned off. Instead I sing hymns at cathedral volume. Doing is so much better than waiting – I feel the beginnings of a lift, a fever in the air, a not unpleasant tension.

Having parked in the multi-storey near the bus station and left the keys in the wheel arch – *why run the risk of having to explain ownership of an Audi?* – I celebrate the return of my appetite with a full English breakfast that tastes divine, smoky and unctuous. My empty plate has only a trace of baked-bean juice.

When Mark drives into a short-stay parking bay at the bus station and looks around from inside the car, I am already walking towards him. The door opens and out spring his long legs. Without the layer of glass, he becomes an apex predator. The jolt of fear short-circuits my nervous system and makes my human electricity run amok. Why did I think I could pull this off? There is a massive difference between a premeditated act and an uncontrollable impulse.

The other times were rash decisions, reflexes even, and therefore on some level understandable, perhaps forgivable. The plea of diminished responsibility while suffering from an abnormality of mind literally exists to allow for such deeds; deeds committed at moments of uncontainable emotion. Whereas this endeavour, like Mark himself, is in a different league.

45

Looking for Mermaids

'You're early,' says Mark, enveloping me.

'So are you,' I mumble into the coarse canvas of his sleeve.

'I couldn't sleep.' The force of him draws my gaze upwards and he swallows me whole.

'Let's get going,' says a chirpy Anna. 'I'm excited to see the sea again.'

With my luggage stowed, doors clunked and belts clicked, we head off.

'We're so lucky the forecast is dry,' I say, keen to blur my unease with a bubbly soundtrack. 'I looked earlier in the week and there was drizzle.'

'I feel lucky full stop.' His eyes leave the road to connect with mine, again. I attempt to match his expression despite the constriction across my chest.

Somehow we chat, aimlessly, affably, both presenting as relaxed, happy, relishing our escape. I owe Frank my fulsome gratitude for teaching me how to expand my lungs against their will. The rigidity of my upper body softens into the seat, into the undulations of our conversation, into the metronomic backdrop of the engine.

'Shall we plan what we're going to do?' We are on the motorway, fifty minutes to go according to the satnav.

'Can do.' I expected a lewd suggestion, but perhaps our recent chasteness has made him cagey.

'What's on your wish list, Mark?'

'I want to take your clothes off.' Ah, that's more like it. My groin – clearly out of kilter with my head – wakes up.

'That won't fill the day.'

'Is that a challenge?'

'I thought we could do that beautiful walk again – along to Budleigh Salterton.' I sing the name.

'Or we could go the opposite way?'

No, no, no – I have studied the map, we are not going that way.

'Are you worried we're already in a rut?'

'I can think of nothing more splendid than being in rut with you.'

'We could have lunch at that café where we met the couple who'd been married forever.'

'They'd be pleased to see a ring on your finger.'

I ignore Mark's comment; I'm never removing my ring.

'I think the menu had crispy duck wraps.'

'I wouldn't want to stand between you and a crispy duck.'

'Wise decision.'

'We could cycle there?' he says.

'But then we'd miss the drama of the cliffs.' I am already a jitterbug, interpreting his objections as prescience.

'True.'

The immediate itinerary agreed, we stray on to Christmases past, on to Mark's eclectic history of car ownership and my funny story about taking a Mandy bomb in school. May as well be entertaining.

'I can score for you,' I offer, 'if you fancy experimenting?'

'Why would I want to escape from this reality?' He places his hand on my thigh.

'Where does Jan think you are?'

'Swapping presents with my sister. What about you? Won't your absence be noticed in that claustrophobic village of yours?'

'I'm having a weekend to myself, getting organised for Christmas.'

'What if I don't let you go home?'

'It's not up to you.'

By late morning a strong, round sun has driven away the morning mist and the day is exactly as advertised on the weather report: dry and bright, not too cold but with a definite breeze. We are driving along the seafront, minutes from the studio, and I'm pleased to note my body is in stasis, my disposition level. A long journey has been an effective way to reboot our relationship. So far, so good.

Mark gets organised: unpacking our luggage from the boot, opening a window to let the stale air escape and turning up the thermostat, putting champagne in the fridge.

'No moussaka this time?'

'I thought we could neck the champagne and then sample whatever the metropolis has to offer.'

'Prawns in Marie Rose followed by a steak?'

'We can but hope.'

My smile disappears as soon as I've shut the bathroom door – the level of fakery, even for a consummate faker, is exhausting. In the mirror I spy a little frown that I pull apart with my fingers.

As I wee, I shut my eyes and let the impending drama play out. Two innocent tourists stray too close to the cliff edge. They are looking out to sea, pointing, their attention firmly on the horizon, unaware that the ground is an unstable platform. A patch of slippery mud, a camber and a meddlesome rock is all it takes.

Having checked there is no blood on the toilet paper, I flush, wash my hands, press my feet into the tiled floor and re-enter the world.

'Oh, goodness!'

Mark is standing in the doorway, in fact, blocking the doorway. He reaches for me and we kiss and kiss. We both know how this goes, except I am no longer an eager bedfellow. Reluctance would be out of character but enthusiasm feels too great an ask. I see a pair of old-fashioned scales, weighing the pain of one last fuck against the reward of Mark buying into my change of heart. The scales decide for me. I slide my hand up his back but . . .

'Much as I would love to continue, we only have daylight until four so how about we reconvene with champagne later?' He kisses the tip of my nose. 'And take our time.'

I sigh, slide past his body and reach for my coat—

'I've got an idea,' he says.

'Which is?'

'Follow me, Anna Banana.' His childish excitement – Dylan wanting to play dog treats, Daisy wanting a ride on Ben's back, Tallulah being tickled by Bridget – brings instant apprehension.

He opens the bi-fold doors and walks to the large shed, painted blue to match the outdoor table, unlocks the padlock and beckons me from my position, rooted on the patio. I don't want to join him. Whatever he is about to show me will be something to do with water. We are not going near the water – we are walking the cliff path and having crispy duck wraps, if Mark makes it that far.

'Come on.'

The hut is very organised: metal shelves run along one side, neatly stacked with wellies, a pump, various boxes, a bucket; on the other side, wetsuits hang from hooks; bodyboards are stacked in the corner and an orange canoe floats above our heads, suspended from rafters.

'The sea is perfect. How about we paddle to the café, Ratty?'

'I'd really rather go for a walk,' I say, repelled by both the idea and the baby talk. 'I'm not a brilliant swimmer.'

'We're not going swimming. These things are as stable as an oilrig.' He reaches up and thwacks the plastic. 'We can hug the coast – hardly need to go out of our depth. Believe me, you'll love it.'

I won't love it.

Hurry up and close this down, says my internal voice.

'I've never been canoeing, or is it a kayak?' His determination is clear from his stance but I give it my best. 'Starting on the ocean doesn't feel like a wise move.'

'In a kayak, your legs are stretched out inside the cockpit.' With one hand he unclips a carabiner, the other grabs a rope, and he lowers the huge orange boat. 'This is a Canadian canoe, which has sit-on benches. Anyone can manage it.'

'I'm way too nervous, but I don't mind watching you from the shore.'

'If you don't like it, we'll come straight back.'

Two wooden paddles appear next, and a trolley with wheels.

The control has slipped; I need to wrestle it back but the doom-filled premonition that accompanied Ben's departure has returned. All I can see is my funeral, Ben's head dipped to hide his grief. The uncomfortable feeling, a stone lodged in my windpipe, is hard to interpret: might be fear, might be worry, could be guilt. If guilt, it is misplaced – *I'm doing all of this for Ben*, I tell an anonymous omniscience.

If (why all these ifs) there was a moment where it would be useful to turn off my internal commentary, it is now.

'Surely no one goes canoeing in winter?'

'Of course they do. They just don't fall in.'

'Is falling a choice?'

'Yes. Don't stand up. And don't lean over the edge looking for mermaids.'

Mark continues to slipstream over all my objections, leaving me floundering in his wake.

'Do you want these?' He holds out a pair of wetsuit boots. 'Or you can take your shoes and socks off and put them back on when we're afloat.'

I dither.

He is standing in front of me, fit and lean, eager, happy, ebullient. I am the opposite, racing to catch up and curate what happens next. His curveball cannot be permitted to throw me. An opportunity will arise, I tell myself. Canoeing won't take all day. Keeping him onside is crucial.

'How long will it take to row to Budleigh Salterton?'

'An hour or so, definitely less than two. There in time for duck.'

'And we'll stay near the shore?'

'Nearish. We'll need to leave a margin to avoid the rocks and there are two outcrops to get round.'

'Define outcrops.'

'Sticky-out bits of cliff – Orcombe Point and Straight Point.'

'Are there life jackets?'

'Too bulky over a coat. We won't need them.'

Willpower dredged from my bowels enables me to smile and summon a perkier tone. 'Okay. But I am reserving the right to bail.'

'Absolutely,' he says.

Ten minutes later, we leave via the garden gate, Mark dragging the canoe on disproportionately tiny wheels, one hand of mine helping to minimise the lurching as we negotiate the track down to the beach.

46

Shooting the Moon

To be fair, the sea looks quite inviting. Unthreateningly flat and borrowing a blue hue from the sky. We grab a coffee and a flapjack from a cute shipping container at the far end of the beach and are about to embark on our maiden voyage when I have an attack of anxiety, necessitating a precautionary loo stop. Mark opts to wait on the beach while I walk to the public toilets.

I lock the door, have the tiniest wee, but don't immediately leave the cubicle because I can't decipher the messages from my body.

My head is irritated by the canoe trip but not dismayed – at worst, the clifftop adventure can wait until tomorrow. However, my stomach is a twisted knot and my mouth dry. I'm not sure what I am most uncomfortable about – the sea is calm, I can swim, there are people around. Unless this is a reaction to the general daredevilry. Yes, that sounds plausible. A combination of nerves and wintry discontent, the vastness of the sea and the unsavoury nature of the looming task.

At the same time as I open the cubicle door a woman pushes it towards me, making me jump. 'Oh!'

'I'm sorry. I thought it was free,' she says, pointing her stripy gloves at the lock.

'No problem.'

We swap places. I press the soap dispenser and lather the entirety of my hands in the manner of a surgeon in a hospital drama, making figures of eight. The stone appears back in my throat. I cough to dislodge it.

My fellow occupant reappears and she too begins the ritual of hand washing. I notice the semicolon tattooed on her wrist and, once again, wish for a release from my own mental overload.

Loitering is weird – I should go, but . . .

'I've agreed to go canoeing,' I say, rolling my eyes at her reflection in the mirror. She has two plaits framing a full-cheeked face that is partially obscured by a huge purple scarf. I put her at mid-twenties.

'Rather you than me.'

'I'm not keen. It's my boyfriend's idea.'

'Are you from round here?'

I shake my head while I choose. 'Cambridge. We're tourists.'

'But you're experienced kayakers?'

'My first time.' I giggle. 'He's a bit of an action man.'

She lets her wet hands drip over the basin. 'Listen, I don't mean to be a killjoy but there's an offshore wind. You'll be out to sea calling the lifeboat before you know it.'

'It looks calm,' I say, in the least confident manner ever.

'That's because the waves are being blown out to sea – trust me, half a mile from the shore it will be much windier and the chop won't be beginner level.'

'He seems to think we can hug the coast along to Budleigh Salterton.'

'Has he got a death wish?'

'Not that I know of. We're quite a new relationship.'

'In summer it would be a great trip, but with the tide going out plus the wind direction, you'll get dragged away from the shoreline.' She puts her hand on the arm of my fleece-lined jacket. 'Do you want me to come and talk to him? I've grown up here and I've seen plenty of rescues. It can be tricky.'

I try to work through the thought that is immobilising me, making me thick and slow and stupid: I may not be the only one with an agenda for the weekend.

Eventually I say, 'It was only an idea. Don't worry, we won't go.'

'Are you sure?'

'Yes,' I say. 'Nice to meet you. You may have saved my life.'

I leave her trying to force her damp hands back into woolly gloves.

The sun is beautiful, greeting me as I emerge to walk the fifty metres of seafront back to where Mark is waiting; fifty metres to calculate the odds of returning safely from our jaunt.

I weigh up his reassurances: that we will hug the coast, that we will hardly be out of our depth, that I can change my mind at any point, against the warnings of, let's face it, a random stranger. Looking at the glorious expanse of mirror-flat sunlit water, I wonder if she exaggerated the danger. Locals love to show off their knowledge – I can't count the number of times the villagers have warned me not to wear shorts in the long grass because of ticks and not to swim in the weir. (Although, to be fair, the warnings about killer cows were on the button.)

'Are we good to go?' Mark's familiar smile switches to a cartoon shark. This flicker between lifelike and caricature adds to my general confusion.

'I'm really not keen.'

The reticence, the unease, the vacillation: it is, of course, because of the baby. But as yet there is no baby, only the possibility of one.

Mark pushes the canoe seawards with his bare foot. 'First sign of a wave and we'll abandon the plan, I promise.'

He leaves footprints in the wet sand but I stay where I am. He turns; the look on his face is impatient verging on irritated.

'Come on, Anna, shoes off. The duck wrap awaits.'

I cannot afford for Mark to have doubts: this is what swings it.

'One wave, Mark Turner, and we're back on the beach.'

'Scout's honour.' He attempts the corresponding hand signal but his fingers won't comply so I help out, reaching to pin his pinkie in place. And kissing it. (*Good girl, Anna, keep things nice.*)

I slip off my trainers and socks and roll up my jeans. I am wearing a long-sleeved T-shirt and a thin sweater under my bulky jacket. Waterlogged, the clothes would probably sink me before the cold precipitated a cardiac arrest. Frank said the rough rule of thumb is that you can stay as many minutes in the water as the temperature, which today might mean twelve minutes, maybe less. In the pool I regularly swim a hundred metres in well under two minutes, so in twelve minutes I might manage half a mile. Open-water swimming can be faster because there is no wall, and therefore no turns, and the salt brings buoyancy, but the wrong attire, the wrong waves, the wrong state of the tide would surely negate any benefit.

'The heaviest goes at the back,' says Mark, as he manoeuvres the canoe into the water.

I don't want him to sit behind me.

Walk away. Or maybe run. Yes, run, Anna. Ben would want me to bolt. Ben wouldn't want me to get into the boat with the tiger. Yet, with only the smallest of gasps, I am also wading through the

291

shallows, toes clawing the gravelly sand in protest at the iciness. Calf deep, Mark holds the canoe steady while I clamber in. A firm push and he has hopped on behind in a manner of someone who knows boats, understands balance and buoyancy, is au fait with the currents and, therefore, the risks.

'Ready?'

Mark has to show me the correct side of the blade to use but we quickly synchronise, me plunging on the right as he does the left. Paddling out from the shore is simple; too simple. I can feel the sea beneath the boat applauding the decision to piggyback rather than challenge its dominance. The repetitive action is soothing, allowing my mind to sieve and sort the silt that has muddied my brain. First, I discard my assumption (my lazy, arrogant assumption) that Mark freed himself up this weekend to enjoy a romp. As the other player in the prisoner's dilemma, wasn't it always more likely that his motivation might be more insidious? But does he intend to frighten me? Or blackmail me into silence? Or, if we are indeed well matched, orchestrate my demise before I attempt the same? The disquiet this brings is a crawling ant, itchy wool, shavings of hair fresh from the barber that make you scratch till you bleed: all light of touch but hard to ignore. I shift on the hard bench, glance back at the beach.

'I don't want to go too far out.'

'Don't worry. You can't drown in three feet of water.' He reaches to pinch my ear lobe and I swat his hand like a fly.

We continue in a straight line, nothing ahead but the deep dark sea. With each extra length the decision over whether to exhibit panic, real or otherwise, and demand we turn around becomes more complex. A hissy fit doesn't seem helpful if I want to appear to trust him. Although a damsel in distress might allow him to be a hero. But could also be annoying.

A jet ski flies into our field of vision on a cloud of spray, roars and circles away, making the canoe stutter. Nausea billows in, but I swallow hard and fix my stare on the horizon.

'Isn't it time to turn along the coast?' Being at his mercy is a mistake. The minute he unlocked the shed I should have dug my heels in.

'I was just about to. Honestly, Anna, relax. This is Devon, not the Cape of Good Hope.'

As I have no instinct for how to manoeuvre, I stop and observe. He plants his paddle as far forward as possible before sweeping it back and away from the canoe in a letter J; the front duly turns to the left. He repeats the move a couple of times to achieve a line parallel with the shore.

'Now, will you please try and enjoy yourself. Look around you. It's perfect.'

My head duly moves from side to side but I am a fish caught in a net, a grid of criss-crossed lines fucking with my focus.

'Keep your eye on the headland and we shouldn't stray far.'

Unlike our previous visit, the sea is not a busy playground full of primary colours. I pray the proximity to Christmas is what has kept people on land rather than any expert knowledge of the conditions.

'Okay.'

Combating the pull to my right involves a modicum of concentration – the nose, or bow as Mark refers to it, takes every chance to veer away from the shore. My shoulder quickly begins to complain at the effort so I shimmy along the bench a little and swap my paddle to the other side; Mark follows suit.

'Maybe tell me next time you're going to change sides,' he says, his voice overly loud.

'Sorry.'

Mark being out of eyesight deters conversation, not that I have anything I want to say. Figuring out either my course of action or his is beyond me – I can't keep hold of the thread. All that is real is the increasingly grey water, the unnatural stripes of red and orange stone that form the cliff, the gurgle of the passage of the paddles. The effect is mesmeric.

Pippa's family played card games. My favourite was black lady: a variation on whist where the objective is to avoid winning any tricks that contain a heart card or the queen of spades, all of which accrue points. (Points are bad – look up the rules, this isn't the time.) In a clever twist, you could also win by feigning losing while actively trying to collect every point card, a move known as 'shooting the moon'. I loved this move, both the subterfuge and the surprise when, late in the proceedings, my opponents would realise and fruitlessly scrabble to stop me. As I roll my shoulder forward, elbow out, to give leverage to my stroke I feel there is a parallel here, if only I could see it.

The trip to Exmouth was, ostensibly, an opportunity for Mark and me to reconnect, two people playing the same game. Unbeknown to Mark, I am pretending. But if Mark is also pretending, the game changes. Two players can't simultaneously hope to shoot the moon because the first one to win a trick containing a points card immediately scuppers the opponent's chances. Therefore, if cards mimic life, my options are to move first or change strategy.

If I was one of those women who lug around a huge bag I might have options. Pepper spray, a corkscrew, a sharp nail file – Milly

294

carries a mini pink Swiss Army knife – but I travel light, just a phone and keys.

'This is Orcombe Point,' shouts Mark. 'When the tide is out you can walk all the way round from Exmouth Beach to Sandy Bay.'

Since I last paid close attention the scenery to my left has changed. We have come far enough to see where a chunk of cliff has been scooped out to reveal a semi-circle of beach. In the distance I can make out stick people and fast-moving dogs.

'We can stop there, if you like. It's a private beach – owned by the holiday camp. Or have you found your sea legs?'

Being given the option brings instant and absolute reassurance. The relief is bliss, flooding me with a chemical antidote to the cortisol that has kept my throat tight and my thoughts feral. I almost want to share my Machiavellian suspicions, my hankering for a handy weapon, my panic, so that we can both laugh hysterically.

'Let's keep going,' I say.

We travel the length of the bay at some speed – 'You're a natural, Anna' – but to navigate the promontory of rock at the end we have to go further out to sea again. As soon as we change direction the canoe accelerates of its own accord, the driving wind luring us away from safety. My nerves rise up – the cliff seems higher, the current stronger, the endeavour more intrepid. I create the map in my head, trace the shape of Straight Point – the long needle of rock was one of several spots that stood out as being particularly treacherous for a careless cliff walker.

'It's quite deep here, Mark.'

'We need to leave a decent margin to make sure we don't hit something – the cliff doesn't magically stop where it meets the water. The rocks continue underneath.'

I peer over the edge but the sea is completely opaque. From nowhere the surface starts to ripple, little humps with the merest hint of white at the crest. Not quite waves, but tremors, carrying advance warning of what is to come. The next time I place my paddle I don't draw it as far back, loath to expedite our passage to France.

'This is the only rough patch we'll get,' he says. 'As soon as we're past Straight Point – that's the long finger – we can start heading back in and we'll be able to see the next stretch of beach.' My peripheral vision catches his arm flung wide, gesticulating towards the two towers of cliff sandwiching a deep crevasse.

I don't linger on the view because it only adds to my alarm. Mark is a risk-taker; I should have considered that before I agreed to get in the boat.

'How many times have you done this?'

'Too many to count.'

'How come?'

'I grew up near here.'

'Not in Devizes?'

'No.'

'Why didn't you say?'

'Honesty hasn't been our hallmark.'

'It could be from here on.' We are both shouting.

'Okay. Why did you join Jan's choir?'

I continue paddling, ignoring the waves hitting the side of the boat, rocking us as we plough through the choppy water. 'I wanted to annoy you.'

'You succeeded.'

'Good – think of it as payback for coming to my house.'

'If you wanted me to stay away from you, why are we here?'

There is no one but us on the water, we are out of sight of the shore; only a birdwatcher, teetering on the edge of the cliff, would be able to see us. If Mark's intention is to push me out of the boat, this might be the place. Panic tries to close my airway but I force a breath.

Keep breathing, Anna.

'What would you say if I said I had a passport in the name of Sofia Hemingway?' I twist my head to look at him. 'That I have considered simply disappearing.'

'With me?' His smile is cautious.

'Yes.' I turn back around and settle my eyeline on the horizon to try to offset the vertigo.

'Who is Sofia?'

'Someone I knew. Someone who died.' I will him to latch on to the idea I am as wicked as him. To believe we might catch that plane to Honolulu together.

'What about Ben?'

'I'm here with you. Doesn't that tell you enough?'

The pause is too long. I wish I could see his face, read his thoughts. My shoulders creep up and my back hunches at the prospect of being manhandled into the cold water. I brace, the paddle mid-air, my lungs mid-breath.

'Keep paddling. I don't want to be picked up by the border patrol.'

I do as he says, fairly sure I have been tested and awarded a reprieve.

We are quiet as we navigate the furthest part of the point and begin the long trawl to the shore. Countering the wind and the current takes considerable exertion, making me hot inside my jacket.

When our labours are rewarded by a clear view of the next beach, I feel my neck muscles relax despite the ongoing pitching of the canoe. The drop in tension gives way to ravenous hunger – crispy duck here we come – and slight euphoria. We have circumnavigated the south coast with its two rocky outcrops and I have not died.

Magic suddenly becalms the waters.

'That's better,' says Mark. 'The wind has dropped because we're closer to the shore.'

An imaginary cox encourages us to up the frequency and ferocity of paddling and we don't disappoint, sprinting across the line.

'Just under an hour and a half,' says Mark, as my paddle scrapes sand. 'Not bad.'

'Why, thank you.'

'We make a good team.'

Paddle abandoned, I swivel, letting my legs follow. I take his face in my hands and I kiss him, kiss with unbridled passion. We stay entwined, afloat on the ocean. Love's young dream.

47

Twelve Minutes

My God, the crispy duck wraps are good. Rich and fatty, doused in honey and sumac but cleansed by crunchy salad. The between-mouthfuls chat is less appetising.

'I've seen people dying from cancer before. There can be a long plateau but once the decline starts in earnest . . .' Mark opens his palms. '*Que sera.*'

'Are you sure you're Jan's main beneficiary?'

His cards are on the table, face up, no more conjecture.

'Yes, I took her to the lawyer myself.'

'But did you see the actual will?'

'I've told you before, I didn't cajole her – this isn't blackmail.' He brushes aside his lock of hair that falls so fetchingly over one eye. 'She has no close family, and no desire to leave her estate to the cats' home.'

Lulled by the easy, convivial chat, by the outdoor exercise and tasty food, by a shared villainy, I almost mention Bartok, Jan's dead cat. The near-slip is useful, hoicking me back onto tiptoes.

'And much as you think she's a nice old lady,' he continues, 'she enjoys leveraging her generous bequest.'

'Will you go through the whole palaver of arranging her funeral and wearing a dark suit?'

'Jan has arranged her own, but, yes, I will honour her wishes and only after she is lowered into the ground will I make hay.'

'Does she really want a burial?'

'She does. Buried in an oak coffin with brass handles – "none of this wicker rubbish".'

I laugh.

'Is Angie looking after her while you're with me?'

'Partly. But she also has someone coming to stay,' he says, 'a lost soul by all accounts, name of Harry.'

'How long for?' I ask.

'Unsure.'

'How do you feel about having another bull on your territory?'

'It might be fun – it might even be fortuitous.'

'In what way?'

'If Jan's last hours were with Harry in charge there would be no need for ugly rumours.' His eyebrows form high arches. 'I'm aware of how our situation looks from the outside.'

My mind leaps on this with the energy of a kid goat. I run through a myriad of ways he could remote-control Jan's murder: lace her porridge with ketamine; leave Agatha Christie-style trip hazards – a ball on the stairs, a strand of wool tied across a doorway; empty her navy and white capsules of paracetamol and replace the contents with rat poison.

'What is "lost" about Harry?'

'A purpose, I think.'

'How old?'

'I'm not sure. Fifties, I assume. He's been overseas for years.'

'Hippy, nomad or expat?'

'Hippy.'

'Love and peace or a stoner?'

'Not sure, maybe the former. Although the latter might be more entertaining.'

'I wonder how the locals will react.'

'Applause, I expect.'

'Depends how hippy. There'll be talk of a commune if he's wearing harem pants.' Choosing attire at odds with Harry's corporate-looking photo makes me feel quite clever.

'What have you got against harem pants?'

'Depends if they come with a ponytail and a poncho,' I add.

The words hang for a second: a speech bubble stolen from Mark's other, other woman . . . but also not a totally atypical description, I quickly reason.

With only a tiny, tiny glitch, I carry on with my theme, 'And a duffel bag. All self-respecting hippies come with a duffel bag.'

Mark puckers his face. 'As long as he doesn't smell.'

'Says the man who drinks Lapsang.'

He smiles. The moment has passed – we're good.

'Aren't you worried he might inveigle himself with Jan?'

'He won't have time.' I can't sculpt a reply to Mark's insinuation that doesn't betray my feelings.

'Talking of time, I've agreed to get married on January the second.'

His laughter is from deep in his belly. 'I like you so much. You deliberately raise the stakes. Goading me, yourself, the world. I can see inside your head, can follow your workings. What did you call it once?'

'Innards.'

'Yes, your innards are not secret, not to me. Not anymore.'

'You think you've solved me, do you?'

'I think you won't be walking up the aisle with Ben.' He tilts his head – so sure of himself.

'Because I'm the type to stand someone up at the altar?'

'Yes. Or maybe the type to disappear part-way and get on a bus still wearing the froufrou frock.'

He is in the right ballpark.

'Do you actually intend to go away?' I ask.

'I'm not sure. I could be persuaded into a London penthouse or a shack on a beach. Persuaded by you, that is.'

'If I'm destined to desert Ben, why wouldn't I do the same to you?'

'You might, eventually. Or maybe I'll leave you. But we haven't actually started yet, have we? Although you've created a deadline.'

Slightly unsure of his meaning, I say, 'You're the one with a schedule.'

'It would be tidier, wouldn't it, if we could dovetail?'

His invitation for me to be complicit in his freedom from Jan makes me choke on an imaginary duck bone. I take the last mouthful of barely warm coffee and order my throat to soften.

'All good?' asks Mark, rolling his serviette into a ball and chucking it into the nearby bin.

I nod.

'We'd better get going, then.'

He kisses my greasy lips, takes my hand and pulls me to standing. As we head back to the canoe, I notice the light has lost its yellowness, the sea is a deep charcoal and the air somehow anaemic.

302

'We need to chivvy up to get back round Straight Point,' he says. 'Once we're the other side we can go on foot if necessary.'

'Do you mean if it's too dark to see?'

'I do.'

'Because the tide will be out by then and we can walk where before we had to paddle?'

'Exactly that; the beach will be huge in comparison to earlier.'

The change in his manner is almost imperceptible, but definitely there. His haste feels like proof of his desire to keep me safe, not cause me harm. He is definitely convinced of our future together. I marvel at what an ego he has, to believe in my affection despite the ring on my finger.

We take off our shoes once more – the shock of the cold makes me hiss – and climb aboard, no tiger this time, just a pussycat, cream all over his mouth.

Reversing our journey is fascinating. The slog to the beach that seemed to take ages is more like freewheeling with the help of the offshore wind. Only when we attempt to circle the point does the sea object. In the space of three or four strokes the gentle undulation becomes a more insistent shove from the side, followed by a dip. There is probably a nautical word but my lay brain thinks of it as being winded; hit then hollowed. I don't like it.

In between strokes our pace drops and the wind picks up handfuls of spray. In no time the denim of my jeans is sticking to my thighs, my feet are unresponsive blocks and my fingers are turning blue; gripping the paddle is increasingly difficult.

'I don't like it,' I holler, as another arc of fine mist lands on my lap.

'These things don't capsize,' he shouts back.

Being buffeted by wave after wave makes me want to sink to

my knees, bow my head and leave Mark to save the day. But I keep paddling, all the while hanging on to the knowledge that we will soon emerge on the other side. Mark knows these waters. All is well.

'Are you worried?' I shout.

'No. But I am quite wet.'

'Me too. Whose idea was this?'

'Mine. But I assumed you'd protest and we'd end up abandoning the trip.'

'Great. Next time I'll know.'

'I don't think there'll be a next time.'

And suddenly the tiger is back, never really went away. My nerve, held all this time, gives way to frenzy, pulse sky high and buzzing in my brain.

'It would be nice in warmer weather.' My voice might not sound as bright as I'd like.

'Have you told Jan about us?' I can almost hear him rifling through the facts once more and drawing a different conclusion. 'Is that why Harry is coming?'

Mark has stopped paddling, so I also stop or we'll go in a circle. With no propulsion, the waves buck us like a bronco. I twist awkwardly around, feet forward but hips askew, head dizzied by the lurching. With difficulty, I maintain eye contact. 'How would telling Jan in any way benefit me?'

'The benefits are many. You take some moral pleasure. You punish me for lying. You, not Harry, replace me in her affection – maybe you have an idea to monetise that?'

I lift both my feet over the seat and swivel to face him. 'If I'd told Jan I wouldn't be here now and I don't think you would be either.' I'm missing something, I know I am. 'Can we postpone this conversation for firmer ground?'

His staring eyes could bore through concrete.

'How did you find her?' he says.

'Who?'

'Come on, Anna. I know you've been playing detective again.'

'What are you talking about?'

Keeping my expression neutral is difficult, given all inside is haywire. Stupid, stupid me. We all tell the same stories over and over. Of course Mark knew about his other, other woman's teenage marriage to the man with a ponytail and a poncho. My ear immediately caught the repetition of her phrase. I should have known Mark had noticed too. Like me, he notices everything.

'Don't bother denying it.' He flicks his hand at me dismissively. 'It's insulting.'

My alarm at being uncovered, far out to sea, floating on plastic, ignites a fury of words, tumbling over each other in the rush to salvage the situation. I choose indignance, not apology.

'. . . can you blame me for wanting to uncover the truth . . .

'. . . I knew you weren't single from the off but I believed in your job, I believed in you, I believed in us . . .

'. . . I only snooped because I couldn't understand where you were when Jan thought you were on a shift . . .'

If I can keep talking, I can keep thinking. Only thinking will save me.

'. . . it wasn't that difficult, you parked your car outside the pub . . .

'. . . I should be the one who is cross . . .

'. . . telling Jan would be cruel, why would I do that?'

On the outside the stream of verbiage continues. Inside I am acutely aware of being in the blind spot of the skyscraper cliffs; aware of the sinking sun, disappearing to shine elsewhere; aware of the deep and no doubt treacherous gully between the two fingers of cliff.

With my hands tight on the shaft of the paddle I gabble on, the pitch of my speech undulating with the peaks and troughs of the waves, which are themselves bolder, messier. Mark seems content to wait for a gap in my monologue. That gap isn't coming.

If we're both pretending, be the first to move: I repeat the strategy in my head but what my move should be I am incapable of deciding. I'd like to take a great big swing at his head with my paddle, but I'm not strong enough to wield the long, heavy shaft with any force. I'm not strong enough to match Mark regardless of how clever, how cunning, how speedy.

The memories come reluctantly: violent fights with my brother, with my drunken mother, with the twenty-something man who thought my fourteen-year-old kiss meant I was game on. I draw on them all, supercharging my rage, letting my fear spiral and bring adrenaline aplenty.

The only way I am a match for Mark is in the water. The thought of plunging into the abyss is more terrifying than Mark himself, but I am a strong swimmer, I have stamina, I have a good style and, if I can find the courage, I will have surprise. In the meantime, still I talk.

'. . . all the evidence said you were a charlatan . . .'

My right hand reaches into the pocket of my jacket, leaving my left holding the paddle. I fold my house keys inside my fist as I have done on so many nights, no matter how drunk. Girls learn this lesson early.

But despite mentally rehearsing a hammer punch, despite picturing the arc of my arm and the jab of my fist, my hand stays deep in my pocket.

Come on, Anna.

Compromising Mark will both help me get him in the water and greatly reduce his chances of emerging alive. A punch and a push. In return for a ponytail and a poncho.

Come on, Anna.

'. . . put yourself in my shoes,' I say, 'no one wants to feel used . . .'

The timbre of my voice has altered, base notes of defeat creeping in. The fear presses down on me. I won't make it home. I won't get married. We won't have our family.

And suddenly I am shouting: 'You arrogant fucking prick!' The return of my estuary accent brings red-hot energy to my whole being. 'I wasn't going to tell you. But you've fucking made me!'

His body is rocking with the swell, but his attention is fixed. Fixed on this Anna with a filthy mouth. He is silent, but he is listening. Slowly and deliberately, I deliver what might or might not be true – 'I'm having your bastard baby' – and feel a grain of control.

His face changes; and that slit of doubt gives me my chance.

'That's why I came away with you.' I lean forward – does he imagine I am going to plead? – but instead my hand rises up on the diagonal and I punch his face hard with the side of my clenched fist, the key blade nice and proud. On impact, his head seems to fly off his neck, matched by ugly vibrations running through my shoulder. The force coupled with the unsteady platform makes me lose my balance and I almost fall into his lap, but recover quickly, grabbing the bench before hitting him again. Bewildered by his lack of response, but unable to think or focus, I form my fist for the third time and notice my hand is dark and sticky. I look across at Mark. Both of his hands are clutching his face; wax-like drips seep between his fingers.

'Mmmmerrrrr!' He roars, flinging one arm towards me and snatching at my neck. I bat his hand away. Only now do I see the damage. One of his eyes is open. The second is not an eye but a dark well, lid half closed. He moans again, guttural.

This time I think I break his nose.

Terror takes over, bringing rashness and dispatching caution. Thoughts zing and fizz. I stand and the canoe quakes on the fevered sea. I know what I have to do.

With one foot on the side, I push down. In an instant the boat has capsized and we are in the water. Water that is strangely viscous, thick and gummy. Syrup water. The cold, too, is baffling: razor cuts on numb skin. I realise he is pulling me, his hand bunching the hem of my jacket. There is laboured thrashing, me or him or both, I can't tell. More limbs than makes sense . . . weighty, wayward limbs. My iron fingers grapple his apart – I hear myself yell – and I push him away. His head dips below the water. Rises again. Dips and rises. His mouth gapes for breath but catches only wave after wave.

Only my hands are moving, dainty little sculls. No feeling in my fingers. I am hanging vertically in the water, suspended like a specimen in a jar, chin tilted skywards. No breath comes. Mark has vanished, leaving me quite alone. If I can't make my chest muscles spread, my mouth open, the bellows suck in air, I'll vanish too.

The canoe, a concave shell, has already drifted away.

Twelve minutes, says the timer in my head. *Twelve minutes.*

My body feels heavy, lethargic, unwilling to try. I continue to hang, little sculls from dead hands.

Seconds are valuable.

I gulp the air and force it down; pain radiates across my front, but I swallow more air, eating it like dry cake. Awareness of my predicament slowly asserts itself.

I picture the coastline, trying to understand the task, and the reward.

Undressing might help. Yes, good idea. I attempt to wriggle out of my jacket but the second sleeve won't release my arm. I sink lower in the water, yank myself free, and then I swim. For the first few strokes my head stays high but old-lady swimming is not efficient at cleaving the water. In goes my face – pain from angry nerves radiates across my forehead – and I start to count.

One . . . two . . . three . . . breathe.

The cold is burning the back of my eyeballs and the lining of my mouth, making my teeth ache and stinging my ears.

One . . . two . . . three . . . four . . . five . . . breathe.

Every twenty strokes I pause, look up and try to get a bearing. I do this again and again to verify that I am making progress, to verify that the huge shard of rock has shifted in relation to my position. Feedback is important – positive feedback has more effect on performance than raw talent: Sofia told me that. I tell myself how well I'm doing.

One . . . two . . . three . . . four . . . five . . . breathe.

My arms are heavy, struggling to clear the surface, hardly reaching forward before falling heavily back down. Down and down. My feet are a long way away, too far for me to ask them to kick.

I am no longer so terribly cold, nor curious as to why.

309

My mind strays, prances through a weekend at Reading Festival with a boy called Damien . . . I have a daisy chain around my neck and he has a bare chest. We're swaying. My feet are in clogs, tan with studs. I loved those clogs. They made a wonderful sound on a hard floor.

I have forgotten I am meant to count. Forgotten to check what I can see. Forgotten why I have to live.

One . . . two . . . three . . . breathe.

Twenty more strokes and I pause again, committing to memory the few details in the homogenous scene – a fatter stripe of red stone, a circle of grey stone, a dip in the ridge. Twenty more strokes and another twenty . . . I narrow my eyes, trying to focus is difficult . . . but, yes, there it is. The ribbon of beige sand, bobbing in and out of view as I bob, and the water bobs.

Land a-fucking-hoy.

I won't die of hypothermia. I might not even catch a cold. The sun, the moon and the earth have worked their alchemy and brought the beach to me. I dip my head again and count, powerful now, but I don't make it past nine. Hands, man hands, crush my biceps, fingers digging into one shoulder. A sharp inhale, brine fills my mouth, scalding my throat.

48

Remain Vigilant

My story won't stay straight so I don't tell it. I stay quiet. The uncontrollable shivering is less violent but a foal-like weakness persists, my jaw is clenched and my tongue too big, my hands are all fist and no fingers. I have no feet. People are speaking but I don't have any attention to spare. My story is the only thing that matters. Keeping it linear, as bald as is acceptable, plausible, assured.

The dry robe is black with a bright blue lining. My feet are in red socks, the heel halfway up my calf – men's socks. They stripped me bare, the couple, stripped me naked on the beach and reclothed me. More people came and I was brought up to the holiday camp, carried in a fireman's lift – firm hands under my bottom. Someone called an ambulance but the wait was too long and I am conscious and have spoken enough to de-escalate the status from Emergency to Remain Vigilant.

'Sofia.'

I look up at the woman; she is wearing a T-shirt. The room beyond my cocoon must be warm.

'Why were you in the water?'

My smile is deliberately small; I look up at the ceiling, close my eyes. The story isn't quite cooked; there are patches of raw that could develop infection. I need my sluggish brain to regain normal speed. Only then will I explain.

'What time is it, please?' My voice, like my body, is shaky.

'Quarter past five.'

I had hoped to be on the way home by now. Had hoped to be able to crawl into bed and wake on Sunday, the demon dealt with, the nightmare over. If I can escape my saviours, that can still happen.

Like mist clearing from the morning fields, like the end of a monotonous sermon, like waking, I become present in the room. Inside the robe I wiggle my fingers, press the tips together and note the feeling. Better. The recovery accelerates; a body scan confirms the return of sensation from my toes to the elastic around my waist to my damp hair, bundled into a wool hat. Only now do I realise it is itchy. I wonder what colour it is, and who it belongs to – the nervous man, his formidable wife or their irritated son? I tune in to their chatter, still shivering involuntarily but, otherwise, alert and alive.

They are meant to be eating out, but could cancel. The man thinks that's what they should do, but the son says there's still time. The woman, brusque, accuses the son of being more interested in chips than the welfare of another human.

'Actually,' I pause while they all turn to stare at me, 'I feel better now.'

I shrug off the robe and am surprised by the bright pink fleece underneath.

The parents speak over each other:

He says, 'Can I get you something to eat?'

She says, 'Do you know where you're staying?'

'She might be local,' says the lad, sixteen at a guess, heavy-fringed with a rectangular face – like Tamsin's Airedale terrier. I am tempted to resume my muteness and rollick in the memory of that lunch in Sofia's parents' kitchen, but instead I straighten up, hone in on the dynamic.

'She said she wasn't from here,' says the mum.

'Might not be staying over,' says the dad. 'She could have come for the day.'

Finally, I catch up with the undercurrent – they think I attempted to take my own life.

'I was canoeing,' I say, intent on controlling the intermittent quivers of my body. 'But I got into trouble around Straight Point.'

The relief shines on their faces like floodlights. They gather round, interested in what possessed me to canoe on a day like today, no longer terrified of what their responsibility might be. I spin the story, more and more eloquent as the sequence unfolds. I scoff at my own naivety and apologise for causing concern, feign distress at the loss of my host's canoe and add some local knowledge to imply a smidgeon of familiarity. It takes a while to attach labels to my memory of the map but eventually I dredge up the name of the long road that runs behind the holiday camp: 'I'm staying nearby . . . on Maer Lane.'

'Well, you landed in the right place then,' says the mum.

Like all good conversationalists, I reverse the attention and they share details of their three-day getaway combining a visit to an uncle in a care home and some walks and, of course, winter swimming.

'You were lucky – I'd only just got out myself,' says the dad.

When I judge we are all satisfied with the situation, I say, 'Thank you so much – I can't tell you how grateful I am. But I had better get going. I've lost my phone – it was in my jacket – but I've got my laptop and my mum will be worried if I don't call.'

'You can use my phone, Sofia,' says the woman.

'I don't know any numbers off by heart.' I attempt a hopeless face.

We spend a few minutes reflecting on our reliance on tech before I wind it up for good. 'Can I drop the clothes back this evening?'

'Of course. Perhaps leave them in a bag if we're out.'

'I'll walk with you,' says the man. 'We don't have a car here, I'm afraid.'

'Really, I'm fine. Although I don't suppose you have any wellies or—'

The boy jumps up from his perch on the arm of the sofa, 'You can borrow mine.'

Wearing his black wellingtons and a red waterproof I thank them again and, with only a short delay for some safety tips that include not kayaking without a lifejacket, I scarper.

Out of sight of the chalet, I chuck my head around to unlock my neck – there's a pleasing crack – before breaking into a run. Setting off like a greyhound is a mistake. The bone-deep chill has left my feet detached from my body and I stumble, so I swap between jogging and speed-walking. The street is dark but I am aglow.

Hello, future, here comes Anna.

Safely inside the studio, I have a hot shower and dress in my own clothes. I allow myself a few minutes collapsed on the sofa to revel in the events of the day – the smile may never leave my face – before rousing myself to address the loose ends. Obliterating any signs we have been in the studio is easy given we didn't unpack. I take the car key from the pocket of Mark's messenger bag and put

314

everything, including the champagne, in the boot. I lock the shed and leave the key on the hook. I refold the end of the toilet roll into a perfect V, as I found it. By the time the canoe is missed, today will be ancient history.

With the heater of the Honda Jazz on full blast, my hoodie up, I sing as the motorway miles take me homeward. My fingertips crackle in their ongoing quest for room temperature.

When the low fuel light shows on the dash I turn off onto an A-road, keen not to feature on the CCTV of any service stations. Mark's wallet has cash, which is a bonus. I fill the Honda and take a second detour to a giant superstore where Mark also funds a sharing-size bar of milk chocolate and a cheap phone. Calling Ben should be top of my list, in case he has been messaging me, or Dee, who may have popped by the house, but Jan takes precedence. As my tingly fingers type in her number, one of oodles I do in fact know by heart, I imagine her in the living room with Harry, a glass of red wine on her side table.

Confiding in her would be a mistake – people can be overly holy about the sanctity of life – but I will enjoy her freedom from being lied to, duped and fleeced when she realises Mark won't be coming back. (Maybe on her deathbed, as she wavers between worlds, I might be permitted to lean over and whisper in her ear. Yes, maybe then.)

My text doesn't elicit a reply so I call her with the phone balanced on my lap, speaker on loud. My mobile goes to answer machine after five rings but Jan's must be set to infinity. I am considering hanging up and calling again when—

'Hello.' Not Jan.

'Hi, is Jan there?' I shout.

315

'Sorry, no, she isn't.'

She is. I know she is. She's always there. I pick up the phone and hold it to my ear. 'Who am I speaking to?'

'This is Harry.'

'Where is she, Harry?'

'Sorry, who are you?'

'I'm her friend, Anna.'

'I'll tell her you called.'

'Hang on, you've made me worried. Is she not at home?'

'I'm not sure I should say. I'm sorry but I don't know who anyone is.'

'Is Angie there?'

The pause is ever-fucking-lasting and super-fucking-irritating.

'Harry, I'm a friend. I know you've arrived from abroad and your mum is in care and you haven't been to England for ages. Please tell me where Jan is?'

'She was taken by ambulance about two hours ago. I didn't ask where because . . . because it's all been a bit of a shock.'

I give up on Harry and call directory enquiries, driving with one hand, pedal to the floor. Doubts would be good, better than good, doubts could weaken the granite certainty that this is all my doing; but no doubts cloud my thinking because the timing is too cute for reasonable doubt.

Mark never intended to dispose of me in Exmouth. Jan was the one in his sights. My role was that of alibi. Except I interfered.

No more complicated than a game of swap, I took Mark, but he took Jan.

'The number for Southmead Hospital, please. Can you put me through?'

While I wait for the call to connect I see the spidergram of my life, white chalk lines on a dusty blackboard. The calligrapher adds details: boxes for places I've lived, pound signs for my many jobs, stick figures for people I've fucked, and little gravestones for the ones who got caught up along the way.

49

The Angel of Death

My brother died when he was eighteen. I was the last person to see him – that might not be a surprise given what I've revealed about myself. We'd both been to a party a few streets away from the terraced house where I rented the attic room but he'd gone on somewhere else. He woke me up by banging on the door like a one-man SWAT team, something he did on a fairly regular basis. (He was, supposedly, still living with Mum.) I let him in and he barged past me, stinking and raging. He was always angry – picking fights in pubs, smacking his girlfriends, pummelling the shit out of me.

The front door led straight into the sitting room. I watched him trip over his own legs and fall onto the sofa, curling into a ball and throwing insults, in between belching and writhing. I wanted him gone, but I was scared of him too; a legitimate fear given we were spawned from the same salubrious gene pool. I went back upstairs but could still hear him, which meant so could my housemates. I needed him to shut the fuck up, so I selected a benzo from my stash with the aim of speeding up his passage into oblivion. He was happy to oblige, would have swallowed flea treatment as long as it was

318

pill-shaped. His eyes quickly gave up on him, disappearing under swollen lids, but his mouth hung open, still cussing, his breath a sweet sewer. I stood there, disgusted by the train wreck he'd become. No use to anyone, or to himself. Was that why I had the idea to help him? Yes, let's go with that. The yellow and green capsule I gave him next was a good one.

I remember looking at my watch – it was nearly six in the morning. I got dressed in denim shorts and a hoodie and walked all the way along the river to Borough Market and had a divine fried breakfast. When I came back the paramedics were there. The sad part isn't that he died, but that he was such a bastard when he was alive.

On the outskirts of Bath I hit a red traffic light. While I wait for it to turn green I turn off the cute videos of Simon and me playing with a hosepipe and the two of us with our faces painted as zebras. For balance, I could trawl through the library and find the nightclub where he punched me so hard I wet myself and had headaches for a week, or the time he dragged me out of Mum's house by my hair, but I don't. Dwelling on the past is always a mistake, the filth collects like thick oily dust – the sort wiping can smear, but not remove.

I leave Mark's car on a side street near the bus station, take my bags and coat and leave his. I hurry to the car park – chucking his keys in a bin en route – and, face shrouded once again, drive away in Ben's car. But I don't go home, I go to Bristol, to the hospital. Jan is in the Acute Medical Unit, the efficient voice said. Family only.

'I'm here for Jan Elsworthy. She's my great-aunt.'

The woman consults a screen. Without any actual eye contact

I'm given directions and buzzed through double doors. The ward is deathly quiet.

Jan is sleeping but her breath seems quick and her cheeks overly rosy. I sit on the chair by the bed and wait for a health professional to enlighten me. Whatever Mark's done to her hasn't worked. Not yet anyway.

Something bangs my knee and I go from collapsed in a chair to bolt upright; my neck sends a wave of distress up my brain stem.

'Sorry.' The nurse is beautiful, titian hair and flawless skin. 'I need to do her obs.'

'What happened?'

'Have you not spoken to anyone?'

I shake my head. She walks to the foot end of the bed, looks at the chart, looks at the monitor. 'We're treating her for sepsis.'

I gasp. 'Will she die?'

'She's on IV antibiotics but the cancer treatment increases her risk – hopefully, she'll be moved to a ward tomorrow for observation.'

While she talks she puts a monitor on Jan's lifeless finger, takes her temperature; the blood pressure cuff inflates, and deflates, the stand holding the IV drip clangs against a bed leg; throughout, Jan doesn't stir.

'Why doesn't she wake up?'

The nurse smiles. 'She's old, she's ill and she's tired. It's nearly midnight.'

I have been asleep for aeons. 'But she will wake up, won't she?'

'Yes, when she's ready. Why don't you go home and come back in the morning?'

It's tempting. 'I just want to hear her speak, then I'll go.'

'She might not be lucid. High temperatures play havoc with the elderly.'

'How did she get sepsis?' This news is a challenge to my narrative – Mark can hardly have grown sepsis in a Petri dish and spread it on her toast.

'She has a nasty leg wound.'

'Not anymore. It was getting better.' Unless he used a dirty dressing of some sort.

The nurse smiles. 'Go home. We'll call if there's any change. Are you the next of kin?'

'I'm not sure. Can you take my number?'

'We've got a Liam Turner listed. Is he a relative?'

'He's her partner but he's away.' I dictate the number of my new phone. 'Anna Harris.'

She glides off but I stay in this liminal space where bodies hover, neither here nor there.

Opposite me, a young man is fast asleep, hinged at the hips with his bottom on the hard chair and his forehead resting on the bed. I decide he is a devoted grandson, good at cricket and engaged to a pretty accountant.

'Anna.'

'Jan.' I lean over the bed, kiss her cheek and take her hand. 'You gave me a fright.'

'Anna,' she says again.

'I'm here.'

She stares but whether she sees, I can't tell.

'There's no need to worry. You're on intravenous antibiotics and they work really quickly.'

321

She nods. 'What about Liam?'

'He doesn't matter. Getting well is what matters.'

'I don't want him there with Harry.' Her voice tails off.

'I can go round and make sure everything is okay.'

'Don't trust Liam in the house.' Her words are laboured, punctuated by little breaths. I can feel her frustration, but I'm not sure what she wants me to do. 'I left money.'

I wonder if she is confused. 'You changed your will, Jan. Mark, I mean Liam, he doesn't benefit.'

'Money in an envelope. For Liam.'

'What for?'

'To go.' Her eyes are barely open.

'Do you want a drink?' I reach for the glass and put the straw between her lips. She sips.

'No fuss. To go, no fuss. In the bureau, Anna.'

She won't be able to settle, not while she's fretting about Mark having free rein of the house and unlimited access to Harry and to a wad of money and, if he chose, the opportunity to have a gander at the revised will. I'd be worried too, if I didn't know he had been neutralised.

It is within my gift to give her peace. I think about that while she sips some more water.

'I wrote a letter.'

'To Liam?' I ask.

She takes a sharp breath. 'I had a bad night. Is it night again?'

'Yes, time to sleep.'

Her eyes close so slowly I can almost see the pull cord, gently lowering the lids.

'Give him the money, Anna,' she says. 'Please. Make him go.'

322

She is pleading with the last reserves she has when she should be fighting the infection, intent on getting better. The mind and body aren't separate; they are interwoven, interdependent. Mark may yet be the death of her.

I put my mouth by her ear. 'Jan,' I say, with a commanding edge. 'Jan, listen.'

And I tell her.

50

Home-made Brownies

On Sunday I am a sloth, barely able to reach for the remote control to swap channels. I do not go to church. I do not get dressed. I eat only carbs.

My exhaustion is hardly surprising. A death-defying sea swim, a very late night and an overdose of adrenaline make quite a cocktail. (I could add in the nourishing of a little human, but still won't let myself believe the raspberry might become a peach, a grapefruit, a great big pumpkin.)

On Monday, by contrast, I have the energy of a whirlwind, hand-delivering a ton of Christmas cards before, randomly, deciding to make brownies to welcome Ben home. (Dare I suspect myself of exhibiting nurturing behaviour?)

The doorbell goes when I'm elbow-deep in the extraordinarily stiff mixture.

The delivery driver shouts my name at the same time as thrusting his device at me.

'Hang on.' I wipe my hands on the tea towel before scribbling an approximation of a signature with my finger and taking the package.

I leave the rectangular box on the bottom stair and, back in the kitchen, give the mixture a final arm-aching stir before tipping it into the traybake tin (borrowed from Dee) and sliding it into the gaping oven.

With thirty minutes before I can take the brownies out, I take the box upstairs to the spare room. My wedding shoes are nicer than I remembered and the smaller size is perfect. I swing my foot to and fro, consider trying on the dress but decide against – I don't want to tempt providence. I am about to shut the wardrobe door on all the wedding attire when my eye catches on the flash of red. I fetch a black bin liner and in goes the entire contents of Sofia's shrine. I tie a knot, to make sure she can't get out, and put the bag in the newly emptied wheelie bin. The act of disposing of Sofia's clothes is cleansing; the whole episode disappears. I was never Sofia; I never wore her clothes or borrowed her fine education.

At half-past three, my baking complete, the bed linen changed and the washing machine whirling, I climb into the back of the waiting taxi. On the journey I play a mindless game on my phone, because my mind cannot be permitted to roam free.

I enter the anonymous building, hand over my payment and confirm my details.

Fifteen minutes after my name is called I leave with a due date and a 2D picture of Baby Harris. I can't stop staring. And I can't wait to show Ben.

Home again, the momentum that has carried me through the day ebbs away and my rusty old conscience steps in to fill the void. It sets to work, taunting me with the many ways Ben might not make it back as punishment for my part in the drowning of a bad man. I invent a car crash on the way down the mountain, see Ben crossing

325

paths with a suicide bomber, watch an aneurysm burst in his brain. I make a troubled teenager drop a breeze block from a high bridge, let a lorry driver fall asleep at the wheel, have Ben swallowed by a sinkhole.

I pace the house like a captive polar bear; barter with a God I don't believe in.

Without Ben, nothing makes sense.

Only when I force myself to concentrate on the television screen does the madness begin to abate and reason return. The undercurrent of unease is to be expected, I tell myself, but will pass. Every hour is another degree of separation from the unpleasantness. Soon the whole affair will vanish into the distance. I let my thoughts come and go and, gradually, I feel less amped, more mellow.

I am weeping along with a woman who has been reunited with her birth mother when I hear what sounds like the back door opening. I am instantly on my feet, brain transposing the image of one-eyed Mark thrashing about in the ocean into an upright waterlogged man currently in my kitchen. As my quiet feet carry me towards the danger, I pick up the solid oak doorstop with the rope handle. In the hall my skin tells me the air has dropped a few degrees. He is really here. Despite everything, he is going to win. I wait for a moment, ears straining to detect his breath, surely quickened by anticipation. The spectre of him roaring as he comes face to face with me makes me rest a hand on the wall for support. I can't gather myself, too splintered by fear. My phone pings loudly in my pocket and I freeze. But Mark doesn't appear.

Courage comes, a survival instinct keen enough to propel me into the kitchen, my weapon at the ready. The back door is wide open, only blackness beyond. I whip around. He has tricked me, is waiting with a knife. The lurid headlines in the paper flash before me.

When I have locked all the doors and windows, opened and closed all the cupboards and looked behind the curtains, I camp on the bottom stair to wait for Ben, just as I did all those nights waiting for my parents to come home.

As soon as I hear the car I fling open the front door. Ben's face is bright under the streetlight, his smile wide, his teeth luminescent.

I run out in my slippers and wrap him in a huge hug. The relief courses through me like amphetamines. Ben has not died. Ben is here.

'Someone missed me.'

Like an excited puppy, I can't stop kissing him, pawing him.

We tumble inside, bulky luggage and the obligatory plastic bag of duty-free alcohol.

'Good time?'

'Brilliant.'

'Knee held up?'

'Absolutely no problem.'

I make Ben a coffee and cut him a square of brownie.

He takes a bite. 'Did you make this yourself?'

'I did.'

'I need to go away more often.'

I shadow him around the house, chatting while he empties his dirty washing straight into the machine, puts all his electrical bumf back in the appropriate places, plugs in his camera card to download his photos. He is such a grown-up. Grown up is what we need.

'I'm done in. Shall we have an early night?'

This is not a salacious invitation; beneath his healthy snow-glare cheeks is a very weary Ben. Knowing Finn and Jamie, the toll on his leg muscles will have been surpassed by the strain on his liver. He takes the stairs two at a time, but I hang back slightly, nerves a-gallop.

He spots it the minute he turns on our bedroom light.

On the pillow on his side of the bed: an abstract image made of black and white and in-between shades.

'Anna?'

A tiny nod. 'About the size of a bumblebee, evidently.'

His smile, his big shiny-eyed smile, is made more beatific by being so unhurried.

He takes a large stride and picks me up, hiding his already wet face in my hair – 'Anna Harris, I bloody love you' – and we kiss and cry and talk and, much later, he drags me into the burrow that is his body and he sleeps. And I lie awake, happy in his arms, certainty blooming.

All is well.

51

Traitor

The noise of the doorbell permeates a vivid dream . . . water, a lagoon maybe, and a pony with a garland. My lids lift enough to note the blackness and drop again.

'Will you go?' I say.

Neither of us moves.

The doorbell goes again, two short rings. Ben lurches across the room and thumps down the stairs. I work out that it is Tuesday, that term is over, that we are having a baby and getting married, that a lie-in is definitely in order. I roll onto my other side, shove the pillow further under my neck and attempt to slip back into my dream – there was a pony and a festoon of flowers but I can't quite grasp the connection. I actively try to recreate the feeling of free-fall, forcing nice slow breaths, fabricating very heavy eyes . . .

'Anna.'

I ignore him.

'Anna, there's a policewoman. She wants to talk to you.'

This cannot be happening – my happy ending cannot be stolen from the palm of my hand. I swing my legs and sit on the side of the bed.

Possible reasons for the unwanted visit fire like bullets: the canoe has been discovered by a passing boat; Mark's body has been washed up on the beach; Mark's car has been found; my phone, or maybe Mark's, has been recovered from the sea; Jan is dead (I don't like this thought); my rescuers have contacted the police, suspicious at my solo-canoeing and non-return of their clothes; the studio in Exmouth has reported a break-in; a mobile speed camera caught me on the way home; there is CCTV of me buying a burner phone; Angie has somehow said something incriminating, or maybe Harry; or maybe Mark is alive.

Oh God. I am instantly transported to my cell, blood gluing me to the narrow bed as I give birth, my wailing ignored.

Despite being bombarded with thoughts, I move at snail-pace. Ben passes me the red fluffy dressing gown no one wears and I put my arm in the wrong hole but don't immediately realise. When I've corrected the problem I knot the belt tightly around my middle. The sensation is good, a reminder of what is at stake.

'What time is it?'

'We slept in. It's nearly nine. I've got a team meeting.' He kisses me. 'Can I tell them?'

'No, not yet. Can we not tell anyone until I'm three months.'

'Not even Mum?'

I can't believe we're having this conversation when in five minutes I might be pushed into the back seat of a police car, head dipped, hands cuffed behind my back. 'I'd rather not.'

He disappears to his office, totally unperturbed by the presence of a uniform, concerned only with his imminent meeting. Oh, the luxury of being a law-abiding citizen.

I go to the bathroom, clean my teeth and splash water on my

face, and smile at the mirror. The act of smiling has been shown to reduce stress, even if that smile is forced. I smile again.

The police officer is waiting in the hall. She is young and looks efficient in her all-black uniform of slim trousers, short-sleeved top and stab vest, finished off with a tidy blonde bun.

'Hi. What's this about?'

'Hello. Sorry to have woken you. I'm PC Darley. Can we talk somewhere?'

'Is my mum okay?' Isn't that what people ask?

'Yes, as far as I know.'

'Do you want to go in here?' I gesture at the living-room door but don't actually move. 'Should Ben come?'

'Just you, if that's okay. For now.'

We walk in and I perch on the chair; she closes the door behind us and takes the sofa, unaware that the seat cushions have seen better days. She sinks further than she expects and we share a smile as she scrabbles into a straight-backed position.

'I wanted to ask you a few questions about Liam Turner.'

'Okay.' I've got form when it comes to being in trouble and controlling panic is rule number one. By the time she has opened her notebook and readied her pen, I am fully prepared: be curious and open, but slow to grasp any suggestion of wrongdoing.

'You know him?'

'I do. He's the . . .' the right word escapes me, 'a companion to Jan Elsworthy.'

'I've spoken to Jan. She is concerned that Liam hasn't been seen for a few days.'

Traitor.

I want to flare my nostrils and scratch the earth.

'How is Jan?'

'I am here to follow up on her concerns.' She smiles but her body language is clear – we are not friends having a chat. 'When did you last see Liam?'

This is a tightrope. Fall on one side and I will be guilty of withholding information. Fall on the other and PC Darley might feel the need to launch a full-scale investigation.

'I might have seen him at Monday's choir practice – we hold the rehearsals at Jan's house because the church isn't free.' I pretend to peruse a virtual calendar. 'Yes, he came and joined us at the end.'

'So, yesterday?'

'No. Last Monday. Yesterday's rehearsal was cancelled because of Jan being in hospital.' She has her head down, writing my words in her notebook. 'The concert is tonight,' I add, to fill the silence.

'Do you ever see Liam outside of rehearsal?' She looks up for the answer. Her eyes dissuade me from lying.

'You won't mention anything to my partner, will you?' I glance at the door even though I know Ben can't overhear.

'Not unless it became necessary.'

'What would make it necessary?'

'If you were in some way connected to the fact that Liam hasn't been seen.'

'I'm not.'

'Okay. Can you tell me about your relationship with Liam?'

'Given that you're here I assume Jan told you that we were close for a while.'

'Can you clarify what you mean by that, Anna?'

'Until recently we were having an affair.'

'How recently?'

'We broke up a few weeks ago. I can't remember the actual date but I could work it out.'

'Can I ask who ended the relationship?'

'He did. I think he took up with someone else.' She is interested in this nugget so I carry on, mean-mouthed and bitter. 'He's a serial womaniser, a cheat and a liar. Women are interchangeable as far as he is concerned.'

'What do you mean by that, Anna?'

Not knowing what Jan has disclosed is like walking with a blindfold.

'He was juggling three of us. I found out about Jan and she found out about a third woman he was seeing.'

'You think he finished your relationship to take up with someone else?'

'No, I think we all overlapped.' I take a deep breath, as though this is painful. 'I'm so ashamed of how I've behaved . . . he was like a drug.'

'So why did the relationship end?'

'I was finding it more and more difficult to find time to see him – I'm getting married, you see.'

She momentarily smiles. An everyday interview has become the stuff of prime-time drama.

'I'm fairly sure he went looking for another naïve woman to fill my slot.'

'Why do you think that?'

'A message popped up from someone – I might be wrong but there was something about his face – I got the feeling she was his next victim.' Tears come with minimal effort. 'He turned me into someone suspicious by all his lying. I wish I'd never met him.'

'Do you know anywhere Liam might have gone?'

I shake my head. 'I know very little about him. He said he had a sister called Carrie but I don't know an address.'

'Where did you used to meet?'

I name a couple of pubs, and the hotel where we stayed over, but omit Woodies.

'I'm honestly happy to help but I'm surprised Jan is concerned. She knows he's a compulsive liar.' I bite my top lip, as though unsure about how much to reveal. 'He told me he was an art therapist and told Jan he was a paramedic but he wasn't either of those things – nothing he said was true. Wherever he is, she's well shot of him. We all are.'

'Can I take a few details of where you've been this weekend, Anna?'

'Why? I said I haven't seen him.'

'I'm simply doing my job. I'd appreciate your cooperation.'

I huff, before deciding to flood her with detail. 'On Friday I had a driving lesson and then went to Bath and bought a wedding dress and had a drink in a bar. I stayed in on Friday night. On Saturday, apart from a walk, I spent the day sorting out stuff for the wedding.' I decide not to mention my visit to the hospital unless she does.

'With your partner?'

'No, he's just come back from skiing.'

'When did he leave and return, please?'

'He left on Friday morning and came back last night – about nine.'

'Carry on, please.'

'On Sunday I stayed in. Yesterday I did chores and baking. Surely none of this is relevant?'

She raises her eyebrows. 'Did anyone see you yesterday?'

'A delivery driver. And I had an appointment in Bristol.'

'Where was that?'

'At a baby scan clinic.' I swear she smirks.

'Can you give me the details?'

I do as asked. 'And you don't have a name or address for the third person in the relationship?'

The police radio crackles and in response to an indecipherable code PC Darley makes her excuses and goes outside, leaving me to stew.

A wave of indignance at the situation Jan has put me in makes me chew on a roar. I only confided in her because she was distressed – you'd think she could have parked her conscience given how unequivocally evil she knows Liam to be. Her reaction is very disappointing and I hate being disappointed. My back teeth are locked so tight I'm in danger of cracking a molar, so I use my fingers to massage the hinge of my jaw.

The lazy label would be to call me a psychopath but I am not one. I don't fit the profile. I form close bonds, am empathetic, can control my temper, have patience and can learn from my mistakes. For fairness, I'll admit to lying excessively and being promiscuous – may as well throw in impulsive and lawless – but there is plenty of room for reasonable doubt. If I am guilty of any disorder it is that I have the confidence to act on my principles. No one mourned my brother, and I don't think anyone, including Jan, will mourn Mark. Such a shame that she has displayed sensibilities that don't concur with mine.

PC Darley lets herself back in. 'Sorry about that. Do you have any details for the other woman?'

'No. Sorry.'

'No name at all?'

'You'd have to ask Jan.' I'd like to know if the police are aware of the letter and the money Jan left for Liam – surely two pretty incriminating pieces of evidence. They must have been to her house, but might not have searched the bureau. I decide to dangle a hook. 'I think Jan was planning to ask Liam to leave. Maybe he read the tea leaves.'

'Could I check the messages on your phone?'

'I lost it on Saturday, I'm afraid.'

She flips back a page. 'You spent Saturday sorting out stuff for your wedding?'

'That's right.'

'But lost a phone.'

'I went for a walk – it must have slipped out of my jacket pocket. I lost my keys as well.'

'Can I see the jacket, please?'

I am officially a moron – lobbing untruths into the air with no idea how to catch them. 'I am beginning to feel hounded by your questions.'

'If you could show me the jacket.'

She follows me through to the hall cupboard where I quickly scan our coats looking for one with a shallow pocket. Ben's navy pea jacket catches my attention. I drag it past the other coats in an attempt to dislodge the line of dust on the shoulder and hold it up in a sarcastic manner.

'Thank you.'

'Are we done? I'd like to get dressed now.'

'Yes, thank you for your help.'

336

I can hear movement overhead and will Ben to stay put.

PC Darley is almost out of the door when she asks, 'Do you have a new phone?'

'I've ordered one.'

'But it hasn't arrived?' I want to thump her pretty little face.

'Not yet.'

Ben appears at the top of the stairs and shouts, 'Everything okay?'

'Yes,' I say.

I send frosty vibes but he doesn't read them, lolloping down to join us.

'Do you know Liam Turner?' she asks him.

'I don't think so. Do I, Anna?'

'He's Jan's partner.'

'No, then. I've only met Jan once.'

He heads for the kitchen.

'If you think of anything else, please get in touch.' PC Darley hands me her card, which I defiantly balance on the domed newel post. I have never been good with authority.

52

Season of Goodwill

Harry finally comes to the door after the third press of the bell. He must have trouble hearing.

'Sorry, I was meditating.'

'Oh, I've obviously come at a bad time. I'm Anna, Jan's friend.' I hold out my hand. 'You spoke to me on Saturday.'

'Yes, that's right, I did. It seems ages ago. I can't keep track of the days.' He is quite flustered.

'It's Tuesday,' I say, 'three days till Christmas.' He smiles.

'Come in, please. Not that it's my house to invite you. Everything is odd, don't you think?'

'I do.' I follow him into the hall.

'I can wait while you finish your meditation if—'

'No, it's fine. Life feels very fluid so I've taken to meditating on and off.'

'It must be strange to arrive in the middle of a medical drama.'

'Surreal. You know, I've got older but this house is completely unchanged.' His face, not immediately attractive, softens. He has thinning hair and a weak chin but nice pale green eyes.

'You've been here before?'

'Yes, but not since I was a boy.'

'How long is it since you were in England?'

'Ten years. I came to my father's funeral.'

'Golly. Your mum is still alive though?' Unintentionally, this sounds like a judgement.

'Yes, I don't know where the time went. All these years I've been in an alternate universe. She's in a facility in Hertfordshire now – I can't imagine her in a little room. She used to like the garden. I need to go and see her but until Aunty Jan comes back I'm not sure what my responsibilities are.'

'Tricky situation,' I say, smothering the desire to smirk at a grown man's use of the word aunty.

'Shall we have a drink? There's wine open. She wouldn't mind, would she?'

'No, definitely not.' Half-past twelve is a tad early but if Harry wants wine, wine we will have.

I follow him into the kitchen, take off my rucksack and my coat and sit at the table. He pours us each a large glass of red.

'I hope I'm not being too inquisitive, but who normally lives here?'

Describing the living arrangements necessitates mention of Liam but I am spare on detail. 'He was due back on Sunday but must have changed his plans.'

'Is he a carer?'

'More of a companion, I think.'

'The police came yesterday – they rather scared me to death.'

'Were you busy meditating?' My jovial tone misses the mark.

'No, I wasn't. I'd been for a very nice walk and they were on the doorstep when I got back.'

'You haven't had the best welcome, have you? Although you're getting to know the emergency services! Sniffer dogs next!'

He doesn't react. Harry and I are not a natural meshing of minds.

'Was it a PC Darley who came?'

'I don't remember the names. There were two of them. A girl – or woman, I should probably say – light hair, I think. She was quite abrupt but the man was very nice and polite.'

'That same girl came to see me this morning.'

'Is Liam missing?'

'I have no idea what's going on.'

'He still has quite a lot of belongings here. I wasn't snooping, by the way. I had to look around to work out where I should sleep.'

'I expect he'll turn up one day with a Canary-Island tan and a giant Toblerone from duty-free.' I am deliberately offhand. 'Have you found everything you need?'

'I have, thank you. If he has gone away, wouldn't he have told Jan?'

'Liam isn't a very straightforward person. Have you heard about the carol concert tonight?'

'Yes, Angie mentioned it. She has been checking in on me.' He takes a generous gulp that leaves a ring of maroon around his mouth. 'I haven't sung a carol since school – I was a boy chorister.'

'How wonderful.'

'No, awful. I was a boarder. They bullied me from my first night in the dorm.'

'I'm so sorry. Kids can be cruel.'

'Do you have children?'

'No, but I work in a school.'

'The other boys weren't to blame. It was the culture of the school that was at fault – it brutalised all of us.'

'I can see why England might not hold the best memories.'

'I don't feel any sense of Britishness, any belonging.'

Keen to move on from his childhood trauma, I say, 'You must have met all sorts running a hostel?'

'Yes. Every species of mankind and, it's a cliché, but every day was different.' He shakes his head. 'I'm not sure whether I can settle down here but Jan has given me the motivation to try.'

'How well do you know her?'

'Now, hardly at all, but as a child she used to take me out on exeat days. She and Gerald were good fun.'

'She's still fun. Have you been to see her?'

'Not yet. The carer, Angie, said Jan is quite confused.'

'I'm going this afternoon.' I go to look at my watch and clumsily send my glass flying. The dark liquid spills all over Harry's lap before he can move out of the way.

'Oh, I'm so sorry. Let me get some kitchen roll.'

I attempt to dab him but I have done a good job – his beige chinos are drenched.

'I'd better change,' he says, standing up.

'You'll need to put them to soak, I think.'

When he has hurried upstairs, I go to the slim cupboard and take the bottle of liquid morphine, slipping it into the main compartment of my rucksack and closing the zip. I then nip across the hall to Jan's study and lift the lid of the dark oak bureau. Two envelopes, both addressed to Liam, one fattened by cash, are propped up as though expecting me – PC Darley and her sidekick clearly didn't bother with much of a search when they came calling. I slot them into the front compartment of my bag and quietly shut the lid of the bureau before returning to the kitchen, tipping my wine away and sitting back at the table.

Harry reappears wearing navy trousers and holding his stained beige pair in his arms. I get up and run cold water in the sink, apologising once again.

With the trousers soaking, we sit back at the table and spend a few more minutes talking about Jan's sepsis and her cancer, about Christmas and turkey farming and the sin that is eating an octopus, before I deem it time. 'I'd better be off.' I get up and, as though it has just occurred to me, say, 'Actually, Harry, why don't you come with me?'

The delay is quite telling . . . murmurs precede actual words. 'I don't know.'

'I'm sure seeing you will cheer her up.'

'I suppose I could.' His enthusiasm is in the minus column.

'We don't have to stay long.' I smile, warmly, at this ungrateful waste of a man. 'Can you drive?'

'Yes, but I don't have a car.'

'How about this, Harry – you drive me in Jan's car and I won't have to get the bus?'

'I don't have insurance.'

'It's an any-driver policy,' I lie.

He really has no choice. I fetch the keys while he attends to footwear and a coat; we reconvene in the hall.

'Actually,' (must stop saying actually when I'm lying) 'Jan mentioned she'd left a letter for Liam in her bureau. Let's see if it's still there.'

I tug him along by continuing to talk. 'It's only a twenty-minute drive to the hospital but it's a complete nightmare by bus.'

Starting with the three drawers is probably unnecessary but I want Harry to be a reliable witness. I open the bureau lid last and stare at the tidy desk space, moving the notebook and flicking through the pile that comprises church newsletters and a few magazines.

'Well, I can't see anything addressed to Liam. Never mind . . . you did say she was confused.'

'It was Angie, not me. Perhaps I shouldn't come.'

'It is the season of goodwill, Harry.'

I bundle us out of the door and into the garage where Harry gets into the passenger seat, which is made funnier by the confusion on his face.

'Right-hand drive,' I say, and he gets out and tries again.

I give directions as though I'm an instructor, making sure he has plenty of warning, but he is a nightmare of a driver. God knows when he was last on a proper road.

'Can you pick up the pace, Harry? The lorry behind us is doing his nut.'

Harry obliges by doubling his speed before braking heavily at the first roundabout. I decide not to bother asking for a lift home.

We park on the third floor of the multi-storey and take the stairs down because Harry doesn't like lifts. The café is right in front of us, which is handy.

'Let's get Jan a drink. The tea is always tepid in hospitals and the coffee is abysmal.'

We join the short queue. 'Do you want something?'

'Cappuccino, please.'

'Anything to eat?'

He looks at the counter display. 'A chocolate muffin, please.' I feel like his mum.

While the barista makes our drinks I put two flapjacks and Harry's muffin into my rucksack. He doesn't offer to pay, simply reaching for his takeaway cup and leaving me to carry the other two.

Back in the main thoroughfare, I say, 'I won't be a minute,' indicating at the door to the ladies'.

'Do you want me to hold the—'

I'm already halfway through the door, still clutching the cups.

Not engaging with the task is the only way I can make myself break the tamper-proof seal of the medicine bottle, tip and stir. I check the initial on the lid: J. Wouldn't do to make a mistake.

The all-female ward is full of what medics call 'the frail elderly'.

'Hi, Jan.' I kiss her cheek. 'I've brought Harry to see you.'

'Aunty Jan.' Firmly in her gaze, he seems to shed a decade.

'Harry, my boy. How lovely to see you.' He gives her a hospital hug, ginger and awkward because of the height of the bed, the apparatus, the risk of causing pain.

'I'm sorry I didn't come before.'

'I'm the one who should be sorry – leaving you to fend for yourself.'

'It's not your fault. I'm glad you're okay.'

'Not bad.' She gently rubs the back of her hand, avoiding where the cannula is taped in place.

I watch them travel through time, skipping through some decades, dwelling on others – she is much better than she was on Saturday night but still not herself. When they reach the present day, I interrupt: 'Harry, do you want your muffin?'

'Is eating allowed?'

'There's not much hope for the patients if it's not,' I say.

As he dives into his paper bag, Jan smiles.

'We bought you a flapjack and a caramel cappuccino.' The items are already on her table but I swing the counter over her legs so she can reach.

'Thank you, Anna.'

'Such a shame you're going to miss the concert,' I say. 'Harry's coming, aren't you?'

He nods, mouth spilling dark brown crumbs.

'Harry had a shock yesterday – the police came looking for Liam.' Having a third person here is genius. No one knows what anyone else knows. 'They talked to me as well. I assume they've spoken to you?'

She says a very quiet 'Yes.' I pretend not to notice her timidity.

'Liam hasn't been seen evidently. But his room is full of belongings – that's right, isn't it, Harry?'

'Seems to be.'

'By the way, we looked in the bureau before we came.' I try a frown. 'There wasn't anything obvious.' I take a huge bite of flapjack.

'There was a letter, Anna, and an envelope,' says Jan.

'I don't think we can have missed it. Was it in one of the drawers?'

I don't know if I am fooling her, or if we are both fooling Harry. I don't know if she recalls the details of our conversation mid-fever or just the bones of it. I'm also not sure any of it matters.

'The letter and the money were on the desk. You would have seen them if you lifted the roll-top.'

'We looked there,' I say. Harry and I share gormless looks.

'Is it important?' he asks.

While I wait for Jan to decide on her answer Harry turns

detective. 'There definitely wasn't anything there. Could Liam have taken the envelopes?'

I stay quiet, hoping for more good fortune.

'Have you seen him?' asks Jan. 'Has he been to the house?'

'Not that I know of, but I've been out quite a lot. Walking, and I went to the pub.' He looks from Jan to me. 'Twice.'

'I've heard they do nice fish and chips,' I say, happy to move the conversation on now the seed has been so nicely sown.

'I had a vegan tagine.'

'Are you vegan?'

'Vegetarian.'

Jan reaches for the paper bag and takes a bite of the solid flapjack. The cup with the black J stays where it is.

'How are you feeling today?' I ask. 'You look better.'

'Very tired,' she says. 'I can't get up.'

'You don't need to. Lie back and let the hospital do its work.' I touch her shoulder; can't resist stroking the soft cashmere of her cardigan. The pang, under my sternum somewhere, is sharp with sadness. She should have been grateful, accepted that Liam was gone and praised the lord. But she made her choice, which has forced mine. She could pretend she was deluded and call off the dogs, but she won't. It's my fault for misjudging her character.

'Do you need anything bringing in? I could come again tomorrow and debrief you on the concert.'

'Aren't you busy getting ready for Christmas?'

'I wasn't offering to stay all day.'

She likes this – the return of banter.

I take my cup with its bold A and test the temperature with a tiny tilt. Not too hot.

346

Jan takes a second bite of flapjack and then she too reaches for her cup.

'Do you think you might be home in time for Christmas?' Harry asks.

There is a moment of silence while we wait for her to answer.

I can almost see myself knocking the hot drink out of her hand and hear my voice joking about how clumsy I am today. I can picture the flurry of hands grabbing the bed sheet, lifting the edge high to stem the flow before a foamy brown puddle forms on the floor. I can invent a conversation where Harry tells Jan how I threw wine over him earlier, necessitating a change of trousers, while I clean up the terrific mess I've made.

But I do nothing.

53

Silent Night

We are all wearing black on the bottom and white on top, although with much variation in flamboyance. I have borrowed one of Ben's work shirts – the alternative was a T-shirt – but the woman beside me has gone full flamenco with ruffles framing her ample cleavage. As our collective voices ricochet throughout the church our choirmaster periodically flashes smiles of encouragement. We are on hymn eight. Nearly there.

'Holy infant so tender and mild

Sleep in heavenly peace.'

Ben is sitting near the back with Dee and Steve. I can't wait for him to take me home. I am in a choir of people but the sense of standing alone, apart, is overwhelming. The compulsion to check my face is not smeared with blood, my shirt is not marked by gun residue, I don't have someone else's skin under my nails, is both crazy and more real than my voice, blending and harmonising.

'Sleep in heavenly peace.'

I need the shutters to close on this never-ending day.

*

'Wonderful, Anna.' Steve kisses my cheek; the warmth from his hand penetrates my cotton shirt but nothing can alleviate the chill inside. 'We enjoyed it very much.'

'Carols have a special place,' I say, taking my puffer coat from Ben. 'Shall we go?'

The crowds, and a few familiar faces, hamper a quick escape. When we make it to the car Ben suggests we have a drink in the pub and Dee and Steve readily agree.

'Can you drop me home?' I ask. 'I've got a headache.'

They all show concern that I counter with a positive: 'A good night's sleep is what I need. You go and enjoy yourselves and have one for me.'

The noise of the catch securing the door behind me is the most enormous relief. I intend to make a hot drink and go to bed but instead I sink to the floor. The drama of being unable to put one foot in front of the other becomes cymbals in my head, clanging and angry. I know what I have to do; am well practised at avoiding the dark corners, the grubby nooks, the ugly crannies by focusing on the good, the kind, the wholesome.

Do that now, Anna.

I close my eyes and try to visualise a country garden, busy with summery flowers and birds and butterflies, but my mind brings me poppies, and poppies bring me Sofia.

I switch to a fern-filled forest, the ground springy underneath, making my footfall soft and silent, but the trees decorate them-selves as I watch. Mark's hand looping shiny barbed wire over one branch and then another, careful not to catch his skin on the spikes. That hand is in the water, tugging at me. I try to shove the hand away.

349

The hand is Jan's, speckled brown with age-spots, reaching for the takeaway cup with the sweeping black J.

The hand is mine, popping a little remedy into my brother's mouth and pressing his lips together.

I need to open my eyes; the only escape is if I can open my eyes. But the lids are glued shut. And I'm back in the place I don't want to go. I am in Russia Dock Woodland.

I am running, faster and faster, catching up with Pippa. I can hear my brassy breath and the beat of my feet. I can feel the pumping of my heart and the hate in my head. I am so angry I can hardly stay upright, my feet prey to every camber and crack, sliding on rotting leaves, surprised by puddles of unknown depth. I want her to know I'm here. But she can't hear me. She will never hear me.

This time the buffering is short, the blackness temporary. The footage, dredged from the archive, decides to load, a premiere for my eyes only.

I am so close, the breath I take is the air she has just expelled.

I am so close, I can hear the rhythm of the music streaming into her ears.

I am so close, my outstretched arm can cross the divide.

I reach forwards, both of us still running. My palms find her mid-back. My fingertips register the bony spurs of her spine. The spine I have rubbed sun cream into; the spine that has given me piggybacks; the spine I have slept against. The action pauses. I want to spin her round and make it a happy surprise. *Ta-da! Your friend, Anna, has come in from the cold.* But I am not in control of the past. And in the past, I am tied taut by a knot of bitterness. Tied too taut to stop. With no thought, only an unstoppable impulse to lash out, I push. I push her really hard, and in an instant it is over.

She is on the ground. Utterly still.

The syrupy centre of a liqueur chocolate pools around her head.

One push. One rage-filled push.

I don't know where the scream starts, or when it will ever end.

I killed Pippa.

And I am so very sorry.

My phone is ringing. A reassuringly ordinary sound, repetitive. I slowly sit up, cross my legs, take in the nondescript cream of the hall walls. Only the hospital has the number of the throwaway phone, written alongside my name in the slot for Jan's next of kin.

If I don't answer, there is still room for doubt. The morphine might have done no more than temporarily slow Jan's breathing; she may not even have drunk the hideously sweet coffee; she may have been sick, emptying her guts before tucking into her hospital dinner. Jan might be lying awake right now, crafting an apology for when she sees me tomorrow. Free from the vagaries of infection, she would be aghast at the fantastic story her unwell brain made her believe.

54

Navy-blue Tulle

On Christmas Eve, Bridget arrives with Daisy, Tallulah and Sasha bang on eleven o'clock. Milly was also invited but she thinks Daisy is less likely to kick off if she's not there when I reveal the not-pink bridesmaids' dresses. Let's hope Milly is right.

'Okay, girls, hand-washing then dresses.'

I inspect their hands and faces, before leading them upstairs to the spare room.

'Do you want to see my dress first?'

'Yes, please,' says Tallulah, who despite being eight to Daisy's ten is the leader of the pack.

They stand – a row of soldiers – and watch me take out the protective silver cover and undo the zip, revealing the spaghetti straps, simple bodice and cloud-like skirt.

'Anna, it's heavenly,' says Bridget, whose style is tailored, verging on stern.

'Do you really think so?'

'I do.'

'It's like a ballet dress,' says Tallulah.

'And so are yours.' I whip out their dresses, delicious little creations with capped sleeves, shirred bodices and ballerina skirts. The paradox is very pleasing, the severity of navy made frivolous by design.

Avoiding Daisy's eye, I say, 'Shall we try them on?'

With no modesty I pull off my long-sleeved T-shirt and bra, slide off my jeans, step into the dress and let Bridget do up the back.

Tallulah, bless her, actually squeals.

'Take your socks off, Aunty Anna,' says Daisy with a giggle.

'Come on, girls.' They throw off their clothes and are, one by one, transformed. Tallulah yanks the bodice away from her body and it stretches before snapping back into shape.

'That looks comfy, Tallulah,' says Bridget.

'It's not itchy,' she says, and Bridget winks at me.

'Is it to keep?' asks Daisy.

'Of course. You can wear it to play dog treats if you like.'

'Not until after the wedding,' says Tallulah. 'We have to stay clean.'

Daisy makes a cross face. 'I know that.'

Sasha's thumb has crept into her mouth.

'Do you want to see your shoes, Sasha?'

The thumb pops back out. 'Yes-th.'

Their faces as they open the boxes are priceless. What little girl wouldn't want silver shoes with an actual heel? They literally can't cram their feet in quick enough.

'Can I take a photo?' Bridget asks.

We pose: me in the centre with Daisy one side, Tallulah the other and little Sasha in front.

'Send it to Mummy,' says Daisy.

Bridget looks at me and I nod.

'Shall we ask Dee to pop up for a preview?' I ask.

'She'd love that.'

I call her and she says she's putting on her coat as we speak. The four of us wait in the hall with Bridget manning the front door. The excitement is like fireworks, bangs and sparkles and unexpected fizzes.

When Dee walks in the girls laugh and flounce about, skirts billowing under happy hands.

'Beautiful,' Dee declares, unashamedly tearful. 'Oh, Anna. Simply beautiful.'

The girls hug their grandma's knees, hips, waist. I look at her adoring face and imagine that same gaze resting on my own child. And, as if beckoned, she comes. A shock of dark hair and perfect little lips that my mind paints ashes of rose.

See, Anna, she is real.

'Thank you for inviting me, Anna,' says Dee. 'You're so lovely to always include me.'

'You're included because you're so lovely,' I say, engulfed by a rapture so keen it hurts.

The dresses are all back in the wardrobe and Bridget is trying to herd the now over-excited trio into the hall, when the doorbell rings. The interruption brings me down with a bang. How dare Anna Harris dream of a future filled with good fortune?

As Bridget goes to open the door, I find my mouth won't shut. I am convinced PC Darley is on the other side, ready to read me my rights, but it is Steve, come to take Dee out to lunch. Bridget takes the opportunity to shoo the girls into her car.

'See you at Midnight Mass,' says Dee, kissing my cheek, and off they go.

For Christmas, Dee is giving Steve a key to her house, taped inside a shoebox so he thinks he's getting slippers. I can't imagine Milly is going to be thrilled by this development. Steve has, I gather, bought Dee a camellia, which seems ever so slightly less symbolic.

In an uncanny parallel, Ben is also being gifted a key: the key to Jan's house. Although until the probate is sorted, he'll have to make do with the cardboard version he'll find hanging on our tree on Christmas morning.

I take my phone out of my jeans pocket and click on Meryl's email for the nth time. I had almost ignored it, assuming it was church business, but this time she was acting in her role as executor of Jan's estate. I'm glad she decided to notify me straight away. As she said, the bequest is life-changing. The will, which was attached, was sweet reading. The bulk of the estate, all mine. And all the more fantastic by being so unexpected, and so unengineered.

Meryl couldn't resist adding a note of piety: 'We reap what we sow', which made me smile. Dispatching Jan was, with hindsight, a kindness. I see that now. All that lay ahead was an increasing dependence on others and pain, plenty of pain. Better this way. Happy hypoxia, they call it, when your oxygen levels gradually ebb – a gentle passing.

I press print and go up to Ben's office to retrieve the papers, which I staple together before placing them in the bottom drawer of my bedside table: the home of Sofia's passport.

Options; always important to have options.

Acknowledgements

I seem to want to thank a few people who live on only in my memory. Mum and Dad whose belief in me had no limits. My friend, Helen Dunmore, who refrained from giving me advice but did once say, 'Make it dark. Make it darker.' My tutor, Fay Weldon, who was always looking to liven things up: 'Couldn't someone tamper with the brakes?'

I also want to thank my city, Bristol. A place that started my love of writing through a council-funded course, subsequently consolidated at the university; a place where Sheila Hannon's Show of Strength performed my monologues and Sara Davies produced my work for BBC Radio 4.

On to the living and breathing.

Thank you to my terrifyingly efficient agent, Caroline Hardman at Hardman Swainson, for sticking with me, and to both Charlotte Greenwood and Miranda Jewess at Viper for sticking with Anna Harris. Thank you also to Rosie Parnham, Kate McQuaid, Hayley Shepherd, Audrey Kerr, Jane Howard, Samantha Johnson and Emily Frisella for their contributions to getting Anna Harris ready to face the world. She looks amazing.

Thank you to my family (the extended version) for being so positive and supportive through the ups and downs, and to my many enthusiastic friends.

Encouragement is everything.